if she's WICKED

WICKED KNIGHTS SERIES

AMELIA HUTCHINS

WICKED

Authored By: Amelia Hutchins
Cover Art Design: Tenaya Jayne
Copy Edited by: E & F Indie Services
Edited by: E & F Indie Services
Published in (United States of America)
10 9 8 7 6 5 4 3 2 1

ALSO BY AMELIA HUTCHINS

The Fae Chronicles
Fighting Destiny
Taunting Destiny
Escaping Destiny
Seducing Destiny
Unraveling Destiny
Embracing Destiny - *Coming Soon (Final Book)*

The Elite Guards
(Part of the Fae Chronicles)
A Demon's Dark Embrace
Claiming the Dragon King
A Winter Court
A Demon's Plaything

A Guardian's Diary
Stands Alone
Darkest Before Dawn
Death before Dawn
Midnight Rising - *Coming Soon (Final Book)*

Playing with Monsters series
(Part of the Fae Chronicles)
Playing with Monsters
Sleeping with Monsters
Becoming his Monster
Last Monster Book *TBA*

Wicked Knights series
Oh, Holy Knight (Standalone alternative POV to If She's Wicked)
If She's Wicked

UPCOMING SERIES

<u>A Crown of Ashes</u>
Coming Soon

*If you're following the series for the Fae Chronicles,
Elite Guards, and Monsters, reading order is as
follows:*

Fighting Destiny
Taunting Destiny
Escaping Destiny
Seducing Destiny
A Demon's Dark Embrace
Playing with Monsters
Unraveling Destiny
Sleeping with Monsters
Claiming the Dragon King
Oh, Holy Knight
Becoming his Monster
The Winter Court
A Demon's Plaything
If She's Wicked
Embracing Destiny coming soon

WARNING!

STOP!! READ THE WARNING BELOW BEFORE PURCHASING THIS BOOK.

Warning: Erie **isn't** a hero; she's the **antihero** in this story.

This isn't a **love** story. It's a **dark** and **twisted** battle of wills and bare bones. They're going to **war** against one another, and it will be **brutal**, chaotic, and **beautiful**. So if you're not into dark retellings of twisted love stories, this isn't for you. Thank you for looking, but I'm an **unapologetic** author of **alpha-holes** and the women who fight back against them. I don't **believe** in instant-love. I believe in putting them through **hell** and making them earn it first.

Second Warning in case the first didn't scare you: This book is **dark**. It's **sexy**, hot, and **intensely twisted**. The author is human, you are as well. Is the book perfect? It's as perfect as I could make it. Are there mistakes? Probably, then again, even **New York Times top published** books have minimal mistakes because like me, they have **human editors**. There are words in this book that won't be found in the **standard dictionary**, because they were created to set the stage for a paranormal-urban fantasy world. Words such as 'sift', 'glamoured', and 'apparate' are common in paranormal books and give better description to the action in the story than can be found in standard dictionaries. They are **intentional** and not mistakes.

WARNING! (CONT'D)

About the hero: chances are you may **not** fall instantly in **love** with him, that's because **I don't write men you instantly love**; you grow to love them. I don't believe in **instant-love**. I write flawed, raw, caveman-like **alpha-holes** that eventually let you see their redeeming qualities. They are **aggressive**, **alpha-holes**, one step above a caveman when we meet them. You may *not* even like him by the time you finish this book, but I promise you will **love** him by the **end** of this **series**.

About the heroine: There is a chance, that you might think she's a bit naïve or weak, but then again who starts out as a badass? Badasses are a product of growth and I am going to put her through **hell**, and you get to watch **her** come up **swinging** every time I knock her on her ass. That's just how I do things. How she reacts to the set of circumstances she is put through, may not be how you as the reader, or I as the author would react to that same situation. Everyone reacts differently to circumstances and how Erie responds to her challenges, is how I see her as a character and as a person.

I don't write love stories: I write fast paced, knock you on your ass, make you sit on the edge of your seat wondering what happens in the next kind of books. If you're looking for cookie cutter romance, this isn't for you. If you can't handle the ride, ***un-buckle your seatbelt and get out of the roller-coaster car now***. **If not, you've been warned.** If nothing outlined above bothers you, carry on and **enjoy the ride!**

DEDICATION

THIS ONE IS FOR EVERYONE WHO HAS EVER WANTED TO throat punch someone, and somehow managed not to. For everyone who is just trying to survive and navigate in this crazy world without high-fiving someone in the face with a chair, mainly because it is illegal, but like, while you're counting to twenty to prevent doing it, imagine that shit happening. To those who are going through a rough time, it's not a bad life; it's just a bad time and it too will pass. To everyone living a perfect life, how the hell do you manage that shit? To my haters, I love thy haters, and I see you, and I still wish you well even though you're an asshole! To my team, my family, friends, and especially my anger management team that keeps my ass in check on the above haters, hey, guys! Still haven't killed anyone, this shit must actually be working! To my tribe, my fan group, unicorns, and people. I see you, you're my world too. To my girls, you know who you are, thanks for always being an ear, or an extra set of eyes on these books, and for loving my worlds as much as I do.

if she's WICKED

WICKED KNIGHTS SERIES

if she's WICKED

WICKED KNIGHTS SERIES

CHAPTER
one

THE INCESSANT BUZZING NEXT TO MY HEAD REFUSED
to stop, no matter how much I ignored it. Turning over
in bed, I glared at the world's evilest invention since the
iron maiden. As I slapped at it, it still refused to stop
squealing as my fingers missed the button repeatedly.
The asshole who had invented this contraption had to
be among the world's most hated people. Now, the one
who added the snooze button, he had more fans, of that
I was sure. Rolling out of bed, I stretched as I began
digging through the endless pile of dirty clothes that sat
beside my bed, scattered on the floor. Someday, I'd get
around to washing or burning them.

I sniffed myself before hauling my ass towards the
fridge, dressed and unimpressed with how this day
was starting off already, considering it wasn't even a
Monday. I piled my unruly hair into a mess of a bun that
wasn't appealing by any means and headed towards the
freezer for the coffee I had pilfered from a store being
ransacked by demons last week. Of course, I'd left the

demon corpses behind as payment, because I preferred to earn the things I took.

My clock started buzzing again from the bedroom, pulling an eye roll from me that almost resulted in a strain as I groaned, flipping through the months on the calendar. A circle had been penned around today, marking it doomsday. I snorted, staring at it as I tried to stave off the fear that came with it. Swallowing hard, I grabbed the pen, bit the lid off between my teeth, and crossed it off. Sealing the pen back up, I tossed it into the trash can and frowned at the calendar again, as if I could light it afire with my mind alone.

Marching back into my bedroom, I ripped the alarm clock from the wall and slammed it against the floor, staring at it. My eyes gazed up at the pictures of the couple who had lived here before the world had gone to utter shit. They looked happy, almost too happy. I really should have removed their pictures, but I enjoyed staring at the blatant lie that they'd lived once upon a time. I'd had to remove their corpses months ago, as I had moved in here. Oftentimes, I wondered what it would be like to have the luxury of belonging to something.

I wasn't wanted by anyone. I had been created to save two races, the druids and Templars, both cursed by ancient witches who had probably been warranted for what they'd done. I mean, the races I was destined to save were assholes; it was as simple as that. When they hadn't been able to find a way around the curse, they'd banded together and created me. The only child ever created from their two races, both who had drunk from the cauldron of Dagda, and then made me. And so the story went. That was over one hundred years ago, and now they were encroaching on D-Day. According to their seers, a female druid and a male Knight had to give birth to a child of both races, without the magic of the cauldron that had been used to create me, of course. The big problem with that? There were no female druids alive or created, except yours truly.

They actually expected me to lie back, spread my thighs, and do as I was told. *As if.* They had made damn sure I knew I was unwanted, that I was nothing more than the bane of their existence, but still, they expected me to save them. *Irony.* I was an unnatural, unwanted occurrence that had one job and one job only. The druids had beaten that into me as a child, reinforcing it anytime I forgot my place. I was evil incarnate, which might have been the only thing they hadn't gotten wrong.

My eyes slowly took in the mess that littered the front room. The piles of books and ancient manuscripts I'd stolen to find a way out of the curse—and to skip over the whole pregnancy issue. The rest of the place was filled with books or scripts that I'd taken from the library to indulge in, as my solitary existence had become smothering. It wasn't that I minded being alone, but the silence of it was unnerving most days.

I pulled open the freezer and reached in to pull out the coffee, smirking at the irate demon who stared back at me. I patted him with my free hand before bringing it back to stifle a yawn. "Morning, Fred. I trust you slept well?" Leaving the door open, I moved to the coffee maker and poured fresh water into it before piling grounds in and clicking it on to brew.

"You will pay for this, woman," he snapped.

I took him in, or more to the point, what there was of

him. I'd found him ripping humans apart and returned the favor. I'd removed his head, but it had continued talking, which was how his head had ended up in my freezer as it was, while his body remained *elsewhere*, probably searching for his head after it had healed from me setting it ablaze.

"I thought we were past this? Remember, we agreed that there shouldn't be any hard feelings. I mean, you *were* eating humans, and eating humans *is* bad. You had this coming, admit it. I'm sure you never expected to get caught or punished for it, but how long did you really think you could keep going like that? No hard feelings, right? We're friends now. You should be trying to make the best of it." I shrugged as he turned red, growling and snapping as he grew way too angry over being caught red-handed.

"You decided that I deserved this. I didn't really have much of a say in this since you cut my fucking head off and tossed me into your freezer! It wasn't as if I could protest or point out how insane you are as you left my body in the trash and lit it on fire," he grumbled, and I winced with a small smile as I pushed the cup beneath the coffee machine and brewed a single cup.

The rich aroma filled the apartment, and I hummed with my eagerness to down it. Watching it fill to the rim as Fred continued his irate bickering and cursing me to the depths of hell, I picked it up and inhaled it into my system. Being balls-deep in an apocalypse hadn't boded well for the cows, so cream wasn't an option. I took a long drink of the hot brew, oblivious to the burning liquid as I turned back around, facing Fred.

"Do you need anything while I'm out today?"

I asked softly before taking another swig as my eyes moved to the clock on the wall with a glare. I was late for work *again.*

"My body back?" he asked, watching me closely as I lifted my brow at his question.

"We talked about that too, and I said no. You wouldn't agree to stop terrorizing the humans, and well, I'm a bitch like that. That is what you like to call me, right? Also, Fred, we agreed to make the most of this situation and become friends," I chuckled as he sputtered while I watched him over the rim of my cup as I polished off the contents. The frown that marred his blue lips was priceless and called to the evil within me. I moved to the sink, washing out the one cup I owned before turning, waving at him as I made my way to the freezer to close it so he didn't stink up the place by thawing out in my absence. "I'll be back later, don't go anywhere," I snickered as his mouth opened and closed at my choice of words.

"You crazy bitch!"

"I'm still not a dog, Fred. I'm also most definitely not in heat either. Also," I called to him through the freezer door before I patted it, "we need to discuss your willingness to allow stereotypes between us. Just because I'm not your kind of normal doesn't make me crazy. We can talk about this when I get home tonight." One last look up at the clock on the wall, and I groaned with how tardy I was to my day job.

It took me less than twenty minutes on foot to reach the Den of Druids, or what I liked to call Den of Thieves, as they never did anything for free. Plus, they overcharged for services they offered the people desperately in need. I hated them, everything about them except what I was, which was magically inclined, and that was only because they'd been forced to teach me. Fighting skills, I had been taught those too. They'd done a lot more than teach me though, but that was in the past. It took a lot of effort to leave it there.

"You're late again," a deep male's baritone cut through the silent entrance as I pushed open the doors and stiffened at the familiar tone.

"Fashionably late," I offered with a shrug as I stared down Frasier, my handler for all things messy. "Had a late night," I said with a tight-lipped smile.

"Indeed," he grumbled as he took me in with a look of derision. "Arthur, from the Templar Knights, has requested your presence today. He needs your help with a mission. There's also Sir Callaghan, who sent this over for you," he said tightly as he handed me the note that simply stated 'Time's up' on the crisp, white piece of parchment that singed my fingers the moment I touched it.

I let it drop from my grasp, staring at the white, singed flesh that the spelled message had burned into them. Great, he'd marked me, and I'd fallen right into it. He was smart, marking me so that he'd be able to hunt me down, which I should have seen coming. The asshole had no idea what he was in for though. I wouldn't be his little booty-call druid, not now or ever.

"Is there any other poisonous shit you want to hand me, Frasier, or was that it?" I snapped irritably as I stared him down. This asshole feared me; he may have hated me, but what I was scared the shit out of him and the others. Out of the druids I was forced to deal with,

he hid it better than the rest, but I could smell it on him. He should be scared; I had a hit list, and he was high on it. He held out another crisp white letter that I eyed before accepting.

"You knew this was coming. You were created for one thing, and one thing only. I told you many times before now that you were created to save us, and your only purpose in life is to serve the Templar Order and their needs. Did you expect it to change? Because I, for one, have been counting down the days until I was finished with you," he said snidely. "That day is today, Erie."

"Yes, yes, I remember the many *lessons* you and the others taught me so often. I remember it all, but then I have been told the same thing over and over since I was old enough to understand it. My question for you, Frasier, is this: as you beat me, tortured me, and placed ink all over my face, did you ever consider that it may make me wish for your races to die out? Because I fail to see why I should care if either of them cease to exist anymore," I hissed as I got up close and personal in his space, watching as he shrank back from me. Sweat beaded on his brow as he watched me, fear permeating from his pores, and I inhaled it like cotton candy at the carnival as it filled the evening air. "You smell good, Frasier."

"You will play your part, or they will tie you down and take turns until one of them breeds that cursed womb of yours, Erie. My money is on Arthur planting his seed first, as he hates you the most." I smiled coldly, unwilling to let him see the shiver that rushed through me with his words. Mostly because I knew they would do it if it came down to that.

"Sorry, but you're going to lose that bet. Callaghan is ahead of them already," I muttered beneath my breath as I started towards the doors. My eyes scanned the document that he had handed to me when I'd first entered. Reading it, I stopped short of the door and frowned. "Are you fucking crazy, or just stupid?" I swung around, staring him down. "The Guild is forbidden to breach, even for me."

"You're not to enter it," he grumbled. "You're to be sure the Fae are otherwise occupied elsewhere. You have that ability, don't you? It's probably just a guise to get you out into the open anyway, so what does it matter to you?"

"Is that because today is the day your doomsday countdown started? Tick tock, Frasier. I do hope you have a great year because I assure you, it will be your last one," I chuckled as I wiggled my fingers in a wave and pushed my back against the door as he watched me.

Outside, I let the cold air wash over my face as fresh snow began to drift down to blanket the world around me. I held my tongue out, catching a snowflake before I closed my mouth and looked around as I felt eyes watching me. Snow was the last thing this city needed right now; as if the humans weren't struggling enough already?

Really, if I could add Mother Nature's ass to my hit list, I would. Hands shoved in my pockets, a target on my back, I headed to the one place the Fae loved to gather: Night Shade. It was a sanctioned bar that allowed creatures of the other realms to seek asylum as long as they followed the owner's rules. I myself wasn't

allowed in there anymore, but it had been worth it. Who knew pixies could be used as darts?

It didn't take long for me to reach the nightclub or find the Fae who gathered around in the large, opulent club. I watched them, wondering what it would be like to be a part of it. To have enough friends that you could barely fit them all into one room. Oh well, I had Fred, and he could never hurt me.

I palmed my weapons and turned away from the club as I felt another presence close to me. I pulled down the hood of the jacket I wore, eying Arthur as he watched me with a heated look that sent a shiver racing down my spine. He wasn't hard on the eyes, but the way he looked at me sent every warning bell in my body off.

"They're preoccupied," I informed the Knight as I watched his slow approach, stopping only when he was mere inches away from me.

"For how long?" he questioned.

"If you like, I could go inside and ask them?" I snorted as he sneered at my answer from where he stood in his pristine armor that glinted in the moon's gaze.

"I am your superior, Erie," he snapped coldly, his narrowed gaze sliding over my attire with disdain as if he could still smell the last job I'd finished on them. He probably could, but finding running water nowadays was a bitch, let alone a washing machine attached to it.

"So you are. That still doesn't change that I cannot foresee when they will finish for the night, Arthur," I grumbled, hating that I couldn't just tell him where to shove his attitude. There were several painful places that I could suggest, and I knew I'd enjoy pushing into most of them.

"And the Guild; is *it* empty?"

"Again, I am not a seer," I chided softly. "I cannot tell you it is if *I* am not inside it, now can I? If you're afraid, I can go with you and hold your hand."

"Drop the tone, female," he ordered as he stared down his nose at me.

I knew what he was after, but I also knew it was no longer hidden within the Guild. When the Guild fell, we'd taken it. They wanted what was ours, and even worse, they wanted to use us to obtain it. As if druids were no more than the creatures who bowed at the feet of the ancient Knights.

I crossed my arms over my chest to ward off the chill of the air; little puffs of steam expelled from my lips as I stood in the garbage-strewn street waiting for him to decide if I had to go play fetch with him, or if his buddies he had hidden within the shadows would begin their chase tonight. I prayed the latter didn't happen, as it would force me to up my own schedule.

"I will retrieve it myself; you're dismissed," he said as he slid his faceguard into place and slowly slithered back to the shadows from which he'd come.

I exhaled the breath I'd held as his power reached out to touch against mine in a show of force and strength. A warning of who was stronger. He'd never felt my power, none of them had. I kept it hidden from everyone, even myself.

Dropping my arms after I'd watched him fully disappear into the shadows, I turned and found Callaghan watching me from where he leaned against an old abandoned building. This one, this one was my bane. He made me warm and fuzzy in places that both

bothered me and made me want to know more about things I shouldn't. Out of all of the Knights I'd met so far, this one was the star of every fantasy I'd ever had. Which shouldn't happen, not with what he wanted from me.

Blue eyes locked with mine as a cocky grin lifted those full, sinful lips up in the corners. Eyes of the clearest turquoise waters watched me as he moved ever closer to where I stood frozen to the spot. His dark blond hair was pushed back, untethered as he often wore it. He was dressed in the same ancient armor that Arthur wore, but where it looked out of place on Arthur, Callaghan wore it perfectly. His heady scent filled my senses as he closed the distance with sure-footed strides that bespoke of power and grace. The sword on his hip drew my eyes, watching the blood-red ruby on the hilt of his blade as it caught the moon's light, glowing eerily in silent warning.

I should have pretended *not* to have noticed him and rushed off, but I was sure he wouldn't have allowed it. This Knight was the highest ranking one I'd dealt with thus far, and his sheer dominance and power always left me shaken when he walked away from our meetings. I was Erie, unafraid of anything, anything *except* the male who was currently giving me a wolfish smile as he strode towards me.

CHAPTER
two

CALLAGHAN

I WATCHED HER EXITING THE DRUID'S DEN, HER EYES burning with ire as she peered down at her fingers and then lifted her wild blue gaze to the skies as the first snow fell. Her pink tongue darted out, capturing a snowflake as my cock jerked in response. Erie had two sides to her, the cold killer who watched you with every intent of ending you, and the childlike woman she let slip out every once in a while. I'd watched her enough to see both, to watch her eyes as she took something in for the first time and her eyes grew large with wonder. There's a side to that woman that I wanted to know while avoiding the other like the fucking plague.

Erie was and would always be the epitome of beauty and grace, but she's also a fucking wrecking ball that would destroy anything that threatened her. She enjoyed her freedom, a freedom I was about to destroy. I hated the idea of watching those eyes grow cold with understanding as she tried to figure out what I'm about

to do to her. I'd scoured the world over, and a few others to be certain there wasn't another way out of this, and now, with the clock ticking down, time was up. I wanted her to come into her power first, to remember the past, our fucking past that was so buried within her that she might never find it again. I still wanted that for her, no matter what had happened.

I watched her walking away from the den, her tiny hands pushed into her pockets as the wind sent her hair into her face. She worried for the humans, something not many cared or bothered with nowadays, and yet she protected them to the best of her ability. I wasn't even sure she knew what she did, or why she felt the need to do it. The girl didn't belong to this world, to this era, and yet here she was, diving into a war that wasn't her own.

The idea of what I was being tasked with sat like a rock on my chest. Knowing that if I didn't do it, someone else would, well, it bothered me to even think of her tied down, raped until she'd become pregnant, and I had no plan of allowing anyone to do that to her. Not when she was mine and had been since as long as I could remember. No, this woman had been mine since I breathed into her premature lungs and brought her to life. In reality, it had started way before that, but that was neither here nor there, and this Erie was so much softer than the other versions.

Still, no matter what had unfolded in the past, or the ages that we'd survived, I wanted her to come to me on her own. I wanted this shit over with, to save the people I'd vowed to protect from certain death if the curse wasn't stopped. If this didn't play out, thousands of innocent lives would be caught in the crossfire. They deserved to live, to grow up without being cursed by the ancient crones that had fucked themselves way back before this world even fully comprehended what they were. We'd warned them to stay out of the affairs of the mortals, and instead, they tortured them. Then those assholes got their noses bent when we refused to step in and save them. Not because we hadn't wanted to, but to bond them to the church would have doomed us all. Not that it stopped it, not with who was pushing it from the shadows to play out exactly how it had. No, one person had wanted us cursed, and she was the epitome of war. And so she had waged it against us and won.

I pulled out of the memories as I watched the lone female who carried the weight of our unknown future with her. She walked away, moving further from me by the moment as she trudged through the litter-covered streets heading to meet up with whatever mission they'd given her today. She looked afraid, and I wanted to pull her close, stare into her beautiful blue eyes, and tell her it would all be okay, but the fucked up truth was, it wouldn't. Not for Erie, not for the child she would carry either. Life wasn't black and white, but hers, it was created in the grey that lay between them. I know it was, because I was the one who created her, or more to the point, brought her back.

I pushed through the doors of the Druid's Den with no warning, enjoying the shocked faces that turned to stare at me. It was white and bland, sterile walls in the antechamber that greeted you as you walk into it, made to disorient whoever entered it. I searched the room for the lecherous asshole who I'd given that girl to mere

hours after she'd been born. To be loved, and yet they'd hated her with every fiber of their very being. Nothing I did made them change how they treated her, not even telling this cold bastard that I intended to take her as my female, eventually. Maybe it was what she was, or that they sensed the evil that slumbered within her, but even so, it didn't give them the right to hurt the child she'd been.

"And to what do we owe this unexpected visit, Templar?" Frasier's tone grated on my nerves, and I wanted to rip his fucking tongue out and slap him with it. I refrained, barely. I allowed my power to fill the room as he swallowed hard, and yeah, I fucking enjoyed the fear I smelled rolling off of him, old and new. Good, she made this pansy-ass, paper-pushing pencil dick cower in her presence.

"Cut the shit, you know why I'm here," I growled, watching as the color drained from his face. It continued, right up until I produced the payment for Erie's living expenses for the last one hundred years. The monthly checks she received for work I'd sent her to do, needing to see her in action, to know her weaknesses and faults. There was nothing I didn't know about her unless you considered her love life, but then I hadn't needed to be privy to that. Who she took between her legs had been her business, just as long as her monthly physical turned up negative for pregnancy. The only thing of hers that belonged to us was her womb, and as long as it wasn't filled, she was free to continue doing whatever she wanted. I'd fought for her freedom without her knowing it. I'd fought for her since the moment I'd brought her into this world.

"How generous, but you're short a couple thousand or more," he wheezed as he tried to hand it back to me. I stared at it before I snorted in reply, watching him step back as my chest rattled, my eyes glowing from within. I wanted to wrap my hands around his throat and watch as the life dimmed to nothing in his dull brown eyes.

As if he could fucking escape me.

"Short? I've monitored every cent you spent on her, which was rather low, considering you spend ten times that amount on those you deem *untrainable*. Not to mention, she's never received a check from you for over one hundred dollars, even though you sent her to do your dirty work often, for *free*. You should be happy I'm not charging you for that, too, considering she is mine and has been mine since the moment she drew air into those premature lungs. Did you forget the agreement? Or the abuse she endured under *your* watch?"

"I assure you that I was not in residence when the blue woad was applied to her face, or when she was taught...I mean, *abused*. As I've told you many times before today, apparently some of the men feared their children lusting after Erie with her unnatural taint or getting ideas that she was...theirs. It was meant to keep her pure until the time in which you came for her. It doesn't really matter either way; she only has one use. Erie was created to spread her legs and take what is given to her. She's nothing more than a womb to be used and then thrown away. What does it matter if she was mistreated or scarred?" he snorted and then groaned as my fist slammed against his face without warning. Bones snapped, the crunch soothing to the monster within me as I watched him slide down the wall

in shock as the pain registered inside the useless organ between his ears.

The moment he climbed his worthless ass back up from the floor, I was in his face, nose to nose with him. "Convenient, you were also absent when she was beaten repeatedly because she drew the eye of a head druid's son, too. And when she was strung up and beaten again, and again," I hissed icily as he flinched with every word I said. My hands tightened around the crumpled collar of the suit he wore; nose to nose I hissed every word, knowing he could hear the beast within me rattling his cage, itching to take him out. "Erie isn't ugly. That girl is as beautiful and wild as the land she is named after. You think those marks you placed on her deter or detract from her beauty? They don't. You abused her and allowed others to do the same. You acted and treated her as if she was no one or nothing of consequence. Then you trained her how to wield magic. You painted the woad of the long-forgotten Celtic warriors onto her face and taught her how to fight, Frasier. Now you're butthurt because she's willing to go to war to be free of you, of us? You think she's going to be easily caught? Nah, you better start praying to your Gods that she can forgive us because she's more than ready to fight for her freedom. You don't build the perfect weapon and expect it not to work. You painted that girl for war, and make no mistake: she will go to war against us. It's in her fucking blood, in every fiber of her being to wage it. She won't just bow down because some man tells her to. No, Erie will wage war against us, and she's got a huge advantage over us in that department."

"You think she will live that long? No, she will be

dead the moment she is no longer needed," he hissed, and I smirked, showing him my teeth.

I let the beast within flex his muscles. My eyes glowed as I stared him down, begging him to make a fucking move, any move, so that I could allow what lay beneath the cold façade of my skin to come forth to collect a pound of his flesh. We've craved his death longer than Erie's been born.

"She is an abomination of the laws and of this world. She was created in an evil so terrible that it was banned from this world by the Gods themselves. She cannot be allowed to live, and the fact that the monster within you wishes her to be his should tell you everything you need to know about her! She is evil incarnate, and if she ever learns to wield it against us, God save us all!" he shouted, and I smiled coldly, because yes, that was my girl. She was evil, so fucking evil that he couldn't even begin to understand what lay within her beautifully twisted soul.

"You touch my girl, and I'll make an example out of you that will never be forgotten as long as this world continues to spin. She is a fucking unicorn, and she's mine. I named her, and when her mother refused to look at her? I was the one who comforted her and promised her that everything would be alright. Erie is mine by right, one hundred fucking percent. When no one else cared about her, I did. I have protected her for her entire life, and if you think it will end because she's accomplished what she was created to do, you're wrong. Let's hope you're not *dead* wrong, Frasier." My hands released him and fixed his shirt as I remained close enough to stare into his eyes. "Now tell me, were

you a good boy? Did you hand her my letter?"

"She took it, and it burned her hands; your spell is well-embedded into her flesh. You can track her at will, elsewhere."

"Good, now give me the rest of the spells I asked for," I ordered as I watched him wiping the blood from his mouth and nose. The bent appendage would never heal correctly, which satisfied the inner beast that watched from within. Once I had the spells and her location, I growled. "What the fuck is Arthur doing summoning her?" I demanded as he handed me her mission log.

"I didn't ask why he needed her," he shrugged. "He called and asked for her to meet him at that location. If you ask me, he intends to get that necklace and place it on her before you have a chance, Templar. You may want her, but he hates her enough to treat her as what she is. Nothing more than a womb," he mocked as he nodded towards the door. "You've overstayed your welcome. Best you get going before he claims that which you crave, Mason Callaghan. While you're throwing out threats, remember this: I raised her; she's very aware of her value and what she is. She will never touch me because that was the first thing she learned under my teachings. Ask her about it, ask her what happens when she doesn't listen or questions me."

"Careful, the monster within me wishes to feed from your corpse, Frasier," I hissed, letting the deep rattle reverberate through the room. "Keep fucking running that mouth and I will let him out to play." He shivered visibly, very aware of what was watching him from within me. As old as he was, not even he would fuck with that which prowled within my flesh. I knew what he'd done to her, and I'd stripped the Knight who was supposed to protect her in my absence of his spurs, along with his power. Right before I took his fucking head from his shoulders for looking the other way as she was abused.

I stepped back, pulling my phone from my pocket as I slid my thumb over it, unlocking the screen. Arthur didn't answer, and he had shit for brains if he thought he could do this without my knowing about it. I dialed the Templar Order, snorting loudly as my father's mistress asked me to hold, knowing who it was before I'd even spoken.

"What?" my father responded within seconds.

"You sent Arthur after her?" I snapped crossly.

"I sent him to lure her to you. He is retrieving the necklace you asked for. She will assume it is something else, but she will be where we agreed within the hour. How you handle it from there is your issue, as long as you handle it, Mason. Her time is up, our people come first."

"I'm en route; if he touches her, I'll kill him myself."

I ended the call, moving towards the location as I pulled up the other half of the spell she took unknowingly. A few whispered words and the paper ignited, burning as I held it until it singed my flesh. I dropped it, watching as it hit the snow-covered path and disintegrated. My girl was inches away from the one Knight who wanted to hurt her, the one asshole who fought me for this right. Fuck him too if he thought he was ever touching her. I'd rip his spine out before I allowed that to ever happen.

Stepping into the shadows, I watched the alluring wench who was wearing the stolen glamour of what she thought was the perfect woman. She was all blonde, blue eyes, and perfect, which didn't fit her at all. Not my girl, no. My girl was created for war, scarred from battles, covered in woad, and those eyes of hers; they searched your soul, ripping it open to see past any fucking armor you wore to your bare fucking bones. Arthur watched her, his eyes greedy as he took in what he thought she looked like, what she showed the world. I knew better. I knew what beauty lay beneath that façade she'd created. Her eyes were of the bluest skies high above Dublin on a warm summer day, hair as wild as the flowers and mixed with red hues as wild and untamed as she was. This beautiful storm of woman, she was of druids of the ancient Celtic warriors, Knights of the Isle of Sky, and this beautiful mess was created of both, and yet she was neither. She was older than both, designed to be the embodiment of grace and beauty, to lure men to their deaths.

I listened as she spoke, enjoying the sass of her words and the light brogue of her homeland. A homeland embedded in her so deeply that it couldn't be separated from her soul. Arthur was so busy staring at the illusion that he missed the way her voice went higher as she lied. I snorted as I rubbed my hand down my face and waited for him to move away. The moment he did, she turned, staring right at me.

"Erie," I murmured, cocky asshole on the outside, a fucking mess inside knowing tonight we fight. She and I, we had history, but however she felt about me, I couldn't let it stop what was coming. She didn't want it, I get it. Monsters had to be caged. The one I'd taken within me was no different. It needed me as much as

I needed it, and we needed her. Like I said, we had fucking history. "Does Arthur need your assistance, or do you just get off on sending men to their untimely demise?"

I drank in the scent of wildflowers that clung to her body. It was a scent that drove me insane at night after I'd watched her fight or worked with her closely. This wisp of a girl was a spitfire as a child, but as a woman... as a woman, she was unmatched in beauty or mind. She was a force that had no equal. Her eyes narrowed, watching me for any sign of danger because she didn't trust anyone, and with damn good cause. We'd dropped the ball too many times, and what she'd become was a broken beauty, but those cracks of hers let the light within her shine.

"The Fae would not dare touch him...too much," she said with cold indifference. "Play with him, yes. Kill him? No. They have enough war to deal with. I don't think they'd ignite your wrath as well. You're all so overdramatic as is. The entire world knows it," she uttered, devoid of emotion as her shoulders lifted and fell in a halfhearted shrug.

"You're a mere girl, Erie. Born of the magic of the cauldron of Dagda to serve *us* and this world," I whispered huskily, watching the anger that entered her expressive eyes. Erie pissed was a beautiful thing, but Erie irate made my dick ache to know how she fucked. I backed off years ago, knowing her adventure into womanhood was hers and hers alone to take. She'd earned it. I'd known my time would come, but now that had changed, and events wouldn't allow me to give her the time she needed.

"I serve no man," she said, a grin lifting those sweet lips that I wanted to taste. That smile was all bite and no sweetness. Fuck if it didn't coil a need that I knew I'd sate soon enough.

She stared me down, her eyes heated as she slowly let that heady gaze of hers drop, and I watched her looking over every inch of me. I grinned wickedly as her pupils dilated, her spine arched seductively, and fucking hell, I wanted to bend her over and make her mine, right here. Right fucking here, with the entire world watching us as I made her mine. We stood in place so fucking long that nothing around us registered. *Me*, a fucking Knight that had never been caught off guard or distracted, until her. I'd been a Knight since before this land we stood on even existed or was known of. Her eyes got stuck on my neck, sliding over it like a caress that I felt all the way to my balls. Swallowing hard, I refrained from doing what I really wanted to do.

"Do you like what you see, Erie?"

"You are rather pretty," she hissed as she admitted she liked me, but I already knew that. I'd caught her stealing glances before, watching me with a curiosity that made me ache to let her explore it further. Not that she would have been ready, which was why I let her be until I knew she was. Every time I'd requested her to come on a mission with me, those pretty cobalt blue eyes of hers found me in the crowd and eye-fucked me until I had the world's bluest balls. Her tongue snaked out, licking over her full bottom lip as her head tilted to the side. "What do you want from me; I know you didn't just happen to be around the area, so what do you want?" Her eyes moved down to her hand, studying her uneven nails. She didn't understand chemistry, because if she did, she'd have that answer figured out already. She tended to get nervous around me, and it was sexy as hell, but the way her eyes sized me up, she wasn't finding me lacking, and I damn sure didn't want to disappoint her there.

"You are aware of the prophecy for which you were created." I stepped closer to her, invading her personal space as her nostrils flared with my scent, one she's familiar with and yet refused to remember. "Your time is near. You will be mine whether you like it or not. It's time we do our parts to protect our people." I continued talking as I backed her up until she was pressed against the wall of the abandoned brick building. "Them or me, Erie," I growled huskily, unable to hide the lust that slipped free with the words I spoke. "If you're mine, they'll never touch you. I will lead them all one day; they respect me. You're running out of time, and they are running out of patience. Are you aware of what Arthur seeks tonight?" Fucking shit comes out all wrong when I'm this close to her; as if I'm some fucking youth trying to slip into her panties. She had a way of getting under my skin, making me unhinged by her true beauty, and the history we shared that she was oblivious to.

"He seeks the witch's cauldron," she snapped as she shoved me away from her. Erie doesn't like people up close to her, or to be touched. It drove me insane knowing why she was like that, knowing I didn't protect her from it. It was a failure that haunted me every fucking morning that I woke up knowing it.

"Wrong. He seeks an amulet we created long ago. One that controls the free will of those who wear it," I

corrected as I was forced to turn to continue watching her as she prepared to dart away if she needed to in a hurry. Erie had the highest sense of self-preservation of anyone I'd ever encountered, and she was not wrong to use it. There was a damn good reason she should fear my intentions, and did.

"So what, he can get some free will of his own? We both know he could use some."

"That's not how it works. It doesn't give free will, it takes it away. He was told to retrieve it so that it can be placed around your pretty little neck. As I have said, they're done waiting. They want to make you into an incubator, Erie. With that trinket, they can do it, and you'd never be the wiser."

She shivered minutely, her pupils responding to her fear, and I wanted to rip Arthur's spine out for instilling it in her years ago. The words slipped over her harshly with no comfort to give her. No pretty lie to make this anything but what it was. Her fate was tied to mine; it had been since before she'd ever drawn air into those lungs from which she breathed. The only way to ease what was about to happen was to help her through it. To offer that which she was afraid to crave: me.

"You could be mine, carry my sons, and remain at my side as my queen, little one," I said softly as my fingers trailed through my hair in frustration that had no outlet. My eyes captured hers with a silent plea in their depths. I watched her closely as the darkness inside of me peered out, taking her in. It didn't see her glamour; it knew she's wild and beautiful. He showed me what they'd done to her because he'd found it beautiful. He'd found it familiar, alluring.

"They have to catch me first," she retorted angrily.

"Arthur called you to him tonight, and what happened? You came. Your mother was from the Templar Order, as pure of blood as my own. In all reality, you should be one of us, but you're not. You're a druid; did you never wonder how that happened? You were handed to the druids to be trained and then returned to us when you came of age; you're of age now. That tattoo on your wrist? *I* put it there. I placed ink into your flesh to bind us together; you and I, Erie. You were born for a reason, and that was to be mine when the time was right. It's here now, and so am I, to collect you."

"You branded me like cattle?" she demanded, and that flash of betrayal that shone in her eyes coiled in my stomach like a snake ready to strike.

"I gave you my signet to protect you," I clarified carefully, even though she wouldn't catch the gravity of the mark I had given her. "You have *my* seal, *my* name on your arm in *our* language. You've worn it since the day you were born. When the witches cursed us, you were created to be our fix that breaks the curse they placed to end our races. Every curse has a fix, and you are ours. If a Knight isn't born once a century, we cease to exist. We serve the same cause, Erie. Don't make this harder than it has to be. You won't ever want for anything. I won't hurt you as the others may do. I will leave you the use of your mind and that smart mouth of yours."

She swallowed a scream that bubbled up, but I sensed it in the way her eyes burned with fire. Blue flames danced within them as her mouth tightened. "When was the last Knight born?" she asked, her chest heaving as the wind kicked up her hair, sending it every

which direction, her magic clinging to her. I allowed *him* to adjust our vision, showing the truth of the beauty before us.

"Ninety-nine years ago today," I announced, watching as she flinched and recoiled without noticing she was. I hated the way her eyes burned with rage mixed with hurt, and yet I didn't regret that she would be mine soon, no, because I'd craved this woman much longer than was healthy for me.

"I won't be yours or anyone else's, Callaghan. This is my life! I'm not something you just claim and then throw away. I'm not even old in druid standards, I'm an infant."

"You're not young anymore, Erie. You're beautiful; you are ready to do what you were created for. I've waited for you to be ready for me. I've given you ample time to come into your powers, and you have," I returned softly, silk lacing every word as I watched her to be able to judge when she was going to attack, because this was Erie, the girl had two settings: Fight or flight, and she tended to lean towards the former more often than not.

She turned around, closing her eyes against the emotions that overwhelmed her. When I stepped closer, closing the distance between us, she turned, staring into my eyes before smiling coldly. Pain assaulted me as I stared down between us, glaring at the dagger she'd stuck between my ribs, straight into my heart. I glared into those pretty blue eyes as the woad on her face was lit from the moon above. My hand lifted to touch her beauty, but she stepped away, leaving me to drop to my knees in the trash-laden street.

"I won't be yours or anyone else's incubator,

asshole," she snapped as she withdrew the blade and stepped away. Her eyes snapped back to mine over her shoulder, as if she didn't know whether to do more or leave me on these streets to rot. She should have done more because now the beast within wanted to play hide-and-seek with her. But it wanted to seek that ass out and show it what rough play was.

CHAPTER three

ERIE

ENTERING MY APARTMENT, I SLID MY SHOES OFF AT the door and opened the freezer to allow my roommate some fresh air. He snarled, and I smirked as I addressed him coolly, pushing the flesh of the dead human I'd buried on my way back here between his lips. Mouth full of the dead, he sputtered and spit it out. I frowned as I placed my hands onto my hips and glared at the head that was propped up by thick ice cubes.

"I had to cut that off a corpse, Fred. You need to eat," I suggested as I jumped on the counter and stared him down crossly. My eyes dropped to the crest and name on my wrist, and I became restless. "It may help that sour disposition you have."

"I have no stomach, woman! Remember, you *left* it behind."

"Semantics, you can still eat, right?" I asked as I jumped off the counter and started pacing. I was agitated, unhinged by the asshole who wanted to claim me. When Fred refused to answer and just continued to glare at me, I shrugged. "I have a problem," I uttered as I faced him.

"I don't care," he retorted.

"How long can you survive like this?" I returned offhandedly.

"Forever," he snapped angrily.

"So if I were to go missing, you'd be okay here until I got back?" I asked, knowing that sooner or later, Mason Callaghan would catch me.

"Free me, and then you won't have to worry about it," he offered.

"Not happening, Fred. You and me, we're friends."

"I hate you, woman. You're the furthest thing from a friend to me, and you're insane. You cut my fucking head off! Remember?"

"You should eat, you're hangry. I need to shower and remove the feel of Templar and his blood from my flesh. I'll be back, don't go anywhere," I said, listening as his foul mouth started up. The things a girl had to do to get a friend these days. I was sure he'd come around, eventually. The moment the freezer door closed, I was back to pacing aimlessly in my front room.

The Christmas tree in the corner was no more than a car air-freshener. But it wasn't like there'd be any gifts to put under an actual tree, so it worked for me. I'd stolen lights from downtown, which now blinked on and off, basking the room in a soft, colorful glow. The couch in the corner was scuffed up, but it had been that way when I'd discovered it here eons ago. Pictures of a happy couple covered the walls, which were painted a lighter shade of grey than I'd have chosen myself. I

preferred all things dark because I was sure that if I had a soul, it was black and lifeless.

Moving into the bedroom, I stripped out of the blood-stained clothes that served as proof that I'd murdered Callaghan. Not that he'd actually die, but wishful thinking and all that jazz. Water dripped from the other room, reminding me that a hot bath awaited my aching bones. Abandoning the bedroom for the bathroom, I exhaled the pang of regret that entered my mind, clenching my heart in a vise. I added lavender to the bath and watched as the water fizzled.

Callaghan was a bastard, but the others who wanted me? The others wouldn't care if I liked it, wouldn't care if it killed me, as long as it added to their lifespan. Was his offer so bad? *Yes!* I wasn't theirs to control or to be used for their purpose. My magic depended on them, but it didn't mean I had to do anything. Shit, my life depended on this happening, and I still didn't agree on it being done. *Period.*

Pulling my hair up, I placed it in a messy bun. I eyed the mirror, taking in the new bruises I'd gotten this week already, and it was only Sunday. Slowly, I stepped into the scalding water and inhaled the calming scent of freshly plucked lavender that calmed my soul. Sitting, I watched as the water rushed out of the tub, covering the floor in a mess.

Whispering a spell under my breath, I watched as more colorful bubbles filled the tub and flowed over the edges to join the growing mess already on the floor. The earthy scents of lavender and magic eased the chaos that ran rampant through my thoughts. Leaning my head back against the porcelain tub, I closed my eyes and gave in to exhaustion.

I awoke in a chilled tub, my eyelids heavy as I sat up and peered at the shadows. A growl rumbled from deep inside my chest as I sat forward, pulling my knees to my chest as I covered my breasts and glared at the shadows that moved.

I felt him then, the heat he permeated along with his intoxicating scent that made my body react in all the wrong ways. It had created some of my wildest fantasies through adolescence, and while I'd never admit that shit out loud, it didn't mean that they had ever stopped either. But I knew him, I knew the moment he got a glimpse of the monster they'd painted me to be, he'd flinch and recoil just as everyone else had so long ago.

"You shouldn't have come here, Paladin. You're uninvited." My tone was flat, lifeless. It was exactly how I wished my body would react to him, and yet that traitorous bitch arched with invitation.

"You shouldn't sleep in the bathtub; that's what they make beds for," he smirked as he moved from the cover of darkness and let his glowing blue eyes slip down my naked frame. Instead of playing dead, my nipples responded, hardening before those glowing blue eyes. "But you are beautiful in what the Gods gave you, Erie," he purred huskily.

"You shouldn't say my name with such familiarity, asshole," I retorted as I stood to my full, unimpressive height of five-foot-nothing. My thick blonde hair decided at that moment to let loose from the ponytail holder that had held it up. I snorted as the taint of his magic cascaded down my back and past my ass. "Don't use your magic on me," I warned, sending a jolt of

electric current at him as I stepped closer. It was ancient magic, pure and simple. It soothed my aches, pleasured my flesh in ways that made me flinch and worst of all, I had felt it before and knew without thinking or examining the magic that it was a part of him.

"You are more than blessed, woman," he murmured as his eyes slowly trailed from head to toe before slowly moving back up to settle on my eyes. "Yet you hide and never allow anyone to see the real you. Show me who you are, Erie."

"And let you see what our people have done to me?" I scoffed as I raised my foot to kick him, hoping to catch him off guard. No such luck. He grabbed my leg, using it to pull me closer. I wanted to break his perfect nose, to rip his eyes out so he could never see what they did to me. I hid the ugliness of what they had done to me from everyone, hating the thought of them recoiling as I did when I peered at myself in the mirror.

"Careful, little one, I like playing rough," he warned thickly as coarse gravel coated each word that escaped his sinfully full lips.

I wanted to taste him, to touch him in ways so impure that the blush of longing smoothed over my flesh before I could prevent him from seeing it. I rounded my body, kicking him with the other leg, which didn't even faze him. Instead, he shook it off before my feet touched the ground and took me to the floor, dropping his hefty weight onto mine, holding me down with it. I stilled, clearly aware of the heat from his massive body as his eyes bored into mine. They dipped to my lips, and then he did the last thing he should have.

He *kissed* me!

It stunned me, left me breathless. The intensity of his kiss and the way I responded to it sent a shiver of need pulsing through me. It sent everything out of whack; my entire sense of self-preservation abandoned me. Heat pooled to a place it only ever had whenever his image is on my mind, and yet here, now, he was creating it! His mouth was sin incarnate; the clean flavor of mint dulled my senses. I moaned against it, unable to pull away as I should have done. The emotions that danced through my mind and body were foreign, uncharted territory that both scared and exhilarated me. His tongue dipped between my lips, pushing past the weak effort I maintained to keep them closed against him. The growl that escaped his lungs was captured by me, and as I moaned, he deepened the kiss, demanding I respond to him. My entire body heated, fire blazed between my legs as a new ache filled me, building as if it could reach some epic height I wasn't aware existed.

I pushed against his chest, which only made him push back, holding me down as a moan ripped from my lips, heat pooled between my thighs. I felt him there, his cock pressing against my vulnerable sex. The tremor that ripped through me at feeling his hardness against my naked flesh made me swallow hard.

Callaghan relaxed into the kiss, moving his hips against me and I groaned as he devoured me. His hand slipped between our bodies, moving down towards my naked flesh and I rolled us, staring down at him as my chest rose and fell with every labored breath I took to calm my response to him. What the ever-loving fuck was wrong with me? Blue eyes that glowed like the River Styx stared up at me triumphantly.

"You kissed me," I whispered huskily as I moved to slap him, only for him to capture the hand. I used the other, unsure of where my brain had abandoned me to go, but it was no longer in this fight, or with me. I stared down at him, acutely aware of exactly how hard he was, and that I had sat directly on it. I was also aware that *it* had a pulse that matched mine perfectly.

"So I did," he purred as he slowly trailed his heated gaze over my heaving chest, pausing as he took in the embarrassing state of my nipples. The heat in that stare melted my insides. "And you taste like I want to fuck you," he uttered as he released my hand to grab my hips. He ground his arousal against my sex, watching every minuscule emotion that played across my face. My hands rested against his steady chest, balancing myself as he rubbed his cock against me erotically. "Would it be so bad with me, Erie?"

"Don't ever do that again," I snapped as I stood up even though his eyes latched to the thin patch of red hair that was slick with arousal. Oops, I'd forgotten to glamour *all* of me.

"What? Kiss you, or make you want it as much as I do?" he challenged with a brutal intensity in his gaze that scared and excited me.

"I don't want you," I hissed. I turned, dismissing him as I pushed my wet hair away from my face. I had done the one thing I knew I shouldn't do; I turned my back on him. He moved with speed and precision. I was shoved against the wall, lifted, and forced to straddle his waist.

"You suck at lying."

"I suck at a lot of things, things you'll never

experience with me, Paladin." I pushed against his chest as my back touched the coldness of the wall. His gaze dropped to my lips before slowly rising to lock with mine. "Put me down."

"Make me," he challenged. "You smell ready for me," he growled as his teeth scraped across my collarbone, sending a shockwave of need crashing down to where I did *not* want it to go.

"That must suck," I whispered through the need that tightened in my throat as my lids grew heavy. "Because I don't want you, Callaghan," I replied huskily. My lips touched against his in a soft flicker of curiosity as my tongue darted out to slowly trace the fullness of his bottom lip.

"Let me have you, Erie," he uttered before his mouth crushed against mine in insatiable desire and every coherent thought I had fled my mind. I moaned as my arms slid up his chest and my fingers trailed through his hair, ripping it backward, away from mine so I could think. "Careful, I can play rough too," he warned. "I don't think you're ready for that, or am I wrong?" Blue eyes the color of the ocean on a bright summer day challenged me. "You will choose tonight before I leave here."

"I choose never in a million fucking years," I muttered flatly, sliding down the wall, pushing against his chest. He allowed it as I marched towards my bedroom, intending to dress. "There has to be another way. The Order can find another way rather than forcing me to do this."

"You still don't get it; even if you find a way out, which you won't because I have fucking tried, you will

be forced to do this one way or another. Every prophecy entangled with this one has come to pass. The Order will not wait to see if it is undone. They won't chance it by waiting to see if we begin to die, Erie. Have my son; you'll be free the moment you have given birth to him, if that is what you desire."

Tears stung my eyes, swimming in my vision as I turned around to face him. Anger clouded my judgment as my hair rose with the electrical current of power that pulsed to life within my soul. It wasn't a secret that my parents, both Templar and druid, had used ancient, powerful magic to conceive me. Dark magic twisted with light, and when I was born, I was abandoned by both as if I was nothing more than trash they couldn't throw away fast enough.

"You think I'd hand you my son and just walk away?" I inquired barely above a whispered breath as my body heated, and this time it wasn't lust driving my pulse to a dangerous crescendo, but rage. "You should leave, Callaghan, before I reach my blades."

"I cannot be killed by you," he countered as he grabbed my arm and twisted it behind my back as he pulled me towards him painfully. "I'm offering you a way to remain free, unchained from a dungeon where you would be kept, bound until you conceived a child. I will not hurt you, nor would I keep you locked up. I assure you that *is* the plan for you. They're coming here right now, hunting you. You're out of fucking time," he growled.

"You think I'm weak? I assure you, I am not. I'm not a fucking damsel, Callaghan. I can protect myself, so take your offer and get the fuck out. I am not bound to you or any of them. Unlike you, I don't care if we die out. This world doesn't need a hero; it needs monsters. They don't need you and your pristine order of crusaders to charge in and save them. Don't you get it? They like destruction. They crave chaos, not order, not security. They're like me, dark and deadly. So take your voodoo dick and get out of here!" I ordered as I yanked my arm free and turned away from him.

The front door was kicked opened and before I had time to react, Callaghan grabbed me, shoving me behind his back as he materialized thick, heavy blades. I peered around his hulking frame, and my stomach dropped as I shrank away from the angry faces of the Templars who crowded into my apartment.

"Release her, Callaghan," Arthur demanded, and I winced as I took in his disheveled appearance. The Fae obviously hadn't been kind to him. *Oops, my bad, asshole.* "She belongs to all of us. Not just you, princeling," he continued as his eyes hooded, heavy with lust as he took in my lack of clothing.

"She is coming with me," Callaghan announced as he stepped further in front of me. "She's agreed to carry my child in her womb; my blood is pure and ancient. Both her blood and mine date back to the first man and woman of the Order, and we will breed a powerful son. She has chosen," he challenged, and his words swallowed any argument I might have held. What the fuck was he thinking?

"Is that so?" Arthur laughed coldly. His cruel gaze stared through Callaghan as if he was taking in my current state of undress. His lips curled with distaste, and he spat on my floor. "That bitch no longer gets to

choose. We all want what is owed to us. She thinks she's above us, but we intend to show her where she belongs: On her back, serving us."

The room exploded in a flurry of motion so fast that I didn't even have time to register anyone had moved. I'd known all of my life that the Knights were among the most skilled killers. Until today, I'd never seen them in action—and I wasn't sure I wanted to ever again.

The glass shattered as light exploded, and darkness engulfed the room. Grunts sounded, and then howls of pain filled the room. The sound of metal hitting flesh was sickening, and as a hand encircled my waist, I struggled against it as I tried to make my brain react to what was happening in my own apartment. Fingers brushed against my naked ass, and I spun against the hold, fully intending to fight my way to freedom.

"Gods, woman, hold still!" Callaghan hissed as he whispered a spell to bathe the room he'd shoved me into in a soft glow. I peered over his shoulder, gasping in air as I took in the grisly scene that bathed my living room in blood and gore.

"What did you do?" I whispered hesitantly.

"I told you, you're mine," he snorted. "Pack, because you won't be able to come back here for a while. You're no longer safe on your own; the Order will begin to hunt us down for what we did unless I can convince them otherwise, but I need your help for that."

"*We?* I didn't do anything! You did this," I groaned. I looked towards the freezer, eyeing it as I considered what would happen to Fred if what Callaghan had said was true. Either way, I'd be slipping away from this asshole to save the bodiless demon. He was my only friend.

CHAPTER
four

CALLAGHAN

I WATCHED HER ENTER MY HOME, UNAWARE THAT SHE took the servant quarters up to it. My *home*, she's in my fucking home and at my mercy. I watched her take it in, her eyes scanning for each escape exit, noting the lack of them. Her lips tugged down, frowning as she noted the varying shades of black with worry. It was all black because I wasn't colorful; my life had a meaning, and I lived by the code of the Knight. Sure, it was done tastefully, but I didn't waste money on things I didn't need. There was also the fact that without her, this is what I saw. Erie was the color to my dark world, the light that lit it on fire.

"Impressive," she hummed as she tossed her bag to the couch and crossed her arms. Her eyes held mine with a pointed look. "Still not sure why I'm here though," she snapped, her voice full of irritation as they searched mine for any sign of aggression. "I'm not giving you a child, nor are we doing it to even try to have one."

I smirked, knowing she may be crude and brash in attitude, but Erie didn't like to swear. In fact, she normally skirted over words if she couldn't find one to substitute it for. "*Fucking*, Erie, say it with me." Her eyes bulged, and I chuckled, noting she was afraid of me. Terrified, even. Her hands trembled as she stood there, and no matter how much she fidgeted to hide it, I still saw it. I was trained to spot fear in my enemies, to know when there was blood in the water. Erie was afraid of me, and it both bothered me and hurt that she had placed me into that category.

"You're not *fucking* me, asshole," she popped off, and I barely contained the need to groan with her crass use of the term. I may not have been in her personal space, but I had spent enough time studying her to know that when she took lovers, she had been discreet, careful for others not to note who they were, not even me. I'd watched, curious to see who they were, but never managed to figure it out, or catch them on their way out of her apartment. "What happens when Arthur comes next time?" she asked through the thickness of her throat.

"He won't come for you again, ever," I returned sharply, more harshly than I had intended to. It wasn't a lie, not really. I would forbid him from even trying, but she assumed I meant he was dead, and the asshole that I was, I let her.

"He's immortal," she argued.

I swallowed past the lie that was about to drip from my tongue. "Even we can die," I muttered, and she blinked as understanding dawned in her eyes.

"The blade you used?"

"Lethal to anyone who breaks a vow to the Knight's Order," I said softly. "And before you assume it will work on me, I assure you, it won't." I should have been pissed off that she was excited over the news, but I wasn't.

"Didn't think it would," she frowned as she redirected her attention to the portrait of me in battle; one of the few left that had survived the crossing into this continent.

"Romania," I answered, noting the question in her eyes as she glanced from it to me. "It's from when the Turkish Empire first invaded. We were there to help those loyal to the church escape."

"Stay the fuck out of my head," she snapped as her eyes watched me.

"I wasn't in your head," I smiled coldly as she watched me, fully aware that I was a predator and she was my quarry. "That pretty face of yours hides very little from me. It's one of the things I enjoy about you. You can't hide what your heart holds. Come; it's late, and you'll need sleep soon."

I heard her heart as it increased speed, palpating as fear entered her veins. For all of her bravado, she was afraid of being this close to me. Not that I blamed her; my intentions weren't knightly, in fact, they were anything but. By now, Arthur and the other Knights would have been here to set the spells, to add the wards, to trap my saucy little vixen.

"This is where I leave," she uttered thickly, if not a little huskily as passion flared to life in her eyes.

"You are being hunted now, Erie. You are not making it out of this one without choosing your future. I see

your gears turning, and I assure you, there's nowhere you can run or hide that we will not find you. There's no place for you that doesn't have me in it."

"Show me where I'm sleeping then," she said, changing the subject as she pulled her eyes from mine, dropping them to the floor.

"In my bed, with me," I announced.

"That's not happening." Her tiny arms crossed over her chest as she watched me.

I had her, I had Erie in my house, and I knew her one weakness. I hated myself for using it, knowing that it would guarantee that this happened, but it would also protect her in the long run. I had no other option, no other direction to take this. Not one that she'd like or be safe from.

"I just killed Templar Knights to protect you. I broke the rules to keep you safe; you will sleep with me tonight so that when I return to the Templar Order tomorrow, I smell of you. You don't have to fuck me, but you have to give me enough that when I turn myself in tomorrow, when I tell them you are willing to allow me access to your body to secure a child, I won't be lying to them."

"I didn't ask you to do that," she pointed out softly.

"No, but the idea of him raping you did not sit well with me," I admitted. "My sword cannot be used on me because I've never broken the law of the Knight's Order. So you have a choice to make. I've given you time to decide, and a safe place to make your choice. Tomorrow you will be handed over to my father to either tell him you've chosen me, or you'll be placed under lock and key until you do what you were created to do."

"You'd turn me over after you just slaughtered your own people to keep them from raping me?" she asked flippantly as she placed her hand on her hip.

"In a fucking heartbeat," I said flatly with fire igniting inside of me. I would, but I didn't have to like it, and it may kill me to do it, but I would. Thousands of lives depended on this, even more if we lost the hold we held in this world and more monsters descended into it.

In silence, I watched the need to pay me back and her self-preservation fighting against one another. She knew what the cost would be if it had played out as she'd thought it had, even though it hadn't. Erie had a moral compass so fucking pure that it terrified me. She never left a debt unpaid, and she always protected those who helped her, even if she didn't like them. I wasn't sure what drove that need, or who had created it, but it was her downfall tonight, and we both knew it.

"Fine," she muttered as she swallowed hard, audibly. "I need to use your bathroom to freshen up first."

I showed her to my bathroom, staring at the door as she closed it behind her, and then stared at the wards around the room. I lit the candles inside the room, dimming the light as I pulled the thick silk navy blue bedspread to the side. I had purchased a large enough bed to fit ten people into it long ago, but I didn't sleep, so it had seemed like a waste other than when I'd fucked someone here. The Knights that held beasts within them never hungered, never slept, and never craved anything—or I hadn't, until one hundred years ago when she'd been born into this world. My eyes slowly moved over the white walls, striking against the navy blue carpet and ceiling that were painted in runes

older than time itself. A gift from the beast I held as I'd claimed this room and apartment as ours.

A noise sounded from inside the bathroom, and when the doorknob turned, I watched it, waiting for her as I felt her emotions playing in her mind. She hated what they'd done to her, thought it had ruined her, but it hadn't. I had waited for this day for seventy-five years, since the day she became a woman. I'd abided my time, hoping with the missions we'd been on that she would come to me willingly again, and yet she held everyone at arm's length instead. No matter what I had done, she pushed me further away.

The door cracked open, and I turned back towards it, staring at her as everything inside of me flexed to move to her, to make this happen right now. The moment she stepped through the door, the world stopped turning as I swallowed past the need that coiled tightly in my stomach. I stopped breathing as I took in her sheer gown, exposing everything beneath it to my hungry stare. Her hair was loose, cascading down her back as she rubbed her arms nervously, like some impish virgin that didn't know how beautiful or alluring her nakedness was to a man. I had to stifle a growl of possession as she frowned and lifted those cornflower blue eyes to meet mine briefly before she dropped them to take me in slowly as heat pooled within them.

Her eyes slowly slid down my body, the tattoos that adorned my chest, my arms, and my neck forming armor over my shoulder blade. The scars that graced it from the countless battles I'd endured before I was turned immortal. Her eyes lowered to the V-line that disappeared beneath the jeans I wore and then flared with fear. She looked like a caged animal about to fight her way to freedom.

"This is stupid," she uttered through trembling lips, and my gaze narrowed at the way her body shook before me.

"Drop the glamour," I whispered, wanting her to trust me enough to let me see what she hid from everyone else. I wanted her to just let one person in this world know who she was, who she really was behind the magic and fear that clung to her like a second skin.

"What?" she asked, momentarily caught off guard by the request.

"Let me see you, Erie. Let me see what you hide from the world," I uttered thickly.

"Never," she scoffed as a growl entered her throat as her familiar anger returned. "This is me."

"No, this is what you show to the world to protect yourself from being judged. This isn't you," I whispered. My tone filled with a layer of need and desire. She wasn't the cold killer right now, this was the other one, the innocent beauty who wasn't sure how to react or what to do. How many other assholes got to see this? To see this softer, naïve side of her that she hid so well behind the coldblooded killer.

"This is the only me you will ever see," she returned. "Take it or leave it, Paladin. I don't care either way."

Paladin, the one thing she knew that pissed me off when she called me it. At least she hadn't lost her fight.

"Come to me," I ordered firmly. "Don't be scared, Erie, I'll be gentle with you…at least for now."

"Callaghan," she warned. Her feet moved forward, but it was timid and out of character for her. I watched

her, knowing something was happening here that terrified her, but I felt it too, knowing that once we went through with this, we'd be bonded. She wanted me, and I wanted her, it was basic fucking chemistry. "How far do we have to go?" she asked.

"Far enough that when I tell them that you're sexually open to me, it's the truth that slips from my tongue," I said thickly, unable to hide the lust that was blurring my vision red with need.

She deadpanned me, her eyes going blank as she waited as if it's the executioner block instead of my bed. I wanted to laugh at her, but I knew her enough to know she'd think it was about her, and not at the frown marring her full lips, or the tenseness of her posture. I pulled her flush against my body, letting my heat warm her. Fuck, she was tiny, and yet a force of nature. My hands cupped her chin, tilting her face up to force her eyes to meet mine. She swallowed hard, loudly as she nipped her lip, waiting for me to make the first move.

I inhaled her wildness; the lavender scented soap she loved filled the room. My body reacted on cue, driven by the need to drive my cock into the heat of her welcoming flesh. She trembled as I lowered to claim her lips, but before I reached them, I moved mine to her ear and whispered against it. I wanted to savor this, to make it last, but this needed to happen a few times tonight, until her womb was filled with my unborn son. It wouldn't be over quickly, not until she knew who owned her pleasure. Her every fucking orgasm would be mine, and mine to give her from this day on.

"Are you scared of me? You should be; I've waited eons for you to be ready for me," I growled huskily before my teeth nipped at her earlobe. "You're afraid of what you feel when you're close to me, aren't you?"

"Just get this over with, Callaghan."

She was fucking trembling like a leaf hanging on to a tree at the end of fall. Her hands were visibly shaking as I tilted my head, watching her briefly before I shook it off. I reached down, lifting the gown from her flesh, exposing her skin to my greedy gaze. Her hands rose, trying to cover her flesh, but I was faster, catching them and somehow managing to stifle the growl that threatened to bubble up and escape. I placed her hands on my flesh and then tensed as she slowly began to explore me, as if she'd never seen anything like me before. What the fuck kind of assholes has she been with? The moment she leaned over and dragged her tongue over the pierced nipple, I lost my ever-loving shit as a deep growl hissed from my lungs. I watched her back up, her cheeks flooding with heat as if she'd done something wrong, and I couldn't fucking think to say anything past the throbbing in my cock.

"I…I don't know what the hell that was."

I laughed.

Fucking brilliant, Callaghan.

In all my years, in all my time with women, I'd never laughed at one who stared at me as if I was the devil. She'd fucking licked me, and I'd growled, and she blushed. I watched the confusion dance on her face, the uncertainty and anger as she hissed.

"I hate you," she scoffed adamantly as she turned away, trying to escape into the bathroom.

I didn't respond; there was nothing I could say to take away what I had just done. So I moved, picking

her slight weight up and tossing her onto my bed. My hands pushed down the jeans I wore as I watched her with a need so red-hot that I couldn't even process it. The moment my jeans freed my cock, her eyes widened, and she flinched, recoiling as if she'd never seen one that large. I needed to find the little boys she'd been fucking and end them. Where the fuck had she found these dolts?

"Jesus Christ, that thing isn't normal," she mumbled as her heart kicked up a notch, drumming to an alluring beat that the wild beast inside my soul knew well.

Grabbing her legs, I pulled her to me as her eyes grew large, rounding as fear leaked from her pores. Her foot kicked out, pushing me back as she struggled to get away from me. "Erie, stop." I lowered my tone, sending out a soothing one that had calmed her down more often than not. I parted her legs, feeling the sheer terror she'd sent out into the room, and frowned. "Gods, you're shivering," I mumbled, angling to rest between her legs as I tried to calm her nerves.

My mouth found her lips, brushing against them as I coaxed her to open to my kiss. The moment my tongue darted between her sinful lips, I devoured her like a starving beast. I went deeper, capturing hers as I fought her for dominance, a dance as old as time. My hands cradled her face, holding her there so she didn't pull away from the kiss. My cock was resting against her belly, and even I knew it wouldn't be an easy fit. She was tiny, but then she always had been. Her hands snaked down, pushing between us as she caressed me, and I struggled to remember the need to be gentle with her. No matter how many men she'd taken, she hadn't ever taken one like me before. I hissed against her touch and broke the kiss, staring down into the confusion marring her face.

I pushed off the bed, giving her more room to touch me, but she wouldn't. My tattoos swirled on cue, sensing the spells that were beginning to combine her with me. They glowed, lighting the room around us in a heady beat of magic and lust unmatched by anything else in this world. I lowered my mouth, nipping one pink nipple and then the next, watching her face as pleasure burned in her eyes. I allowed my teeth to graze over her flesh, enjoying the hiss that was stolen from her lungs as pleasure burned through her.

"Callaghan," she whimpered huskily, her voice sexy enough to force me to lose control. Her body cradled mine, allowing me to push my cock through her wetness to know she was more than ready to take what I needed her to. It continued to grow, even though I pulled back the magic, knowing she'd be a tight fit at first.

"Erie," I laughed huskily as I watched her eyes light with need, lowering my hand to trail through the pink flesh of her sex. My finger pushed into her cunt, and I struggled to maintain focus as I watched her reaction, judging her preparedness. Another finger sunk into her heat, and I fought to keep that growl at bay. Her sweet flesh pulsed around me, sucking my fingers deeper until it was all I could do, to watch her as she came undone.

Magic filled the room, sending mine into the tattoo that I'd given her to a deep blue glow. Mine added extra power as the spell around us worked to create a bond unlike any before it. I watched her eyes grow wide as a scream escaped her lungs. She rode my fingers, wild

and hurriedly as she took what she wanted, and I wasn't about to start complaining because fuck, she looked so fucking beautiful coming for me. I watched as she floated back to earth, and her eyes grew hooded from the orgasm and magic that claimed her.

"What the hell, Callaghan! You, you almost killed me…" she accused as she shivered, the orgasm receding. I blinked, staring at her through narrowed eyes as my mouth opened and closed, watching her as she continued to tremble with the aftershocks of it.

"It was only an orgasm, Erie," I uttered carefully, and now I knew I'd be finding those assholes and murdering them. "Your body is responding to my touch, coming undone for me. It's as natural as the fire burning in your depths for me." I laughed huskily as I looked down at her with a cocky smile lifting my lips. "Ready to feed the wolf, kitten?" I pushed against that tight opening, staring into her eyes before I leaned over, stealing a kiss to bring her back over to mindless need as I thrust into her body without warning. Her scream ripped through the room. My cock battered against something that was hard as fuck to miss. I stared down at her, shocked and sure that I'd just plowed through her hymen without realizing she'd still had one. I winced from her body's grip against mine and tried to withdraw, only to discover it wasn't fucking happening. Fucking hell, what the fuck? No wonder she had been shaking so badly, she'd never had a dick in her entire life, and I'd just battered through it like nothing. Her head was thrashing from side to side as she wailed like a fucking banshee as her body gripped my cock so tightly I feared it would cut it off. *"Fuck!"* I seethed, unsure what to do to get the fuck out of the vise-grip tightness of her pussy that was convulsing around me painfully.

Of all the motherfucking things to discover now? This wasn't it. How the fuck had she forgotten to mention this small detail? I couldn't even backtrack out of her flesh because it was locked around me, sucking me deeper as if the spell was working, and yet her body was fighting the need to feed it magic. So I was stuck, balls-deep in the tightest cunt of my life, one that refused to stop cutting off the circulation to my cock as it throbbed around me, sucking me deeper into her body.

"Jesus, stop moving, woman," I uttered thickly as my cock threatened to empty into her just to free itself of her tight sheath. It was a fucking iron maiden-like box that sent spikes into my cock as it pulsed. "You should have warned me of your innocence," I gritted out as sweat trickled down my face while pain mixed with pleasure, and magic pulsed through us. Her sweet noises threatened to undo me even more as I watched the pain flashing through her eyes. I swallowed hard, my hips needing to let loose to batter her flesh enough to get free.

"Move, bitch!" she ordered as she continued to rock, unable to stop without her body burning with pain from my oversized intrusion. "Callaghan, get out of me. You're ripping me apart!"

"Erie, hold the fuck still," I gritted out through clenched teeth. I didn't know what I wanted more right now, to kiss her for being untouched, or to bend her over and spank her ass for not bothering to tell me she was. There went the idea of taking her again; she was untried

by man and would be too sore to do more tonight after I'd finished with her. "I'm not asking. I'm telling you that you're too tight. You should have fucking warned me that you were a virgin before you let me fuck you. Your body wasn't ready for me, and now you need to hold fucking still before I do end up ripping you apart, which will make this really fucking suck for both of us. Now hold fucking still," I roared as I held her hips still, needing my brain to focus on the fact that we were stuck together, like fucking *stuck*.

"Callaghan," she whimpered through tears that blurred her vision as I stared down at her. I watched her with hatred at myself for putting her through this pain, pain I could have lessened for her, had I known. I could feel the blood from where I'd pushed through the barrier, but worse, from tearing through it brutally because I hadn't known it was there. "It hurts, make it stop. You're breaking my *vagina*!"

"It's…not broken, little one," I gritted out through clenched teeth as I leaned over and rested my forehead against hers, staring into the pain-glazed eyes while I fought the beast for control; the spell continued to fight against us all with the need for us to breed. "You're too tight, relax for me. Relax so I can give you pleasure."

"*Relax?* Are you fucking serious? You just tore me apart, and you want me to *relax*? It aches, dammit. Make it stop!" she snapped crossly. As if this wasn't her fault too? I had thought her skilled in sex, shit, I'd given her enough space to do just that, and yet she was a fucking virgin. Most women weren't afraid to sing their praise at being pure as they headed towards a bedroom. Not Erie, no, she waited until you were balls-deep into her before you figured that shit out for yourself. The woman was an enigma, a beautiful hot mess that most women craved to be, and yet she thought it made her less. It didn't, it made her so much fucking more than she would ever know.

"You're fucking perfect," I growled possessively, unable to help it from slipping out. My hips began to rock slowly. I moved at a tempo that was slow enough not to hurt, and yet fast enough to make her body react to it to lessen the pain. Moments, it took moments before her mouth opened and her eyes began to widen as pleasure took precedence over the pain. Every single thrust was painful as her body continued to fight me, and yet eventually, slowly, I unlocked, and her arousal coated my aching cock to allow me to please her needs.

"Ooh, oh hell," she whimpered wantonly as her eyes rolled back in her head, her mouth open to form a perfect *O*. "More," she pleaded as her eyes closed, stealing her beauty and her reaction to my cock from me.

No fucking way that shit was happening, little fighter. Not after seventy-five years of waiting for this moment. "Open your eyes and look at me," I demanded hoarsely, my voice a mix of need and pain as I watched those wonder-filled eyes open on command. Fuck, she was perfect, from her perky tits to her tight pussy that clenched against me. She was everything I'd expected, and a few shocking surprises more. My darkness latched on to her, craving the purity that seeped from her pores as I fucked her, bringing her over to my world slowly. I surveyed her reaction and felt as her body adjusted to what it wanted and craved from me, and I fucking gave

her more. Her legs wrapped around my waist, giving me more depth, and I took it. I took it fucking all, hitting against her womb as the spell seeped in, combining our need as one brutal goal. The statues lit up around us but she was too far gone to notice them, and I didn't care if they worked because my only goal was to watch her come undone for me with my name on her pretty pink lips.

My mouth lowered to hers, and she went wild with need. Her tongue caught mine, fighting me for dominance even though she was clearly unskilled enough to take it from me. Fuck if I wasn't turned on that she was trying, and yet everything inside of me demanded I claim her, own her, make her fucking submit to me and give me everything she was. I watched her climax rip her apart and slowed my hips, locking her into the endless pleasure that allowed me more access to her depths. I watched her coming undone for me as her nipples hardened and her back arched off the bed, her mewling noises sending a pulse through my cock with every whimpered moan of pleasure. I pulled her up as I slowly turned her over, watching as she presented that perfect ass to me like a gift. Nudging her legs apart, I pushed into the tight, aching flesh that once again sucked me in deeper than ever before. My hand landed against the softness of her ass, watching as she bucked against me, my other hand slowly pushing against her spine, dancing along the lines of the elaborate, delicate woad that covered it. Once my fingers sank into her hair and grabbed a fistful, I pulled it hard enough that she knew I did. I smiled at her heavy-lidded glare before my mouth claimed hers even as I lost control, riding her body without care as it pushed against mine, accepting what I gave it until I exploded into her tight, needy cunt. I leaned over her as I struggled to catch my breath, to gain some semblance of control. Fuck, she'd made me crazed with need, coming undone without warning like some stable boy going at it with a maiden for his first time.

Lifting up so I didn't crush her with my weight, I stared down at her, her head buried in the blankets as if she didn't plan to face me after what we'd just done together. I frowned, withdrawing from her pussy to find my cock covered in the blood of her innocence. Fucking hell, there was too much. If she'd warned me, I would have spent hours preparing her for my thick flesh instead of tearing hers apart with an eagerness I couldn't control. I climbed from the bed and stared at her perfectly heart-shaped ass.

"You bled everywhere," I muttered as my hand scrubbed down my face as I stared at her red, swollen flesh that pissed me off more than it should have. "You fuck like you fight, woman." I hated myself for hurting her, but I was pissed at her for keeping that shit to herself when I was on a need to know basis.

I crawled onto the bed, intending to pull her up with me, but she ignored me as she ripped the blankets from the bed and padded across the floor to the empty couch.

"Get your tits back in this bed," I demanded as I smirked at her mussed hair and porcelain skin that was covered in red marks, my marks from claiming that ass. I preened inwardly with the knowledge that I'd claimed her first, which was something she'd never forget.

"Go fuck yourself, Paladin."

If she's W̶ICKED

I smirked as her angry eyes challenged me while she touched her abused flesh and winced. She'd be sore for days, and I couldn't even pretend to not like that idea. She'd feel me there, between her silken thighs where I'd owned that sweet cunt until it was swollen from being fucked by me. Her clumsy fingers slid through her sweet, bruised folds and her eyes lifted to mine, and I smiled, but it was all teeth. Fuck if I wasn't already hard and wanting to be in her tightness again already.

"Why would I do that when I have you here?" I laughed as I watched her frustration play out on her face.

"That won't happen again," she muttered as she lay on the couch and pulled the covers over her head like a petulant child. "Everyone makes mistakes; you were just mine."

"Is that so? Maybe you should try it a few more times to be sure it was a mistake."

"I'm going to bed now," she growled.

"Night, Erie," I chuckled.

"Fuck off, Callaghan," she groaned.

When I finally woke up, it was to find her gone, escaping from the Templar Order stronghold with the ease of the most skilled assassin. My gaze settled on the fertility statue that was moved from where I'd placed it. The pulsing wards beneath my bed hummed, warning of an attack, and a smile flitted across my face. Oh yeah, my little imp had let me pluck that treasure and then snuck out like a thief in the night. As if she thought this shit would work for me. Game on, little hellion. I was ready to hunt.

The fucked up part though, the part that hurt was

I knew she found Arthur and the others alive outside of my apartment when she awoke from being with me. I knew why she ran, and that she wouldn't be easy to catch again now that she had learned the truth of my deceit. I had her, and I fucked up. Story of my life with that little Goddess, it was what we did. I smiled as I lay back on the bed, gripping my cock as I swallowed past the ball of need that grew in my throat, replaying last night and how amazing she felt beneath me in my mind.

She wanted me, I'd heard it in her tone and in the way she screamed for more and pushed against me. It may not have started out that way, but she didn't hide her need after the initial pain had fled and pleasure had replaced it. She fucking roared for me, and I wanted her again already. The smile that curved my lips as I thought about her wincing every time she moved today was more wolf than man, and the rattling in my chest confirmed that he too had enjoyed what we'd done to her. We hadn't even begun to play with her yet or to show her why the Gods made men and women with parts that connected perfectly. I hoped that she fucking ached and that when she did, she thought of what I'd done to her and craved more.

CHAPTER *five*

ERIE

Walking home was painful, physically so but emotionally draining on top of that. I replayed hearing Arthur, who was supposed to be dead, speaking to other Templars about Callaghan's smoothness in getting between my legs. I'd thought he would die, or worse, so I'd made a sacrifice, and for what? That's right, nothing. They'd been in the next room, right beside where I'd lain with him. I groaned as pain arose in places that I didn't even know could hurt. It was a reminder of what had happened with that traitorous, no good, lying prick.

I couldn't believe I'd been trying to save him, and he'd probably laughed as my honor code had become my own downfall. I stepped over a corpse and eyed it, noting the rapid decay of the body before I shook it off and continued my walk of shame towards the empty apartment complex. By the time I'd finally reached it, I'd already buried three bodies and had cursed that man to a painful death more times than I could count.

Once inside the complex, I slammed the door closed and screamed until my voice grew hoarse and the anger of what I'd done dissipated a little. Moving through the destroyed room, I frowned as I took in the destruction that they'd done to it with their ploy. There was blood everywhere, meaning he'd hurt them even if he hadn't killed them. That, at least, made me feel a little better. It didn't, however, take away the guilt I felt at having ruined the dead couple's home.

Stepping over the scattered debris, I opened the freezer and backed up to jump onto the counter with a yelp of pain as my lower region ached. The man had a wrecking ball penis, one that destroyed vaginas. In fact, I still felt him everywhere, as if he hadn't ever withdrawn from my flesh. The heat of his lips still burned against mine, only making the betrayal I felt worse.

"Good morning, Fred. I hope you slept well," I uttered.

"Slept? No. I was praying for the first time in my entire existence. I don't *pray*, but I prayed that whoever was in this apartment had slit that pretty little throat of yours and that you were bleeding out. Pity that they failed, and that you're here, alive…still. They are most unskilled at murder; had I the use of my body, I would have loved to teach them, with you as the victim, how pleasuring it would be, therapeutic even," he pouted. Or…at least I thought he did, his lips were blue and so was his face, which was almost comical, and may have been, had I not been indulging in self-pity.

"I had sex last night," I uttered as a frown marred my face as I slowly lifted my eyes to find his glowing red while he watched me.

"And you think I care? I don't. I'm also not a girl, and do not partake in the lesser things of your humiliation after a lame fuck."

Ignoring him, I continued. "I mean, I thought he was different than the others, but he's worse. Yes, he's been the star of every fantasy I've ever had, but then he broke my vagina, and I found out that he's worse than the others." He hadn't betrayed me in those fantasies. He'd been the one I had wanted forever, and yet I'd known the moment I let my guard down, he'd destroy me. They always did.

"You did hear me when I said I didn't care, right? Because, to point it out, my feelings have not changed," he muttered.

"I gave him my virginity, Fred! Shouldn't that have meant something more to him?"

"Good God, you were a virgin?" he exclaimed. His eyes traveled to the top of my shirt since it was as far as he could look from his vantage point in the freezer, and then lifted them back to my face with a frown. "What a waste. We could have sacrificed you to bring more of our kind over here. What were you, the oldest virgin in history?"

"Focus, Fred." I snapped my fingers in front of his face as I growled. "I gave him something that was only mine to give to him because I'd thought he may die since he protected me last night, which was why I didn't die. Turned out, he hadn't killed anyone at all. He'd just used my own honor code against me, who does that?"

"A brilliant man, that's who," he snorted as he rolled his eyes and started to shake his head, which didn't exactly work out since he was propped up on ice cubes.

"So did it at least hurt? Please tell me he wasn't gentle with you. Did you scream? Was there a lot of blood? Please tell me you are in excruciating pain from it."

"Of course it hurt, he has a wrecking ball penis in his pants," I snapped. "I mean, it actually hurts to walk. Is that even normal? I had to walk all the way back to you with a constant ache to remind me of him! I thought that shit only happened in books and movies, not in real life. *And!* That son of a bitch had fertility relics set up in his room, which I'm not even sure why I'm surprised, but I am. His entire focus is to knock me up, and can't a girl just enjoy her first time, but no, not with him. Yet I trusted him, which I'm telling you now, won't ever happen again."

"Why the hell would he want to do that?" he scoffed. "Unless he wanted a child so he could eat it as you watched him. That would be a valid reason."

"Eww, no," I shook my head as a shiver raced down my spine. "It's because I'm the cure to saving the Templar and druids, who earned their fate, I'm sure. I mean, they're assholes, and isn't that reason enough to die? I was just created to save them, but did anyone stop to consider anything about how I would feel? No, nope, all they thought about was their own needs. Not one of them even thought about how my life would be with their curse hanging over *my* head. I wasn't even a part of it."

"*You're* the child of the cauldron of Dagda?" he asked, his tone serious as he watched me. "You can't be fucking serious."

"I am," I admitted as I stretched my neck and winced as my apex burned with pain. "Is it normal to hurt this much after sex?"

"If it's done right," he smirked as he watched me. "How large was his cock? It was huge, wasn't it? Did you scream? I love it when they scream because it hurts, yet they beg for more."

"He was more than just huge." I rolled my eyes at him. "It was like *run away from it because it is a one-eyed monster that will rip you in half* cock," I uttered as my cheeks flushed at the reminder. "He didn't even see if he could fit, and then he was stuck inside of me. It felt like I was being torn in half, and out of everything I'd ever imagined doing with him, that never happened, ever. He ruined everything, my fantasy of him, my vagina, my faith in him, and any trust I may have held, all destroyed." My eyebrows creased as I pouted, my heart aching with what he'd done, and my inability to ignore the draw I felt to him. Plus, again, he'd ruined my fantasies of him, which were so much better than reality.

No, in my fantasies he'd been perfect. He'd coaxed my body to readiness, and there'd been no pain. He'd said all the right words, done all the right things and it had been beautiful! Instead, he got stuck in my vagina. Of course, I also didn't have any fantasy of him betraying me either. So that said a lot about how much they could be relied on to be even semi-correct. Fantasy was so much better than reality. Reality only let you down and left you a ruined mess.

"Did he fuck you in the ass, too?" he snickered.

"No! That thing would never fit there. Oh my God, that *is* a thing?" I asked incredulously as I tried to picture it. My mind played it out, and my ass tightened with fear. Nope, not happening; not with that wrecking ball thingamajigger in his pants. I seriously needed to dig through the couple's porn collection more so that I had more of an idea about sex and what to expect.

"Wish I had found you unprotected and as innocent as he had. I'm actually jealous right now. I'd have stripped the flesh from your body and then taken you until you knew what true pain was," he said wistfully.

"Eww, Fred. Focus, remember, he broke my vagina? This is about me, not you right now. Try to think of others besides just yourself for once. That type of thing is why you're in my freezer in the first place. Hurting humans is bad, we don't hurt them. We definitely don't take off their flesh and then do *it* with them," I muttered. I jumped down, hissing as pain erupted from the motion and closed the freezer door. "Think about what you did, and when I open this door again, you better have a new attitude on life."

"Or what, you crazy bitch? You'll cut my head off and keep me in a freezer until I see the error of my ways? You will die for this!"

"We're friends now, and it is my job to teach you right from wrong. Who else has ever tried to help you out as I am?"

"You took my fucking head knowing that I couldn't die!"

"No, I only assumed that you couldn't. I didn't know for a fact that you would survive. I can't foresee the future, but I knew we'd be great friends if you did. See you in a little while; I have to go wash the stink off of me. I can still smell him on my flesh."

"You didn't know I wouldn't die? I hate you even

more right now!"

"You hangry again, Fred? You sound it; maybe I should find you a Snickers bar to eat," I called from the other side of the freezer door as I turned, heading towards the bathroom while an explosion of curse words sounded from him. I stripped out of my borrowed clothes and entered the bathroom, throwing wards up before I turned the hot water on, crawling into the bath to scrub off the scent of betrayal. I lit a few candles with a flick of my finger, painting runes across my flesh until it burned with power, and yet that fucking ache refused to lessen as the water washed away the proof of them. I lifted my eyes to gaze to the door as the wards pulsed in warning. Callaghan's stink reached me before he rounded the corner and came into view, all sexy as sin.

"You left," he growled thickly.

"You need to leave here, *now*," I growled back, dismissing him as I sank into the heated water, disappearing beneath the suds to ignore him. His growl echoed through the water as the air expelled from my lungs. I didn't want to face him right now, or ever. I wanted to hide the shame I felt at falling for his freaking ploy. My lungs burned until I was forced to come back up for air. I slowly emerged from the water, only to discover he had made it past my wards and stood above the tub, staring down at me. *What. The. Fuck?*

I stood up and stepped out of the bathtub as I pushed him out of my way. Glaring at him, I left the room, dismissing him with a snort of anger and rage. Water sloshed everywhere in my haste to place as much distance between us as possible. I started to put more wards up in my bedroom when he grabbed me and shoved me against the wall hard enough that my teeth rattled.

"I killed for you," he hissed, but even he knew he lied. His eyes burned as he watched my reaction, probably hoping I hadn't heard the others on my way out of his apartment.

"You must think me the biggest idiot, asshole," I seethed as I glared up at him. "Did you have fun playing with me last night? Was it fun to watch me struggle and choose you over myself? Did you enjoy me beneath you as you hurt me even though you lied about it all?" I whispered through the constriction of my throat as I fought to keep the tears at bay. "Congratulations, Callaghan, you won. You got further than any man before you ever has, does it feel good? Do you feel like the almighty conqueror now? Was it fun for you to watch me buying into the lies you fed me, to use my own honor code against me? I'm guessing you enjoyed it and that it didn't bother you at all since you slept soundly and untroubled afterwards." When heat flared in those beautiful blue eyes, I growled angrily, more at myself for still wanting him than at him. "Get out, just get out and leave me alone. You're just like them, only worse."

"Erie, two races depend on you carrying a son. Until we're sure you are pregnant, they won't leave you in peace. *I* won't leave you in peace, because lives depend on it."

"Oh, they will leave me alone, or they will all die horribly," I uttered angrily. "I'm warded against them and you now. Anyone stupid enough to attempt to rape or force their will against my own will die. You seem to have missed the part where I am a master of wards."

"You cannot ward against us," he laughed as his eyes searched my face and then narrowed. "Wards can only be placed on places, not people."

"Try it," I hissed. "I dare you to, Callaghan. Taste me," I whispered huskily as my hand slid down my body, which no matter how much he pretended, he couldn't ignore. Those sweet baby blue eyes watched my hand as it pushed against my sex. His jaw clenched as he lifted them to mine, smirking as he shook his head.

His mouth slanted as his eyes narrowed and held mine. "No one has the power to ward against us entering their body. Least of all you, little druid," he answered huskily as his finger brushed the hair away from my face. "You belong to me, you have from the moment you sucked air into your premature lungs and opened those pretty blue eyes of yours," he said forcefully. "And I will never let anyone else lie between those thighs. You, and me, Erie? We're mated now."

"Bullshit," I muttered.

"You didn't look at the wards above the bed very well, did you? Those weren't just fertility wards placed on the ceiling and floor. They were druid wards to lock two souls together as one in the mating ritual of the druids themselves. I promise you, you're mine forever. Last night wasn't just about getting you into my bed; it was about claiming you in a much more primal way. Now, more than ever before, you are mine in every possible way. No, I don't fucking care if you like it. I made sure you were safe by any means necessary. Yes, I'd do it again in a fucking heartbeat to keep you that way."

"Like you did with Arthur? Am I safe from him as

well?" I countered and watched his eyes narrow even further. "I must look like the biggest idiot to fall for that bullshit," I laughed as I shoved against his chest. He didn't budge. Instead, he placed his hands flat against the wall, trapping my body between them as he lowered his mouth to hover over mine. A chill raced down my spine as I licked my lips, wanting to taste him. I craved him; I craved the contact he offered like a fucking junkie needing a fix. He was the drug that could send the pain below and ease it until everything was numb again.

"I never said I played fair, little one. I did what I had to do to protect you," he uttered before his mouth brushed against mine. "I'm not sorry for last night. You are, and were, everything I imagined you would be and so much more."

"Kiss me," I whispered, waiting for him to do just that. The moment his lips fully touched against mine, he jerked back in pain. I smiled against the look of shock as pain registered in his eyes. His body went rigid and then straight as a board as the wards rushed through him, taking him to his knees. I followed him down, smiling as my tongue pushed past the stiffness of his lips, delving and rubbing against his. "I am unlike anything you and yours have encountered, Paladin. You think I owe you and your people something? I owe you nothing," I hissed as I pushed him and watched him fall to the ground.

An electrical current rushed through his body, leaving him helpless against anything I wanted to do to him. I knelt beside him and ripped his shirt open, smirking as I watched his angry glare following my movement. My tongue darted out as I lowered my lips to his ripped body, licking the pierced nipple before I nipped it between my teeth. "You play dirty, but guess what? So can I, and I sure as hell won't play by your rules. Your people and the druids did nothing but treat me like a freak, like I was nothing more than an animal. Like an animal that needed to be whipped into shape, and so they did. Do you know what the druids did to me?" I asked through tears that slid down my cheeks to splash on his golden flesh as I continued to smile through the pain those ugly memories brought back. "They tattooed me in ink, strapping a helpless child to a chair as they branded me for hours. They made sure I wasn't wanted by any man so that I was bound to jump at the first invitation to be *used* by you and your Knights. I killed them, Callaghan. I followed the ones who branded me, and I ripped them apart; don't think I won't do it to you too."

"Release me," he gritted out through clenched teeth.

"Release your own damn self, Templar," I mumbled as I lifted to my knees, intending to leave him in pain on my floor. "When you have managed to do so, leave. You and your kind are not welcome in my life. The next time any of you tries to force me into anything, I won't just leave you in pain, I will start hunting Templars one by one. You may not die, but you can be cut into small pieces and eaten," I warned with a saccharine smile on my lips.

I started to lift my body up only for his hand to grasp my hair and pull me back down to him. He watched me struggling against him, unable to get free. He chuckled as he held my struggling form against his, staring into my eyes with a hungry look. *Impossible!* He should be immobilized by the wards, and yet he was *literally* holding me with the strength of ten men *by* my hair.

He rolled us on the floor, trapping me beneath his burdensome weight as he watched me struggle. "I told you I like it rough," he warned. "Give me an excuse to fuck you like a beast, any excuse to take you without control. I fucking *dare* you," he shouted.

His hips rolled, and I gasped as heat shot through my core. I growled with frustration as I fought to get from beneath him. Why wasn't he screaming in pain? The wards were good, great in fact, and yet he was fighting them, but how? I frowned as I bucked against him, hitting his thick cock while he smiled down at me with something else in his turquoise eyes watching me from within. I swallowed hard as he ground his erection against the wet heat of my core that clenched with readiness in response. The tattoo on my wrist glowed brilliantly; his matched it as he continued to watch me struggling beneath him.

"You want me, sweet girl," he laughed coldly. "Your wards only work if you don't want me."

"I don't want you!" I seethed, hatred dripping from my lips.

"Liar," he chuckled huskily as his eyes searched mine. "I know it, and you know it. Your wards are good, I'll give you that much, but I'm better than most at being able to break through anything you can throw at me. I always have been. Even now, you want me buried deep inside that tight, welcoming heat. I can smell it, your anticipation, the way your body weeps for me to bury my thick cock into it over and over again. You are so fucked, Erie. I've never craved anything as much as I crave the need to be with you."

"I hate you," I cried as his forehead pressed against mine, his eyes boring into me with carnal knowledge.

"You don't have to like me to fuck me, Erie. I was gentle last night, but this I promise you: next time you won't walk away so easily. You'll crawl, you'll beg me for more. Hell, I'll even oblige you and maybe even let you suck my dick for a little while between pounding that sweet, tight pussy you are trying so hard to protect from me."

"You're a bastard," I screeched as I pulled power to me and sent it sailing into him. Blood splattered on my face as I shoved what little was left of him off of me. He was nothing more than a puddle of blood and singed severed flesh. "Asshole." I wiped his flesh from my face as I sat up, smiling at his mangled corpse.

He had no idea what he was fucking with. None at all. I lifted from the floor, wiping the blood from my face as I sat back on my haunches. I didn't bother dressing before I moved to the freezer and opened it, staring at Fred, who winced.

"Still alive, I see," he pouted.

"I have serious men issues!"

"Oh, honey, you are the issue. Maybe if you were less slice and dice, you may find one willing to stick around longer. From the sound of it, you didn't let him play, and therefore, you are the issue, not him. But that's not you, you prefer to blow them up, and then you come crawling to me, and say guy issues? He sounded pretty clear, he wanted to fuck you. I wanted to hear your screams. Pity, none of us got what we wanted, now did we? Oh, that's right, you did."

"He only wants my womb!"

"No man wants a womb, woman. We want what comes before that pesky womb gets filled."

"Not him, he wants me to carry his son. He wants me to save them when they couldn't even help me, knowing that I suffered. It's bullshit."

"You know, not that I care, female, but if he's got a nice cock…what the hell is the issue? Who cares if he wants that womb? Make him earn it, and hell, I'll even help you. Because that's who I am, the helpful demon willing to help that pussy get lit, but first, I'll need my body."

I snorted as I stifled a laugh. "Damn, that was smooth. I mean, you almost had me, but you lost me at womb."

"Bitch," he growled.

"Demon," I shrugged.

"That's the best you have?" he snorted.

"I had a very lacking education. It wasn't as if they wanted me to talk back, or just talk at all," I explained, pulling another piece of Callaghan out of my hair and tossing it aside. "I think they need to be reminded of who I am and how I was created."

"I think they're aware of that, hence the wanting to be in that womb of yours. To them, you're the Holy fucking Grail. To them, you're everything that will keep them alive."

"I'm more than just a womb, Fred. I'm also insane," I smirked as I closed the freezer door and padded towards the bathtub as I wiped off another patch of Callaghan that clung to my shoulder, hoping the water was still warm.

CHAPTER
six

TWO DAYS BEFORE CHRISTMAS, AND THE DRUIDS JUST kept handing out mission after mission while everyone else prepared for the holiday season. Not me, because I wasn't given time off, not that I had anyone to spend it with or anything. Callaghan had yet to regenerate, which was a testament to my magical skills, and made me have a skip in my step. He may have been one of the strongest Knights ever born into the Order, but even his kind had to regenerate an entirely new body if they died. Even the strongest had to come fully back from wherever the Knights went to when they died.

I watched the Fae coming and going from their notorious nightclub that seemed to draw the dangerous and unwanted creatures of nightmares into their doors. Vlad was known for enforcing laws and rules by wards, and my prey was about to enter his domain. That meant I was about to walk inside and break his laws, but hey, a girl had to eat, right?

Druids only paid when you finished a mission, and

I'd been hunting these creatures down for weeks. They fed on children and innocent women and were notorious for leaving them in disarray, or on display with pieces cut off of them. The last one I'd found had her tongue removed and branches shoved into her arm sockets. They'd used a rope to string her up by her neck, leaving her to stand on her tiptoes or hang to death. They'd known she'd die; she'd have had a fighting chance with arms, but without, she faced certain death.

That had been two days ago, and since then, I'd not slept or eaten while I hunted them down. I stared at the doors of the club as I studied the wards, biding my time as I waited for the creature and his cronies to show. This was where they'd picked the last three victims up, and since they were Fae, it only made sense that they were creatures of habit.

The issue with it being at this club was the Witches Guild castaways were inside. They were oblivious to what those inside did while pretending the world was right when everything was wrong. I got it; they had been through hell, and no matter what anyone did, you couldn't entirely close the holes that stretched daily, letting everything imaginable slither through.

Well, they couldn't, but *I* could ward them enough so nothing could escape. Not that I wanted to, not while I enjoyed killing those who preyed on weaker species. I reveled in it. It allowed me to test my boundaries without harming innocents. The druids had rules which I was forced to follow, and the Knights Order had even more rules than they did. I had no limits other than being able to be killed, which sucked, but I only ended up dead if I failed. I wasn't about to fail and end up pushing daisies.

My prey strode up to the doors of the club, hooting and hollering as they strutted with the joy of hunting their victims. Remaining in the shadows, I lingered as the doors opened, revealing some of what was inside. It included Callaghan, who sat at the bar talking to Vlad, King of Vampires. *Great!*

I swallowed hard, considering my next move. To get to my prey, I had to drop my glamour to hold focus while fighting the wards and them. Callaghan to see my true self, which no one ever did, but the Fae were masters of wards too. They had powerful magic which had been used to create the wards that kept the peace inside the nightclub.

Would he recoil from me as everyone else had done? Would he stare in horror once he saw what I looked like? *Probably.* I let the glamour drop, pulling the hood over my unruly mess of crimson curls. Stepping away from the building, I hunted the monsters that preyed upon those who couldn't defend against them.

The doors of the club sparked as I pulled them open, ignoring the curious stares as I entered. Maybe I'd been wrong, and it hadn't been Vlad I'd seen through the doors. My eyes scanned the bar, and my hope sank as I took in the silver-eyed male who was pouring Scotch into Callaghan's glass.

I pushed the heavy cloak off as the wards felt my presence. The moment they did, I sent a jolt of power pushing back at them. My other arm threw the entire crowd against the walls of the club, all except Callaghan and a blonde female who stood over babies, who luckily seemed immune to my magic. Who the fuck had babies inside a nightclub? Pausing, I added wards between me, my prey, and her. I stared at her before my gaze lowered to the babes who had been warded away from her, which she wasn't happy about.

"Erie, stop this now," Callaghan warned, and I lifted my gaze to his, watching as he flinched. Ah, there it was. The repulsion at seeing what he'd begged to when he'd had me at his mercy. I threw my arm at the blonde again, watching with unease as she didn't budge from where she stood, pulling power to her as she watched me back. "Stop this."

"No," I uttered as I started placing wards around the little ones as the blonde moved towards me. I moved my fingers, adding even more wards until set after set of magical barriers stood between us. No matter what she was, she wasn't getting through them. I finished protecting the children and then blinked in wonder as the little girl walked right out of it. "Back inside," I urged. "It's for your protection," I explained, and I swear she smirked and tilted her chubby face to the side as if she was considering my words. One minute I was alone, and the next she was in my arms. I held still, uncertain of what the fuck was happening. Her small hand touched my cheek, and she smiled. She vanished from my arms, and I watched as she nodded platinum curls and moved back into the safety of the stronger wards I'd placed.

I exhaled my relief and turned towards my prey. The leather I wore covered my breasts, my waist, and barely covered my ass, but it was the outfit I'd worn since I had been a mere child. It was what the Pict women wore to battle. Every tattoo was laid bare to see, everything I was exposed. Usually, no one lived to tell what I looked like,

but this time everyone, including Callaghan, would live to tell the world my shame. I called forth my swords, listening as the others spoke.

"If she attacks, she will die, Callaghan," Vlad growled.

"What the fuck *is* she?" a male asked.

"Impossible, the druids birthed no females," another muttered as he struggled to get off the wall.

I closed myself off to their words, rounding on the monsters that stood motionless, frozen by the magic I'd cast. I released them from it and watched as the biggest one moved into swift action, rushing right for me. I let him come right at me until I jumped, flipping into the air to take his head with my blade. I threw a smirk at Vlad and wiggled my brows for him. His wards were good, but mine were better.

The second guy sent out a burst of power, calling forth multiple versions of himself. I twirled my blades and started forward, slicing through the clones one by one until nothing but bloody pulp remained. He called more to him, and I rolled my eyes, dropping my blades as I brought my fingers together, snapping them. The room emitted in raw, uncut power as the clones exploded into pink mist as if a bomb had exploded.

The last male watched me, his sunken eyes slowly trailing over my ruined body. Scar after ugly scar covered it, and that which wasn't covered in nicks or abrasions was covered in ink. I called my power to me as I cracked my neck, stepping closer to him.

"It is forbidden to harm us here!"

"And yet you hunt those weaker than you right inside this very room? The last victim was left to teeter on her tiptoes with a rope around her neck. Her tongue had been removed, and you'd replaced the arms you had ripped out with tree branches. Is this not true?" I called back angrily.

"She was *human*," he spat out as if it was vile to even slither over his tongue.

"She was. She's no longer of this world because of you. She died on that leash you tied her to, and now here I am, hunting you. The Guild may have fallen to rubble, but they're not the only ones who enforce the laws in this world. You will die screaming," I informed before I rushed at him, whispering a spell that made my hand sharper than any creature's claws could hope to be.

My hand slipped through his throat carefully as I grasped his tongue and pulled it before I flipped over his shoulder, wrapping it around his neck before I kicked him to the floor and went down with him. There, I lay beside him, braced on my elbow as I stared at him. He screamed, but no words escaped, only muffled cries.

"You see, I enjoy slaughtering monsters that hurt weaker species. I don't know…" I sat up, turning my head a bit as I peered at him. His tongue was longer than I'd thought it would be. His eyes were wide with pain, and blood oozed out of his wound and mouth as he continued to screech in pain. "I think it's an improvement from how you looked before. Don't you?" I asked before I straddled him and smiled down at him. "I think so. What was that?" I asked, moving my ear closer to his mouth. The only noise escaping sounded as if he was encouraging my trip to hell. "No. No, I won't because this is where *you* die," I chuckled as I sat back, tossing a curious gaze at the female who had been unaffected by my magic. Whatever the fuck she was, she was strong. I could feel her power rippling against the wards as she worked with Callaghan to undo them.

Turbulent ocean blue eyes held mine as I brought my dagger down into the creature's skull, ending his suffering. I stood up slowly, letting Callaghan see every detail of my body before I stood nose to nose with him, only the ward between us.

His hand pushed through the wards before I had a chance to react and wrapped around my throat. I winced and then laughed darkly. "Do it, end it," I uttered through the crushing hand that held me.

"Drop the fucking wards, Erie, now. Those children are sacred," he growled.

"Those children are protected by me at the moment," I replied through a whispered breath. "I only hurt those who hurt others. The Fae dropped the fucking ball this time. They allowed monsters to use this club to become a hunting ground. They become fair game when they do stupid shit." I punched him in the crotch and watched as he dropped to his knees.

I moved to a sign that said 'Last Work Accident 999 Days Ago' and winced as I erased it and replaced it with a zero. Pushing to the bar, I leaned over it and grabbed a bottle of tequila, using my teeth to remove the cap. I tipped it back, chugging from it in an unladylike way as I tried to wash the image of Callaghan's disgust from my brain.

"Are you done yet?" the female asked.

I lifted a dark brow at her question and then followed her gaze to where the bloody corpses covered the floor. I flicked my wrist, sending their bodies to the trash bins outside. I dismissed her as I let the room move back to normal, releasing everyone, expecting a blade to pierce my heart in retaliation. I welcomed it.

It didn't come.

"Erie," Callaghan growled against my neck before he kissed the soft column.

"Touch me and die, Paladin," I warned as I spun around with the bottle still in my hand, my legs spread to house his wide frame with my elbows resting on the bar behind me in a relaxed pose.

The Fae stood with weapons out, the children in the arms of a winged creature who watched me with a lethal look.

"You flirt with death, female," the winged creature snapped.

"I did my job," I replied nonchalantly. "Three humans in two days," I explained as I wrapped my legs around Callaghan, forcing him to get closer as he ignored the ugly bits of me by staring into my eyes. "One was *thirteen*, which, if I'm not mistaken, is illegal to be inside this club, and yet she was. She died from puncture wounds they placed with knives. She survived until they inserted one into her…"

"There are children present," the blonde hissed.

"*She* was a child," I threw back.

"A lot is happening around here, and that isn't an excuse," Vlad injected. "It's a fact, some have slipped into the club unwelcome by us, we will be more careful with what we allow into our sanctuary."

"You could start by closing the fucking gaping hole in your world," I laughed. "Just a thought," I offered before bringing the bottle to my lips and downing some.

"You think we haven't tried? Anything that touches it makes it grow larger." The blonde woman's foot tapped the floor angrily as she watched my movements with careful purplish-blue eyes.

"Ward it," I suggested.

"Well shit, why didn't we think of that?" she hissed as she threw her arms out wide. "Oh, wait, we did. It cannot be done."

"*You* can't do it," I laughed while I watched her, sizing her up as I tried to figure out what the fuck she was.

"But you can?" she laughed.

"She can," Callaghan muttered. "If she can ward her pussy against me, she can ward anything."

The blonde's eyes went wide as she looked between us. "She's yours?" she asked.

"He wishes, well, probably not now that he's seen me," I laughed soundlessly, staring anywhere but at him. "He just wants my womb."

"To save *our* races, Erie," he snapped.

"I don't have a race!" I screamed as I shoved him away from me and slid off the chair. "Don't you get it? Look at me! Your people didn't want me and threw me away like fucking garbage, and the druids made damn sure I knew that I was nothing more than a monster. They tortured me until there was nothing left, and when I thought I'd finally be free of them and die, they spelled me from death. They took pieces of me to figure out how to recreate what I was, and your people were no different. I am their fucking science experiment; nothing more, nothing less. The only purpose I serve is to kill and be your incubator, Callaghan. You tell me:

why would I care if both races die out when they've done nothing but hurt me?"

"You were protected by me," he ground out through clenched teeth.

"Was I? Or did you think I was because I learned to hide what I was a long time ago? You've watched me since the moment I was born and yet you never wondered why I hid? Buy a fucking clue, because you may know what I let you see, but you will never know me. I am more than just something you and your people threw away and used as they saw fit."

I was so busy screaming out all of my pain that I hadn't noticed he'd gotten closer to me, or that he held anything in his hands. I started to step back, but he moved before I could manage a single step, taking me to the floor as he slipped something over my head. I pushed away from him, about to dare him to kiss me again and see if he liked the upgrade I'd done, when he spoke.

"Remove the wards from your body," he demanded, and I did without question. My eyes went round with horror as I opened my mouth to replace them, only for him to stop me before I could. "Leave them down."

"No, Callaghan," I whispered as my throat constricted and tears burned my eyes. His thumb traced my cheek as he stared down at me.

"You left me no choice, Erie. I won't let my people die. I can't."

CHAPTER *seven*

CALLAGHAN

THE MOMENT SHE'D WALKED HER ASS INTO THAT BAR, they'd marked her for death. I'd felt it, and it had terrified me. That girl was fire, an out of control inferno that was set ablaze in rage. I'd lit that fuse, but the moment she'd entered that club, she'd sealed her own fate. I watched her fight with the skill of the most expertly trained Knight, each movement chosen to do fast, easy damage that left her opponent incapacitated. There was one way to get her out of this one alive, and I'd use it.

I'd do anything to protect that girl, no matter how much she pissed me off. If I wasn't trying to save her, she'd never have killed me as many times as she had. She was my fucking kryptonite. I couldn't hurt her, and so she killed me. I wouldn't abuse her more than she had already been, but time was running out, and I'd given up too much to let our race fail now. I'd vowed to do whatever it took, and what had been asked of me, the cost, it was everything. One girl couldn't be allowed to stand in the way of losing and giving up everything for something these people had no part of doing.

ERIE

There are moments in your life where you look back and reflect on things you should have done differently. Things you *could* have done differently. You reflect on it at the worst possible time, you imagine doing something else to get the expected outcome you desire. Like right now, for instance, I was wishing I'd taken Callaghan apart piece by piece instead of blowing him into pieces. I wish I'd done it so that his rotting body was still inside my apartment, slowly decaying.

Instead, he was watching me closely. The Fae stood inches from me, weapons drawn, and I was unable to do anything unless he told me from the moment he'd said "stand still and listen." My eyes moved quickly, fearfully, but my body? *Frozen.*

"Jump on one foot, Erie," he purred, rolling the 'E' in my name as it ran off his tongue in a silken caress.

I jumped like a fucking rabbit as my heart thumped, pounding violently against the cage that held it from running away. Tears threatened to escape as rage pulsed inside of me, a stupid fucking trait that I loathed. Crying was a weakness, one they wouldn't understand. They wouldn't know that when the tears left my eyes, it meant some motherfucker was about to die. They'd think I was some colossal crybaby.

"Stop jumping and come to me," he smirked roguishly, his ocean blue eyes slowly watching my reaction as my body jerked to do as he bid.

"I'm going to rip your tongue out through your chest

and wear it as a scarf," I growled.

"No, no, you're going to do whatever I tell you to do. I warned you what would happen if you didn't choose. You can hate me, but I won't let my people die because one female doesn't want to help when she can."

"It's *my* body," I hissed. "I don't want to be a mother, Callaghan. Have you *been* outside lately? It's not a pretty place. I have no plans of letting you touch me again, so tell me, Knight: will you break your honor code to achieve your goal? Because I assure you, I am not willing no matter what this necklace tells you. And you lied; I am very aware that I am not the one in control," I spat out as I stopped in front of him, close enough to smell his woodsy scent.

"Kiss me," he uttered as he wrapped his arm around the small of my back and pulled me closer. "Like your pretty little life depends on it."

I couldn't stop the tears that fell, couldn't stop myself from doing as he instructed in the room full of creatures that would live forever to remember it. I rose on the tips of my toes, claiming his lips before pulling his full bottom lip between my teeth gently, sucking it before my tongue pushed past it. Mine touched his, finding it and dueling with it until I moaned as heat washed through my body, white-hot desire igniting like flames leaping from a gas-lit stove. His hand pressed against the back of my head, holding me to his heated depths as he devoured me until I wasn't sure what I wanted more, air or him.

He pulled away, and I struggled to get back to him; my one focus in life was to continue kissing him. I fought his hold as he watched me struggle to kiss him, like some blooming fucking idiot who couldn't live without him.

"Stop," he whispered thickly as he stared down at me with something raw in his gaze. I dropped my hands and stepped back, turned to run from the room, only to have his fingers wrap around my wrist. "You will not leave my side unless I otherwise order it."

My eyes closed as my feet stopped mid-step, forcing my body to hit the floor with the momentum of my dead run cut short. On the floor I waited, not bothering to rise as my shoulders slumped and my mind raced with what this meant.

He could keep me forever as a pet; all he had to do was order it. Or even worse, he could tell me to fuck him, and I would without hesitating. I was at his mercy, which was the last place I'd ever wanted to be. I could, however, kill him if he forgot to order me not to. Interesting…if I had free will to do what I wanted, I could still survive this.

I stood up, knowing he hadn't told me to. I turned around and glared at him as a smirk lifted my lips.

"You will not harm me, druid," he seethed before I could summon the magic to do just that. "Ever," he muttered as his hand lifted and scrubbed down his face, his shoulders slumping. "Can you prevent creatures from getting out of Faery?" he startled me with his question. I stared at him, aloof and curious to know why he cared, and yet he hadn't demanded I answer. "Answer me, Erie!" he shouted, and I nodded.

"I can, but I won't," I replied as I stared at him through narrowed eyes.

"Tell me how you can close it."

"I cannot fully close it, but I can ward it to prevent those who wish to do humans harm from escaping." I wanted to bite my tongue off, but unlike his, mine wouldn't grow back.

"Then let's go do it, shall we?" he asked, turning to look at the blonde who watched us with something dark in her eyes.

"Will it harm us if we leave Faery through the portal?" she asked, and I stared at her blankly.

"Will it harm them?" he asked.

"If they intend to harm humans, of course," I said, barely above a hiss of air as I stared at her. "They are Fae; are they not?"

"That's not your concern," he replied heatedly as he stepped closer. "What happens to those who enter it, wishing to do the Fae harm?"

"That depends on the wards I cast, asshole. Pink mist or maybe worse…those who cannot die may enjoy a much slower death."

"You will cast wards that do not harm them, do you understand me?"

"It's not like I have a choice otherwise, is it?" I seethed. "I'm your bitch now. You can literally do whatever you want to me, or make me do whatever you want. At least until you can't, right?"

"What does that mean?" he asked hesitantly.

"Every time you order me to do something, it loses its magic. Which means eventually, I will kill you, Paladin," I chuckled. "And I'll enjoy bathing in your blood."

"Years, Erie. That is how long it will take for the magic inside that amulet to wane, and we'll have a lot of fun between now and then. There's also the fact that you're druid and Templar. You want to know why you're so powerful. You're both types mixed into one little hot mess. You hold ancient bloodlines inside your veins, blood most druids and Templars would kill to have been born with, and yet you have both running through you. So you may kill me one day, but not before you give me a son who will save our people. *Our* people," he hissed. "Now go sit at the bar and have a drink, and do not leave your seat for any reason until I tell you to. I'll be right back."

I moved to the bar, jumped on a stool, and stared at the bottle of tequila I'd been drinking from, which was now sitting on the other side of the bar. I watched Vlad move to where I sat. He placed his hands on the bar and lowered his face to mine.

"I don't let people fuck with anyone inside my club, woman," he hissed meaningfully.

"Kill me then," I offered. I stared into his swirling silver eyes and swallowed hard. "Or hand me the bottle of tequila so I can drink myself stupid; one or the other, please?"

He stood back, crossing his arms before he finally exhaled and retrieved the bottle, placing it in front of me. I grabbed it, tipped it up, and chugged, ignoring the burn that traveled down my throat as I drank deeply, enjoying the warmth that swirled through my body, numbing my senses. I set it down and gazed up at him, watching as he whistled through his lips and shook his head.

"Had I known what they had done, they'd have died a lot slower than what you gave them. You gave them

mercy; I assure you, when someone breaks my laws, they pay for it."

"You were aware of what was happening. You followed them, and yet you didn't stop it. I watched you, Vlad. I watched you walk away from it. Tell me, what was more important than saving her life?"

"Someone I liked very much took her own life that day. I was called away to help."

"Did you save her?" I countered.

"No, we lost her."

"Then you should have saved the one you were closest to. Life sucks; you don't get to abandon one to save another. You save the one who needs you, not the one you have to leave to save. Life isn't that easy. It's messy as fuck, and her death is yours to carry now. Not mine."

"You think you could leave a friend you cared about to die so easily?"

"I'd have to care about someone in order to answer that, now wouldn't I?" I said tonelessly.

"You have to have someone you care about; everyone does."

"I was kept away from the other kids in the center where I was raised. I wasn't allowed to speak to the others or learn with them. Druids and Templars are like water and oil, yet one force. I had both of them inside of me, and no father wanted their son soiling his reputation with someone created to become a Templar's whore. At least, that's what was inside their minds when I read them. They were mortals, easy enough to penetrate their thoughts with what I was. Immortals like Callaghan were a different story. I was meant for one thing, and at that, I was unnatural to them. So how is it I'd care for any of them?"

"You're more fucked up than the last two girls who sat here and told me their stories," he muttered. "Drink," he ordered. My hand latched on to the bottle, and I gulped it down without stopping until he realized what he had done. "Stop, you will drink when you want to."

I slammed the bottle down and turned to search for Callaghan, finding him right behind me, listening in on the story I'd told Vlad. "Anyone can control me?"

"Don't worry, I'll protect you, Erie," he smiled. "From everyone but me," he chuckled.

I shifted to launch myself from the chair but stopped cold, unable to leave it. He moved to me, stopping right in front of me. Nose to nose I stared into his eyes. "I hate you!"

"I know you'll probably always hate me after this, but what's done is done. You're mine now; you're my mate whether we like it or not. The Fae have agreed to allow you to try to ward the broken portal. You will not place anything on it that can harm any of them. You will set it to deny entrance to their enemies while preventing the Fae from leaving Faery without the King's permission. Can you do that?"

"Callaghan," I said as I shook my head.

"Can it be done?"

"Yes," I answered, not bothering to tell him that while it could be, it may be the last ward I ever placed in this lifetime. But it was fine with me; I'd get out of this life of slavery one way or another.

CHAPTER *eight*

FAERY WAS UNREAL. WHERE I STOOD WAS THE CLOSEST I'd dared to get to the fractured portal. I hadn't realized just how large it was, but the view I held was breathtaking. Twin moons stood high in the violet sky, and the sunset splashed over mountains and beaches that called to me. Flowers swayed in the moonlit field, and my hands itched to touch them, to pet the soft velvet petals. I shook my head, dispelling the urge to do just that.

Faery was deadly; everything about it was created to lure innocent humans into its beauty, to feed from them. It was a place you went to but never returned from. It was a void as big as the one in my soul that ached to be filled. The only difference being that, where I longed to find somewhere I belonged, it ached to consume those stupid enough to enter.

"You can start now," he growled as he watched me take in the beauty.

"As you wish, master," I laughed coldly.

"How long will it take?"

"Hours, days, years, who knows? It's larger than Spokane and the smaller cities that surround it. It's bigger than I heard it was."

"How long?"

"I don't fucking know!" I growled as I turned around to face him. "That isn't a hole anymore, it's a fucking crater. I can't tell you how long, not even if you demand it, because honestly, I have no idea how long it will take. It could take years if you keep demanding answers for shit I don't know. Now leave me be so I can figure out what to do, Paladin!"

He stared at me as the tick in his jaw hammered, his body tensed, and I shook my head. He could demand all he wanted; it would be the last one he ever got. I moved my fingers, testing the air around me. It pulled back, and I stalled, throwing a curious glance to the Fae who watched me.

"You said you tried before, and it grew larger?"

"It did," the blonde agreed softly as her eyes bored into mine cautiously. "It's too much for you to do alone, we can help." Synthia was her name if what they'd called her at the bar was correct.

"You can't, you're connected to it. You touch it, it expands. It's triggered to run from you. It's not from the gates opening; it's unnatural. Someone created the fracture," I explained as I bent down, running my fingers through the dirt that divided our world from theirs. "These," I said, pulling out glass fragments, "are something placed in the ground to sever the walls that kept our worlds separated," I finished, standing to drop the shards into her palm.

Her violet eyes scanned the fragments before she groaned. "Relics; someone used one of the relics to sever the veil between our worlds. It's the Stone of Destiny," she uttered as she turned to the golden-eyed man who was never far from her side. "They used our own relics to open the world to the outside, to create chaos."

"Stone or no stone, my ward will not stop it from growing. Only prevent them from leaving it in its current state. If it grows, that part which gets larger will not be warded."

"Then you can come back and ward it," Callaghan announced beside me.

I smiled as I lifted my eyes to Synthia. "I will do what I can, but I make no promises."

"According to Grandmaster Kreseley, you're the only one with enough skill to do wards of this magnitude. Start; we're wasting time, and you and I have unfinished business to attend to."

I faced away from him to do as he bid. My power roiled through the atmosphere, pulling from everything around me until my hair electrified and power raced through the marks that graced my flesh. Unlike the Fae's, mine was unnatural, as unnatural as the stones that had been used to tear the fabric of Faery and undo the veil that divided the worlds. The air crackled with it, and lightning exploded above our heads, thunder clapping loudly directly above us.

My fingers danced as I became lost in the pleasure of warding the worlds, one against exit and the other against entry. Unfortunately, I wouldn't be able to add any consequences for those who sought to hurt humans.

Hours passed, and those behind me came and went

as I worked tirelessly to magically ward the gaping hole that allowed monsters into my world. I heard voices, felt their presence, and yet I noticed nothing. If I was going out, at least I was making a difference before I did, not that anyone would care. Well, Callaghan would be upset about my womb, but not me.

I felt the exhaustion, nausea swirling inside my stomach as more time passed. My body sagged as I neared the end, and I felt his hands supporting my weight as my hands dropped, yet my fingers still moved with the magic that pulsed through me. Well, it did, until my ears popped, then my nose, and when I opened my eyes to see, red covered my vision.

I laughed soundlessly as I tried to gain focus, to clear my vision. My hands stopped without warning, leaving the invisible strings of magical protection wards attached. My knees buckled, and Callaghan whispered my name. He sounded far away. He shook me, muttering something too softly for me to hear.

Trying to speak ached, and something warm and wet covered my face as it bathed my body in it. I felt my body falling faster than it ever should as blackness descended, stealing away all of my senses.

"You will not die, Erie, do you fucking hear me? You will not die; I order it!"

CHAPTER
nine

BRIGHT LIGHTS FLASHED ABOVE MY HEAD, BLINDING
me. Machines beeped somewhere close as I brought my
hands up, covering my eyes as I struggled against the
nausea that violently hit me. I moved over the edge of
the bed, retching until nothing remained in my stomach.
I stared down at the expensive loafers I'd just thrown up
on and lifted my heavy-lidded stare up to Callaghan's
angry face.

"You should have fucking warned me," he seethed
as anger burned in his gaze.

"I tried," I uttered as I laid back down and hung my
forearm over my eyes. "I tried, asshole. You didn't *let*
me answer. Magic has to have a consequence. I cannot
cast a two-way door, not without it taking its pound of
flesh from something. You forced the outcome. It is on
you, not me. Maybe next time you ask for my magic,
you'll think before you demand something. Don't
place my magic into your rulebook, because it sure as
hell doesn't fit there, nor with the druids," I whispered

through cracked lips.

"You could have warned me," he uttered as he bent down and flicked his wrist, saving his loafers. I eyed his expensive suit and winced. I gazed around the room we were in; the sterile scent itched against my senses. Christmas lights covered the walls while creatures milled through the hallway that led into my room. "An entire day, Erie. You've been asleep for an entire day without any sign of waking the fuck up." He answered my question without me having to ask it.

"Did you miss me?" I whispered as my eyes grew heavy.

"You'd like that, wouldn't you?"

"For one single person in any world to miss me?" I mumbled as I peered up at him. "Maybe, maybe not," I shrugged and my tone grew stronger. "It's almost easier alone."

"You don't know the difference," he growled. "You've never been alone, ever. You've always had a Knight protecting you, even when you thought you were alone."

"I don't buy that," I scratched out through the sandpaper of my mouth.

"Sit up, we're leaving," he ordered, and on cue, I did, even though it was a bit slow. My legs draped over the edge as I faced him, noting my lack of dress as I did so. He grabbed a gown, helping me into it before he placed a bathrobe around my shoulders and then cradled me in his arms as he headed towards the door. Footsteps sounded down the hallway and then Synthia was there, halting our clumsy escape.

"She isn't well enough to travel," she pointed out.

"We have rooms here, upstairs. You may use one if you wish," she offered as her eyes traveled over my disheveled appearance. "Eliran, my healer, will be close if she has need of him as well if you remain here. She's still healing, and in no condition to travel, Callaghan."

"I didn't finish your wards," I mumbled. I hadn't finished, and she wasn't letting me leave until I had, which just fucking figured.

"They're working and rather well at that. What little that wasn't finished is easy enough for the guards to patrol. I do not need you to finish, but I'd rather you stay to regain your strength than wade through Faery and its potholes in your current condition."

I blinked and then stared up at Callaghan, who considered her offer. He nodded but then paused. "She needs a bath and clothes to wear tonight," he said gently, and I felt a strange sensation in my chest as he spoke softly to her.

"She can use some of mine, and the room I had made for you is accommodated with a pool in it. It's larger than a condo in most large cities. It can soothe her aches as well, as it does have water from the Fairy Pools. Now, we can stand here all day talking, or you can follow me, and I will show you to it. Which option would you prefer, Erie?"

I lifted a brow and almost swallowed my tongue when she directed her question to me instead of Callaghan. "Here," I admitted, hating being closer to him than I had to be.

"If you will please follow me; and Callaghan, put her down. Her feet work just fine, you oaf," she threw over her shoulder as he started after her. He set me down, and I swayed on my feet, holding on to him to remain upright but noting she slowed as I started forward. I could have kissed her for giving me the respite from his touch, along with the name she'd called him. Maybe I did need a friend?

I followed her until she stopped in front of a set of doors and stepped to the side, allowing him to proceed as her eyes locked with mine. One moment I was dressed in a gaudy hospital gown and the next the sensation of butterfly wings fluttered beneath the robe as my hair rose with the awareness of magic being cast while she dressed me with her magic.

"A girl's outfit is her first and best defense against a man," she shrugged as I narrowed my eyes at her in uncertainty. "Use what the Gods gave you, and the bathing suit, as well, which will fit your curves perfectly. Men are unable to think beyond a woman's body on a good day, but dressed in a suit that shows its best features, and they're left one step up from a brainless caveman."

I frowned at her words as I smoothed my hands over the robe and suit I felt beneath it. I turned towards the room, watching as Callaghan did an inspection of the room and the setup before I turned and glared back at Synthia. "I'm not with him willingly. I don't think my outfit will help out much," I pointed out with a shrug. "I will kill him eventually."

She waved a single hand in the air, and everything around us froze. I gawked at the magic that vibrated around us, sizzling as it singed and popped. I struggled to close my jaw and get it up off of the floor, where it was trying to become a permanent fixture.

"Tell me what you see when you look at me, Erie," she demanded as she crossed her arms, which pulsed with brands that vibrated with magic.

"A rich, spoiled bitch who has everything handed to her on a silver platter," I chuckled, unafraid of flirting with death because I was very aware she was so much more than she was allowing me to see. "Someone who is loved," I added, hating the heaviness in my chest as the words left my lips.

She silently raised a dainty brow and then slowly nodded. "What you see is what I allow you to see, so your assessment is fair. It's easy to judge a book by a cover, but what lies beneath the cover isn't always as pretty. I was like you are now," she said as she held her other hand up when my mouth opened to argue our differences. "I was thrown away by my parents, but under very different circumstances. Mine was actually trying to protect me; yours are just soulless assholes who could use a blade through their hearts. But what happened to us is a lot alike. I was trained within the Guild to kill, to be the best at enforcing the laws. I was used, mistreated, and yet I am stronger because of it. I had little control over my destiny since others mapped out my life before I was ever conceived. You feel as if you don't belong to anything because you're a mix of two races, two races that don't want you, and yet their fate lies within you. That's your greatest leverage, Erie. You hold the fate of their world in the palm of your hand; use it. We're off point here, and he will not remain frozen for much longer. I run a sanctuary for the unwanted. I now run the Spokane Guild, a place where lost and unwanted things can find acceptance for their unique gifts. You're lost, and right now you think I'm insane, which is legit fine with me. Life isn't fair, but sometimes you have to take control of it yourself. You think the necklace holds you prisoner, but does it really?"

"I am unable to do anything other than what he tells me to with it on," I growled.

"Anything he tells you to," she nodded carefully. "But unless he tells you not to specifically do something, you're not unable to. Down this flight of steps is a garden that leads to a portal, Erie. That garden is sacred and very important to me." I blinked at her rapidly as the crease on my forehead furrowed. "Do not harm any of mine on your way out. And do not disturb the garden, either. Think my offer over and let me know when you come to a decision. And, Erie, Merry Christmas." She smiled sadly before she waved her hand, unfreezing time before I could ask her what the hell she'd meant.

"This will work," Callaghan said as he turned to look at us, narrowing his eyes while taking in our positions. "Come to me, Erie," he said, and my feet moved even though I wanted to run in the opposite direction. Once I was flush against his muscled chest, I stopped. His arms draped around me, pulling me closer. "We will remain here until dawn. Thank you for your hospitality, Synthia."

"I'll leave you to it," she said, turning those purplish-blue eyes to me long enough that I worried my bottom lip between my teeth.

CHAPTER Ten

THE ROOM WAS SHEER ELEGANCE. MY GAZE SLIPPED from the large four-poster bed that was swathed in a wispy cloth which held a thousand tiny crystals that reflected the candlelight to the circle pool in the middle of the floor. White carpet covered that same floor, soothing against my aching feet as I eyed the indoor pool longingly.

"Strip, then get into the water, Erie," he ordered. "You have blood and debris in your hair still."

My hands moved to the robe, pushing it from my shoulders as a quick intake of breath sounded from Callaghan. Peeking up at him, I stalled or tried to as my hands lifted to the silver strings that held the bathing suit up around my neck.

"Leave it on," he amended as he grabbed my hand and walked me towards the water. I was wearing a skimpy bathing suit which did little to hide my body. It hugged my waist, crisscrossing over my chest to cover my breasts, but they were hardly considered covered.

The bottom was a thong which exposed the gentle swell of my ass cheeks. "Gods," he growled as he released my hand to allow me to slip beneath the water. I dug the pieces of gore from my hair and bathed quickly, ignoring his looming presence.

I stared up at him as I sank into the soothing, warm, rose-scented water. It was infused with healing powers that delved into my aching body. A gasp which unraveled as a moan escaped my lips, and then the sound of clothes hitting the floor made me look up to find him stripping.

"There's not enough room for you in here," I grumbled.

"Then you can sit on my lap."

There was plenty of room in the round pool, but Callaghan had a way of eating space with his full frame. My vision swam with lust as he slowly stripped and stepped into the pool of heated water. I swallowed hard, hating that I was stuck here with him.

"Like what you see?" he asked, and I bit into my tongue until I tasted blood.

"Yes." the reply stole from my throat, filled with anguish at being unable to *not* answer him.

"Do you want to fuck me?" he asked with a smirk, his sexy, heavy stare made my body react in ways it shouldn't have. It ached for him, even though I hated him.

"Uh-huh," came out as a moan as I closed my eyes against the heat that mixed with hunger in his oceanic depths.

"Come to me," he said thickly, running his tongue over his lips which caught my hungry gaze. I moved towards him, settling between his legs as his fingers

found my chin and forced my head up until our eyes locked in silent battle. "Are you fully healed, Erie?" he asked, his other hand slipping beneath the water to rub his fingers against my heated core.

"I am," I uttered before my mouth lifted to capture his, shutting up his stupid line of questions that I didn't want to answer. His hands released me, raising to my hips as he rose, carrying me from the water with him. It splashed over the pristine carpet, sloshing everywhere as he took us to the bed.

The swimsuit top was removed, exposing my naked breasts as he lowered me onto the soft bed, never ending the soul-sucking, toe-curling kiss that both took my breath away and left me boneless. His arm pushed between us, ripping the swimsuit bottoms off while stealing a pain-filled yelp from my lungs.

I felt him pushing against my opening, and for a split-second, my brain came hurtling back from space and I placed my palms against his chest, testing his weight and sheer strength as he pulled back, staring down at me.

"Tell me you don't want this," he urged.

"I don't want this," I replied instantly as his eyes narrowed and dropped to the necklace as he glared at it.

"Tell me what you want, Erie," he changed tactics.

"I want you to fuck me like you hate me, bitch," I snarled as I lifted my legs, winding them around his slim hips and pushing him inside as a scream of pain ripped from my lungs. "Now," I pleaded as I rocked and twisted to accommodate him.

"Like I hate you?" he laughed huskily as he rolled us, gripping my hips as he lifted me and pushed me down further on his thick, vibrating cock. His magic pulsed through the air, thick and hot as it slid over my body. His hands continued to use my hips to guide my lithe form down on his rigid cock. "Ride me," he demanded. "Don't stop until you come for me."

My hands landed on his broad chest, my hips moving as my feet rested against the bed, and it took seconds to combust and shatter. I whimpered as my eyes closed while his hands came up to knead and pinch my nipples before he spun us over, trading our positions. His hands gripped behind my knees, pushing my legs up until I groaned with how full he made me feel.

He rested between my legs, rocking slowly at first, and then faster. "You want it rough, don't you, sweet girl?" he questioned, and I agreed, watching his eyes darken to a dangerous hue of blue. "Jesus, you're a hot fucking mess," he groaned as he pulled out, only to thrust forward with more momentum. I whimpered at the deliciousness of pain and eroticism his movements caused. "You want me to hate-fuck you, don't you? Because it will make it easier for you to hate me when the sun rises in the morning," he purred thickly while his hands moved from my legs, slowly up my body as he leaned over.

His fingers caressed my throat before his mouth touched against mine, claiming my lips hungrily. His other hand moved to my hair, yanking it back hard, mercilessly, as his kiss heated up until I no longer cared if he allowed air to fill my lungs. The fingers around my throat tightened, and fear licked the inside of my brain. If I'd had any common sense, it had long ago left me, so instead of bailing and begging him to stop, I growled,

because I was kind of digging it, and sometimes you just had to test your own boundaries.

Callaghan's mouth left mine bereft as it moved away. His hands continued, one applying pressure as the other pulled my hair. He used it to move my body on his slick cock, utilizing the juices he'd forced from me to slide in and out until all I could do was feel him there, using me.

His hand slipped from my hair, reaching around my throat until he stole the air entirely from my lungs. Eyes burned into mine as he fucked me until I whimpered from lack of air as he fucked it out of me. Lights exploded behind my eyelids, from dying, I was sure. My lungs burned, but it didn't fucking matter because I was quaking with every thrust of my body, which forced him into mine like a well-oiled machine. His mouth slammed against mine, teeth nipping my lip softly as I opened my eyes to fight against his hold. The moment his tongue entered my mouth, I inhaled as his hand released. I sucked the air he fed me deep into my lungs as my body shivered, the orgasm leaving me mindless and coming hard around his thick cock over and over as his magic played with my clitoris.

"You're a fucking savage," he growled. "You are as beautiful and wild as the land you were named after," he murmured while he pushed me down, releasing my body from his and positioning me in front of him as he wanted. "And you're mine, Erie, say it," he purred thickly as he pushed my legs apart and settled behind me.

"I'm yours," I whispered barely above a breath.

His hand trailed up my back as he threaded his

fingers through my hair, pulling me back until I was bent painfully, staring up at him. "I can't fucking hear you," he moaned as his cock entered me, filling me until I opened my lips on a moan. His mouth touched against mine briefly before he pushed me back down, gripped my hips, and fucked me hard and fast until all I could do was bury my face in the sheets, biting them as pain touched pleasure and became everything. I yearned for more, for him to reach the darkest places inside of me. I wanted it all, to feel him there with me, bringing light into the darkness I'd been born into. I lifted my ass, giving him further depth, and as I did it, my body lifted, and something hit the bed.

I lifted my head from the sheets and stared down at the necklace. My heart sped up as I grabbed it, hiding it in my palm until he tensed behind me, groaning as he found his release. He started to move, and I turned around, lowering my mouth to his cock. I licked the sensitive edge, slowly moving up his body with kisses. My teeth nipped against the silken 'V' that sat above his massive cock. I kissed all the way up until my mouth claimed his hard. His hands moved to my hips, lifting my body up to savage me again, already hard and ready for more.

My hand threaded in his hair. My arms settled around his neck as he slid my body onto his. I cried against the soreness and fullness as he hissed his approval. I retook his mouth, momentarily forgetting my purpose as pleasure burned through me, red-hot.

I pulled my mouth away, jerked the necklace over his head, and screamed, "Do not remove the necklace!"

"The fuck?" he demanded as he pushed me onto

the bed, staring down at his chest where the necklace glowed beside his other amulet. "You fucking bitch," he snapped.

"Do not touch me," I hissed as he lunged to do just that, still erect and full with his arousal as mine shone on his silken shaft. "You will not tell anyone you are wearing it. Understand?" I whispered thickly as I stood up, knowing he'd kill me now for sure. "Tell me you want me, Paladin."

"I want you, but I don't need the necklace to admit that," he snarled as he stood up. His cock bounced as he walked towards me. "Tell me to fuck you again," he hissed thickly. "Tell me to finish what you started and see what happens, little druid."

"You think I won't?" I laughed coldly. "Lay on the bed, on your back."

I watched his spine stiffen as he moved to the bed and did as he was told. "Do you want me?" I asked, slowly prowling closer to him.

"I've never pretended otherwise," he admitted. I stepped onto the bed, placing my feet close to both hips as I knelt down, straddling him. His hands didn't move; he didn't move. "Come on, big girl, say it."

"So you can hurt me?" I asked carefully.

"No, so I can make you sore enough to remember who the fuck you belong to when you leave me here. So tomorrow, when you wince, you think of me, and the next day after it. I want to fuck you so damn hard that my dick is imprinted in your womb, and you remember who claimed you first."

"Fuck me," I growled, not intending it as an invite. I was pushed down so fast that I wasn't even sure how it happened. His body pounded with inhuman speed against mine until I was whimpering and screaming his name to the Gods above us. His mouth crushed against mine in a painful kiss, meant to punish. I brought my hands up to push his mouth away, but his hands captured them, slamming them against the bed as he refused to release my lips. He was fucking me silent? I wasn't sure if I should be okay with it, but fuck, he was sexy when he was pissed off! He pulled back far enough for me to gasp air and instead of issuing a command, I screamed... "Yes, fuck yes! Harder, you bastard," I demanded, and he did.

Magic slithered up around my nipples, applying painful pressure. It pinched against my clit, sending my body twisting away from it as the already sensitive nub pounded with the impending orgasm. He jerked tautly, and I screamed as the hardest, most violent orgasm of my entire life bowed my back and shook the world around me as it tore through me. I moaned against his mouth, biting his full lip as he groaned and hissed while his own orgasm continued.

The moment he finished, he fell off of me onto the bed beside me. "Run, little druid," he laughed. "Because I know how to remove this damn thing," he admitted before turning to stare into my eyes. "When I do, I will hunt you to the ends of the world to claim you. Remember, don't harm her people on your way out, and don't touch anything in the garden because it will kill you. But Erie, know this, there's nowhere you can hide from me. No one who can stop me from getting to you, or finding you, little one. It's no longer just a quest for our people. It's fucking personal now."

"Sucks when the shoe lands on the other foot, doesn't it, big boy?" I lay beside him, stretching out as I eyed the room for clothing. I expelled the air from my lungs and sat back up, only to be gripped hard around the wrist and shoved beneath his hulking frame. "Let me go!" I screeched, but he didn't. He stared down into my eyes with something dark and brooding as the necklace glowed between us.

"It was created by the Templar Order, Erie. *My* fucking Order," he hissed out as it glowed brighter in warning. "I'm going to enjoy punishing you when I catch you. I do enjoy hunting pretty little things down and claiming them," he uttered before his mouth claimed mine. I didn't move away from his kiss, not until he pulled away, claiming my bottom lip between his teeth and drawing blood. He sucked it, the fire in his eyes igniting further as I reacted to it.

My legs spread, inviting him for more, but he didn't indulge. He watched me, and then rolled off of me, unable to ignore the magic that pushed through the necklace demanding he did as I said.

"You will remain here until sunrise," I instructed. "After that, you will destroy the necklace and *then* remove it. If you come after me, Callaghan, I will kill you. Happy hunting, Paladin," I muttered as I turned around and grabbed the robe, slipping it over my shoulders on my way out of the room.

Outside the room, I paused, leaning against the door as I struggled to calm the furious reaction that thundered inside of me. That man had been wild, unmatched in lust, and a fucking beast in the sheets. If he wasn't who he was, and I wasn't the one thing that could save his people, we may have had a future—*if* I actually liked him. I could admit I enjoyed his cock and body, but him? He was a rich, entitled, good-for-nothing prick. It was too bad, really, a waste of a good dick. Maybe it was a good thing he was my first though, because he'd set that bar rather high.

I followed Synthia's instructions as I made my way into the garden. The moment I entered it, I screamed. A dragon literally flew over it as a woman with dark hair bounced a small boy on her lap, reaching for that fire-breathing, honest-to-Gods dragon. It flew back over us, and I hit the ground with my naked ass in the air.

"Oh, oh wow, you're naked," throaty laughter sounded, and then the sensation I'd felt earlier covered my body. I jumped to my feet as I kicked myself for being the world's biggest ninny and stared at the mother and her child. Was she pregnant with a toddler? Hadn't I heard that the Fae had conception issues I'd envied? "You must be Erie; I am Ciara, and the dragon who is now showing off for you is my husband. The door is right there," she nodded her head towards a thick door guarded by what looked to be mutes. "They won't stop you. Us women, we tend to stick together in times of need. You are free to leave if you wish it."

"Definitely." My tone was devoid of emotion or fear as I moved towards the guards, intending to fight my way out if I had to. They shocked me by opening the gate, which had a dark-haired male barring my way. I'd known it wouldn't be this easy.

"I'm Ristan, I'll be your tour guide to the portal as our world will try to keep you here, and as Synthia promised, you are free to leave."

"Why the fuck would you do that? Isn't Callaghan your friend or something?" I countered.

"Use 'friend' loosely and you have what he is to us. He helped us when we were in a rather tight space," he smirked. "Not a good sort of tight place. You smell like you fucked him."

I blinked and his sudden change of subject. "That was rude."

"Hey, tour guide here," he groaned as he waved his hands down his tightly coiled body. I followed those hands as I took in the *Demons do it Better* shirt he wore, down to his Doc Marten shit-kickers. "I didn't say I wasn't an ass or polite. You smell like you just got fucked, and you have welts around your neck. My kind of freaky deaky sexy bitch," he laughed throatily. "Fuck, I wish Olivia would have our kid already. These mood swings are hell on our sex life."

"You're a demon in Faery," I pointed out offhandedly.

"I am half-demon, anyway," he agreed as he started forward, and I had to run to keep up with his long strides. "My other half is Fae. And here we are," he said with a wave of his hand at the portal.

"Where does it lead?" I asked, turning to eye the rising sun. "Shit…"

"You should probably run; he's already coming for you. Can't say I blame him any," he mused as he reached over, grabbed my shoulder, and started me towards the portal. "Good luck, druid," he laughed. "I'm sure we will meet again if Faery brought you to us."

"Faery didn't bring me here; he did."

"Faery has indeed brought you here, druid. She calls to everyone who enters, and I assure you, she led you to us for a reason. Five minutes."

"Five minutes?"

"Until he is here," he chuckled. "See you soon, female."

I hadn't considered the fact that time moved differently inside Faery. Or what time it had been in general when I'd given him the order. I turned back, eyeing the demon that smirked and wiggled his fingers at me oddly. I slipped through the portal with one thought: Callaghan was coming for me, hunting me. So were the druids and Templars. I didn't intend to let any of them catch me. Not now, not ever. I was Erie, born of two worlds that could never control me, and I'd be damned if he thought he could.

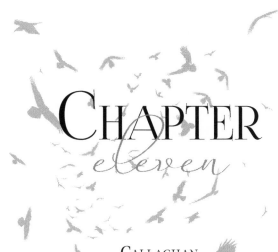

CHAPTER eleven

CALLAGHAN
FOUR WEEKS LATER

I STARED OUT OVER THE STREET, WATCHING THE GUILD for any sight of the little imp who'd slipped my watch in Faery. I knew she was within, protected by the Fae. Not that they could protect her from me, not with the mark brandishing her flesh. I felt her pain, knew it like I knew my own. I'd betrayed her trust, but then she'd been moments away from being attacked by those within that bar, and I would have gone to war to protect her. She was and always would be my downfall, since way before she'd drawn air into this new body of hers.

I could still feel her body beneath mine. The lavender and mint that clung to her flesh as I fucked her without mercy. She'd come undone for me, bending and twisting to take more with a hunger that drove me over the edge way too soon. Then she'd placed the necklace over my head, shocking the ever-loving shit out of me. I wasn't even sure why I'd been surprised since, if anyone could fight her way out of a corner, it was that girl.

Sure, I could have fought harder to hold her there, withstanding the pain of the necklace. It would have been easy enough, but I hadn't wanted to break her, and if I was honest, I wanted her to want me on her own. I didn't crave some fake fucking relationship that the necklace demanded she abides by. I wanted her, the wildness that she freed as she took what she needed, what she wanted. I wanted those eyes alight as she came on my dick, riding it with abandoned need.

She stepped out of the Guild, and I watched her graceful movements as she paused on the steps. A frown tugged at her bottom lip as she turned, staring back at the doors with something foreign in her eyes. Erie didn't get attached to people; she didn't reach out for help either. Seeing her evolve made something inside my chest ache from within.

Several moments later, she was heading away from the Guild as if it too had scared her. As if she'd noted the same thing I had just whispered in my head, and now she ran from it. I didn't blame her, people sucked. She'd been put through hell, abused to the point that when I'd discovered it, I'd been unable to reach her. That hadn't been in the plans I'd made for her, and yet she'd emerged even stronger than she'd been. For a whispered moment, I'd thought she'd emerged from her cocoon, but she hadn't, not yet.

At the tender age of fifteen, I'd gone to the Druid's Den to check in on her. To see what progress she'd made in school, to see what new thing she'd discovered. What I had found hadn't been pleasant, far from it. The moment I entered the observation room, it was to find

a broken, beaten girl lying in a pool of her own blood. Bile had escaped my lips as I'd inhaled the filth of her cell and the excrements that came with the sickness of what had been done to her.

They'd beaten her, whipping her until the flesh was open on her back, her spine exposed. They'd continued, snapping it until it had severed and for what? Because some little boy had gotten too close to her, and then they'd forced all the adolescent boys into the stands to watch as she was punished for his crimes. All because Erie was different, unnatural to them.

Afterward, instead of helping her, or allowing the healers to tend to her, they'd locked her into a glass room. One that allowed the others to watch as she'd healed, but that took weeks or even longer with the damage they'd done to her spinal cord. So she'd lain there, in her own blood and waste as they'd watched, dehumanizing her while she compartmentalized what they'd done. She was so alone and broken that I'd come undone, freeing the beast to punish those who had tarnished what was ours.

I'd gone unhinged, murdering each and every one of the adults who had wielded that whip against the child she'd been. I'd let the monster out to play with them, and oh, had he. She was his; he'd whispered it to each and every one of them as he'd ripped them apart that day. I'd taken her from there, bringing her to my home as I summoned the healers to help her. It had taken almost an entire year to heal her body. Every part of her had eventually healed except her mind, and from that day forth, she never let another person get close to her. No one touched her, and when she walked by them, they stepped away from the madness they had placed into her mind.

They'd broken her, so fucking deeply that she never even knew it was me who washed her, who tended to the sewing of her flesh. It had been me who held that slip of a girl against my chest, singing hymns from Ireland, pushing her hair from her face as I begged her to come back to me. I'd done everything I could to save her, to keep her as more than just the womb everyone thought her to be. I'd wanted that fire within her to blossom, and it had taken me more time than I'd ever imagined getting even a whisper of a flame to light in her soul again. When the flame had finally come back, I fed it promises of a better life if she could just hang on for me. I'd purchased rare soap that smelled of the lavender that grew wild in Ireland, and to this day, she wore it without knowing why.

They'd sheered her wild, beautiful red hair, butchering it until her scalp bled from where they'd cut it. Barely having grown tits to be noticed and she'd had the boys all hard for what she was becoming, and they'd blamed her. She was created of the cauldron, magic in the purest form, and I didn't question the beauty she had been blossoming into, but then I'd seen it before; the wild red hair that was natural to Ireland, and the bluest eyes that had once smiled without knowing it. To this very fucking day, they didn't smile. They held pain, a pain so fucking deep that it couldn't be erased. They watched everyone with distrust, took in everything around them. She expected everything bad to happen to her as if it was how it was supposed to be. That girl trusted no one, not a fucking soul, not even me, who

had spent the last ninety-nine years protecting her, only to fail over and over again. The moment I'd been called to follow orders, something always befell Erie in my absence. I'd fought to get her brought to the Templar Order compound, but they'd refused. To them, that girl was a monster, and to the druids, she was an unnatural thing of ugliness that didn't belong. To me, she was the most beautiful fucking thing in the world.

There was a reason she was born so wild and free, of the darkest magic this world had ever known. A deep darkness so wild and so forbidden that even the Gods had taken notice and banished it. But Erie wasn't just anything; no, she was reborn of the cauldron that not even the deadliest of creatures would drink from. The cauldron was a thing of great power, with the ability for rebirth and reincarnation. It was wild magic that brought back either the purest of heart or the darkest souls. There was no in between for it, and so we'd pushed her parents into it, knowing she would be who they created. And so she existed because we'd demanded it.

I'd held her moments after she was born. I'd found her abandoned on the floor, still in the placenta of her birth, unmoving. I'd pushed my own air into her premature lungs, holding the infant who couldn't have weighed more than three or four pounds in my hand, staring into her beautiful blue eyes that watched me, filling with the life I breathed into her. The nuns hadn't wanted to touch her, hadn't wanted to look upon what they thought was pure evil. They'd left her on the floor where her mother had birthed her, helping her to get away from the evil child she'd helped create. I'd taken her away from that cold, dirty floor, and the moment

I stepped into the light, her tiny blue eyes had locked with mine in silence. As if everything in the world had settled into place and was right again.

From the moment I'd walked outside of the crumbling building and held her beneath the Scottish sun that kissed her flesh, I knew she would be mine. Her tiny finger had wrapped around mine, and she made the tiniest of noises while she watched me, as if she felt it too. She hadn't cried once, hadn't squirmed as she gazed up at me, as if she sensed that her fate was connected to mine.

The seer who had watched us together cackled, her withered face crinkling as she moved closer to where I stood. She stared at me, cradling the tiny, premature girl in my hands with care. What a fucking sight we had to have been, her covered in the blood of her birth, and me, covered in the blood of my enemies, standing there beneath the sun of Scotland. I'd withdrawn my cloak, wrapping her in it like the most precious holy relic as the old crone watched me, her dull eyes sparkling as if she knew something I didn't, and maybe she did.

"And what will you do with it?" she wheezed.

"It? She is precious," I argued, hating the way she'd already been treated.

"Is she? Or is she only precious because without her, your kind will cease to exist?" she countered. "She cannot be both."

"She will be cherished by all."

"No, she will suffer for what she is, of that, you can be certain. That girl will know more pain than most people will see in a thousand lifetimes. You gave a sacrifice to create her, will you honor it, or will it have been for

nothing? It was the greatest sacrifice a man can make, and yet you stare at her as if she is more than the cure. Her life is as cursed as you are, Sir Knight. She hasn't even been given a name, and her own mother birthed her onto a floor and left her there to die, alone. And so her life begins anew, with new pain and suffering, but what will you do to stop it? Or will you wait until it is too late to reach her?"

"A name is just a name, as I have held many throughout the years, seer," I argued.

"So you will not name the wee thing?" she asked as she reached out, touching the child's forehead with the woad she'd produced from magic.

"She will not be a warrior," I uttered as I stared at the blue cross that had been painted onto her tiny forehead. It matched her blue eyes, which stared up at me. I lifted mine to the cross, sparkling on top of the ancient church on the edge of what had once been a Celtic stronghold. It had once been a glorious place, filled with laughter and the sound of strong, brave men preparing for battle. It was old, decrepit, and falling to ruins. It was where *she* was reborn, time, and time again.

"You're wrong; she is certainly a warrior by birth. She is barely formed, four months early from the womb of that uncaring whore who birthed her. She is a child of Ireland, born from the flames of those who have come and gone before her, created from wild, unimaginable magic. She will be wild, this little wee thing. Your people and the druids are going to break her, but she will rise from it stronger than either of you will ever know. Would you like to see what she will become?" she asked, and I swallowed.

"You can show me the woman she will become?" I inquired.

"Indeed, I can show you what she will become, but not what will make her into that. The future is always changing, and with it, what forges us to become soft, hard, or unfeeling."

Her hand grabbed mine and we were no longer in the fields outside the crumbling church in Scotland. We were in a strange place filled with corpses that littered the ground around us. A woman with wild red hair and the purest blue eyes I'd ever seen turned around, staring through us as if she couldn't see us. Her face was painted in the woad of the ancient Pict warriors. Her heart-shaped face was soft, delicate. Red lips the color of freshly drawn blood smiled, transforming her into the most beautiful woman I'd ever seen in my entire long lifetime. She was beyond beautiful, she was fierce and smiled through her eyes with the purest joy that cut through me as if I could just reach out and touch her, and she'd heal me.

"She will be a beauty, born of the magic of Ireland to heal two races that will both use and discard her unless you protect her, Sir Knight. So name her, and watch over her to ensure she remains of the light, for if she tastes the darkness, you will lose her. Something created of wild magic will never be tamed or fully broken, but she can be turned."

"Erie," I uttered as I stared down into the eyes that watched me. "She will be named Erie from the land of which she came. She will be mine to protect from this day forward."

"If it is true, mark her. Give her your protection;

bind her to you in a way that cannot be argued. She will need you; her road will not be an easy one. She is hungry," she whispered as she produced a glass vile and handed it to me. I accepted it, staring down at the blue liquid within.

The monster inside of me sniffed, assessing what it was, and then smiled as he forced my eyes back to the tiny girl who had yet to close her eyes.

"See that you do not fail her, for if you do, you will lose her."

"She will have my insignia upon her before the sun sets on this day."

"And that of the beast within you, for he has chosen her."

"Chosen her?" I countered carefully, sensing she was not what she said she was.

"You hold his mate in your arms." She vanished before I could ask anything else.

Back in the present, my eyes lifted to find Erie entering her apartment building, her head down, shoulders slumped, as she did her ritual to see if anyone had disturbed her home before she slid the iron grates over and crawled through it.

The Templar Knights wanted her brought in, but none of them wanted to chase her down. No one in the Order understood her past or cared about her. To them, she was a womb. To me, that girl was everything. She was the infant I held and named beneath the sun of Scotland. She was my past, my present, and my future. To me, she was the budding woman who was torn apart, the one I put back together and prayed that she would come back to me. No, she wasn't just a womb, Erie was my fucking salvation, and I knew it to my soul.

CHAPTER
twelve

ERIE

I WALKED INTO THE APARTMENT AND TOOK OFF MY bag, heading to the freezer to open it. Fred glared at me as I smiled at him. He'd been growing easier to deal with since I'd almost died a few times and the realization of what would happen to him if I did sank in. Plus, I knew he was beginning to enjoy our conversations.

"Still alive, I see."

"I'm literally spelled *not* to die, Fred. Trust me there, for a while; I tried a lot of ways to skip this portion of my life."

"Unsuccessfully…I could help you with that. So, did we get hit by the wrecking ball again?"

"No, I've been busy elsewhere. Besides, I told you, no more wrecking balls for me. I prefer to do things myself."

"If you're going to tell me about it, you should know I'm a visual learner."

"Smooth, Fred. Are you hungry?" I asked, opening

the fridge to examine the old milk carton and the three cubes of butter that sat in the fridge. I closed it, grabbing my bag as I slung it over my shoulder and stared at Fred. "I have to go out again for food, do you need anything?"

"My body," he groaned. "How long do you intend to keep me here?"

"Until hell freezes over," I shrugged. "You did very bad things, and you're still unwilling to say they were bad."

"If I admit it, you will let me go?" he asked.

"No, I just said you were still unwilling to admit it. I didn't say if you did, that I'd let you go."

Demons, they never did listen when you said things. Fred was no different. Although he did seem interested in the size of Callaghan's wrecking ball penis, he still had a lot of things to work on. I closed the freezer door to give him some alone time as the swearing began and I headed towards the door, but the moment my hand touched it, I felt the jolt from the wards. Exhaling as the wards pulsed to life inside the apartment, I frowned deeper.

I peered over my shoulder, dropping my bag as I moved to the window, peeping through the curtain to watch as men in full Templar gear surrounded the building. Fucking hell! I rushed back towards the freezer, pulling Fred out as I stuffed him into my bag. I wouldn't freak out; I wouldn't. I told myself over and over inside my head.

"What are you doing? You *touched* me!" he complained as I moved into the bedroom, grabbing the few pictures I had of Ireland and the lavender soap from the bathroom before tossing them into the bag as well, on top of Fred. Once I had the few items I needed, I rushed to the wall behind the bed, sliding the hidden panel I'd built open and slipped through it. Seven more just like it had been cut through other apartments that still held the remains of those who had lived in them until finally, I reached the fire escape.

Once I was on the fire escape, I went up towards the roof, silently making my way through the metal ladders as I reached the last one, and peered down at the men who watched the exits below. I eyed the building next to us, a greater distance than anyone should leap, and started running as Fred wailed from the backpack he'd been stuffed into, screaming for help.

"Shut up, Fred," I hissed. "The first thing that they will do is wash you in holy water. Trust me; it's not what you want. Your body? That will be the least of your concerns with those holy jackasses." He went silent as my feet hit the edge and I launched myself towards the next building. My fingers grasped the side, and I swung momentarily until I hefted my body weight over the edge and rolled onto the roof, hiding behind the lip of it that rose just enough to hide me as the door to the other rooftop was kicked open.

I listened as the Knights moved onto the roof of the building next to us. After several tense moments of calling down to the Knights below us, they went back inside. Had they been following me from the Guild? I shook off the knowledge and possibility before rolling my eyes at my own stupidity. Of course, they had been because I carried a womb of freaking gold. Or, at least to them it was. I was their mother-freaking Holy Grail, wasn't that what Fred had called it?

I crawled on my stomach towards the broken door of the rooftop and listened to the noises within. Silence greeted me, utterly chilling silence that took me away from the rooftop, back to the glass room I'd once lain inside, dying over and over again. I exhaled, pushing the fear and pain away as I whispered a silent prayer to the Gods of old, praying they helped me escape the fates that Arthur had spoken of once my time came. Bile pushed against my throat as I closed my eyes and sank my teeth into my arm to prevent the panic attack from spreading to my mind. It took several moments to calm the fear, and the pain I'd inflicted to gain control abated. Exhaling, I took back the control that had begun to slip away.

I wouldn't be tied to a bed and raped, left there as they watched me bleed out again. Once inside, I pushed through the hidden panel and closed it behind me, doing the same thing with the escape route I'd planned eons ago until I entered the last apartment. There, I opened the window and slipped across to the next building, doing the same thing through it until I was inside the abandoned shopping center that sat on the edge of a main area of Spokane, and entered suburbia.

The Hot Topic store had been set up by me the moment the grid had fallen. The large bed hidden behind a wall of corpses was to keep my scent from being discovered. I tossed the backpack off my shoulders and withdrew Fred and the lavender soap, holding it to my nose to calm the rapid beating of my heart. I had never figured out why it soothed my mind, but it did.

"They've begun hunting you in earnest," he grumbled as I placed him onto a pillow and grabbed the cooler of ice I'd refilled every day for him, just in case it was needed. I'd snuck in here just for him, and to pile more bodies up as the days closed in on me. "For a woman, you do think ahead. I would say I'm impressed, but I'm not."

"Quiet," I urged as I stared at him before moving to place him into the cooler. "Be glad I remembered you, or you'd be making bubbles in holy water right now."

"They do not carry around holy water," he scoffed.

"They drink it," I said as I lifted a brow. "They have to; it is part of what keeps them immortal. Inside every canteen or water bottle they carry is, in fact, holy water. They would enjoy sending you to the crossroads, and we all know you would be cursed to walk endlessly as a spirit if they did. Hell is here, and as far as I know, Heaven closed those gates a while ago. Those who die are cursed to nothingness. Would you rather I send you there now?" I asked, hoping he didn't wish to actually die, or leave me.

I had no one, and while I didn't mind being alone, having him around helped ease the endless hours of nothingness that I lived in, helped them pass by faster. I turned and looked at him as I stood, pulling the backpack back on as I stuck the soap in the pockets of the jeans I wore.

"What are you doing now?" he asked as I prepared to close the cooler.

"We're not staying out in the open tonight. There's a room in the walls here. It's the room that they used for security, it has bars, and I've fixed it, so it's safe enough for us to sleep in. This is just where I wait to see if anyone is trailing me. I'm not an idiot; I have had this planned for the last year."

I closed the lid before he could argue and slid the cut wall over, slipping through the narrow space before I pulled him in behind me. Carefully, I slid it back as I listened. The walls here were heavily warded by me, my sanctuary that I'd worked on for the last year and a half as my time dwindled down. Even with the humans alive, I'd begun painting the walls. I'd prepared the apartment buildings as well, waiting for one unit to go vacant before I cut the hole, working my way through them until I'd planned the perfect home for me, one that had an escape route in every room.

The hallways were silent as we walked through them, even within the slimmer parts that weren't made for human passage. I slid away from the wires, ducking and dodging debris until we turned right, heading down an even smaller hallway that led to the room. Inside of it, I paused, noting the bars of soap and the ice machine that was tiny but should be able to produce enough ice to keep Fred comfortable, and then set him down.

Pictures of Callaghan and the other Knights covered the walls. Next to each picture were the details that I knew about them. The first time I'd met them or ran a mission with them, I had begun taking notes on each and every one of them. I skimmed all of the photos, noting who was outside my building tonight, but that wasn't what I focused on. Callaghan hadn't been with them, and he'd been there almost every time I'd ever had to deal with the Templar Knights. So, where was he? Why hadn't he come with them to capture me?

Unfortunately, those who had entered my apartment would be writhing in pain on the floors about now. I'd placed undetectable wards that not even their oldest Knights would sense before they went off. I had no plan of not fighting back and had used everything in my arsenal to send that message loud and clear tonight. They'd be too cocky to notice the carpet had been freshly placed. It no longer was covered in the blood Callaghan had left when he'd pretended to save me. Beneath it laid ancient runes, ignited by anyone entering my home without invitation.

The outside of the door literally was a warning written in Gaelic to the Knights. Most of them could read it but chose to ignore the past entirely. They shouldn't because I was paying for their past crimes that I hadn't committed. Had they lifted a finger to help the witches who had been burned or murdered, they wouldn't be cursed today. But long ago, they'd turned their heads and pretended it wasn't happening, and so started the witches revenge against the Templar Knights.

"Erie, do you know what you are?" Fred asked, and I undid the lid of the cooler, staring down at him as I inhaled the bar of soap I held against my nose.

"Does it matter?" I scoffed in a low voice.

"It should matter, it should matter a lot."

"How would you know what I am?" I asked as I watched a smile play over his lips.

"I'm going to tell you a story of how you came to be alive, daughter of the cauldron. I'll start at the beginning since you're slow on picking up the clues of what you are, should you choose to become it," he said with an ominous tone as he let the air around us fill with silence before he finally began. "Legend has it that on Friday the 13th, in the year 1307, King Philip IV ordered

the arrest of the Templar Knights, along with the druids who had resided in his own court. It started before that day though, a few years before it, as we demons liked to play. Two years prior to that warrant being issued, the witches had begged the Knight's Order to help them hide from persecution of their crimes, ending with many deaths that were carried out by the Knights themselves, by order of the Pope. Not willingly, of course, as they had made many deals with the devil to remain in power, but to stave off persecution or suspicion of being spelled by the witches themselves, the Knights carried out burning those women.

"It was a fucking massacre that bathed the land in blood. The Knight's, having previously warned the witches of what would befall them if they continued meddling in the lives of mortals, fought back, of course. The witches refused to follow the orders of the Knights, and instead of listening, they became crazed with changing the course of history and began murdering humans relentlessly in front of others, who carried those stories to the Pope and the King. But it wasn't their fault, not really. You see, demons had been ordered by a very powerful Goddess to inhabit the witches, and rein chaos that would set many other things into motion. As they did, chaos erupted, and that brought every eye in their direction. Their action under the guise of the witches drew the eyes of many officials, sealing their fate. The Knights were called upon to rid the land of the blight the witches had created. To remove them from power, and dispel the humans who had been enthralled by them. Bloody business that it was, the Knights were forced to either do as they'd been ordered by the King and Pope, or stand trial with the witches. The druids, having also been called to help the witches when the Knights had refused the witches, then joined the Knights in driving out the evil that had swept over the lands like a plague.

"The witches were enraged that they were being burned for doing nothing wrong, other than housing demons, then turned their curses upon those who they blamed for the slight against them. They gathered together to have enough power to ignite a curse that would follow both the Knights and the druids through bloodlines. It started with the higher ranked Templars, forcing those beneath them to flee from their homes and hide deep in Scotland. Of course, I'm getting ahead of myself. I forgot the burning Templars, didn't I?" Fred chuckled as a shiver ran up my spine.

"On Friday the 13th, 1307, King Philip IV ordered the arrest of the Templar Knights. Of course, most people assumed he was trying to escape the debt he had accrued from his war against the English, when in fact, he'd been under an enthrallment spell, spelled by the covens. I can still smell Jacques Dé Molay's flesh as it burned. The man was more than just a myth; he was a legend among the first Templars who were rumored to hold something evil in their souls. I went to watch him burn, but the man, while on fire, cursed the King, the King's line, and the Pope himself. Impressive feat while being burned alive, don't you agree?"

"Sounds disturbing," I uttered as I stared at him, still holding the forgotten soap in my hand as a chill raced up my spine.

"Oh, it was. Because Jacques Dé Molay wasn't alone in cursing them that day," he smirked as his voice lowered with his story. "Unbeknownst to the bystanders who watched the Templar Knights burning, other Knights stood witness to the crimes of the church and King. A group of Knights so feared that not even the King and his armies dared fight them. Sir Callaghan, one of the first Knights of the Order of the Templar, watched as his idol burned alive for crimes that he did not commit. After that, he ordered the massacre of every remaining coven in France and England. The druids, knowing that they would burn alongside the Knights, hid and allowed the world to believe they'd been eradicated. Callaghan was relentless as he brought the witches to task for burning his Knights at the stake. There was a rumor that he sought one female out, someone he'd once loved who may or may not have started the entire mess in the first place. Unfortunately, he vanished before it could be discovered as fact or fiction.

"The witches, knowing that Callaghan was immortal, had to figure out another way to stop him. They called on Hecate to assist them in their greatest hour of need, and she answered their call with a curse. One that could only work if the entire bloodline and Order of Knights and druids were included; a pentagram that needed each point filled to be complete. So the Knights, druids, witches, and two sacrifices to a darker power had to be included in this curse. The witches killed two other supernatural creatures to take out the Knights and druids. To this day, no one knows which or if it is the monsters that the Templars took within them. We do, however, know that it came with a cost, as most things do. To gain the strength they needed to fight the witches' curse, they agreed to house a greater evil within them.

To prove they were worthy, they each had to sacrifice what they loved most in the world on an altar to the evil beings. Once they had proven their worth, they were told what the cure was and how to obtain it, and given a beast to ensure that they succeeded."

I stared at Fred, knowing his story was off a bit, but then he was a demon. They all told different tales of what unfolded in history, their own version of the truth. He was wrong though, Callaghan had secrets, and he'd merged with it long before the day his idol and mentor had been burned on the pyre. Still, I listened, as often there was truth in their version of the past.

"That brings us to you. The witches cursed the Knights and the druids to a plague that would ravish their people slowly until even the youngest of them suffered from it. This plague, it wouldn't only turn the immortals to mortal beings, it would start with the weakest of their race, the babes, and then work its way through them until the mightiest of them fell. To escape that fate, they had to make another sacrifice. They knew that they would need a female druid to carry the child of a Templar Knight to term: you. The only issue was, she had to be pure of blood and created of magic that was so evil, no one would ever touch her for fear she would create a likeness of herself and set this world on fire. Apparently, they didn't realize or think of how far the Knights and druids would be willing to take things during their desperation to survive. There was also the fact that druids didn't birth females, but they knew how they could accomplish it. In comes the darkest evil this world has ever known.

"They gathered the womb. A female who was of

the purest blood of the Order, Jacques's own daughter. A druid male of great magic, one who was respected and loved by his people," he hissed as he watched me. "They were forced to drink of the darkest magic in their darkest hour of need. They fucked until they created you, a monster, unlike anything this world would ever know. You were born under a blood moon, left in a pool of your mother's blood. It was where the Knights found you, born too early to survive, and yet you did. They took you to the druids, to be trained in magic and to become strong enough to endure and survive, through the coming of the witches, for they will come to end you, Erie. Of that, you can be sure. You are the only way that this ends, either with a child buried in your womb, or you buried in the cold ground. But there's more. You are the Queen of Darkness, mistress. Should you choose to wield it, that darkness inside of you would call to every creature who resides in the darkness, even me. You are everything evil, created from the most evil thing in any world that ever existed."

"That's a cool story, Fred," I muttered as I lay back onto the pillows, considering what he said and then dismissing it.

"Mistress, it wasn't a story. Should you rise, the riders will come. If you choose darkness, this world will become yours to take," he crooned as if he was salivating at the idea.

"And where do you fit into this world?"

"Me, I'd be at your side, of course."

"Of course," I muttered beneath my breath as I brought the soap up against my nose, inhaling it. I reached over, closing the cooler before I stood back up, pulling down Callaghan's portrait. My finger touched his cheek, studying the unguarded look in his eyes. My cheeks heated as I realized what I was doing and, setting it aside, I pulled a few bars of soap out of their boxes, placing them along the edge of the room as my heart started to increase its pace, my mind processing the tiny room I was inside. I wouldn't panic. No, I grabbed the last unwrapped bar of soap and held it to my nose as I laid back on the bed, peeking through my lashes to study the picture as sleep took over, taking me back to the nightmares that I never fully escaped. "The Queen of Darkness, my ass," I muttered sleepily as I closed my eyes, ignoring the tight confines that I'd chosen to hide from the Knights within.

CHAPTER *thirteen*

I WAS ON FIRE, MY BODY A BLAZE OF UNSATED NEED AS my hand rubbed the place it ached the most. All night long, fantasies had played out in my dreams until the pull to touch it became a need I couldn't ignore. I swallowed a moan as I found it wet, drenched with the fantasies of Callaghan and his touch that played out on repeat in my head.

It was as if he had used magic, a spell that ignited a need so red-hot and violent within my core that one caress had my fist against my mouth as I exploded. My spine arched off of the exercise pads I'd stacked as a bed, and my heart pounded wildly as the orgasm pulsed through me. Heat flushed my cheeks as I realized what I had just done, and who I had imagined when I'd come undone.

"Flicking that magic bean, mistress?" a deep voice pulled me from the haze of lust as I eyed the cooler with irritation. "If you brought my body to me, I could add the magic bean*stalk* to it."

I didn't reply as I sat up, aware of the sweltering heat of the room and the fact that it shouldn't be hot at all. We were almost to spring, but it was still weeks away, even with the snow blanketing Spokane, and yet it was so suffocatingly hot in the small confines of the room that my hair clung to my neck. I wiped away the sweat that covered my neck and stared down at the mark on my wrist; it was glowing as if it was the reason my body had been out of control.

Bringing it up to my eyes, I watched as it began to grow, sending a single tendril of what resembled a delicate tattoo of a vine racing up my forearm to wrap around it, like delicate tribal art. He hadn't just tattooed his signet onto my flesh; he'd marked me in a deeper way than that. It didn't burn or ache, but it was definitely his fault.

I leaned over, pulling the cooler to where I sat as I opened it, staring down at Fred, who smirked at my flushed cheeks.

"Still alive, I see," he repeated his usual greeting as he watched me, knowing what I'd done with a dark smile on his lips.

"We need to set boundaries," I muttered as I reached into my bag, pulling out the only tube of lipstick I owned, and painted my lips as I spoke. "If you hear anything you shouldn't, pretend you didn't, okay?"

"You mean if I hear you masturbating, I should ignore it? No."

"Fred, this isn't a negotiation," I grumbled.

"I don't care," he chuckled. "Remember, I'm not here because I want to be, I'm here because you cut my fucking head off, woman."

"Are you still upset about that? I thought we were past that, what, with me being your Mistress of Darkness and all," I exhaled, staring at him. He looked peckish, and I frowned.

"You are past it, and yet I am still here unable to murder you as I want to do, badly."

"Friends don't kill friends, Fred." I stood, grabbing the jacket from my backpack before pushing my arms through it.

"Where are you going? And we are not friends!" he hissed.

"I'm going to get some holy water," I announced as I zipped up the pack and shoved the straps up my arms.

"Whatever for?" he exclaimed.

"Because I think you need an exorcism."

"I am a demon! You do remember that, right? Woman, you're not right in the head."

"Don't stereotype me, it's not nice!"

"I call it as I see it, mistress."

"I am not crazy."

"Are too," he muttered.

"Am not!"

"You're infuriating!"

"And you're a head without a body, asshole!"

"Ouch, that one hurt."

"Good!"

I pushed through the wall and then paused, turning back to slam the lid of the cooler down as he grumbled some more. Men were so infuriatingly annoying. I'd saved him from being drowned in holy water by those asshole Knights, and he still pretended he didn't care about me. Men!

I slipped through the walls and paused inside the store, staring into the darkness that seemed strangely off. It shouldn't be this dark, it was still morning. Some light should have been entering through the store's glass ceiling, and yet there was no light coming in. Only darkness that seemed inhumanly dark and smelled of magic.

Slowly, I exited the room and walked through the many corpses. Pausing at the exit to the store my hideout was located in, I swallowed hard as a dark shadow moved deeper in the outlet mall. I slid against the wall, following it as it moved further and further away from me.

At the divider, where the escalators moved down to the subfloor of the mall, I watched as the shadow grew larger than life against the candle it had just lit. My eyes narrowed as I tried to make out what it was or who it was. I should have turned around and gone scouring for food and holy water, but instead, I followed it.

My footsteps sounded louder than they should have, but then my heartbeat was pounding loud enough to wake the dead as I hunted whatever was hunting the darkness below. I reached the bottom, stalling my movement as I waited for it to round a corner. My guess was, demons were trying to move into my new home, and that wasn't happening. Not on my turf; but how could they have bypassed the wards I'd placed to make them feel uncomfortable here?

They were the same wards painted on every church wall throughout history. Humans thought that demons couldn't enter them, or they'd burst into flames. Not true, they didn't enter them because they were so heavily

warded that the demons would back away, sensing the trap laid to catch them. The demons who didn't heed the wards or warning went boom, but that was simple science and runes.

I stood on the other side of the hall, blocked by the wall. I prepared to go around it as the light continually moved further away. Stepping past the protection of the wall, hands grabbed me and pushed me against it. I kicked out, landing a well-placed knee to his nuts as a string of curses erupted in a hushed whisper. Turning to run, he grabbed me, yanking me against him as he covered my mouth with his hand.

My teeth sank into flesh, and even more hushed cursing began. I bucked against him as he took me to the ground, blue eyes glowing in the darkness as he rolled us towards the wall. I hissed as his arm tightened over my chest, knocking the air from my lungs while I fought to breathe.

"Erie," Callaghan breathed against my ear. "There are others here, so stop fighting me, now. Unless you'd rather go with them to breed?" he uttered.

I inhaled his heady scent of woodsy masculinity as something hard pressed against my back. I elbowed his ribs, smirking against the hand that held my mouth silent as voices reached us. A shiver rushed through me as my name was muffled on their words. They were checking each store, searching for me, and fear for Fred flashed in my mind.

The hand over my mouth released it, and I tried to roll away from him. He followed me, pulling me against him as he pushed me into an abandoned storefront. His eyes took me in, and, nostrils flaring, he tilted his head, as if he could smell the shit I'd done earlier on my flesh. A guilty blush covered my cheeks as I slowly stepped further into the store, away from him.

"You smell good enough to fuck, Erie," he chuckled as he prowled forward, his white cloak with the red-cross of the Templar on it marking him a Holy Knight. "How was your dream last night?" he asked.

"You starred in it," I hissed huskily. "You did turn me on though, so much that you ended as a splatter which painted my walls. It was ecstasy," I replied icily.

"You smell like lavender," he growled as I darted one way, only to have his elbow knock me back as he smashed me against the wall. He held me there, staring into my eyes as something else prowled beneath the surface, watching me. Maybe Fred hadn't been telling me a story, or maybe I only imagined it because of his story?

"What do you want?" I seethed.

"I want to wreck that tight pussy," he shrugged with a wicked smile on his sensual lips as a glint of mischief entered his eyes. "I know where you sleep, Erie. I know how that messy head of yours works. You think hiding with the Fae will save you? It won't. Nothing and no one can save you from me, of that, you can be sure."

"Callaghan," I uttered hoarsely, my tongue darting out to trace over my lips as his eyes burned with need. "You forgot one thing," I hissed huskily as his mouth lowered towards mine.

"And what is that?" he asked as those lips brushed against mine. His tongue tested my mouth, testing my resistance or lack of as a hungry growl escaped his lungs.

"I'm not your fucking plaything," I uttered against his lips as the poison began to sink into him from the lipstick I wore. I followed him down the ground, staring at him and tilting my head as his eyes grew hazy. "You don't know anything about me," I laughed darkly, pushing his body against the floor and then straddling him, watching him as he struggled to breathe. "I'm unlike anything you've encountered, and more pissed off than the Scots against the English pricks who coveted their lands and mounted their wives." My core rubbed against his massive cock as I settled onto him. A moan left my lips as blood and spit exploded from his lungs. Eyes widened as he watched me use his cock while he died beneath me. "I do enjoy killing you, though," I admitted begrudgingly.

"Run," he uttered through the blood that filled his lungs.

I turned, sensing the others as he whispered the order. I pushed off of him, dragging him with me as I slipped through the walls. Once inside, I pushed my hand against his mouth and listened as heavy footfalls entered the store from the other side of the false wall. Eyes heavy with death, he watched the panic racing through me as I once again settled over him, pushing my hand against his nose and mouth, preventing air from getting to his lungs.

His eyes grew vacant, and something inside of me hurt as I watched the life leaving him. Something strange and foreign sat against my chest, and I scoffed at it, staring at him. I wiped the blood and spit from his lips and leaned down, letting my nose rub against his still warm flesh. My hands pushed through his soft hair, and I smiled. Dead, he was pretty good-looking. It was really too bad he didn't animate as Fred had, but then I couldn't have it all, now could I? I stood up, realizing I was fondling a corpse, which was a hard limit for me.

I eyed the next secret room and smirked as an idea formed in my head. The footsteps receded, and the voice vanished as I dragged his corpse with me. Dead, he was peaceful and almost tolerable. Pity he wouldn't stay that way. I pushed him into the closet and closed it, smirking as I leaned against the door, wondering where it was that he went to when he died, or where he popped up when he returned from the grave. *Meh, too much brain work*, I thought as I started through the walls towards the exit.

CHAPTER
Fourteen

PAIN ASSAULTED ME; THE LAUGHTER THAT FOLLOWED *brought tears of shame to my eyes. I cried out as lash after lash tore through my flesh. My hair clung to my body as my feet slipped in the puddle of blood beneath me. My blood. My feet pushed against the cold concrete, pushing up only to continually slip as the whipping continued. I begged them to stop, admitted I was the one who instigated the kiss, even though I'd never wanted it.*

The burning in my spine was brutal, all-consuming as scream after scream was ripped from my lungs while the children I'd grown to call friends watched me, enjoying the pain I received. How could they do this? Didn't they see it was tearing me apart? I whimpered, crying as I pleaded for my friends to help me, begged them to tell the truth of what had happened, and yet they refused.

They took turns, each one offering to wield the whip against my flesh. My shirt was ripped open, exposing my breasts. They spoke around me, pointing out my deformed features from being beaten, my impurities that made me different. The Headmaster grabbed my face, his fingers crushing my jaw as he held it up, showing them my ugliness as his other hand ripped the skirt off of my body. One by one, they came up to tell me how ugly I was, those who I'd called my friends. Some slapped me, others spit in my face as my blood continued to slowly drain from my body.

"She is Satan's whore, created to lure you to the sinful ways that lead you down a dark path. This creature was created from lust, from creatures that should never procreate, and yet here she is, this little slut who begs you to the darkness between her pretty thighs. Her red lips beckon to you, begging you to take what she gives so freely, don't they?" The Headmaster asked as he walked behind me, ripping my head backward as new pain began. Those I'd called my friends watched him, letting their eyes drift to my nakedness with disdain and sneers as his hands roamed over my breasts. "The devil's tits and flesh call to you even now, don't they? What lies between this pretty flesh is certain death. This creature was created from the cauldron of Dagda. A magic so deadly, so vile, that it was banished from the land by the Gods," he shouted as his nose pressed against my neck. "That is why you must not see her as one of us, but see her as what she is, a creature of evil who lures you to her so she can murder you," he laughed coldly as he released my hair and moved to stand behind me.

The crack of the whip warned me, but it didn't matter. The cattail sliced through my spine and piss ran down my leg as everyone laughed. My legs gave out, and my body refused to work as I hung there, finally oblivious to the pain. The sweetness of the darkness beckoned me into its embrace, and there, I found home.

"She's pissed herself," Kaden laughed.

My *best* friend.

The one I'd spent my days defending from the other kids, announced my shameful action, and tears pushed against my eyes. Everyone I thought cared about me was watching, laughing, and enjoying the pain I endured at their entertainment.

Long after it ended, they came, laughing as they pounded against the glass room, where I had been placed on display. I couldn't move. No healers came to fix me, no one cared that I'd bled out each time my body tried to heal itself.

I screamed, bolting up as bile pushed from my lips and my stomach emptied out onto the floor. My hands touched my back, discovering it closed and healed. Sweat stuck to my hair, the room pushed in on me, and I stood up, reaching for the soap before I dropped to my knees, inhaling it as I fought to get out of the past.

Everything inside of me trembled and mixed together—fear, hatred, embarrassment as the chanting continued even after I'd awoken from the nightmare. I screamed, I screamed so loud that if anyone had been close enough to hear it, discovery would have been a guarantee. I didn't stop until I was crying, screaming as hatred and self-loathing became second nature, my place of comfort. I moaned as sandpaper slid over my tongue, my fingers flexed, coming back covered in blood as I stared down at my palms where my nails had torn through flesh.

The knife beside the bed caught my eye, and I moved

to it, grabbing it with one hand and sliced it through my leg, exhaling as the familiar pain bit through my flesh. It was comforting, the pain that eased my guilt at being what I was. Knowing I was created to be hated, to be rejected, to be loathed from the magic that planted me into that cold whore's womb.

Blood dripped from my thigh, and I sat back, resting my head against the wall. I chanted what I'd been taught, that I was ugly, wrong, evil, unlovable, and meant to save them all. I was the devil's spawn, and the moment my purpose was finished, they'd end it. I almost wished it would be that easy.

"You okay?" Fred asked, and I ignored him. "Hey, listen, mistress. We all got some fucked up shit we had to survive. You're going to be okay, at least until I get my body back and murder you."

"Go to sleep, Fred," I urged.

"I don't sleep, asshole."

"Pretend that you do," I uttered hoarsely.

"If you're going to cut yourself, can I at least watch and pretend that it's me giving you pain?" he inquired thickly, muffled by the cooler.

"Fred?"

"Yes?"

"Do you know what I did to the last person I considered to be my friend?" I asked.

"No, and I don't entirely think I care to know, either."

"I murdered him, quite violently, too. I waited until he went into the woods to train on his own. I found him out there, all by himself, and stuck him through the stomach with a spear, missing every vital organ on

purpose. Afterward, when he woke up, he realized he no longer had arms or legs. I then took his malicious tongue from his mouth, and I cooked it as he was forced to watch me. I stabbed him nineteen times through his flesh, again missing every vital organ before I used my blade to seal the wounds. As night began to fall, I took his eyes. In those silent woods, I took everything from him that he'd ever used to hurt me. That was over seventy-five years ago. You're my first friend since then."

There was silence from the cooler as I stared down at the healing wound on my thigh. I pushed the sweat-drenched, sticky hair from my face and inhaled the copper of the blood with the lavender, swallowing hard as I pushed the memories away, burying them deep into my subconscious, where I didn't feel or see them anymore.

Seventy-five years ago, everyone I'd ever trusted had turned against me, hurt me. I'd been beaten, pissed on, spit on, and harmed every way imaginable minus rape, and I'd only escaped that because I was the spawn of the devil to them. I'd gotten back up. But when I had, it had been as an unfeeling, uncaring, murderous monster who had embraced the anger within. It had taken ten years to kill—or track down and then meticulously murder— everyone that I had called my friend, anyone who had wronged me.

I'd changed that day. In more ways than I'd thought I would, but trusting people, that was what had gotten my spine severed, my mind broken; and the boys who had cut me as I lay there in my own waste, they'd taught me that friends could destroy you. Friends, the people you trusted the most, were often the ones who destroyed you in the end.

My hand moved to the pile of soap, and I picked one up, pushing it against my nose as silent tears burned in my eyes. Save them? No, I wanted to eradicate them all. I wanted to watch them as they realized they were doomed to the very fate they expected me to save them from. There was no good in them, nothing to preserve in that race of monsters. They'd earned their fate, and I'd help whoever had cursed them to it. That was my destiny.

CHAPTER

fifteen

I DIDN'T LEAVE THE ROOM AGAIN UNTIL I WAS NEAR
starving to death and exhausted from staring endlessly
at the walls. Every time that nightmare visited, it took
days, if not longer, to get back up from the haunting
memories. It wasn't a sign of weakness, I told myself
over and over again, because eventually, I'd believe it.
I wouldn't, of course, because life didn't work like that.

Instead, it fucked you every chance it got. It knocked
you down, and every time you got back up, it hit
harder than before. I'd left the Druid's Den years ago,
preferring life on my own even though they'd dragged
me back each time I'd left, beating me into a bloody
pulp to instill the fear of God in me, and yet every time,
I'd run again. It had become a default setting, to escape
them, to live away from the horror that awaited me at
their hands.

I knew Callaghan had been the one to stop the last
beating, showing up as I'd been tied in the gathering
room, strung up like a spring chicken with my clothes

off. They stripped me every time, to show the ugliness, I guess, and expose how unnatural I was. He'd come in, covering me with his cloak, and whisked me out of the room, and I'd thanked him by punching him.

Reflexes, that's what I'd told myself, but in the silence of the room where he'd watched me dressing, I'd found comfort in his presence, and that terrified me. It had been something I never wanted to feel again. I'd promised myself never to allow anyone to get close to me because the moment I did, they'd have the power to destroy me. I wouldn't ever give another person that power over me.

Then came the day when he started prepping me for what was to come. How my destiny was to save their races. It proved where he ended up on my list, right at the bottom of the very long list of people I wanted to watch die. Yet every time I found myself at the end of a blade held by a Knight, he'd stayed their hand. As if he thought he was doing me a favor.

Still, the comfort of his voice as he spoke had seemed familiar, and no matter how much I tried to place him, I could never find him in my memories before he'd saved me from a beating. It was as if he was there and yet had erased them from my mind. I'd let it go years ago, not bothering to delve deeper into the mess of my psyche. There was too much bad shit in there, and nothing good came from opening those scabs. So I built a wall, and I put everything that didn't make sense or seemed off behind it.

I popped open Fred's cooler and stared down at him as I lowered to the floor, hating that towering above him made it hard for him to see me. He didn't speak, and at

first, it scared me. I grabbed his hair, yanking him out and then exhaled as he shouted.

"What the fuck?" he demanded.

"I thought you died," I admitted as I placed him back in the ice and scooped more I'd been making into the cooler.

"Unfortunately, no," he uttered in a pissy tone. "No such luck there."

"I'm heading out to gather food," I announced, watching him as I placed the ice around him. "I have to go to the Guild, to see if I can find anything out on the witches who cursed the Templars as well, so I may be a while."

"Don't care," he said as his tongue pushed against a stray piece of ice as he adjusted it.

"Wish me luck," I muttered.

"Die, please," he responded.

"You do know that if I die, you will remain here, in this cooler, forever," I said as I tilted my head, studying his dark eyes. He was handsome, or had been. It was unfortunate that I'd had to take his head because he enjoyed harming people. "Right?"

"You forgot to ask me if I care," he snorted as he pulled his tongue back into his mouth and stared at me as if I bored him.

"Okay, well, I hope I make it back so that you don't have to be rotting inside a cooler forever. Alone. Without me. Forever," I grumbled low, under my breath.

With that, I slipped on my backpack and started out of the room. Outside the wall cutout, I paused, turning around to close the cooler lid to keep him safe. I pushed the hidden panel back into place and made my way to the exit, watching the storefronts for signs of anyone being present before I slipped from the protection of the corpses which had begun to stink in their thawing state.

I moved silently through the hallway, stepping over the other rotting corpses that I'd eventually get around to burying when I found the time. I was a firm believer that no one should be left to rot or die alone, but this world wasn't for the weak. The weak died as the corrupt and vile creatures slithered into it, more and more.

Pausing at the open main doors, I watched a headless body ramming a pole repeatedly and frowned as I exited the building, moving towards the mutilated headless corpse. Fred just didn't get it; he wasn't leaving me, and I wasn't leaving him.

He made the ideal friend, and I enjoyed our conversations. He had no arms to hurt me, no way to do so in any shape or form, and until he saw the errors of his ways or I figured out a way to die, he was stuck with me.

Thick black wings were mere stumps that stuck out of his spine. I winced at the damage I'd done as he'd watched me from where I'd placed his head on a spiked fence, making sure he understood that his body was lost to him. I slipped my backpack off, pulled out the kerosene, and doused him, putting it back into my backpack before I flicked a match and set him ablaze again. I watched for mere moments as it patted itself, finally dropping to the ground to roll towards the frigid river as I started in the opposite direction.

I made it ten blocks before I noted the tail on me, and began dipping through alleyways and then buildings until I was running as fast as I could towards the Guild. I rounded a building and hit something hard, bounced

off of it, and rolled on the ground, moaning as I touched my face. I remembered what had been behind me and jumped back to my feet, expecting a fight, but there was nothing there. I stared at the empty space as the hair on my nape rose.

I peered around, searching the shadows before I started forward again, knowing something was here, and feeling it to the very pit of my soul as I continued on. I hit my max speed and was almost within sight of the Guild when I hit it again. I winced as I dropped to my knees and holding my face, I looked up to find Callaghan there, watching me through angry slits. Shouting sounded behind us and he moved, grabbing my arm until I thought it would be ripped from the socket as he pulled me into the nearest building.

"Asshole," I seethed as I felt my face for damage.

"I believe the words you're looking for, Erie, are *thank you*," he growled as he pulled me up a flight of stairs, pushed me through another building, and then slammed me against a dust-covered wall.

"No, I'm pretty sure I meant what I said, Callaghan."

"Poison lips, really?" he snarled as he pulled something from his pocket and pushed it against my lips. "Of all the ways to kill me, pushing that sweet flesh against my cock as I died probably wasn't the best thing. I come back with my memories, every fucking time. You were getting off on my *corpse*."

"I mean, that's not entirely true. I did play with you a little, but corpses are a hard limit for me, so there's that." I blushed, uncertain what else to say about my fondling his dying body. So I shrugged and dropped the subject, praying he would too. My gaze strayed to his lips as I licked my own and then felt the numbness when

I swallowed. My body started to sag as he smirked, watching me with a dark look in his gaze.

"Yeah, Erie, I can play dirty too," he crooned as he trapped me there with his leg holding me up, staring at me as his fingers pinched my chin, lifting it.

"Bastard," I hissed as my eyes grew heavy and my head rocked to the side; I moaned. The poison was slowly moving through me as he watched me. I should have freaking known better. Instead, I'd figured he was testing my lips for poison. "No wrecking ball penis," I uttered.

"What?" he asked as a smile lifted his mouth, and his eyes lit with laughter.

"I will kill you again," I swallowed as my legs gave out and he caught me. He picked me up, hoisting my slight weight as he carried me deeper into the abandoned building.

"I know you will, but I've decided I enjoy this cat and mouse game we play. Just to be clear, you're the mouse."

"But I have the pussy," I whispered.

"And it's a very nice tight pussy, one I intend to use very often, little druid."

"Don't call me that."

"What, a druid? You have the blood of both races in your veins."

"I'm the spawn of Satan," I laughed, or I thought I did.

"You're not, and even if you were, demons all started out as angels before they fell," he growled, or I thought he did. Darkness swam in my vision as all coherent thought left me.

CHAPTER
sixteen

MY HEAD POUNDED AS I PRIED MY EYES OPEN TO figure out where I was. I licked my lips, cringing as the vile taste of the concoction Callaghan used to subdue me hit my tongue again. Lifting my head, I peered around the decrepit room as I tried to get my bearings while I took stock of my position on the bed. My arms were chained, held above my head and secured to a metal bed frame. My legs were chained as well, positioned to be open, and yet I still had room to close my knees together. I yanked against the metal framework, moaning loudly. I struggled to get free and then hesitated as a dark shadow moved in the corner, catching my attention as he slipped from the shadows into the dimly lit room. My head dropped onto the feather-soft pillow as I watched him slowly walking towards the bed, staring down at me, surveying me while I came to the sad conclusion that there was no escape.

"Morning, beautiful," he uttered thickly as he bent over, kissing the inside of my thigh, while I took in the gown I now wore. "You were starting to worry me. I feared you wouldn't wake up," he admitted as his fingers trailed over my thigh, following the same path his mouth was taking. His tongue snaked out, working closer to my sex, his eyes burning with naked desire as he watched my reaction to his heated kisses.

"Unfortunately, no. I fear after I slit my wrist the first time, the druids made sure to steal death away from me. I'm spelled to never be able to die, but then you know that already." I frowned, watching as he lifted the gown and ran his fingers through my naked flesh. His tongue created a fire of need, and I stifled the shiver that rushed through me as he continued to leisurely explore my body. "So what's your plan now, rape me? Keep me here, tied to this bed as your whore? How knightly of you, bastard," I hissed as I watched his mouth curve into a dangerous smirk and he lifted up, pulling a metal medical tray closer to the bed. I yanked on the chains, ignoring the bite against my flesh that burned as it chaffed my skin.

"I don't rape defenseless women, Erie," he uttered as he retrieved a syringe and bit off the orange cap. Those burning blue eyes slowly moved from the syringe to me as he smiled sadly. "Trust me, when I fuck you, you will want it. When I use this *wrecking ball* penis, as you so lovingly referred to it, it will be because you want it. That tight pussy craves it, doesn't it? Your wetness gives your need away."

"How, by drugging me?" I demanded as I stared at the needle he held. My heart raced, pounding in my ears as I watched him with a fear that consumed me.

"This isn't to make you want me. It's to make that

womb of yours more acceptable to carry my child. It's merely a fertility drug."

"Don't you fucking dare," I seethed as I increased the fight to get unchained, to be able to fight back against him. I twisted, crying out as pain ripped through my arms and legs, as angry tears threatened to leak from my eyes. "Don't do this."

"It wasn't my idea," he admitted in a low, pain-filled tone. "You're unwilling to hear reason or help me solve the problem. I can't let my people die, Erie. I'm not asking you to like it, I'm asking you to help me save the children of my race. Those who had no part in the past crimes, who will be among the first to die when the curse begins to play out," he whispered thickly as he stared down at me. "I can't watch them die without doing anything to save them. Not when the cure is right here, within my grasp."

"They don't deserve to live!" I snapped as tears slipped free and ran down my face. I closed my eyes against the pain I saw swimming in his Nordic depths.

"They are as innocent as you are, woman. They are babies, children, and women that will all perish if I fail them. Would you have me sit by and watch them die? They've not even begun to live and yet they're already growing sick as the curse begins. I can't do nothing and allow it to play out, I won't watch them die," he growled as he studied me. "If it were just my men or me, I'd help you escape. That isn't the case here. Innocent lives hang in the balance. You do not see the bigger picture. You're only thinking about yourself and what you will have to endure, but you won't be alone. I'll be with you."

"No, I'm not selfish! I don't want any of you to live!

You don't deserve to use me after what you guys did to me. I don't deserve this. I didn't get a choice in any of this. No one even cared about me until my womb was ready to be filled. No one has ever loved me or even treated me like I was a person. I am *nothing* to you people, nothing but a womb for your salvation to be born from."

"No one has ever loved you, Erie? No one?" he asked softly, turning his turquoise blue eyes to hold mine with a sadness I didn't understand. Those eyes stared straight to my soul, and I looked away, unable to meet them.

"I don't need or want love anymore. You and your kind taught me how unworthy and unnatural I am. The druids taught me how ugly and how wrong I am. Now you want to tell me that I am beautiful, for what? So you can plant your child in my belly and do the same to him when he is born? I'll never let him take root inside of me, Callaghan. I will cut him from my womb before he is ever put through what I was. I'll never let you do this to me, do you hear me? I will cut your son from my womb!" I sobbed as I turned my eyes back to his, watching as the tick in his jaw began to thrum wildly while his anger ignited.

"*When* you conceive, not *if*, Erie, I will keep you locked up until our son is born. I won't stand by and watch innocent people die because you can't see the bigger picture. This is bigger than you or me, and children do not deserve to pay for shit that was done in the past. I wish there were another way, but there isn't one. I'm sorry, but this is how it has to be," he growled as he watched me shaking my head. I looked away from him again, shielding the unease I felt from him.

He pushed me over, turning me onto my side without warning as he pushed the needle through my flesh. I whimpered as the syringe was emptied and then another was pushed into the same place. I bit into my lip, feeling his hand as he rubbed the tissue before he turned me over, staring down at me as he pushed the last one into my stomach, never tearing his eyes from where he emptied it.

"I hate you," I whispered through teeth that chattered as the drugs rushed through me. He pulled the needle out and set it onto the tray, pushing it away from the bed.

"No, you don't. You just don't realize it yet," he said as he stood up, moving to sit in the one chair the room had to offer. "One day you will remember everything, and we will decide where we go from there," he replied as he sat down, resting his arms on his knees as he folded his hands out in front of him, staring at me.

My body shivered violently as heat washed through me. I whimpered as it became too much, sweat beaded on my brow and my back arched off of the bed. I yanked on the chains, moaning. Everything seemed to spin around me as the drugs rushed through my system. The tattoo on my wrist began to pulse, glowing brightly in the dimly lit room, and I groaned as my eyes rolled back in my head. In the silence of the room, I cursed him to hell as everything began to burn my skin. The gown was too heavy against my sweltering flesh, and I whimpered as my skin grew flushed and sweat caked it to me.

Time passed as he watched me, never leaving the chair as I suffered before him. His eyes seemed to glow from within as if he, too, was affected by the drugs that coursed through me. Hours passed as I suffered in silence, never screaming or begging him to end it, not until he moved, settling his weight on the bed beside me. I turned towards the heat of his body, long since having grown cold from the chilled air and my slick flesh. His hand snaked out, slowly drawing a pattern on my belly as he stared into my eyes.

"I know you didn't have an easy life, and that the druids treated you harshly," he whispered, and I snorted in response. That was putting it mildly. I dismissed him, turning to stare at the wall as I ignored what his touch was doing to me. "It isn't them I am trying to save here, Erie. I'm trying to save innocent lives that have never done wrong before." His hand continued to draw the pattern above my womb as if it was a bulls-eye to mark what he needed from me. "I don't want this for you, for any woman. I searched the world for another way out of this. I wish there was more time, but it isn't a luxury we have."

"Let me go," I whispered thickly, heat pooling between my thighs as his fingers continued to dance over my belly. I exhaled a growl as he bent over, kissing the hip he had exposed, watching me respond to his touch. He didn't stop; his hand lifted the gown until it was bunched up against my stomach, exposing my wet, needy flesh to his eyes. He stopped his kiss to slip between my legs, watching me as he towered above me, his fingers lowering to slide through the mess he discovered there. His dark blond head lowered, his tongue slipped through the trail his fingers had just taken, and a scream slipped past my lips as pleasure

ripped through me. "What are you doing?" I demanded as I lifted my head, watching his mouth as he sucked my clitoris between his lips before he let his tongue flick against it to a steady beat that sent pleasure coursing through me.

He laughed against my sex, and I moaned as he increased the speed of his tongue, flicking the ball of nerves until I was trembling with need. My throat expelled noises that sounded more animalistic than human as he pushed a finger into my pussy, and then another as he watched every reaction to what he did play out on my face. I felt my body clenching around them, sucking him deeper as he worked me into a need that painfully grew out of control. His tongue danced around his fingers as he released my clit. The noises his mouth made alone forced the white ball of pleasure to begin dancing its way towards the surface. I rode what he offered, rocking my core against him as it continued to throb and the impending orgasm built.

His mouth lowered, sucking against the nub as his teeth slid over it. That sucking motion combined with his tongue brought out the scream bubbling from within as the orgasm exploded, forcing my spine to lift from the bed, and I begged him for more. It didn't stop; he somehow kept me suspended there, in the throes of that orgasm as my body sang and buzzed with a pleasure so hot that I feared I would melt into a useless pile of flesh when he finally released me. His eyes burned into mine with a knowledge that both excited and terrified me as he smiled around the flesh he held with his teeth.

My head dropped to the pillow as I wiggled against him, needing more, needing what he had yet to give me.

I didn't care if it was the opposite of what I needed or wanted. I needed his cock so I could have the sense of fulfillment he created when he fucked me. I needed to be stretched and filled, and I only wanted him to do it.

"Callaghan," I moaned. I held my legs open, rocking my body against his fingers that continued to tease me as they slowly wiggled against my entrance.

"Beg me to fuck this pretty pussy," he uttered as he sat up, pushing his jeans down while his other hand pushed up my gown. The moment he'd finished, he pinched one nipple as he watched the pain that filled my eyes. "Come on, little one; show me how dirty you are. I know you want to be fucked. Can you feel how wet this pussy is for me? It's wet because it wants to be filled until it aches from it. You want my cock, admit it. You want it to stretch your tight cunt wide, to plunder its depths until you come around it. Tell me to fuck you, Erie, to write my name so deeply inside of you that you no longer understand what your fucking name is, and never forget mine. You can do it, show me how fucking dirty that sweet mouth of yours can be for me. Tell me to fuck this cunt until I destroy who you were before you knew what it felt like to be claimed by me."

"You need to wash that mouth of yours out with soap. You're so dirty, Callaghan," I whimpered as I watched the smile spread over his generous lips. "Stop smiling, asshole, I'm serious; it is very, very dirty, boy. I think you have Tourette's."

"You have no fucking idea how dirty I am, little girl. I've had to watch you grow into a woman without touching you. I waited for you to be ready for me, to be woman enough to need me in the way I need you," he smirked as he leaned over, letting his heavy cock slide over my opening while he sucked a nipple between his teeth, nipping the bud. I lifted my needy pussy against the heaviness of his cock, craving the friction. "I have dreamed of taking you since the first time those blue eyes locked with me in a crowded room, and you bit that fucking lip. I wanted to taste it, to see if you were as sweet as you promised to be. I stood there, watching the men as they flirted with you, and you watched me long into the witching hours. As if you wanted me as much as I wanted you."

"Callaghan," I whimpered as he continued to hit against my clitoris, his cock brushing against it over and over again. I spread my legs further, and he smiled, lifting up as he reached back, producing a key to release my feet from the chains before pushing my knees up against my chest. I watched as he braced against them, using them to spread my core as his thick cock pushed against my opening.

"You're so beautiful, little one," he uttered thickly.

"Don't lie to me," I growled as I looked away from his heavy stare.

"I'm not fucking lying to you. I wish you could see yourself through my eyes. You think that woad takes away from your beauty? It doesn't, it just adds to who you are, and made me crave you a long time ago. They painted you for war, and make no mistake, sweet girl; you are war to the very marrow of your being. You're an ageless beauty, as wild and untamable as the land you were named after. You're more than a womb to me, Erie. To me, you're everything," he uttered as he pushed into my body, only to pull out partially and watch as I wiggled against his thickness.

"Move, Callaghan. This is an entirely new type of torture," I moaned as I wished for his words to be true, but I knew they weren't. They were pretty lies meant to lower my guard, to make me think other than what I'd been taught. I knew better than to reach for things that could never be. I'd had that lesson beaten into me repeatedly until I'd known it by heart.

His hips rocked as he pushed into my needy flesh, and I moaned as my mouth opened to let it escape. He stretched me full, muscles burned from his entrance, and he watched the emotions dancing over my face as the orgasm threatened to take hold. He thrust his hips against me, fucking in hard, slow thrusts that took me towards the edge of oblivion—and fuck, did I want to reach it with him.

He leaned over, capturing my lip between his teeth as he hissed and pushed into my body deeper than before. I felt my sex tightening around him as it ached from fullness, and his tongue pushed into my mouth, following the beat his hips took while he plundered and dominated me effortlessly. I was seconds away from the rapture when something exploded into the room.

My ears rang, and I blinked to clear my gaze as dust thickened around us. Callaghan peered back, over his shoulder, and then he growled, moving his hand as an energy ball of magic exploded from it, sailing towards the doorway while his hips rocked against me. He started to pull away, and I whimpered, still writhing beneath him as pleasure consumed me. Boards splintered and broke apart to rain down against us as he shielded me from the debris with his body.

His hand lifted up, pushing his large cock deeper into my body as he spoke above me. His mouth moved, but nothing registered as my body clenched against his. Something splattered over my face as my hand came free of the chains and I looked up, staring at him as blood dripped from his mouth, splattering over me. He struggled with the other hand, working the lock as he sputtered, coughing up blood that sprayed over my face.

"Callaghan," I mumbled as my sex-driven thoughts turned to what was happening.

"Run, Erie," he uttered as he peered down, looking through his stomach where a giant hole the size of a softball had been made. I looked through him, staring at the demon that lifted from the floor. I hid beneath his body, still impaled by his cock as I tried to figure out where to go. His head turned, and energy slammed into the demon as he rolled off of me, turning to look towards the doorway, where two more loomed, waiting for the invisible wall to fail.

I sprung from the bed and grabbed my bag. I slipped my arms through it as I righted the nightgown. My eyes dropped to stare one last time at Callaghan, who now stared sightlessly back at me. My gaze swung to the doorway as I ruffled through the pocket of my bag, and, producing the kerosene and torch that I held up, flicking it to life as I walked towards them. The wall gave out, and one shot towards me.

Pain erupted as the demon reached me, tearing at my arms. I held the flame up, burning him and me as I tried to inflict the most damage I could. My magic flickered to life, and I hissed as his nails tore through my arms, knocking me down as he followed me to the floor. I rolled against the floor, trying to escape the fire and fluid that covered him and me. I stood up, trying to pass over him as he grabbed my ankle, slowly crawling on top of me as the fire burned us both.

Screams ripped from my lungs as his molten hot hands slid over my arms, burning the flesh from them while I sent my magic like a missile aimed right at him. He exploded, but the other demon took his place, grabbing my burned arm, taking the seared flesh off the bone as I screamed and let the magic within me loose. The demon stepped back, tilting his head, and then it popped. I watched his body drop to the floor, and I started forward, red-hot pain filling me with every step I took. He reached for me, grabbing my leg as I kicked away from his claw-covered hand.

He gave in, and I moved from the room, swaying as I rushed to the window and jumped from the second story onto the concrete. Bones broke as I landed against the pavement, pain ripping through me as I struggled to get back up, staring around to find my position and then held on to the building as I limped towards the Guild. Almost to it, hands grabbed me, and I screamed as I turned around, swinging wildly and lashing out. I whimpered as I took in the sapphire eyes that watched me with uncertainty. I sagged with relief, and a whimper escaped as I trembled and shook forcefully from the pain.

"Erie, fucking hell, girl, what the fuck happened to you?" Zahruk's deep growl sounded as he backed up, raking his gaze over my damaged body as I swayed on my feet with the last of my strength. He was one of the few people I trusted, one of the people from the

Guild. "I got you, you're safe," he said gently as he held his hands up in a non-threatening way. "I'm going to pick you up, and it's going to fucking hurt like hell. I'm going to need you to try not to scream, because there are demons all around us, which I'm guessing from the looks of it, already found you once. Let's not give those evil fucks a second go at ya, yeah?"

I nodded and winced as I braced for him to do just that. He looked at my flesh, noting the parts that weren't crispy, and then carefully picked me up, starting forward as I buried my face in his shoulder, crying against him as pain burned violently through me. I bit into his shirt, sending the scream against his flesh as I was no longer able to stop it. I inhaled, gagging, and the scream continued as the scent of burning flesh grew repulsive to my senses.

"You're fucking beat the fuck up, girl," he muttered. "What the fuck happened?" I wasn't sure if his small talk was to keep me alert or to keep him from throwing up as he inhaled the cooked flesh.

I shook my head, begging him silently to hurry so he could put me down. I needed sleep to heal, to recoup from the damage that had been done. I closed my eyes as I felt him moving up the steps, each one becoming more painful until he reached the doors, shouting orders as we walked through them.

"What the fuck happened to her?" Adam's voice echoed as I was set down, but held on my feet, Zahruk steadying me. "Jesus Christ, what the fuck. Did they try to cook her?" he demanded as we moved past him slowly with Zahruk guiding me carefully.

"Get Eliran here, now," he ordered as voices

sounded.

"What happened…what the hell?" Synthia's voice was sharp as she echoed Adam's words, confident as she moved to me, inspecting me, and I swallowed hard. "We need the healer, now!" she screamed at those around her, turning her eyes back to stare at me as she smoothed down the panic that filled her eyes.

"Demons," I uttered as I started to fall, only for Zahruk to catch me and cradle me against his chest.

"Take her to the dome; it's clean and sterile. She can be tended to there. Adam, Lachlan, go get Eliran, we'll need more than what the healer here is capable of to heal her. Lucian and his men should be here shortly with the witches on the busses; they may have a spell to ease the pain."

"I…heal," I whispered as I swayed, barely able to remain upright.

"Yeah, but not without feeling it," she replied sharply. "You're missing half of your fucking arm, and you look as if you were cooked alive. You need help."

"That hurts," I muttered and looked down, staring at the exposed bones as Zahruk tried to hold my hand, needing me to follow him. "I lit demons on fire, attacked. Window…jumped," my fragmented sentences didn't make sense, nor would they until I'd healed. "Dead," I uttered as my mind went back to Callaghan, and the fact that he'd shielded me so that I would survive it, even though he hadn't. We'd been too busy to even think of being disturbed. It served him right, and I wouldn't feel bad, even if I did.

"And did what with the demons, Erie, play who can burn brighter?" she asked as she helped Zahruk leading

me into the room with the dome in it. There was so much pain, pain that filled my mind as I screamed against their touches. They tried to help, but even that was painful as they helped me onto a bed, Zahruk peering down at me. Synthia's touch sent the pain away, and she refused to let go until the healer had been summoned and drugged me as I slipped into oblivion.

"Sleep, Erie, we have you, girl. You're safe."

CHAPTER
seventeen

I AWOKE TO A HAND TOUCHING MY FACE AND GROWLED. Opening my swollen eyes to peer up at the male healer, who lifted his hands while staring down at me with a cautious look in his own. Mentally, I replayed what had happened and where I was. My arm moved, and I hissed as pain erupted from the simple motion. I groaned as I looked down at the bandages, soaked with healing salve that now covered them generously.

"You're badly burned," he gently explained as he went back to applying cream to my face.

"Erie, this is Eliran, our healer," Synthia said from where she sat beside the bed I was on, her hand on my leg, as if she was somehow holding the pain away from me, at least for the most part.

I turned, staring at her, and groaned at the worry that displayed over her face. I wasn't used to seeing anyone worry about me, and that bothered me. "Why do you care?"

"About you? I don't, I care that you're hurt and you

needed help. You came to us. I don't have to care about you to realize you were running from something and needed our help, even if you wouldn't ask."

"It's stupid to help people," I whispered as I closed my eyes against the pain the healer's touch was creating.

"Is it? Because I see a girl who has been through hell, on her own for so long that she refuses to allow anyone to get close to her. I can respect that, but I will never leave you in the street to rot. You have your issues, I have mine. I'm in the business of saving people, I think you are too. You can stay here and heal, you won't have to repay us for it, or even owe us. I won't, however, stand by and watch you suffer because you think you're too tough to need help. We all need help here and there, and this time, I am in a position to offer it."

"I kill people for a living," I stated, testing her boundaries.

"I killed a lot of people too, and will continue to do it so long as there is bad in the world."

"I kill because it gets me off," I uttered, watching her face as she swallowed and narrowed those violet eyes on me.

"No, you don't. You kill because you are given a name on a list. You kill the bad people because they don't deserve mercy. You didn't walk into Vlad's club to do harm to anyone who didn't deserve it. You did what you came to do, and you made sure no one who was innocent got harmed in the process. I know you, Erie. I know you because I was you. You have an honor code, one that is embedded in the very genetic code of your being. I've watched you, and not once have you murdered anyone who didn't deserve it. I'm guessing this is a test, and you don't expect to pass what you think is our standards, and I'm telling you, we don't have any. I'm willing to bet you want me to reject you, but that isn't going to happen. Life's a bitch, but there's no way around that, no matter how much we wish it otherwise. Rest, recover, and then if you want to leave, you're free to go." She stood, nodding to the healer, and then to Zahruk who watched me from the corner.

"What the fuck are you looking at, asshole?" I demanded.

"Roadkill," he smirked. "Pretty roadkill, but roadkill all the same," he chuckled. "Or it might be BBQ, I haven't really decided which you most resemble or smell like yet." He shrugged.

"You don't have many friends, do you?" I countered, and I winced as the healer began trying to apply the salve to my upper arms. I inhaled through my nose and exhaled out my mouth as I bit down the scream that threatened to bubble up.

"Pussy," Zahruk said as he moved closer, looking over the seared tissue. "I probably have the same amount of friends as you do, crispy."

"Fuck you," I snarled as I started to sit up, only for him to gently push me back down, before taking my hand in his and holding it as I watched him.

"Pain tells you that you were strong enough to survive it," he whispered as he brought my hand to his mouth and kissed the inside of my palm. "It reminds us that pain eventually ebbs, while the strength we gain from it endures. So get those big girl panties back on, because this shit is going to hurt. There's no way around it. That salve will help the tissue heal with less pain, and from the looks of it, you need it."

"You suck at motivational speeches," I whimpered as more salve was applied while Zahruk continued to hold my hand, even though I had to be crushing his. Eliran continued silently, changing the bandages as Zahruk mouthed off, distracting me from the endless pain.

"I'm better with weapons and killing shit," he shrugged as he leaned closer, staring into my eyes.

"Noted," I hissed as a scream bubbled up from my throat.

"This is going to be painful," the healer warned, and I watched Zahruk nod towards him as those sapphire eyes came back to mine.

"I got you, girl," he said, and I screamed as he stood, staring down at me, holding me there while everything inside of me begged for death. My body trembled, quivering as he pushed the salve into the destroyed flesh to ensure it healed quickly. "That's it, give it to me, good girl," he whispered as he brought his mouth down against my ear. "Sleep, Erie," he urged, and I blinked as my eyes grew heavy with the need to do as he'd whispered.

"I can't," I muttered through a sob.

"Yes, you can, you're safe here. I got you; you're protected from the bad shit. I'll stand guard so that you can sleep and heal. I promise."

I didn't get a choice. Blackness filled my mind, even as I fought against it, struggling to remain awake to know what was happening to me. His lips brushed my cheek as he continued whispering those words, over and over again until his magic filled my mind, overriding my instincts to guard myself, to stay alive.

CALLAGHAN
TEMPLAR ORDER STRONGHOLD

I dodged left as a group of children moved through the hallway, running as they chased one another, laughing hysterically. Children ran around unchecked as they played among the rooms of the lower levels. Stopping, I watched a boy as he helped a small girl up, who couldn't have been older than three, from the floor, where she'd fallen down. He smiled down at her, cheering her on as they started back into the chase. I swallowed hard as I reminded myself why this had to happen. Why creating a child with Erie would happen whether she or I wanted it to. Besides, the idea of having a redhead with fiery blue eyes who talked back to me made my chest ache with longing.

That girl...for seventy-five years I'd stood by, watching her, trying my best to protect her when she had needed it, until she'd begun to blossom into her beauty. I'd done my best, and yet every time she had needed me the most, I'd been called away. I'd come back to find her broken by those who were supposed to protect her. My jaw ticked with the hatred and anger I'd felt for those who had harmed her, and had used my absence to inflict that pain onto her. It hadn't been easy to travel back then, and those missions could take up to an entire year or longer. That meant they'd had an entire year in which they'd used to abuse her.

Pushing off the wall, I headed up the winding staircase that led to the upper level. The room was already packed with the older Knights, as well as a few

of my crew. I tossed the notebook onto the table and leaned against it with my palms flat and my eyes boring into my father's. Douglas, the man who had given me life before the dawn of mankind had ever awoken to become a race.

"Fucking demons," I snapped.

"It changes nothing," he argued.

Douglas stared at me, his eyes narrowing as his frown deepened while I stared him down coldly. I lifted from the table and rose to my full height, knowing what he wanted. It wasn't fucking happening. Not now, not ever.

"You knew eventually that time would run out for her. I told you countless times not to intervene or get attached to that girl. She was created to birth a son to the Order, even if it wasn't with you. I didn't want this either, Mason. She deserves better, but innocent lives are at stake. We had three more premature babes born last night, along with two infants who perished from the sickness that no one has any idea how to heal yet. Our time has come, and we must use the cure to escape the fate that even now is hunting and taking out the weakest of our race."

"We don't even know if the sickness is tied to the curse," I growled, pulling a chair out to sit down, hiding the hands which balled into fists at knowing he was right. "It could just be a mere coincidence since it isn't time for the curse to start attacking us."

Lance scoffed, his turquoise eyes finding mine and locking with them. "We don't know that it's not the curse, either, brother. We don't know shit, other than Erie is our cure, and you're getting nowhere with her.

In a year, we end. There will be no one to lurk in the shadows and keep the darkness from devouring this world. Hell, we have a fucking apocalypse outside, and if the darkness comes, no one will ever be able to get this world back upright, and you fucking know it too."

"Did you succeed in the injections?" Douglas asked.

"When has Mason ever failed, even if the mission wasn't one he wanted to succeed at?" Rhett asked as he smirked, pushing his dark auburn hair away from his face. When my father just stared at him, he laughed. "Ask stupid questions, you get stupid answers."

"I injected her with the drugs and my dick, and then the demons showed up. So you tell me, how the fuck am I supposed to get her pregnant with them now hunting her? I assure you, I wasn't their target."

"And how did she escape?" he asked.

"I used my body as a shield to protect hers. I don't think they got her, but she isn't holed up in that outlet store anymore. She isn't anywhere that I can find her."

"And the assholes at the Guild, did she run to them?" Douglas asked.

"She might have, or maybe she's fucking being tortured by the demons who tried to kill her. It's unclear where she went, but I can tell you she took down two of them. They're in the lab being dissected to figure out which breed of demon they belong to." I pushed up from the table to pace the floor, hating that I didn't know if my body had shielded hers enough to give her a fighting chance, or if she was being tortured yet again because I'd failed to save her.

I'd used my body as a shield, unable to do more than that as I unhooked the cuffs that held her there,

and what did the little imp do? She continued moving beneath me, as if her sole purpose in life was my dick, which wouldn't have been a bad thing, had there not been fucking demons attacking us. I'd used my magic to buy her time, and it was time she'd used well, yet it had cost me. I'd lost my spine watching that nymph fucking my cock while we were under attack. Right up until I'd been fatally hit and had to roll her from where she would have happily died sated. It had been worth it, right up until I'd come back and been unable to track her past the fact that someone had picked her up, and they'd taken her somewhere heavily warded.

"So she's missing," Douglas frowned as he rubbed his temples. "If she had been here, this wouldn't have happened."

"If I may interject here," Grigori said. "She's been fucked twice, and may already have the cure growing in her womb. Or, we may bring her here as you desire to, and she fights us. That means she is less likely to breed anything. Erie is special, very much so, but what everyone seems to forget is that she was created. Yes, she had a mother and a father, but both were pushed into that cauldron and drank deeply of it to create that girl. Both also died within days of her birth. It was a miracle she survived, considering the violent way she was left, abandoned. Had Callaghan not had the foresight to see it through, we'd all be cashing our checks and counting down the days until our end was here. What I am saying is, if you corner her, and she fights back, this may end before it's even begun. Erie is a ticking bomb, one that doesn't even know what she is yet."

"Still, we cannot protect her if she is out there on her

own. We won't know that she's been bred, or if she carries his child until she shows it. Not to mention, they're out there hunting her. The witches are awakening, and so begin the games of finding them before they find her. I assure you, my son, if they do, she will be destroyed."

"Arthur is hunting them, isn't he?" I asked.

"Arthur went off the grid the day Erie walked out of that apartment. As far as I know, he's joined the others who tire of doing things your way. He doesn't understand why she isn't caged and fucked until she is bred like any other animal. When I refused to see the errors of my way and decision, he left along with a handful of others."

"She's a living thing," I uttered as I turned around, staring at him. "She's delicate. Those assholes put her through hell, and you knew about it. You knew about it, and you refused to let me bring her here. I could have changed this. I could have had her as my wife, had her never know what she'd been created from or for. You refused, and now you want to lock her up and have us take turns fucking her? No, no, that is my mate. When we take mates, it is forever, and if you refuse me her, the beast inside of me will rebel."

"We all took a vow to do what was needed to secure the future of this Order. Some of us lost a lot more in this deal, and I understand your need, Mason. There's a larger picture here though. I understand that you are attached, but more so, that which crawls beneath the surface is lured to her wildness, which is also why I am giving you three more months to plant your child in her womb. At that time, if it isn't finished, we will move to the next plan. Mason, it isn't because I want it to be so,

but because I cannot watch us die out for the sake of one woman. Your team does, however, have free rein to find the others and bring them back to stand before their judgment. We cannot afford rogue Knights out hunting our only chance of survival. God forbid they set her into motion and light her fuse."

The door to the meeting room opened as the scientist strode in, dropping a pile of clay onto the table. "They were created and controlled by magic," he said as he swallowed hard, and audibly.

"The witches are in play," Douglas said as he sat down and exhaled. "Time is running out for all of us."

CHAPTER
eighteen

I WATCHED THE SCIENTIST PLACE CLAY HUSKS ONTO the table as they explained the logistics of what had attacked Erie and me. I'd been otherwise distracted by the sweetest pussy on earth, uncaring of who watched us or invaded that bedroom and knew I was making her mine, but that had been stupid. Not fucking her, that was *all* right, but what happened after it, and everything else, if I'd been more careful, we wouldn't be working to track her down and figure out what had happened to her.

"My guess is the magic that created them is old, ancient if my calculations are correct. You were right to assume the witches have surfaced, as not many could manipulate this type of clay. It's rare, but not unheard of unless you add in this generation and variables of the bloodlines being watered down. Now, if this had occurred in the 1600s, I would say it was any witch alive, but it is not. You need to ward against those who cursed us because we believe it is they who now hunt the cure."

"Erie isn't named *the cure*, her name is fucking Erie Callaghan," I snarled violently. "Say it!"

The scientist watched me, swallowing as his throat bobbed up and down once before he spoke again. "They're hunting Erie Callaghan down. My guess would be to kill her before we have succeeded in lifting the curse. You will need to find her quickly and protect her because, with the amount of magic that was placed into those demons, I'd say they are fully juiced and ready to fight us."

"And you're sure the witches were controlling these?" Lance asked, watching the scientist as he shoved his fingers through his already mussed hair.

"Positive, the shrapnel that they pulled from the bed and walls was made of the same clay. Meaning they used magic to create a walking bomb. The first demon by the door, he was probably the one who exploded, as he was in pieces. The second one was burned as if something set it on fire, the third one was more whole, but something fought it hard to get away from it."

"Not something, someone. Erie set it on fire and then fought to get away from them, but did she get away, or did she end up getting caught?" I asked out loud, even though it was to myself rather than the room.

"That would explain the human flesh that we found embedded in the clay," he agreed as my stomach rolled.

"How much flesh?" I countered as I rubbed my hand over my eyes and then stared at him.

"Enough that she wouldn't have been able to get very far if she had escaped on her own," he said as he scratched his head and stared at the wall. "If she escaped at all, she couldn't have made it more than a few blocks before she would have bled to death. I know she can heal, but this magic was created to kill her. It's a game-changer."

"So you're saying they don't want her alive, they just want her dead?"

"I'm saying, if you hadn't used your body to shield her, we'd be topping the endangered species list."

"So witches who can control minions without placing themselves into danger are chasing Erie, and we have no idea where she is," Lance said as he steepled his fingers together and stared at me.

"She's also wounded," Cain pointed out.

"And that makes her an easy target," Rhett agreed.

"Not to mention, she may already be pregnant," my father added.

"If she had been pregnant, I don't think she would be anymore. With the volume of blood in that bedroom, mixed with the flesh collected from the demon, she'd most likely have miscarried if she'd been so."

"You know that for sure, even with the spell we did to ensure she is strong enough to endure the druids who abused her? Erie is very strong, not to mention I had just injected fertility drugs and more protection spells into her fucking womb before we were attacked."

I wanted to snap his neck with those words. The pain she had already suffered when I'd been dispatched to deal with a group of rogue Knights, or some other fucking emergency, was enough. Every time I'd returned, she'd been abused, until I'd tied a druid up, slicing him open as the others watched the beast within feeding from the meat on his bones. That had put an end to the torture,

but not the beatings. Mostly because she hid the bruises behind small smiles or a shy glance that made me forget everything else in the world even existed. She did that to me, made me forget the bad shit, filling it with her innocence that the world cruelly took away from her. Until she'd left the druids to hide anywhere she could only to be dragged back and beaten.

The day I walked into that room and found her naked, held up by wires that had sliced through her flesh, I'd lost it. I'd murdered enough to start a war, but I hadn't cared. I'd have eradicated them all from this world if I hadn't been pulled off of them by the men who were my brothers in arms, my brothers who held monsters within them as well.

I'd taken that girl into a room and stood silently as she'd dressed, her shoulders bowed in defeat. It had taken everything inside of me not to pull her close and promise that something like that would never happen again. Not as long as I drew air into my lungs. But I couldn't promise that, because I knew eventually I'd be the one to break her.

"Are you with us, or is that brain of yours balls-deep in that little imp of yours, Mason?" Rhett asked, not bothering to look at me as I lifted an angry glare in his direction. "She's out there wounded, and we're in here yanking our cocks and playing with clay, gentlemen. We're fucking Knights. We kill shit to make sure those who have earned it survive. I say she's earned it, don't you?"

The doors opened, and Hugh walked through them, covered in blood that stood out strikingly against his white cloak. He tossed a head onto the table and frowned. "Arthur doesn't have her, of that, you can be certain. Tiberius, Galen, and Shawn are all going to be detained for a few days, but the rest of us are ready to help hunt whoever is next on the list."

"The Fae," I growled. I sat back down, pulling Arthur's head towards me as I did. "I'm guessing if she was dying, and she knew demons were giving chase, she would have run to them because they'd protect her and she knows it. I almost hate to say it, but I hope she did, as they would keep her safe, and it is the one place that the witches wouldn't dare to attack again after they trespassed against the Horde King and pissed off a Goddess. I've already lied to both Synthia and Ryder, who as most of you know are Fae, about what and who we are once, and it wasn't something I enjoyed doing. No, let them help her if she is indeed with them. At least we know she is safe. I don't want the Fae knowing what I am unless it's absolutely necessary. They'd yet to make a comment about us being Knights instead of Paladins, which means either they've missed the hints, or they're choosing to ignore it. Either way, we have enough shit to deal with already, let's not add them to it."

"Just fucking what we need," Hugh scoffed as he sat down and poured two fingers of Scotch into his glass. "They're on the no-kill list still, are they not?"

"Do you want a full war against them?" Uther growled as he slapped the table and then poured himself a drink.

"Ladies, do you need a moment to collect your balls, or can you listen to me?" I snapped, pulling the bottle away, pouring three fingers into a glass and swirling it around as I watched it.

"If you were not my brother in arms, I'd show you the inside of that pretty head of yours, Callaghan."

"If you could, you would have done it eons ago. Don't challenge me, you never win, Lance. Uther, I want you stationed to the west of the Guild; Lance, you're on the east; Hugh, take the south; and Averred, you will follow me and take the north. I want to know if anything comes in or out of it. I want eyes on the other location we know she frequents, and I want the rogue Knights captured unharmed if possible. I don't want to be hunting bodies while we hunt Erie." I was tired of Arthur dying and coming back, only to have to spend the time to hunt the bastard down again when he regenerated.

"And what happens when you find her?" my father asked.

"Then I station one of my brothers at each location, and we guard her with our lives. If she has miscarried, her body will need to heal, and so will her mind. If by some miracle she is pregnant, then she will be moved into my apartment permanently even if she is unwilling. I won't take a chance of her cutting my son from her womb as she has threatened to do."

"And Carolina? Will you keep your wife somewhere else?"

"My wife has no part of this. We've lived separate lives for hundreds of years, father. She lost her right to be my wife when she decided to leave me because of what I had to sacrifice for this Order, so don't you dare ask me about my fucking wife. She's hated me too long to ever change that now."

"And her children that they assume are yours?" he

asked sadly. "Will you tell everyone the truth of their parentage, or continue pretending they are yours to protect them from the stigma of being bastards?"

"Their fathers know who they belong to, it is time they learned the truth as well. I've shielded them long enough. I claim Erie and any child she bears for me, but Carolina is not my wife, she has not been for centuries, and we no longer have any reason to pretend otherwise. If or when she needs my protection, she knows she will have it." That was a given, but mainly because I'd kept her protected from the one being that had hunted her. That was on me because I'd known better than to take a wife while the one I had craved was trying to get back to me.

"You do realize that Erie hates you, yes?" Uther asked, chuckling.

"Do you remember when we pretended to be mortals, and we married women who hated us all the time? I've seen love grow and flourish from the largest hatred in this world. I've felt her anger as she rode my cock, so I know there's hope there. She may hate me, but she doesn't hate my cock, or how she feels on it."

"You could just tell her what you did the day she was born. There's also that other time you plowed through every one of those evil fucks who beat that girl and saved her. It took you long enough to bring her back, and yet you made them pretend it was less time. You did spend almost an entire year bringing her back, only for her to repress those memories so fucking deep into her thick skull that you probably couldn't even knock them free now. Tell her the truth of who has been protecting her this entire time. Every girl wishes she had a knight

to protect her, and she had one, so just tell the woman the truth, brother."

"Why? So she will love me for it? I didn't do it so that she'd love me. I did it so that she would survive. I named her, Uther. I gave her my name on that rocky crag. I expected it to protect her; my name and my insignia should have been enough. I failed, and she will not see it as a service; she will see it for what it was. I failed her over and over again as I left to do my duty. No, when she remembers it, she will hate me even more than she already does now."

"You're too hard on yourself," Douglas said. "You protected her, even against the odds. You're a Knight first and always because you took a vow that is written in the blood of our kin, of our ancestors. You don't have any other choice than to go when you are called to duty."

"You don't know Erie at all," I argued. "Erie isn't going to think that it was anything but a failure. Not when it was she who paid for it in her blood. You never saw what they did to her, you only heard it secondhand. They stripped that girl and beat her until her spine snapped and she pissed herself in front of those she called her friends, her family, as they laughed at her. I may have murdered the men who allowed it to happen and those who took part in it, but she hunted down and tortured over fifty boys, viciously. That is who you think to trap, the one woman on this godforsaken earth who has had no one who ever cared if she lived or died. The girl should have been cherished, treasured, and instead, she was abused. So you think bringing her in and tying her up is the answer, father? She'll die fighting to remain free. She would burn to ashes and rise as something this entire world would cower in fear before because that is who she is."

No, Erie had a slumbering monster inside of her, and if that part of her ever awakened, God save this world because she'd burn it down. I knew what she was, who she was, because I'd brought her back. I was a selfish prick, but she, she was the woman I'd craved since the beginning of time, loved since the beginning of time, and God save me, I'd brought her back with the only power strong enough to manage that feat.

Erie wasn't just going to allow herself to be captured, and if she ever tapped into what slumbered inside of her, we were all irrevocably fucked. This world wouldn't be ready for her, but the thing was, I'd bring her back before I allowed those cackling hags to kill her. I'd force her to come back if they got close to her again, if they didn't already have her. I growled as I lifted from my chair and grabbed my helmet.

"Knights, we ride," I said. I watched them nodding as I turned, heading for the door. "Lucifer protect us because God won't anymore."

CHAPTER nineteen

ERIE

I STOOD ON THE STEPS OF THE GUILD, STARING UP AT the lightning storm that had begun late last night. According to the Fae, Heaven had fallen, but to me, it seemed impossible. It wasn't as if we weren't already balls-deep in enough shit already. I turned as I heard footsteps behind me, watching Zahruk and Synthia as they came to stand beside me.

"Thank you," Syn said as she remained at arm's length from me.

"For what?" I asked, noting the way Zahruk watched me with a smirk lifting his lips. If I didn't know better, I'd swear he was trying to hump my leg.

"You didn't have to help us with Lucifer or place the wards up against Lena, but you chose to. You even fought alongside us afterward, which was nice to see."

"That wasn't fighting, she spent the entire fight complaining because she couldn't ride the dragon," Zahruk joked, and I glared at him, shaking my head.

"There was a dragon in the middle of that fight. You could warn people first, and then they might not sit and gawk at it for an hour. Besides, I didn't get to ride it. That's like pushing candy at someone and telling them they can sniff it, but can't lick it."

"Blane doesn't like to be ridden, but if you want a dragon to ride, saddle up, Erie. I got one that you can take for a spin."

"Is that a dick reference? Are *you* asking me to ride your dick?" I asked, staring him down with a frown as I tried to figure out what he'd meant by that.

"Do you want to ride it?" he asked.

"No," I uttered with a silent laugh as I shook my head.

"Then, no, it wasn't."

"Are you two done flirting?" Synthia asked as she stared between us.

I blushed and shook my head. "I don't flirt."

"Nor do you help people, but you just helped us." She smiled as she reached out to hug me.

I ducked, wincing as I danced around it. "Don't touch me."

"It's a hug, friends hug each other."

"I don't hug, and I don't have friends." My stomach dropped as her smile flitted and then turned into a frown. I frowned deeply, mirroring her emotions. "I don't need people. I don't need anything. I did this because I won't leave while owing anyone anything. If tomorrow I leave this world, my debts have all been paid."

"You're fucking cold, Erie," Zahruk said as he yanked me close against his chest before I could dodge it. "It's just a fucking hug. I don't give a fuck if you want friends, you've got them anyway. You need us, find us. Be careful out there, crispy. Thanks for not being an asshole."

I pushed him away and glared at him as if he'd grown another head. "Did you just grab my ass?"

"Would I do that?"

"Yes! Yes, you would. Hugging me is unacceptable. I don't like to be touched, ever."

"If you end up burned to a crisp again, I'll hold your hand through it," he shrugged, those sapphire eyes glowing as he watched me. "Don't let them snuff out that fire, sweet girl. You fight for yourself, even if you don't think you're worth it. You are. You're a rare breed. Stand tall, Erie. Don't let them see you fall, and if you do, you take the fucking head off the one that watched you fall."

"What does that even mean?" I asked, watching him as he smiled widely, shaking his head.

"You're going to need to stick around more often. You have no idea what sexual innuendoes even are. You can't take a compliment when it's given, and someone needs to wrap that ass in a blanket and warm you up. You're cold as ice, don't let them win. Erie, you're more than that. You're better than that. They beat you down, and you still got back up. That's the only thing that matters in the end. It isn't about how you fall; it's what you do when you get back up that people remember."

"I need to go. Fred is probably rotting."

"Who is Fred?"

"My friend."

"Why would he be rotting?" he asked. "And I thought you didn't have friends?"

"Oh, because I cut his head off and kept it. He needs to be iced so that he doesn't rot." I watched his mouth open and close several times before he nodded as if he understood.

He didn't. No one would ever understand that friendship had never been something I easily gave, and every time I had, it had ended with me paying for it with blood. I waved at them, walking backward before I spun around, starting down the steps as I headed north, away from the Guild before ducking into an alley and starting a roundabout way through the city towards the shopping outlet.

Once I made it half a mile from the Guild, I caught sight of Fred's body again as he felt blindly around the side of a building, and I smiled at the naked, headless demon who was trying to find the head I'd taken. I had to give it to Fred, he was relentless.

Entering the area around the storefront, I paused, turning to look over my shoulder. I blinked, clearing my vision as I stared beyond the veil of this world and noted the souls that watched me, whispering to each other as if I couldn't hear them.

Something was up, something that made the hair at my neck rise, and my skin crawl. I walked through the closest ones, listening as they continued talking, oblivious that I'd passed through the living world into theirs.

"They will want to know where she is," a young female said. Witchling markings covered her arms as she exhaled, sending her secrets into the world of the living by way of fog that would go to whoever she wished.

"She is different, can you feel that?" The male voice

echoed as he reached out, touching my arm, which caused the flesh to react and break out in goosebumps. "She is magic in human form. I see why they want her."

"They're selfish; she has pain in her eyes. She doesn't deserve to die for what she is. Wild beauty mixed with the magic of an entire race. They will die if she rises. It is foolish to meddle in the lives of those who have suffered as she has."

"And why is that, Katria?" he asked.

"Because she's learned how to survive," she smiled sadly as she touched my hair. "Those who survive merely on instinct are more dangerous since they don't survive because they need to, they do it to make those who have harmed them pay in blood. She is part of the Dagda, reborn in another form."

"Evil was released into this world to save those of pure heart. It wouldn't be the first time the Knights used evil to right the wrongs of the past. This though, this one is going to let something else into this world. Something that no one can stop," the male muttered. "I think she hears us."

"Impossible, no one crosses the veil and lives."

"Oh, I can hear you. You can tell whoever wants me to come and get me." I smiled as they vanished, the other souls following their lead as they sensed the intrusion.

What else could go wrong today? I turned, staring at Fred's body as it continually ran into the side of the outlet. I poked around in my bag as he ran into the shopping carts, tripped over bodies, and crawled around on the trash-covered ground before I remembered that I'd used the lighter fluid on the other demons. Exhaling, I withdrew the daggers before I pulled the backpack on and started the process of destroying his body again. It was becoming therapeutic. Once I had finished, I used hand sanitizer to wash off my hands.

Slipping inside, I inhaled the ghastly scent of the bodies and moved to where Fred had been left, opening the cooler lid to smile down at him.

"Miss me?" I asked.

"I was afraid that someone had finally figured out how to kill you, mistress."

"You stink." I turned to the ice maker, pulling out the ice as I proceeded to dump Fred's water into the bucket and add new ice into the cooler.

"You were gone a long time."

"I had things to do, I told you that," I explained.

"You were hurt?" he countered.

"I was," I replied.

"Good, because leaving me here to float in a cooler is an entirely new low for you, female."

"I like mistress better."

"Woman, female, unwanted spawn of the devil himself," he hissed as he pouted.

"Aww, did you just call me an angel?"

"No, no, I did not! I would never refer to you as an angel. You have darkness in your eyes; I know, because if I had my sexual organs, I'd stroke them as I stared into that alluring abyss of pain that shines from within you."

"You have pretty eyes too, Fred."

There was a noise outside the door, and I paused what I was doing. My hand pushed the cooler closed, draping a blanket over it as I turned, looking around for a weapon and finding none. Shit. I grabbed a bar of soap, and when the Knight opened the door, I chucked

it at him. I knelt down, grabbing more that I pelted him with as he watched me through the visor of his helmet.

"Are you fucking throwing soap at me?" Callaghan's deep voice asked as his head tilted.

I stood, taking in his full armor and white cloak with the familiar red Templar cross down the back. Swallowing hard, I backed up, noting there was no exit, nowhere to run from him. Fred spoke, his words muffled by the cooler, and Callaghan's head moved towards him.

"Don't you fucking touch him! You back off now!" I screamed as power tore through the room. The walls began to shake and tremble as everything inside of me snapped. It hit me so hard that I didn't have an outlet or a target, and I held no control over it. "He's my friend! You get away from him right now!"

Callaghan stepped back, his hands lifted in surrender as he watched me. The air was thick with magic, evil, dark magic that pulsed through me raw and unchecked as I stepped forward, growling, I pushed everything into the magic, sending him shooting backwards as I lifted my hands.

"No one fucks with Fred!"

"You tell him, mistress," Fred muttered from inside the covered cooler.

I turned, staring at the cooler as the buzzing in my ears became unbearable. I stumbled back, dropping to my knees as I brought my hand up to wipe away whatever was dripping from my face. Staring down at my hand, I winced at the crimson stain that marred my flesh. Stars ignited behind my eyes, and I fell forward as everything went black.

CHAPTER
twenty

MY ENTIRE HEAD FELT LIKE IT HAD BEEN BOUNCED OFF
the concrete a few times, and then had been run over
by a truck. I pushed away from the cold, wet thing that
touched my face and winced as I found a hand attached
to it. Cold sweat clung to my clothes as I swallowed bile
that threatened to explode from my lips. It touched me
again, and I stared up into the greenest eyes I'd ever seen
before. I watched him with curiosity until it dawned on
me that they were in my space, in my hideout *with* me.
My eyes immediately moved to where Fred had gone
silent, his cooler hidden beneath the blanket I'd placed
over him. Some resemblance of calmness filled me until
I pushed that incessant hand away from me again.

I knew this guy. He was one of Callaghan's men;
Uther, that was his name. Sir Uther Mackinnon, one
of the few men who Callaghan had brought with him
on missions. I pushed his hand away again as I started
to sit up, only for him to push me back down gently.
My gaze swung to the hallway as coughing sounded,

and I stared at the other Knights who were too large to stand in it, and yet had crowded into the hallway all the same. I swallowed hard as I lowered my stare to where Callaghan's body remained on the floor, lifeless.

"What happened?" I uttered thickly past the dryness of my mouth.

He smirked, pulling his canteen out as he held my head up, forcing the water over my parched lips and tongue. Uther didn't speak right away as he watched me drink his blasted holy water until I coughed from taking too much. I rubbed my temples, and I was finally allowed to sit up, which showed them the stickiness of my white shirt and lack of bra beneath it. His eyes slid down to my hardened nipples as a frown tugged on his lips.

"I'm guessing you used the magic of the cauldron by accident and it kicked that skinny little ass of yours," he chuckled as he stood up, pulling his gaze back to mine.

The Knights wore full Templar Knight Armor, their swords strapped against their waists in their scabbards as if they'd stepped out of medieval times and into ours. My eyes settled on the crimson cross as one of the Knights turned in the hallway, bending down to hoist the corpse over his shoulder as he removed it.

"I did that?" I asked, noting I had no memory of it. The only thing I remembered was the anger, the need to protect the only friend I had—everything else was blackened out of the memory. "I didn't mean to," I whispered as I brought my hand up to my forehead, watching the others as they stared me down.

"That would make one time of killing him an

accident," Uther huffed as he leaned against the wall, staring at me like he couldn't figure me out. I was in full glamour again, hidden beneath the blonde façade of the lady I'd envied as a teenager. Somehow, it felt as if all of the Knights could see through my guise. "It really gets annoying when you kill him, and then we get to stand around and wait for him to return to us."

"If he would just stay away, we wouldn't have this problem, now would we?" I argued as I pulled the drenched shirt away from my flesh and continued to glare back at him. "It's not like I'm the one chasing his ass down, now, is it?"

"You were created to save us, little monster. They promised us that you'd be pure of heart and soul. A beauty unmatched by any other creature," he hissed as he watched me. "You were supposed to be docile, gentle, and unable to tap into that power that created you, and yet I'm willing to bet my balls that you just used it to kill Mason. That was the fear that controlled the vote of the Order when we voted to take you from the druids. You're unpredictable. Unsafe to those around you, created from the greatest evil this world has ever known," he droned on, watching me as if he expected me to wield that power to fry his ass. It was tempting, but I'd only used it a few times before, and it scared the shit out of me. I'd pushed it behind that wall I refused to examine too much.

I smiled as I stared up at him, moving closer to where he stood, and I inhaled deeply. "I'm aware of what I am. I don't believe it would have mattered how unpredictable I was either, not really. I may have been an unknown, but what the druids did to me, well, no

child deserved that. And the Knights, with their white capes and code of valor, well, you were no better than they were. You abandoned me like I was nothing but trash, leaving me to be abused at the hands of those bastards. You and your kind created me, in case you forgot that tidbit. I never wished to be born, Sir Uther. I never wanted to be of this world. I was never asked to play a part in this, and yet I was dropped from my mother's womb and left on the floor to die. I *am* evil, of that, you can be sure, I do not pretend otherwise. Pray to your weak God that I do not wield this power inside of me often, for I may enjoy it. You and your kind do not deserve to be saved. You left me to suffer, to survive in a world that constantly reminded me that I *am* nothing, that I *am* unwanted and unloved. They told me that my differences didn't make me special; that they made me nothing more than a monster. I was a child!" I hissed through tears as I stared at him, so angry that I felt my heart palpitating like thunder against my ribcage. "Do not expect me to come willingly to save you and yours, for they left me to die on the cold floor like the animal they said I was. No, no, the animals were given mercy, were they not; a quick death, so that they did not suffer. I wasn't given that, I was just tortured endlessly, abused, and beaten if the mood struck their fancy. You never cared about me, so why should I care about you? You do not tell someone that they are a monster, and then expect them not to become one," I laughed as my tongue slipped between my teeth, and I watched the anger play out across his features. "That is my only warning to you. Now get out, and stay away from me."

"And you think anyone cares about your woes, girl?

You had a rough go of it, Erie. We all know that, but who the fuck do you think was there to help pick you up every time they knocked you down…"

"Say another fucking word, and I'll kill you myself, Uther." Everyone turned around as Callaghan's deep voice echoed through the hallway. "Leave, go guard the doors to this place, and do not disturb us or come if you hear screaming."

"You need to tell her," he snapped back as his lime-green eyes burned into mine. "Maybe then she'd stop fighting you so damn hard."

"Not another fucking word, Uther," Callaghan warned, his blue gaze locked with mine. He was pissed, his shoulder hit against Uther's, and the other Knight smiled with those shamrock green eyes as he watched me. "Got something to fucking say?" Callaghan hissed as he stared the other Knight down.

"No, but I think you need to address the issue before it reaches further than our ears and eyes. If she can access the magic of the cauldron, this is a whole new ballgame," he muttered as he pushed off the door.

"Go watch the doorways. I want this place searched. I want to know if a fucking rodent is creeping within these walls. Now go," he growled, turning those Nordic blue eyes to me, staring me down as the tick in his jaw intensified.

"You think you are safe with her?" Rhett asked, his eyes watching me as if he expected me to explode and murder them all.

"I think she doesn't know what the fuck she just let out of the bag, and it needs to be handled delicately," Callaghan growled.

"Handled? You don't handle that type of magic, it handles you," Rhett argued.

"Are you going, or do you want to stay and watch this play out?" Callaghan countered.

"I got time, and she's divine. Not my usual type, as you know. Redheads seem to be explosive, too hot to handle."

"I think you all should leave now," I interjected into the conversation. "You're not welcome here."

"Too late for that, sweet girl, you just let Pandora out of her box," Callaghan uttered as he let his gaze drop to the see-through shirt I wore.

I stared at him, knowing that he wasn't leaving after I'd used that power against him, and while I knew I could harness it to send them all running, it left something stained across my soul every time I wielded it. I swallowed, and I watched the others retreating down the hall, waiting for him to speak again as he watched me like he wasn't sure what to do with me.

"How many fucking times, Erie?" he demanded once we were alone.

"How many times what, Callaghan?" I whispered as I chewed my lip and rubbed my arm; I lowered my gaze to the floor.

"How many times have you used that magic before?" he snapped.

My eyes flashed to his as I shook my head. "I don't know," I replied honestly.

"When you killed the young druids, was it you, or was it that magic that you hid so fucking well from us?" he growled huskily. "And if so, what else are you hiding from me?"

"That was me," I admitted as my eyes rounded, staring at him. "You knew that was me?"

"I knew it was you, yes," he admitted.

"Mistress?" Fred's voice filled the room, and we both turned, staring at the blanket-covered cooler.

"Not now, Fred," I uttered. My eyes swung back to Callaghan as my hands trembled, and his slowly narrowed as he stepped closer towards the cooler. "Callaghan, no!" I hissed as he pulled the blanket off of and kicked the lid open with his foot, staring down at the demon.

"Is this wrecking ball penis guy? He's hot," Fred said with a silky tone I'd never heard him use before.

"Erie," Callaghan uttered. "There's a decapitated demon head in a cooler, what the fuck?" he demanded.

"He's my friend," I whispered as my throat tightened and my eyes burned.

"It's a demon," he muttered as he dropped his foot and then recovered the cooler with the blanket. He turned to stare at me.

"I know what he is," I said as I tilted my head, rubbing my arm harder as I stared at the floor. "He's my friend," I repeated softly.

"He's not your friend, he's a demon for fuck's sake, woman," he growled and stared at me as if I was crazy.

"I talk to him, and he can't hurt me," I whispered thickly. "He's all I have."

"You have me," he snapped.

"I can't trust you," I hissed harshly. "I can't trust you to want me for more than what I can do for you. You're a Knight first and foremost, and you would do anything to save your people. I come second to that in your world, always."

He didn't argue as I frowned, watching him. "Come with me, woman. We need to talk," he muttered as he rubbed his hand down his face, staring at the cooler and then back at me.

"We can talk here," I assured him, not wanting to leave the room with him.

"I'm not talking to you about what just happened with a severed demon head in a cooler," he argued. "You do realize that if he is alive without the use of his body, he's a fucking High Prince of Hell, right?"

I shrugged as I nodded at the door, needing to get him away from Fred. "I'll follow you."

"Take me to the other room you have in this place," he ordered.

"No way," I said as my eyes went wide as I held his heavy stare in challenge.

"Erie, I can find it from the outside hallway. I just figured we'd do this your way."

"Fine," I said begrudgingly as I reached for my backpack.

"Leave it, you'll be back," he ordered.

I stared at him as I exhaled and shook my head. Once out of the room, he walked inches from my back, his heat radiating through me as the close confined hallway gave me little room to escape it, and when my pace quickened, so did his. I turned around too quickly to tell him to back off, and lost my balance in the small space, tripping backward as he captured my hand, pulling me against his chest and stared down at me as I was slowly forced against wall as I watched the shadows playing over his features.

"You should be more careful," he uttered, still refusing to release my hand as his thumb trailed over my palm, sending my heart into a rapid beat that hit against the ribs holding it. "You're flushed," he whispered hoarsely as he watched every subtle move I made. I shook my head, and I started to speak, but he released my hand, circling his hands around my waist as he forced me up. My legs wrapped around his waist, forcing my breasts against his chest as a cocky smile flitted over his lips.

"What the hell are you doing?" I asked breathlessly.

"Making sure you don't trip again," he growled as he paused, pushing me against the wall, his mouth brushing against mine, seeking permission. My hands pushed through his hair as I watched his eyes glowing from within. My mouth closed the distance, touching against his before I pulled back, watching the smile spread over his mouth as his hold on me tightened. His forehead rested against mine, and then he whispered into the confined space, "Erie, you have no idea what you've done."

"I thought you wanted me to kiss you," I uttered breathlessly. I pushed against his chest as something tightened in mine.

He laughed huskily as his eyes danced with his amusement. "I do, that isn't what I meant. You can't use that magic, Erie. It wasn't meant to be used." His eyes searched mine, and then he pulled back, letting me slide down his chest.

"I can't control it all of the time," I admitted, uncertain why I was. He didn't deserve to know the secrets I held; no one did. "It doesn't matter."

"Don't do that," he said as his knuckles brushed against my cheek. "Don't deflect this. This is fucking serious. That magic that you used, it was forbidden by the Gods, Erie. It cannot be used, because it will draw evil to you."

"Afraid I'll become the Queen of Darkness, Mason?" I uttered as I watched him.

"You've never used my given name before," he growled as his mouth lowered, hovering inches from mine.

"I didn't," I said as I inched forward, needing to taste him.

"You did," he whispered breathlessly as his mouth crashed against mine and he picked me up, rushing us towards the wall that slid open, using his foot to push it out of the way, never moving his lips from mine as his tongue caressed and stroked it with fervor.

I moaned as he dropped us onto the bed, lifting up and pulling away from me, and I gasped to get fresh air. I watched as he revealed the wall of muscle that danced over his abdomen with every subtle motion he made. Savoring the tattoos that my tongue itched to taste as the reality of what was happening came crashing down on me.

I rolled out from beneath him, staring at him as he smirked from where he lifted to his knees. My gaze dropped to the huge cock that pushed against the armored pants he wore. I exhaled shakily as I shook my head, uncertain what the hell I had just done. It hadn't even registered that I'd been flirting or allowing him to touch me until he had begun to strip his body bare.

"This isn't smart," I muttered. "A bed, you, me,

no shirt, this isn't good, Callaghan," I said, unable to filter my words. He didn't reply. Instead, he watched me like he was trying to calm the same reaction that I was experiencing as we sat there, both ready to pounce if the other so much as moved a muscle.

"You don't kiss someone like that unless you're inviting them into your bed, Erie," he growled as he held perfectly still, staring at me.

"I wouldn't know, Callaghan. You're the only one to ever kiss me in my entire life," I replied huskily. "It's not like I've had a ton of experience or lured men to my bed before."

"Never?" he asked, and the pride that lit in his eyes made me want to punch him right in those soft, kissable lips of his.

"You have no idea what I have been through," I uttered, and my stomach turned as the memories rushed to the surface. I leaned against the wall, staring at him.

"Would it matter to you if I did? Would it matter to you if I had tried to protect you and failed anyway?" he asked, and there was something in his eyes that made me hesitate.

"No," I whispered as I closed the emotion off and pushed the feelings deep into the back of my mind. "It doesn't change anything."

"Didn't think so," he shrugged and he lunged, catching me as I started to move, but he was faster. "Kiss me like you did, Erie. Kiss me like you want me."

I pushed at him as I watched his eyes searching my face. "I don't want to make a baby with you."

"We'd make a beautiful baby together," he shrugged. "This isn't about breeding right now. This is chemistry,

sweet girl. Let me bring out that dirty bitch that you're hiding."

"Bitch?" I stuttered.

"She's in there, just waiting to play with me," he urged as his mouth lowered, kissing the inside of my thigh until my mouth opened and my hand flew to cover it, biting down as I stifled a moan. His hand slipped between my legs, ripping my panties off as he lifted his head, jerking me onto the bed with my back against it while his mouth descended over my flesh. I pulled his hair until he was looking at me, my chest heaving as I struggled to maintain some semblance of control.

"I thought you wanted to talk?" I squeaked breathlessly.

"I want to fuck you," he uttered, lifting to stare into my eyes as I watched him. He lowered his head to mine, turning as his tongue drifted over my lips, pushing past them to claim mine in a slow, heated kiss that pulled a moan from my lungs without warning. His knee pushed my legs apart, grinding against the needy flesh that he'd left unsated. He broke away, staring down at me. "You like this, you just don't know where it fits in that mess of a head," he chuckled as he lifted up, ripping open the shirt I wore. "I can show you right where this fits into it."

"That was my shirt," I growled as his head lowered, catching a nipple between his teeth before he applied just enough pressure that pulled a surprised hiss from my lips. "Callaghan," I warned as the small room became too hot, filled too full with his dominating presence. His tongue worked swirling motions around my nipple until he moved to the other one, pushing my skirt up with ease as his fingers pushed into the arousal between my legs.

I pushed against him, needing him there as the dull ache turned into a ball of need that refused to lessen. His hand moved slowly, and I needed more. I needed him. I pushed him away, fighting his pants to free him as he watched me. He pushed the wild hair away from my face as he allowed me the control to free his cock.

"You're a needy little thing, Erie. Show me what you need, tell me what you want," he uttered huskily.

I ignored him, working to free his cock. The moment it was released, I swallowed hard and laid back, pushing my skirt off as I closed my eyes. What the fuck was happening to me? I whimpered as he moved down, settling between my legs, his mouth descending on my flesh, lapping at it hungrily.

I screamed out as pleasure rushed through me, his tongue pushing hard as he sucked against the ball of nerves between my legs. I expected him to slide up my body and enter me, but he didn't. My hands found his hair, holding him there as another orgasm began to build. He was relentless as he licked and sucked, pushing his fingers into the tightness of my body over and over again until I was begging him to stop as pleasure washed over me blindly and violently.

"Such a naughty little thing, Erie," he chuckled as he lifted his head, mouth glistening with my pleasure on it. He climbed up my body, kissing his way to my mouth, where his lips tasted of me. His tongue pushed into my mouth, capturing mine as he rubbed his cock against my opening, then he pulled back to watch me as he began to push into my body. "You like when I

fuck this pretty, tight cunt, don't you?" he growled as he slammed into my body and I arched up off the bed, screaming as my body burned from his entrance, where he stretched me full. "You have the tightest pussy I've ever had the pleasure of fucking. I'd stay here forever, fucking this tightness if I could," he uttered as he sat up, using my hips to hold us together. "Look at how you grip my cock, sucking it off even without moving."

"Move, asshole," I urged through a huskiness I hadn't known I could achieve.

"Watch me fuck you," he growled as he reached over, pulling my hair until I was forced to watch as he withdrew from my body. My body gripped him tighter, clenching down as he slid in and out of my flesh, coated in my arousal. "Look at that sweet flesh, how your cunt is wet with your release, one I gave you. You want more?" he asked as he held himself halfway out of my body, slowly rocking against the slick heat that needed him to just fucking move. He pulled out even further, using his free hand to push against my clit, pinching it hard enough that I uttered curses as my body trembled around his. "Tell me what you want, Erie," he demanded as he pulled out until only the tip was cradled in my flesh.

"I need it," I pleaded.

"Tell me to fuck your cunt," he demanded. "Tell me to ruin this sweet haven until it knows me by heart."

"Callaghan," I hissed breathlessly. I lifted up, claiming his mouth, and allowed another inch to sink into my wanton flesh. A moan escaped my lips as the need to ride his cock blossomed into an addiction.

"Nuh-uh," he chuckled as he pulled back, trailing his

tongue over my lip before his teeth nipped at it, pulling it between them. His hips pulled back as he sucked on my lip, holding my hair as he moved my mouth to give himself further access. "You can do it, sweet girl. Let me hear you tell me how you want this monster cock to fuck that sweet, tight cunt. Tell me you want me to wreck that pretty pink flesh. How you need it so fucking deep that you'll never forget how we feel together."

"Fuck me," I begged, and he shook his head, refusing to release my lip.

"You can do better than that," he laughed darkly. He pushed me down, lifting my hips as he wrapped his arm around me and pushed his finger against my ass. "I'll fuck this too," he warned.

"Oh, hell no, you will not!" I uttered thickly as he pushed into it, forcing a scream of pain to erupt as he sank his finger into my ass.

"It only hurts for a moment, then it will become pleasure that you will crave," he said, dropping his head to suck on my nipple as I adjusted to the fullness of him poking into my backdoor.

I groaned as I rocked, trying to make it lessen the pain as he held his finger still. His dirty talk had turned me on, and yet I wasn't saying what he wanted, what he craved. He was a nasty asshole who was well aware of my need to not say things like that, ever.

"I'm not giving you what you crave until you tell me how much this sweet pussy needs to be fucked by me. You feel that, don't you? That's your tight cunt begging me to fuck it, but your mouth just isn't moving, Erie. It wants to be fucked, so tell me what you need from me."

His mouth lowered, dragging heat over my

collarbone as he kissed it. His kisses continued to my neck, slowly driving me crazy as he ravished me like I was something to cherish. I moaned, rocking my hips with wanton invitation, but nothing worked. His finger continued working my ass, and I swallowed a scream of frustration as he moved to my mouth, lowering his forehead against mine to stare into my eyes.

"Woman, you are the most perfect thing this world has ever created," he uttered as he pushed into my body, only to withdraw just as quickly. "You want that cock, don't you?"

"If you don't do it, I will cut it off and use it myself, Mason!" I snapped in frustration, which came out broken with need.

He chuckled as he removed his finger and watched me, his cock pulsing with a need I knew he had to feel. He smiled, revealing dimples while he watched me writhing in need for what only he could give me. His eyes flashed with heat, glowing as he once again pushed into my body and then slowly pulled out.

"Please, please fuck me," I urged as I pleaded for him to just destroy me.

"Please fuck what?" he asked as his fingers slowly slid down between us. "You can do better than that, Erie. I have heard you pissed off before. I know what that dirty tongue of yours can do."

"Fuck my pussy," I whimpered.

"No," he said as he sat back, staring down at my pussy that was stretched with the tip of his cock in it. He withdrew, using it to slap my flesh repeatedly, each slap of his velvet length, sending me closer to the edge. His other hand slowly pushed against my throat, watching me as I watched him. "Come on; tell me to fuck that naughty cunt, and I'll let loose on it, I'll make you scream and take you to heaven."

"*You're* a cunt!" I snapped. My hands fisted in the blankets as I stared up through angry eyes.

"So you *can* swear," he laughed darkly, pushing against my throat, taking my air from me as he watched me. He leaned over, capturing my lips as he pushed into my body and rocked his hips. A pulse started in my head, the lack of oxygen burning my lungs as sweat clung to our flesh. I didn't care if I could breathe; I just needed him to wreck me, to let loose and give me what I needed from him. His hand left my throat as his mouth left my lips, and he pulled out of me, watching me as I wiggled against the thick head of his cock readily.

"Fuck my cunt, you fucking bitch, Mason!" I snapped as a smile that was all teeth spread over his mouth.

"Bitch?" he inquired. "I assure you, there isn't an inch of me that resembles that statement, which I'm about to show you. You were a good girl though, so this one is for following directions."

He pushed into me as he leaned over, bracing himself on his hands against the bed as he started to move slowly. He watched me, staring down into my eyes as he began pounding into my flesh. I exploded, calling out his name as the orgasm took control, and everything else faded away. I was screaming, crying, and giving him everything back until he tensed above me, uttering my name while he exploded, drenching me with his cum as it spurted into my needy core.

Callaghan laughed huskily as he rested his head

against my chest, flicking my hardened nipple with his tongue while the orgasm continued to send tremors through my body. I wrapped my arms around him, wondering why I'd been so oblivious to the pleasure of the flesh when a pinch ignited in my stomach. I pushed him back, staring down to where a needle protruded. I pulled it out, staring at the empty syringe as he watched me.

"What did you do to me?" I whimpered as I stare up at him.

"Someone has to protect you, even if it is from yourself," he uttered.

I pushed him over, staring at him as I struggled against the betrayal I felt. Schooling my features and my reaction, I let my fingers trace over his abs as he watched them. My head lowered, kissing his stomach as it tensed against the innocent touches.

"And you think I need your protection? That I can't protect myself?" I whispered, hiding the anger that tightened in my throat.

"Erie," he warned gently.

"I earned it," I whispered. My fingers wrapped around his thick cock, watching his eyes as he watched me back with suspicion. "Relax, it's the only thing about you that I actually like," I uttered as I bent down, tasting the thick head as he grabbed my hair.

"There're some things that not even I will forgive, woman," he warned.

I pushed the thickness into my mouth, stretching my jaw as a hiss exploded from his lungs. He sat back, pushing my hair from my face as I tried to take more of him into my mouth. The man had an ungodly huge cock. I lifted up, pushing it deeper into my mouth as I went down, working my hand as I hollowed out my lips, watching him. I lifted, kissing the side of his cock as he closed his eyes against what I was doing.

"Ride me, Erie. I need to be buried inside of your sweetness," he growled as I continued. I moaned as my eyes moved to the syringe, and my teeth scraped against the delicate flesh of his cock.

"Callaghan," I whispered as I watched him open his eyes and smile down at me as I cradled his cock between my lips.

"Erie?" he chuckled huskily.

"Don't ever touch me again," I growled as I bit into his cock, watching as his eyes widened, even as his hand reached for my hair, yanking it painfully as he fought the hold I held on his cock. Blood pooled from the wound, filling my mouth as I held on to it, even as he slammed his hands against my head to dislodge me. I held on, ripping tissue as I screamed with anger at what he'd done.

"Erie, stop, you fucking crazy bitch!" he demanded, and I did, backing up as he covered his mutilated cock. I smiled, letting the blood drip from my chin as I watched him bleeding out on the bed where I'd just given him a piece of my fucking soul, and he'd taken so much more than I'd given him permission to take. "Fucking bitch, I was trying to help you!"

"I am not the one who fucked me over. You are. I gave you a piece of me, and you repay me by betraying me. I knew I couldn't trust you. I guess I just needed to be reminded of it."

I sat back against the wall as tears streamed down

my face, watching as he moved around, grabbing the blanket to stall the blood that soaked the bed.

"You won't like me when I come back, Erie."

"I don't like you now. You're just like everyone else. You use me, and the moment I lower my guard and think you might be different, you prove me wrong. It's what happens when you let people into your life. You let them in, and they destroy you. They destroy everything you allow them to touch until there is nothing left, and then when you're at your weakest, they send you to despair, where you have to crawl through hell to get out."

CHAPTER
twenty-one

I PACED MINDLESSLY OUTSIDE OF THE LAB WHERE Eliran was running a test on the remaining serum in the syringe used to inject me. I hadn't washed my face off as I had bolted from the room, running blindly through the hallway before I'd climbed through the vents, rushing to the roof where no Templar had been stationed.

"You look like you tore something apart with your teeth," Zahruk growled, sapphire eyes lowered to my lips as the others stood around, staring at me. "I'm guessing there's a dead Templar somewhere?" He watched me, frowning when I didn't reply. "At least tell us how you did it this time," he urged.

"I bit his dick off," I whispered.

He laughed until his mouth dropped open and he stepped backward, putting distance between us. The others made strange noises and stared at me. I turned to look at him as he took in the bruises that covered the side of my face where Callaghan had fought me off. Not that I blamed him, I *had* been biting his cock off.

"Gods, Erie, there's some shit you just don't do to a man." Zahruk's hand scrubbed down his face as the others around us agreed. "Tell me he earned it."

"Erie, I have the results of the substance in the syringe," Eliran said as he walked over to me, his eyes surveying the damage to my face.

"Fertility drugs?" I asked.

"No, it's a suppressant. A way to make magic inactive, if you will," he explained. "The strange part is that it has an enhancer in it as well. I'd say it was meant to protect whoever had been the intended target or patient. There wasn't enough to run more tests, but I did run it for fertility drugs, and there weren't any in it. I can check your blood again if you'd like me to. See what the drug is doing in your system if, by chance, you were the one injected."

I stared at him as my ears rang with his words. "He's going to kill me," I whispered. *I'd* fucking kill me. No one argued it as I closed my eyes. When I opened them, I nodded. "Thank you, Eliran. I owe you a debt."

"No, you don't. You should let me check you, you're covered in blood."

"It's not mine," I frowned.

"Erie, you took some pretty good blows to the head. You should let me make sure you're okay."

"I'm fine, I've had way worse," I admitted absently, unable to process what or why Callaghan had tried to help me.

"Those were tended to by a healer. I'm a skilled healer; there's no reason for you to suffer."

"No, Eliran. This one I earned." I turned to leave, and he grabbed my arm. "Don't touch me!" I screamed as Zahruk stepped closer, perceiving me as a threat to his brother. "Please, please don't ever touch me."

"I'm sorry," Eliran whispered as he stepped back, staring at me. "I had no idea you had red hair," he said, and I frowned as I looked down, taking in the unruly mass of curls and wild hair. I lifted my face to find Zahruk studying me.

"Not everyone is offended by what the druids did to you. You're rather wild and beautiful. There's nothing you need to hide from us; we're all covered in scars we didn't ask for. You need to stop thinking as if they destroyed you with that pretty woad, and start fucking living. Stop being a fucking crybaby. You're better than that," Zahruk said.

"They did this to me when I was a child," I growled defensively.

"And? So what, Erie? They painted your flesh, but they can't touch your fucking soul. Only you decide what touches that."

Callaghan had, even though he'd needed his mouth washed out with soap. I couldn't even lie to myself about it. I looked at Zahruk and nodded, not bothering to answer him as I left them all in the newly built labs that they'd been working on to get the new Guild up and running. I wasn't even sure why they did it, other than they seemed to need to keep moving forward.

I pushed through the outside doors and stopped on the top of the stairs, staring down at where the Knights stood, waiting for me. Swallowing hard, my gaze met the Knight who stood in front of the others, noting the way the anger rolled off of him. I closed my eyes, exhaling as I considered what to do, or where to run. I watched as one of the other Knights stepped forward, setting the white cooler at his feet, staring me down.

I stepped forward, my eyes glued to the cooler as I moved to stand in front of Callaghan. His hands fisted at his sides as I refused to meet his angry stare.

"Take her, and the cooler." His words were cold, filled with something I'd never heard from him before. I turned my head, staring as Rhett stepped forward, his helmet barring me from seeing his eyes as his hand closed around my arm.

"No fight left in you this time?" Rhett asked.

"Would it matter?" I asked. "Would anything I want matter?"

He didn't answer me, his hand tightening as we walked towards the waiting horses. I was pushed onto one, and I waited for Rhett to mount behind me, but he didn't. Instead, Uther moved closer, grabbing my hands as he bound them in front of me.

"Can't say you didn't deserve this," he uttered as he looked up at me. "You need to remember the past."

"My past is filled with torture and horrible shit that never should be remembered, ever. Why would I ever wish to remember any of that?" I demanded.

"Because between it, when there was a calmness that scared you, he was there," he muttered.

"Who?" I asked.

"You fucking done, Uther? It doesn't matter; it wouldn't change anything," Callaghan snapped as he pushed the other man away and pulled the rope tight, pulling a hiss from my lips. "Onward," he shouted as I turned, staring at Zahruk, who watched me from the shadows. I nodded to him, watching as Callaghan followed my stare. "You think he can save you? I assure you, not even the Fae will stand between you and me. Not because they wouldn't want to, but because even the Gods cannot and will not save you from me. Nine months, Erie. Nine months and you can walk away and live your life."

CHAPTER
twenty-two

INSIDE THE ORDER'S COMPOUND, I WAS SHOVED INTO A shower by a woman who would have given the men a run for their money. I could have fought, but what was the point when they had Fred. Callaghan knew if he took him, I'd go. He'd exploited the weakness I'd allowed to slip without meaning it to. He had used it to bring me here, to bring me to this place where I was nothing and no one other than a womb to be used.

I showered and slipped into the green scrubs they gave me, not bothering to use glamour to hide the marks that marred my flesh. I turned, eyeing the woman who flinched as she took in the pain clearly visible without the blood covering my face.

"This way," she said. Silently, I followed behind her as we made our way through white hallways and rooms lit by fluorescent lightbulbs that buzzed. Men moved about as others stood guard at every exit we passed. "They've tripled the guards and sealed every way in or out of the compound just for you. If you're thinking to escape, know that it won't happen."

Her words didn't deserve an answer, so I remained silent until we stopped in front of a room. I was led inside, and once there, I stared at the chains that adorned the medical bed. I jumped up on it, sealing one hand before I held my other out as she sealed it. Her chocolate brown eyes held mine briefly before she shook her head and stepped back.

"They will be in shortly to run some tests."

"Callaghan?" I asked.

"He is not within the compound at this time," she said. "He's gone hunting."

"Oh," I said.

"She's ready," she said into an intercom. Her eyes rested on me a moment before she turned, leaving the room and me in it.

Men moved into the room. One that seemed familiar, and then Rhett slid inside, leaning against the wall as he positioned himself to observe. I watched as a tray of needles was laid onto another tray. A shiver snaked down my spine as one of the men in scrubs stepped closer, wrapping a band around my arm before he tied it off and then pushed the needle into my arm. Tube after tube was filled with my blood as he undid the tourniquet and then slid the needle out, then he pushed the tubes into a machine, and they started spinning.

"Her urine was negative," he said to the other man. He pushed a button on the machine and then read the paper it spit out. "Blood is negative, as well."

"I figured as much," the older man muttered as he turned towards me, lifting my shirt they began to inject needle after needle into my stomach. "This will keep

her subdued, as well as safe to remain in the compound. The other injections will create a fertile uterus for the fetus."

"How many fucking shots do you plan to give her?" Rhett growled as he watched them.

I moaned as my body became numb, and my mind turned fuzzy. My mouth was dry, like the entire Sahara Desert had decided to relocate to it. I closed my eyes, laughing as I envisioned the desert and the sun covering my flesh in heated kisses while animals danced around us.

"The fuck is happening?"

"Side effects of too much of the nulling medication would be my guess. Douglas wanted her unable to use the magic within the compound. The only way to manage that is to almost overdose her on it. He was aware of it."

"This is going to piss Mason off," he uttered.

"Mason is on board with the plan. He said she's unsafe here," he argued.

I didn't care. Pink bunnies were bouncing and dancing around me. I laughed louder, my hands moving to catch them as they continued to dance just out of my reach. Unicorns played in the waves on the beach and Fred was bouncing over the sand as he made his way to where I lay, watching them all frolic. *Frolic?* What *the* fuck? I blinked, turning to stare at Rhett, and his head grew larger, expanding as his hair shook. My gaze narrowed as I took in the wrongness unfolding.

"Help me," I whispered. "Help."

More and more drugs were injected. I turned my head, throwing up until everything went haywire. My body bucked and lifted from the bed at an odd angle, slamming against it as the chains on my arms sliced through my flesh and foam started to explode from my throat. The room spun around me, and my scream erupted as pain ripped through me until everything became too much.

"She's overdosing," the male said calmly, pushing a syringe into my chest.

"Mason didn't agree for you to fucking kill her, and she doesn't come back like we do, assholes. She has to fucking heal completely from within. That's enough fucking drugs."

"We need to finish the fertility medications," he said calmly as I lay there, staring at the wall, foam continuing to drip from my mouth. "She has to be fertile when Mason returns, or Douglas will want to know why and who stopped it."

"Fine, but nothing else," Rhett snarled. "She can't cast or ovulate if she's dead, and if she's dead, so are we."

Hours of shots and temperatures taken later, I was unchained from the table, and Rhett helped me to stand up as the room spun around me. He supported my weight as he washed my face off and then tossed the rag into the trash bin.

He moved us down winding hallways that led deeper into the compound, underground with flickering lights. I swallowed bile as memories and hallucinations started to combine. I muttered to Fred, but when I looked up, it was Rhett, and even though his mouth moved, I couldn't make out what he said past the ringing in my ears.

Once we reached the lowest level, he turned on

the light and cameras beeped to life in each corner of
the room. He moved towards the glass room that sat
in the center of it, and I screamed, fighting against him
as everything inside of me came to life. I scratched,
ripping at his flesh as I sobbed and screamed while he
pushed me into the room and slammed the door closed
behind me. He watched me as I stared out at him as a
sob of horror erupted.

"No, not again, no!" I screamed. I ripped at my
hair as I fell to the ground, screaming as fear and pain
collided, and then everything just stopped. Blackness
consumed me as memories replayed in my mind, and
I stared, unseeing, through the glass at the kids who
laughed and hurt me, watching me die over and over
again.

CHAPTER
twenty-three

I WASN'T SURE HOW LONG I LAY THERE ON THE COLD concrete floor. Hours, days, longer? It seemed endless. Men would come, prod me, check my temperature, and then just as quickly as they had come, they vanished again. I know I stopped living on that floor. The fear and pain that had taken me back to my childhood dug in so deep that I couldn't escape it. I couldn't move to get up off of the floor. I lay there, unmoving, uncaring what happened as memories flooded my mind, slamming in harder with each one.

Rhett would come once in a while, speaking to me through the glass, but I never talked back. I wasn't sure if I even blinked anymore. I never answered any of them when they spoke, because they weren't real. None of this was real. I stayed on the floor, unable to move as if my spine had been severed again. Days into my captivity, I heard him.

A pounding on the glass forced my sightless eyes to focus, and they touched upon the blue eyes as familiar as my own. I pushed off the ground, staring at Callaghan as he shouted for the key. His eyes filled with pain as he took in my dirty body, my matted hair, and I growled, walking towards him weakly. His hand turned flat against the glass, and I stared at it before I looked back at him.

"I'm getting you out of there," he growled, and I laughed.

My head slammed against the glass as I stared at him, watching the horror play out on his face as hit after hit smashed against the glass until it cracked. I dropped to my knees, staring at him while the room spun around me. My body dropped and then shouting erupted. I exhaled the pain, breathing in death, the familiar tang of it soothing me to the nothingness I craved. Everything within me closed down, even his touch as he grabbed me from the cell and started carrying me to the medical ward.

CALLAGHAN

I'd killed Arthur over and over again, hunting him and his men down until the fight within me fled, and yet Rhett's incessant calls continued. I'd ignored it, knowing damn well it was about her. The one woman in this world who could kill me, and I couldn't bring myself to fight her anymore. I'd ignored it over and over again until Uther had slammed his hand against my chest.

"Your girl is in trouble," he growled.

"She isn't my girl anymore," I snapped coldly. "She doesn't want me; I can't keep dancing around it with her."

"Nah, she doesn't. She doesn't want anything. She won't eat, she doesn't speak, and she pissed herself," he snarled back.

"What?" I asked as I wiped the blood from my sword on the cloak of the last traitor I'd slaughtered moments earlier.

"You heard me; she isn't functioning. They threw her into that fucking cage, and she just stopped *everything*."

"What cage? She's supposed to be in my room, which I'm sure she has fucking destroyed by now."

"Your father wouldn't allow it until you returned. It was too much trouble to have her that far away from the medical ward; something about temperatures and tests. He tossed her into some fucking glass box that Arthur had made last year to house magical beings."

"What fucking box?" I demanded as I started for my mount.

"Apparently, he had a room made of glass. Said that it was needed for a special breed of magic wielders, and had the scientist build it last year."

"Is Erie in a glass fucking room? Tell me they weren't that fucking stupid!" I shouted as everything inside of me went deadly calm, and I imagined her inside of it, locked into that fucking room she'd been placed in as a mere child.

"Your father assured them that it would withstand her magic in the event that the injections didn't work."

I rounded on him, punching him in the face even though it wasn't his fault. "Erie was in a cage like that when I found her after they'd snapped her fucking spine while beating her. Why the hell would he do that?"

"I'm guessing because Arthur told him it would

hold her, should you fail to impregnate her."

"Let's fucking go," I snapped as I mounted the horse, taking off before the others had a chance to catch up. Once they closed in around me, we rode through the clusterfuck apocalypse as if the riders of hell had been freed and were given chase. "How long has she been in there?" I shouted over the thundering hooves.

"Since she got there," Uther answered, and my stomach flipped before it sank.

She wouldn't be easy to deal with after being in that cage, if she even fucking came back from it this time. Last time, she'd been so fucking gone by the time I'd found her that she'd wasted away to nothing more than an emaciated skeleton, unable to die.

At the gates, I shouted out the orders, never slowing the horse until I was at the steps, pushing past those who watched or waited to see what we brought back. The hallways were crowded as I forced myself through them, heading directly to the elevator and slamming my finger into the button as the others caught up to me.

"You need to calm down; you can't help her like this." I glared at Uther, the one man who should have told me the moment he'd learned of it. "No, no, you don't get to put this shit on me or anyone else. I wasn't the one who ignored the calls or the emergency notifications that Rhett has been sending you for days. You ignored it because you're fucking furious that your girl isn't yours at all." We entered the elevator, and I glared at him. "I don't know what you want me to say. I get that what she did was harsh, and out of every time she'd ever killed you, there had never been malice involved until now. That girl is fighting for her freedom, something she knows she needs, and yet realizes she's never tasted. Even England realized the horror of that when the Scots refused to kneel. The Irish were the same, a rare breed that doesn't know how to surrender."

We hit the bottom level, and I pushed past them, heading straight for where they'd have placed the cell. I could make out her matted hair, the filth of her clothes, and the weight she'd lost in the few days I'd been gone.

"Where's the fucking key?" I snapped, staring down at her as she lifted those sightless eyes towards where I stood. "Erie," I whispered as I watched her stand up, rising to her feet. I flinched at the emptiness in her eyes as she placed her head against the glass where my hand rested. "I've got you. I'm getting you out of there."

I turned, staring at Uther, who was flinching and recoiling against the mess she'd become. I didn't care if she was covered in filth; I wanted her out of the fucking box right fucking now. I turned, looking back at her as her head slammed against the glass. Blood covered the glass as, again and again, her face smashed into it, her sightless eyes glazed over.

"Bloody hell," Uther whispered. "The fucking key now or I'll take your godforsaken nuts!" he shouted into the intercom as the room exploded into motion. Her legs gave out, and then she fell to her side, blood pouring from her mouth, nose, and eyes.

The moment the door opened, I was inside, picking her up, rushing her towards the medical ward. I didn't say a thing. Uther shouted orders as I placed her on a table and pushed her hair away from her face, hissing as I took in the swelling and shattered bones in her cheeks and forehead.

"Move," the medical staff shouted, but I didn't fucking budge. I kneeled, holding her hand as I prayed to the Gods to save her, to bring her back from where she'd gone in order to survive the cage again.

"We're losing her," the doctor shouted as Uther grabbed me, yanking me out of their way.

"You can't save her, and neither will our God. He abandoned us when we agreed to betray him and the Holy Lands. He won't be answering those prayers." Uther's stare held mine as frustration tore through me.

"Neither will fucking medicine," I snapped, pushing the doctors away from her as I picked her up. "I need holy water, help me, Uther," I demanded as I moved towards the elevator.

"She will die," the doctor snapped.

"She will not die; Erie was born dead until I brought her to life. I brought her to life again after that, and I will do it again. I will always bring her back to me."

CHAPTER
twenty four

I MOVED INTO THE BATHROOM, NOT STOPPING UNTIL we had entered the shower and Rhett turned on the water, staring me down. I wanted them out of here, but to save her, I needed them. I hated that I'd trusted anyone else with her, and yet I'd needed space so that I hadn't gone off on her, or done something irrevocably bad that I wouldn't have been able to take back.

"Turn on the hot water," I requested as I sat on the floor, pulling off her light blue scrub top. The bottoms took effort, and Rhett didn't hesitate, moving into the shower beneath the spray to help me remove them. "Beneath the cupboard is the lavender soap, hand it to me. What the fuck happened, Rhett?"

"They brought her into the medical ward and started the injections to null her powers," he said as he bent over, digging through the cupboard until he pulled out the boxes of soap, the same ones I'd had made and left where she could find them for the last seventy-five years. "They pushed too much, and she OD'd badly,

and I made them stop pushing it, but fuck, it was bad. Your father ordered it, and no matter what I said, they wouldn't listen. They didn't stop the fertility drugs, and afterward, I put her in that fucking box as I was ordered, and started calling you. You didn't answer."

"You should have called Uther sooner," I snapped as I used the soap to wash the filth from her, water running red with the blood that seeped from her head.

"It's not like I did nothing," he argued. "I sat beside that cell, and I did tell your father that he was breaking her by placing her in there. I was with you the last time this happened, and I remembered it. I fucking put her in it, Mason. I did it because I don't have the power to override your father, only you do, and you left us," he swallowed as he grabbed a washcloth, pushing it over her head, which was already beginning to mend. "She isn't pregnant," he stated, dropping the cloth into the shower and staring at her in horror.

"The last fucking time this happened, it took almost an entire year to bring her back, and he still did it." I couldn't believe he'd be so fucking stupid, or that he would let Arthur build a replica of the same fucking room the druids had put her in as a child when it had been Arthur's fault the last time she had been caged.

Uther snorted from the doorway. "He didn't care if she was coherent, Mason. To him, she is merely the cure. There is no person attached to it, no soul. He doesn't know what you have been through to save her, nor does he fucking care. He only agreed to allow you time because you are his son."

"I gave this girl my fucking name," I growled.

"You gave that girl your heart the day you cut her

from the rotten placenta that still held her. Before then, way before then, if we're going to be honest here," he returned softly. He walked over to the tub, nodding towards it as the younger lads entered, dumping the buckets of holy water into the tub while he turned on the hot water.

I watched them in silence as they worked together, adding the raw lavender into the water while candles were lit around the far edge of the tub. Erie hadn't moved yet, hadn't made a fucking sound, but she was warm, still alive.

"Don't you fucking leave me," I uttered against her ear. "Stay with me, Erie, stay with me." My throat bobbed against the words, and the moment the lads were finished, I lifted her and moved her to the tub. Uther held his arms out, and I stared him down, unwilling to let him take her even for a moment.

"You can't get in the tub with your armor on, asshole. Give me the girl and get undressed so I can hand her to you," he growled, watching me closely. "It isn't like we haven't done this shit before. She's just older now."

I shook my head, handing her slight weight to him as I ripped off the soaked armor and clothes, before stepping into the tub to take her, uncaring that Rhett was about to make monster dick remarks as he snorted.

"Of all the blessings you got, I envy that one the most," he snorted, his eyes alight with silent laughter. "How the ladies would love me even more if I wielded that sword."

"You think it a blessing?" I snorted as I settled into the water, lifting my arms to accept Erie's unconscious form. I position her between my legs, holding her head out of the water as I cradle it against my chest. The moan that escaped her lips punched me in the gut.

"I think the monster within you made sure it was larger than most. Although, I'm still the better lover," he shrugged as he spoke. "I'll guard the door, I'm guessing that you don't want anyone else inside your apartment?" he asked.

"I don't want anyone coming in until she's healed," I agreed.

"And Arthur?" Uther asked.

"Fuck him, he can't get to her while she's here, now can he?" I challenged as my hand cradled her chin. I took in the damage to her face. It was swollen enough that she hardly looked human, let alone female.

"You need to face the fact that she may have brain damage after she smashed her head against the glass," Uther said as he knelt. Staring at her, he reached out and touched her forehead. "You may have to kill her, and pray she comes back quickly."

"Erie didn't smash her head against the glass, at least not consciously. They placed her into an exact replica of the room she was locked within for months. Her mind snapped; combine that with the drugs they gave her and she wasn't aware of what she was doing. She was only trying to get out of the cage, away from it. Her mind probably told her that death would be easier than allowing her mind to break again. That was her flight kicking in, the need to survive whatever happened at all costs."

"That's some fucking instinct," he replied as he grabbed a towel and dried his hair off. "You do know that if she doesn't come back, you'll still need to do what is needed, right? He won't let everyone die. Neither would you, no matter what happens. We swore an oath to protect them, to do it at all costs. The price you paid, Mason. The price you paid to keep us alive, to have that girl born, it was the highest cost of any of us. You can't let that sacrifice be in vain."

I closed my eyes against the memories that his words evoked. The memories of a blue-eyed child who smiled at me as if I'd hung the moon just for him. No, Rhett was fucking right. I wouldn't let my son's death be in vain. His life was the cost I paid to allow the cure to be created, the same cure that would save our people. Carolina had cursed me to hell for it, and I hadn't blamed her for it. Our son's life was taken so that others could live.

"Get the fuck out," I uttered as I inhaled the smell of her hair, drinking in the scent that was my sanity. She may have used the soap to escape the past, but to me, she was the escape from the sins I'd committed to save the Templars, to protect the guardians of the Outer Realms, who defended mankind against those monsters getting into this one. No matter what our past had been, she was my salvation, my home.

We kept the other monsters out of this world, and if we died, this world would be lost. Not to mention, we protected this realm from the invasion of other races, like the ones that the world thought were wiped out so long ago. So I'd done what it took, kept a promise that I'd made thousands of years ago. When the witches had cursed us, I'd made a deal with the druids to save both of the races from the curse. But it had come with a heavy price, one that had taken a piece of my soul,

and I'd killed the one thing I had craved the most soon after. The cure, it had cost my son his life, and with it, I'd watched everything fall apart until I'd walked into the decrepit church to ensure it wasn't all for nothing, only to find Erie unmoving in the placenta they'd left on the floor.

Evil, the nuns had called her. Satan's blood; no, no, she was much darker than that. She was created of the oldest magic in this world. I'd knelt, pulling the sac away from her, and then lifted her from the cold, icy floor. She hadn't moved, born premature and too tiny to survive in a world that cruel and unforgiving. My mouth had covered her face, and I'd blown my air into her lungs, and then closed my eyes as I'd prayed to any God who hadn't abandoned us. When I'd looked back down at her, wide blue eyes stared up at me, unhappy that I'd stolen her death from her. As if she'd sensed the life she would live even at the first moment it began.

"I'm going to tell you a story, Erie."

CHAPTER
twenty-five

ERIE

I LISTENED AS HE SPOKE, UNSURE WHETHER IT WAS true or not. The sound of his voice comforted me, sending the pain away as his hand stroked over my ribcage. I could feel Uther watching from the doorway, where he protected his lord master while he tended to me.

"It was a beautiful day," Callaghan uttered thickly. "I had just whittled a wooden sword for Evan. A small one, as he was only a tiny lad of five winters. I watched him light up as he took in what I had made him, and at that moment, I never loved anything or anyone more than I did him. My son, with my eyes and my hair," he said hoarsely, adjusting his hold, cradling me closer as if I gave him comfort.

"He died the night I gave him that sword. The cost I paid to create the cure for what the witches had done to our people. I'd made a deal with the druids themselves to heal our people and save us all. I knew they had the cauldron, and so we worked together to save our sorry asses. If we died, creatures like the ones that lived outside of this world would be free to bring war and plagues of which this world had never known before. We agreed to protect this world, and our race is the one thing that stands between the walls of this world and the ancient ones from cracking and crumbling. Lucian Blackstone, his seal only brought down a few walls, lesser walls. What we protect is so much more, so much worse.

"There once was a maiden, one so beautiful and pure that to look upon her was a privilege men died for. She ruled a race that protected this one from invasions and worse things than you could ever imagine. She brought men to their knees with a simple look, but she left this world. We continued to protect it, no matter the cost, and we became the Templar Knights. While the world thought we merely protected pilgrims, we protected the realm from the monsters who sought to destroy it."

I heard Uther exhale as Callaghan kissed the side of my head. "The witches were among the creatures who wanted the others to enter this world, to bring those who challenged them and their magic to their knees. The witches sacrificed humans to these monsters by the village-full. They slaughtered women, children, and men as a sacrifice to the monsters that they wanted to bring here, but we had sealed the gates, preventing it," he whispered. "When their actions drew the eye of the king and others, we were called to hunt them down and deliver God's justice upon them. We'd warned the witches to stop, to quit before it became too late for them, and yet they refused. As dawn approached, the Order set them afire, burning them at the stake as a warning to any others brazen enough to continue their foolish evil ways. We'd predicted the curse, having already agreed to pay, whatever the cost, in order to secure the line, keeping those who needed and deserved the cure, safe from the darkness.

"On that day of my sacrifice and all others to be paid, I grieved, and as I did, I knew hate for the first time. So I did what was needed of me. The druids agreed and told me of the cauldron and where it would appear during the moon cycle. They told us how to secure a child of both races. They told me of the evil and light that it would create, the purest of both races mixed into one female, who would be mine. I raced to Scotland where the cauldron was hidden, while Uther and Lance set about finding your parents. Jacques's own daughter was your mother. Your father was the strongest, highest ranking druid of age who could father a child. They were pushed into the cauldron and drank of the darkness within. It wasn't a fast process. I waited in the village for weeks, and then months, until rumor came that they'd emerged. They weren't the same people who had gone into that cauldron. Your mother was pure when she'd gone into it, but something changed. They nested as if they had grown something evil inside that cauldron.

"Then her belly began to grow round with child. I still waited with my men to see what we had done. We waited to know if we had cursed this world to its end. On the day you were born, a great storm filled the world. It was unlike anything the Knight's and I have ever witnessed. I made my way to the church, knowing whatever was happening, it was the center of it all. I entered the church, and there, on the floor, was this

mass of blood and muck. I bent down, touching it, and this tiny perfect face was inside of it. I freed you, I freed you and then I blew air into your tiny premature lungs. Erie, you never cried. You just stared at me as if I had somehow cheated you of death. This tiny, fierce little female glared up at me with bright blue eyes and red hair and looked as if she wanted to beat me. I named you outside of that church; I named you after the land from which you were created. Erie, Erie of Ireland, with eyes the color of the skies after the rain had gone and the sun had filled the land; with hair as wild and untamed as the land itself.

"I took you to the druids and left you. They were warned of how precious you were. I marked you with my name, giving you my protection to ensure no harm came upon you. I left you there, thinking you would be treasured by all. I stayed close enough that I often was able to watch you as you grew. You were the wildest child I'd ever seen. So fearless as you did everything the other children couldn't do yet. I went to war though, and when I did, everything changed. I returned after ten years, ten long years and not a day had gone by that I hadn't received a report of the progress you'd made. Lies, every fucking one of them had been lies. On the last letter I had received as the battle ended, I noticed that it no longer spoke of you. Only that the female had shown darkness and had left them wondering who your true parents had been. You had mastered what their most skilled druids could not. You excelled at everything you ever tried to do. You fucking terrified them, and when I figured that out, we rushed back to you.

"I found you in a glass room, beaten and broken," he swallowed as he exhaled. "Just like the one my father put you in. When I found you with the druids that day, I left you with Uther as I hunted them down and allowed the monster within me to feast on the flesh of those who had tortured you. I killed them all, and I know I stole them from you, taking your revenge. I couldn't stop it because to me you were just an innocent girl who had the misfortune of being the purest, most beautiful thing this world had ever created.

"We took you from that place of hatred that day, to my home, where I bathed you in lavender to rid your body of the filth you laid in for months. You were unable to die, but you might as well have been dead to this world. I fed you, held you, and sang to you of the land of which I'd named you after. I pleaded to any God who would still hear my prayers to heal you. I begged them to take me in your place should they be merciful enough to listen. Eventually, your body healed, but your mind was so far gone that nothing I did brought you back. One day, as I sat in my bed, cradling your unmoving body as I am again today, you looked up at me as if you had never been gone at all.

"You asked me once if I knew it had been you who murdered every male druid you'd ever befriended, and I did. I watched you hunt them down. I was there, Erie. I watched you cut them up as you took everything that they had used to hurt you from them. Only once did you ever see me, and the look in your eyes was the darkest magic of creatures staring out of the most perfect blue eyes." His thumb trailed over my cheek as he pushed the hair away from my face.

His chest trembled beneath me as he sat up, pulling me with him, and he whispered against my neck. "On that rocky cliff that I named you upon, I felt you with me. I felt something so deep inside of me stirring that it terrified me. You are the mate to that which crawls beneath my flesh. You were created for me and me alone. You were born of the greatest sacrifice, and the monster within me knew it long before I did, how much you would come to mean to us. That first look into your eyes and everything clicked into place like a puzzle that had been scattered coming together by a power greater than anyone could ever know. In the woods, I felt it again. I should have been abhorred by what you did to them, and instead, the monster within me preened, as if he couldn't have been more proud of you for finally fighting back." He lifted me without warning, and I groaned as my head swam, my vision blurring as Uther accepted me, allowing Callaghan to step out of the bath and reach for a towel.

"Is she awake?" Uther asked, his shamrock green eyes watching me. I mumbled as I struggled to lift my head.

"No, she's not back yet," Callaghan said as he grabbed my chin, tilting my eyes to where he could see them. "Her pupils are blown," he muttered. Uther held me up as Callaghan wrapped me in a towel, slowly picking me up, before he walked us into his room, dimming the lights as he placed me on the bed. When he'd finished with the lights, he crawled into bed, naked, pulling me against his flesh. "That day I came to collect you, I knew you were beyond my reach. I knew you'd never come to me willingly, and neither I nor my men blame you. We failed you, called to duty by the Order, and every time I returned, you were worse off, farther to reach. One day I watched you outside of the Druid's Den, and your eyes were dead. As if there was nothing that could reach you or change what you had become. Two days later, I watched you at a fair as your eyes lit up with the wonder of a child. You watched the rides as you inhaled the cotton candy that filled the air. You were filled with wonder. I want to watch you look at me like that, Erie. I want to watch you look at the son we will create with that wonder in your eyes. I promise you, he will be loved," he whispered huskily.

I closed my eyes, unable to hear more as sleep took hold and memories replayed in my mind. He was there, through everything, and yet he'd failed to help me. He'd always chosen duty to the cross above all else. I inhaled the lavender as my mind wandered to another time, where every instance he'd told me of us replayed, but so many more.

Callaghan had spent my entire life protecting me. He'd healed me without telling me. I remembered him in the woods, but it hadn't been him. It had been a winged creature, one who promised me that I was his and that one day, everything that happened to me would fade away as he loved me *again*. Callaghan had huge leathery wings that had welcomed me into them, and his mouth had brushed across mine, and I'd felt the truth he'd offered. The issue was the promises he had made me were of a darker world, one devoid of life or humans, only other creatures that I didn't know or understand: A world where he and I ruled side by side, in the land of the damned that had long ago died off. A race that hadn't made sense, and yet I'd craved to be among them. To know their world, and their story because somehow, I knew I belonged in it with them.

CHAPTER

twenty-six

His hands touched me, holding me as if I was a shattered, broken thing that his touch could heal. As if he held onto me tight enough, he could hold my broken pieces together. It hurt, knowing that he'd always been close to me, protecting me, and that I'd failed to ever notice him there; that every time I fell, he picked me back up.

I could have been honest and told him I had full access to my brain, but I didn't. I lay there in his arms, replaying the memories of him that I'd forgotten as he slept, unaware of the turmoil rushing through my mind. Escape was a must, but I wouldn't leave without Fred.

I exhaled as he pulled me closer, cradling me into the comfort of his body that smelled like heaven. The rich scent of masculinity and earth and wood, as if he was created of the world itself, and no matter how much I tried to ignore it, I drank it in like an addict, unable to get enough. My eyes closed as my body pushed against his on instinct.

His growl resonated deep from his chest and escaped his lips. Callaghan's fingers dragged over my hip, dancing over my flesh as I pretended to be incoherent. He rose, placing kisses against my shoulder as he slowly pulled away, leaving the bed silently. I listened, hearing the door close behind him as he left the room. I continued to pretend to be asleep as arguing ensued from the other room.

I knew the voices, knew his father was demanding he finish the job or he'd find another Knight willing to mount my incapacitated body. Callaghan shouted back, his tone murderous as he defended me for what his father had done. It lessened the blow to realize he wasn't willing to mount me in my current state and that unless they wanted a fight, they'd back off.

Doors slammed, and then Callaghan was in the room, his scent drifting to me. He paced the floor, only stopping to touch my face as he pulled the blankets over my shoulder. It was an intimate gesture that offered comfort as he moved to his closet, shuffling through it for clothes before he entered his bathroom, leaving the door open as he turned on the water.

Music started, and I opened my eyes, listening as the water flow was disturbed by his body. KALEO's *Way Down We Go* played from within. My eyes closed once more, imagining his hands as he ran them over his flesh with heady soap, creating his scent that I craved.

There was also the familiar scent of lavender that clung to my flesh. I swallowed the memories of another time, another place that I'd been broken.

He'd held me, singing the hymns of the Celtic people as I'd lain in his arms, a broken shell of the

budding woman I'd been growing into. He'd held me as my innocence had been shattered. As my mind slowly worked to piece back what had been broken. This man who gave me freedom, but also took it away, terrified me.

How had I missed the familiarity of his touch? Forgotten the heady scent of his body that I'd once craved as an adolescent girl who had felt his arousal without knowing what it was. Back then, I'd been old enough to become his wife at that tender age of fifteen; in fact, I'd been older than most wives, and yet he hadn't taken what I'd offered him.

I remembered it now. My clumsy kisses as I'd tried to coax him into hurting me. I'd needed to feel his hands while he'd punished me for what I was. I'd craved the darkness of him, begging him as I climbed his body, naked with a crazed need to be hurt by him.

His hands had bitten into my hips, growling with raw hunger as I'd begged him to make me a woman. He'd refused. He'd told me he would never take me like that, in my current state. I'd ripped my clothes off in front of that man, climbing him until he pulled me off of him. He'd stared at me as if I was crazed, but his hand had cupped my face as he'd fought against his baser need to do as I had asked of him.

Those fingers had drifted to my tits, touching them as he'd stared me in the eyes, and then the look of disgust on his face had been a brutal slap in the face. It had told me the truth of what he'd thought of me. He'd pushed me away from him and stormed from the room as if the hellhounds had broken free of the underworld and were chasing him. I'd cried myself to sleep in the bed we'd shared, dejected, and ashamed of myself and who I was.

Still, he'd returned that night and held me, whispering into my ear of what I would become, and how I'd understand when I was older. I didn't. I didn't understand any of it, other than the rejection. I'd thought the beating I had earned might have been my fault, which my ugliness might have brought that boy to me. I was bad, everything inside of me so vile and ugly that not even the Knight who fought to bring me back would touch me.

The water turned off, and I sat up, staring at the door as he exited with a towel wrapped around his hips. His eyes locked with mine as the music continued to play. I let the blanket drop as he moved deeper into the room.

"Erie," he whispered softly as he moved towards me.

I pushed the covers from the bed, staring at him as he watched me. He stopped at the edge of the bed, staring down at me with an unspoken question in his turbulent turquoise depths. I watched as he ran his hand over his mouth, staring at me as I decided the next step.

"I'm not a child anymore, Mason," I whispered huskily.

"You don't have to do this," he said, watching me as if I was an apparition that would disappear if he blinked.

I stood up slowly, knowing I wasn't fully healed, but I was healed enough to decide I wanted this. The room filled with his magic, and I stifled a moan as I pulled the towel from his hips. His mouth brushed against mine, and he lifted me, kissing me as if he could put every emotion he felt into it. It was brutal and beautiful.

Chaos filled us as I captured his tongue, sucking against it while he slowly lowered us to the bed.

"Mason," I whimpered as he pushed against my opening.

"God save us, woman," he muttered as he pushed into the wetness and slowly drove his need inside my welcoming heat. He stretched me until I moaned against his hungry mouth, lifting my hips to take him into my body. He was raised up on his arm, pulling his mouth from mine as he stared into my eyes.

He was slow, careful with me as he took me over the edge, watching as I arched off of the bed and exploded into a million pieces of broken glass. I rolled him, staring down into his glowing eyes as he watched me. My hips lifted, rocking against the massive cock that throbbed against my insides. His hands lowered, settling on my hips as he let me set the pace, watching, I stared at where we joined.

He didn't speak, not even as I rode him until I threw my head back, screaming to the saints as I came undone around him. His hands lifted me, slamming my body down on his too thick, too large cock that only forced another orgasm to shatter me around him. He worked my body, watching my face as wonder and chaos pushed through me, and I couldn't seem to escape the pleasure that coursed through me. The moment I thought I would die from the bliss he gave me, he rolled us, slamming his mouth against mine while he pushed into my body with utter slowness that drove me mad.

His hands captured mine, pinning them above my head. He continued to kiss me, his tongue slowly devouring me as it followed the rhythmic tempo of his cock, and the music seemed to grow louder. That same song played in the room, filling it as he fucked me until we both screamed, our bodies releasing together.

He stared down at me with a look I'd never seen in his eyes before. I swallowed a sob as he leaned over, placing soft kisses over my face and he grew hard inside my body. He didn't stop taking me until we were both boneless, unable to go on. When we lay there in the silence of the room, I curled into his heat, tracing my hand over his chest.

"I'm sorry I bit you," I whispered huskily. "I thought it was another shot to create a child," I admitted. "I thought you betrayed me."

"Erie, I can't say that I won't make a child with you, or that I will stop trying to save my people. I sacrificed what I loved most in this word to achieve this goal. I won't ever stop."

I nodded. "I won't ever stop fighting you, either."

"I never expected you to," he admitted.

"Why didn't you tell me you saved me before?"

"I didn't want you to think you owed me. I didn't want you to ever feel as if you owed me for that, because you don't. I failed you, and that is why you were there in the first place."

"I tried to be with you then, but you rejected me. I need to know why."

"Because you weren't ready for me," he uttered as his fingers drifted over my shoulder.

"I knew what I wanted," I whispered.

"No, you wanted to feel loved. You wouldn't have felt loved if I had fucked you. You'd have felt used. I wanted you that day; I wanted you so fucking bad. You weren't ready for me, not really. I'd have broken you with how much I needed you, and you were so fucking frail already. I wanted to write my name on your soul, but you didn't have one yet. I knew the look that filled your eyes, swimming in your vision. The need to destroy everything that could save you, which right then was me. You wanted pain, to be hurt because it was what you knew. I wouldn't let you add me to the list of people you wanted to hurt. You would have, Erie. You were self-destructing, and you couldn't see it, but I could. That was why I remained close, watching as you murdered those boys. I found you in the woods, naked, bathing in their blood, and there was nothing human left in you. You don't remember it, but I took you from those woods and locked you up. I brought the human inside of you back into this world."

"I remember," I stated as I lifted and stared down at him, letting my hand drift over his chiseled, hard chest, touching over the tattoos I'd once found different and vile, that I now found appealing. "What I don't understand is why you named me Erie Callaghan, if you knew my parents and who they were."

"It seemed right," he uttered as his fingers trailed over the curve of my breast, skimming over the nipple before he lifted his head, claiming one. I moaned as he lifted me, pushing me down on his cock, and a throaty groan escaped past my lips. "I don't know why, Erie, but I know that even then, I knew you were mine. I felt it as I stared into your eyes as if everything in the world had just fallen into place, and you were created for me." He lifted me, slowly directing me down until he was buried within the heat of my body. "You are mine, that much I do promise you." I heard the lie in his words, but I wasn't sure what, or which it had been. I didn't much care at this moment either.

"Is that so?" I asked, staring down into his eyes.

"Does this not feel right to you?" he asked as he lifted me only to slam me back down hard against his length.

"Just because I fucked you, doesn't mean I agree to be yours," I warned softly as I let him control the speed with which he took me.

"Mmm, there she is," he chuckled as I screamed and he slammed into me punishingly. "I wouldn't assume anything with you," he whispered hoarsely. "But I do expect you to come on my cock, again. How many times would the next one make, sweet Erie? How many times has this tight cunt come for me tonight?"

"I lost count," I moaned through the beginning of an orgasm.

"Start counting," he urged as he rolled us and started moving with purpose. I exploded and whispered his name, over and over again as he took me soaring to the clouds. "Good girl, now do it again for me."

CHAPTER

twenty-seven

"WHAT AM I SUPPOSED TO WEAR?" I ASKED AS WE climbed out of the shower. I was sore from his insatiable appetite to have me at his mercy, screaming his name. But I wanted normalcy, whatever that was. I needed to leave his little room and get fresh air, feel the sun on my face, and just live. Not remain camped out in his bedroom for the rest of my days.

In fact, if he had his way, I was sure I'd never leave the bed, and neither would he. It had been endless days of us doing the same routine: bathing, eating, sex, and more sex. Not that I was complaining; if there was one thing I liked about him, it was what he did to me in his bed for endless hours. The soreness between my legs was a small price to pay for that.

"You don't need clothes, Erie," he chuckled as he picked me up and set me onto the smooth countertop of the bathroom. His thick cock slid through the heated folds of my flesh, finding it already wet and needy to be filled by him.

"I want clothes; you cannot just expect me to sit in bed and wait for you," I countered as I pushed him away with my foot, letting my knee drop to the side so he could see just how wet and needy my pussy was for him. "No clothes, no sex, Callaghan," I moaned as I pushed my finger through my pussy, sliding it into the heat of my body.

"You think you can stop? Half of the time we fuck, you're the one who instigates it," he mused as his eyes watched my finger with smoldering heat. His hand stroked his cock as he waited for me to concede and cave to my baser needs.

"I want clothes, but I also want Fred brought up here. After you've done that, you can fuck me all you want, Paladin."

"No," he said as his hand stalled, ceasing his endless stroking that I'd been watching with a hunger I couldn't hide in my gaze. My eyes lifted to his, finding them narrowed with anger as he shook his head. "Fred, as you prefer to call him, is a High Prince of Hell, Erie. He is a fucking head demon in Hell's army. That isn't fucking happening, ever. You have no reason to be dressed. I prefer you naked and waiting for me when I return to this room."

"So, I'm still your prisoner?" I whispered as my hand lifted to the edge of the counter, and I jumped off. I watched all the emotion flee from his face as coldness replaced the lust.

He turned, striding from the bathroom as I followed behind him, unwilling to let him avoid the issue. He moved into the closet, grabbing clothes that he brought out and placed on the bed. I swallowed the anger that pulsed through me, red-hot and violent as he ignored me.

"You're not leaving here. End of discussion," he growled as he began dressing.

"So, I am your prisoner, to have and to fuck whenever you desire it?" I asked carefully.

"Erie, I wouldn't do that," he snarled as he watched me move towards the door, intending to leave the room stark ass naked.

"I'm your whore!" I screamed as everything came crashing down on me. I spun on my heel, heading out of the room as I growled from deep in my chest, entering the outer room without warning; his men's sharp intake of air told me they'd seen everything he refused to allow me to cover.

"Get the fuck back in there," he demanded angrily. "Look away, assholes," he snapped, following me until he was inches away.

I opened the cupboards, slamming them closed as I searched for the coffee. My breathing was chaotic as I realized I was to him, and it played through my head. I'd given myself to him, it was something only I could give, and he'd taken it, yet I was nothing more than willing flesh for him to use when he wanted? Oh, hell no. Let's not forget his main goal to put his child in my womb.

"Don't fucking move, Erie," Callaghan warned thickly, his voice strangled as he gave warning.

I had just started to turn around to tell him right where he could shove his order when the air around me grew thicker, turning deadly as I was picked up and bent over the counter with my ass in the air. Claws slid over my flesh, and I groaned as my hips slammed against the marble. I was unable to touch the floor with my toes as I remained there, knowing that whatever was behind me was deadly and powerful. It slithered over my flesh with magic as claws bit into my skin without pushing through. A whimper of fear left my throat as something leaned against my back, kissing its way up my spine until it whispered huskily against my ear as heat skimmed my flesh.

"Hello, pretty," he hissed as he kissed my ear and dragged his heated lips over my neck.

Hands slid to mine, slipping through as I watched. Black claws longer than my fingers slid over my flesh, pushing against my hands that lay flat on the countertop.

"You shouldn't have tried me," he warned. "Now you will be punished, sweet girl," he laughed huskily, his voice altered as he kissed the back of my head. "It's time you learned who you really belong to."

His hands left mine, twisting my head until I looked into glowing blue eyes that I knew intimately. His eyes were familiar, which told me that Callaghan was a part of this thing, but that was where the familiarity ended. His skin was black as night, covered in glowing blue tattoos that matched the markings of my face. I swallowed a sob as he watched me take him in, from the leathery black wings that expanded behind him to the fact that he was well over seven feet tall. He stared down at me with a wicked grin, enjoying the fear that exuded from me. He released my hair as his hand slowly pushed against my spine, watching me tremble at what was happening. Magic slithered over me, raw and electrical as it created an ache deep in my center.

My eyes closed as his finger slid over my ass, and

his knuckle slid through the slick mess of longing that I couldn't hide. I expelled a cry as he continued to rub against it, slipping those lethal claws precariously close to the delicate flesh of my pussy. His heated breath followed the path his fingers had taken until it warmed my flesh, pushing his tongue against my opening.

"My dirty little girl," he growled as his tongue pushed into my body and a shock of pleasure ripped through me.

I screamed as he laughed darkly, using his tongue inside of me as it curled and touched places no tongue should ever be able to reach. It swelled, filling me until I moaned as my body trembled around him. Noises filled the room, his and mine, as his tongue fucked my body, and I let him. I exploded without warning, and he made a noise as if he'd tasted the most exquisite delicacy created by a five Michelin-star chef. He didn't stop, his hand slid up my spine, gripping my hair as he pulled my pussy back into his face and continued fucking me until I was sobbing while the most terrifyingly beautiful orgasm ripped me apart.

"So fucking pink and delicate," he growled as he withdrew his mouth from my pussy and pushed something too large to fit against my opening, and into me. Whimpering, I pulled away as fear slithered up my spine. "Oh, sweet girl, you will fit me. This cunt was built to house me, and we will fit together perfectly," he warned. He pushed my head back down against the counter and his other hand lifted my hips to rest on the cold marble. He rubbed against my flesh, his wings cooling my skin as the air around us was displaced by their movement. "So soft, so fucking wet for me," he laughed, pushing into my body. My throat opened, and I screamed at his sheer size, pain consuming me as he stretched my body beyond its limits.

I shook so hard that my teeth chattered as his magic opened me further. His hand pushed against my ass as he flooded my body with his cock. I whimpered as my entire body shuddered violently around him, my hands slapping against the counter. It ached, and yet it filled me so completely that I wanted more. I wanted everything, even if he killed me to accomplish it. I wiggled my hips as he gripped them, using them to push deeper into the welcoming wetness of my pussy.

"More," I demanded huskily as he snorted his approval of my shamelessness behavior.

"Such a naughty little cunt," he growled as he withdrew from my body. "You want me to fuck that sweet little pussy until it purrs for me, you naughty little bitch?" he crooned as he flipped me over, forcing me to stare into the pure evilness that I craved.

"Yes," I breathed as my hand slid down, stroking my flesh as the orgasm threatened to take control of my mind. His hand captured mine as he smiled down at me with white, blunt teeth before they extended into fangs, exploding from his gums. That mouth lowered, skimming over one hard nipple as he licked and sucked it into his greedy mouth.

His cock pushed against the wetness that craved him, but he only fed me an inch as he sucked against my nipple hungrily. I moaned, and I rocked against him, trying to take more than he was giving me.

"Mine, Erie," he growled. "You are mine. Allow another to see what belongs to me again, and I will slaughter them all as you watch me," he growled harshly, slamming into my body without warning, enjoying the scream that ripped from my throat as he filled my body too full. He stretched me, watching me as I screamed and came around his thickness, my body jerking beneath him. "You will never escape me, for you were created for me and me alone, female. You are the queen to my king, and if you ever try me again, I will hold you down and fuck this sweet, tight cunt until you know nothing else. *He* may let you tempt the others with your sweet flesh, but I will show them exactly who you are and who you belong to," he snarled as he lifted me, sliding me down further onto his rigid cock, cradling my ass, and moving me away from the counter.

He knew it was too much, and yet he enjoyed the pain he gave me. He watched my mouth open and close, body trembling uncontrollably as he held me impaled on his inhuman cock. He grew still, testing my limits as those glowing, otherworldly eyes watched me come undone brutally around him. He lifted me slowly, staring down at where he stretched my flesh to extreme, painful levels, and then his gaze drifted to mine, holding it as he slammed me back down hard, punishingly. "You come so fucking readily for me, so fucking pink and sweet. I could drink that cunt for hours, fucking it until it was nothing but soreness. Would you like that? Would you like me to fuck that delicate flesh until it aches with pain? Answer me, woman."

"What are you?" I demanded hoarsely as another orgasm threatened to take away my ability to think.

"I'm your husband, the monster for which you were created," he laughed huskily as he lifted me from his cock. I whimpered from the loss of his heat as I was placed on my feet. He smiled as I backed up, finally able to think without him pushing me over the edge of sanity with red-hot need, allowing him to consume me. He stalked me as I walked backward, my eyes never leaving his as my bare feet moved over the tiled floor. "I am the protector of the sacred races of Ireland, but more than that, I am your husband first and foremost. You reek of fear, sweet girl. Did you really think that you were created to belong to *him? He* is only a part of this body, the part that was needed for you to accept me in your new one," he laughed cruelly.

My legs hit the edge of the bed, and then his hand lifted, pushing me back until I tumbled to the bed. Those glowing eyes slid over my flesh, leaving a searing trail where he took me in, drinking up the sight of my breakability.

"Do I scare you, woman?" he asked as he watched me through ancient eyes.

"Yes," I uttered thickly, swallowing past the lump growing in my throat.

"Good," he smiled as he continued to watch me. "Get on your knees, because I plan to fuck you until you beg me to come, and if you're a good girl, I won't hurt that sweet, tight cunt that clenches around me so nicely—well, not too much."

"I won't beg you for anything," I whispered. I watched him narrow his eyes as I scooted further onto the bed, unable to look away from his terrifying beauty.

"Oh, my sweet girl, you will beg me for everything. I am lust in the rawest form. You know that already, hence the mess that is trailing down your thighs from

your need to be fucked. Your body knows me, it remembers me. You will too eventually, sweet girl," he said as he lay on the bed while I watched him. I sat back on my haunches, waiting for him to make a move. "Give me that wet pussy; I want to fuck it with my mouth as you take my cock into the tightness of your throat." He reached and grabbed me, not waiting to see if I did as I was bid to do.

His hands held my hips as I sat awkwardly onto his mouth. He chuckled darkly beneath me and pushed my head down until my lips slid over the thick head of his cock. A moan exploded from my throat as his tongue entered me. Continuing to moan, I licked around him while I tried to figure out what the hell he expected me to do with his inhumanly-sized penis that tasted like heaven as I licked my juices from it.

My hands wrapped around his cock and I moaned, forcing my jaw to relax as he slowed his tongue and stalled his movements. His cock shrank until it slid into my mouth. I forced him further in, clumsily stroking him with my tongue as his magic swept over me.

"You're not mortal, Erie," he whispered, sitting up and pulling my ass with him while he pushed his cock further down my throat. My hands landed on his thighs as he used my waist to lift and pushed me down, fully controlling my throat as if I was a toy. It felt wrong, as if it shouldn't work, and yet every time he lifted me, I took more into my throat as he fed it to me. Eventually, he leaned back as if he was showing me what he expected from me. His tongue grew and swelled in my pussy until I was moaning around his cock, which continued to grow as he grunted against my opening. He filled my throat until air couldn't get through. His throaty laughter was the only sign that he was aware of it. "You have an amazing throat, woman. Now suck it as I fill this tight cunt. Do not come, or you will not come for hours afterward. I almost want to force you to come, just to watch you suffer as you beg me."

My eyes widened as I fought for air, unable to get it into my lungs as he continually adjusted his size while his mouth fucked me. One minute he was too big and all I could do was swallow his massive cock as tears streamed down my face, my eyes watering from the fullness, and the next he'd allow me air as his cock hit against the back of my throat. His tongue filled me as he licked the spot that seemed to be the center of my being until I was crying out around his cock.

Fighting against the need to come, his magic wasn't fair; it was torture. He knew what he did, knowing my body couldn't withstand his magical assault as it tightened around my nipples and clitoris while his hands pulled my hair, pushing and pulling me as he used my mouth to fuck him.

He laughed as he increased the assault on my cunt and I screamed around his cock, coming undone so violently that all I could do was sob against the thick shaft in my mouth. My body clenched and unclenched, trembling as the beautiful, earth-shattering orgasm ripped me apart while he continued licking, locking me into endless violence of the pleasure he delivered. Once he released me, he drew back, lifting me until I faced him, poised over his cock. My head rolled as I stared down at him.

"Bad girl, now I have to hurt you."

"Please," I whispered. I leaned over, scratching my nails down his chest as I claimed his mouth. "Fucking destroy me."

"My pleasure," he uttered as he pulled his mouth away, grabbing my hair to force my gaze to his cock that he pushed against my opening. I was dripping with readiness, an endless ball of need that he knew he'd created. "Watch me fuck you," he ordered, not giving me an option to do anything else. He released my hair, lifting my hips as he grew. My eyes widened and then lifted to his as fear entered my mind. "Eyes on that needy cunt. You watch me as I stretch it, fucking it until you know who owns this naughty, pretty pink haven," he purred and smiled harshly, waiting for me to do as he bid. The moment I did, he pushed me down as his hips lifted, and I wailed. My body violently exploded around him, clenching as the orgasm ripped me apart. I screamed while he continued to lift me, driving my body hard as he controlled it, lengthening the orgasm until I felt myself drifting into nothingness. "Unexpected, but fun, *wife*," he uttered as his gaze dropped to my stomach. "You will give me a strong child."

My eyes closed as his claws slowly retracted, and his finger began to play with my clit, working small patterns into it. "Do you know why Mason watches you so carefully when he is fucking you? So that I can watch you as well, so that I can learn you. When he tastes that naughty flesh, I also taste the sweetness of cunt, which weeps so willingly as I add an inch or take one away to give you exactly what your perfect body craves. I fuck you; I will be the only lover you will ever know. You were created from the cauldron, the symbol of the womb, a magical creation of rebirth and much, much more to those who worshipped it. The Mother Goddess blessed you and your womb, assuring me that it would hold my son within it. You will give me a son, Erie. There is no other choice here."

"I'm dying," I uttered. He continued to keep me on the verge of oblivion as he rolled us on the bed until he was staring down at me, our bodies joined in the most primitive way a man could know a woman. I watched as he rose to his knees on the bed, gazing down at the place where we connected perfectly.

"No, you will never leave me again," he hissed gutturally. "You won't ever die on me again. I ensured it this time," he laughed darkly, his finger lowering to my clit, working my flesh while he added more inches of his cock until I thrashed my head against the bed, my hands fisting the covers to remain on it through the endless pleasure he fed me. "You're right where I want you," he hissed as he increased the pace of his fingers, only stopping to prevent me from falling over the edge. "I know that you feel your tight cunt pulsing, begging me to fuck it. It wants you to beg me; it craves what only I can give it. You want me to lose control and fuck this tight, naughty pussy, don't you? All you have to do is beg me to fuck you."

"Please," I whimpered as I rocked against his cock, even as he looked down to watch me.

"You're so delicate, so pink," he uttered as his thumb pinched my flesh. "Tell me to fuck this cunt, to fuck this delicate flesh until you know exactly who you belong to."

"Fuck me," I whispered huskily, unwilling to fight

him as his magic flooded over my flesh. Sucking against my nipples and clitoris, he smiled coldly, watching me as every inch of me was pleasured by his control. "Please," I whimpered through chattering teeth.

"Mine," he growled. He leaned over, claiming my mouth and started fucking me harder without warning. My body ignited as moisture flooded my core. I was coming undone so violently that everything inside of me was misfiring, and I screamed until I couldn't scream anymore. I felt him growing, pushing my body to its limits until the orgasm ripped me apart, sending a rainbow of colors dancing in my eyes. He crooned his praise, and all I could do was wrap my legs around him, watching as he fucked my flesh until it was sore and bruised.

His hands lifted me, pushing me further onto his cock as he took me into his arms, forcing my legs around his waist while his wings curled around my body, creating a cocoon which held me. His mouth claimed mine, quieting the screams that ebbed and flowed as he stroked my body to a brutal need that threatened to consume me, only to allow the release over and over again until I could only be held up by him, unable to so much as move while he took what he needed and more.

I fell asleep the moment he released me and didn't wake up for hours. The sun had set behind the mountains when I lifted my head, staring at Callaghan, who watched me where he sat in the shadows of the room. I swallowed hard as I felt the soreness of my body, the rawness between my legs, and the moment he moved, I flinched.

"Erie, you're safe."

"No, I'm not. *He* claimed me, I can feel him inside of me," I whispered as I dropped my head into my hands.

"He did, you're his mate. Erie, you're also my mate," he mumbled. He sat down on the edge of the bed, dropping his head as he stared at the floor. "Never taunt him with other men. He's the only thing strong enough to kill another Knight. Those men have stood beside me since the Order was first formed, and even before that when Gods roamed Ireland. Don't push him; you won't like his methods compared to mine."

CHAPTER
twenty-eight

CALLAGHAN WATCHED ME, HIS HANDS STEEPLED IN front of his lips as he waited for me to speak. I wasn't sure I could manage words. I'd been bent over the counter, taken by whatever beast he held within him. And I'd wanted it. I'd begged for it, allowing the beast to bring me over into whatever darkness he had carried with him. I opened my mouth to say something, anything, and the only thing that escaped was a moan and more silence. *It had wings!* Beautiful black wings that had matched its flesh, and yeah, I'd licked and tasted that flesh as I'd thrown inhibition to the wind and let loose on it, giving him everything I was as he fucked me. It had felt familiar, strangely so.

"You weren't hurt?" he asked softly as he studied me.

"Ask that question to my body," I whispered as a tremor of fear and excitement rushed through me. "What the hell was that, Callaghan?" I demanded more firmly, finding my voice as the fear subsided, replaced by anger.

"Nothing you need to know about right now," he said as he turned, looking at me.

"He was just balls-deep in my vagina, I think I'm on a need to know basis," I argued. "That creature within you? It just fucked my lungs. I'm pretty sure I'm on a need to know basis with him."

"You begged him for more," he uttered as he inspected me, noting the red marks that his beast had left on my flesh. "I was right there with him, fucking you. There's no separating us when we're with you. You are the one thing we agree on, Erie. Don't leave this room like that again; I won't warn you a second time."

I watched him rise to his feet as he moved into the closet to grab a shirt. Swallowing hard, I glared at his stiff back. I stood up, taking the sheet with me as I marched towards the closet he'd just disappeared into. I yanked down one of his shirts as he watched me and pulled it over my head.

"I said you could stay naked," he growled harshly.

"And I don't care, asshole. It's not enough that you have me locked inside your damn bedroom at your mercy, but now you want to take away everything? When does it end, Callaghan? When will it be enough! When will I have given you and your people enough of me that *I* can be free?"

"Never! You will never be free of us, Erie. Ever," he snapped, and I flinched as he grabbed the shirt and tore it off of me. "You will never leave here, don't you understand that? You have one fucking job to do; that's it!"

I stared at him as his words slapped against my mind

like a battering ram. I swayed on my feet as I swallowed the emotions and lifted dead eyes to his. I was nothing to him or his people. I meant nothing to anyone, and I never would.

"Fine, *Master*," I uttered harshly as I walked out of the closet, leaving him in his anger to stew within it alone.

"I'm not your fucking master," he hissed.

"Slaves have to have owners, they refer to them as Master, *Master*," I whispered as I lay on the bed, facing away from him.

"You're being childish," he snapped. "I didn't mean what I said," he amended as he swore before he pulled on a shirt and moved to the bed. He sat beside me, reaching for my hand, which I allowed, but gave no effort to hold his. "I didn't mean what I said, you know that."

"You did, you meant every word of it," I returned as I scooted away from him and slipped beneath the covers.

"I'll be back in a few hours," he said.

"Whatever," I muttered as I closed my eyes.

"Do you need anything?"

"Freedom?"

"Anything else?"

"Fred," I replied.

"Anything I can actually fucking get for you, Erie?"

"No, just leave me alone. I don't need anything from you. I don't want anything from you, Callaghan."

"Can you just forget what happened and go back to how it was last night?" he snapped and leaned against the wall, staring at me with a hungry gaze.

"You mean when I gave myself to you so foolishly?"

I laughed coldly. "Never," I uttered through my clenched teeth. "Never as your prisoner or whore," I whispered on a choked breath, turning to show him the deadness of my stare.

"Fine. Have it your way, Erie," he growled as he left the room.

Once he was out of the room, I sat up, listening to the voices in the other rooms. A few quick orders and the door slammed behind him. I moved into the bathroom, blasting the music as I dug around beneath the counters, scouring for whatever I could find. I entered the bedroom, watching as the door began to open. Grabbing the sheet, I pulled it over myself as Lance peeked into the room, his eyebrows lifting as he took in the sheet I wore.

"Everything okay?" he shouted.

I nodded, watching him as he frowned, not looking convinced. I dropped the sheet and turned around, smiling as the door closed in his haste to follow his orders. With the outer door closed, I stood just inside the bathroom, holding the scissors against my chest. Once I was certain he'd gone back to his post, I set to work.

I cut up his entire wardrobe, from his expensive suits to his band tees. I left one item alone inside his closet, and that was a child's uniform. More than likely, it had belonged to his son. I backed out, setting my sights on his dressers as I smashed the fertility statues into dust, the bass of the music covering the crashing noises. I tore the sheets off the bed, sheering through them as I stabbed the mattress, ripping it open until feathers exploded from it and the pillows. The pictures on the walls, the couch that I cut open and pulled the

stuffing from, I pushed in front of the door, along with the dresser drawers.

Entering the bathroom, I smashed the mirror until I had several sharp pieces that I placed on the side of the tub. I lit the candles and picked up the radio alarm clock, plugging it into the socket next to the bathtub. I positioned several jugs beside it and then placed the lavender soap next to the jugs. I leaned over, turning on the water to the tub as hot as it would go.

I slipped into the water, picking up a piece of glass before I leaned over, cutting the inside of my thigh until the water turned pink as it ran down my leg, into the tub. I drained just enough water to do what was needed and sat in the water as my blood spiraled through it, turning it red. I cut the other thigh, and then my arms, wincing as the familiar sting of pain offered a sense of relief. Pain wasn't a stranger, not to me. It was something familiar, like an old friend coming to visit.

Once the tub was filled with blood, I reached for the ammonia, emptying the entire jug of cleaning solution into the tub, followed by the entire bottle of bleach. I heard the door, the pounding as the vapor rose like steam, sending the poisonous gases into the air. I wrapped my arms around my knees, pulling them to my body and I peered over them as Lance entered the bathroom, staring at me in horror and then wincing as he took in the blood that dripped from my wrists.

I coughed as the gas reached my lungs, burning them until I coughed up blood, splatting it against the wall. He backed out with his hand over his nose, slamming his fist over the alarm as he ran to get help. I stood up, swaying on my feet as footsteps sounded from outside the bathroom, and then Uther, Rhett, and Lance were all there, all wearing mask as they watched me. I turned, lifting the electric alarm clock and I smiled coldly at them.

"Erie, don't you fucking do it," Rhett pleaded. "Jesus Christ," he uttered as he took in the damage I'd done to my body.

I coughed violently, sending more blood into the water as my lungs liquefied. More feet sounded, and Uther disappeared, returning with Callaghan in a mask similar to the others. I stared at him as he watched me, sparing a quick glance around the room before those turbulent eyes settled back on me.

"No!" he growled, but he didn't dare move.

I stared him down as the others held him back while he struggled to get to me. I frowned at what was about to happen, but if I wanted to find myself, this was how I would do it. That darkness within me waited to be awoken, and you had to lose yourself if you wanted to find who you truly were. I would eradicate who I had become to unleash who I was supposed to be.

I dropped the alarm clock into the tub with a smile and then fell back as it sent electricity rushing through me. My head cracked against the tub, crunching as my back arched from the shock that tore through me, and then everything stopped as I stared at Callaghan's pleading eyes, the others holding him back while he tried to get to me.

CHAPTER
twenty-nine

CALLAGHAN

MACHINES BEEPED AND THEN STOPPED FOR HOURS. Her body was fucked, sliced apart by glass, electrocuted, and her lungs had liquefied from the poisonous combination of the chemicals she had knowingly mixed together. We all sat around the wall, watching as she died over and over again while her body tried to heal itself, but the damage was extensive.

I'd done this to her, pushing her past her limit. In order to keep her safe from those who hunted her, or from her trying to escape, I'd created a prison for her. I'd smothered her until she'd chosen death over staying with me. Commotion in the hallway drew my attention, and I rose, moving to stop my father before he entered the room and could see the reality of what Erie had done to her body.

"She's healing," I stated coldly.

"Is she? Because the healers say it may take weeks for her to heal enough to continue fucking you. Did you tell her of the past, is that what changed?"

"No, the monster inside of me decided to play with her this morning," I snapped, and his frowned deepened as understanding dawned.

"But you did tell her about the past you shared?" he asked, and when I nodded, he snorted. "I'm going to guess that you left out the other parts," he snapped back. "The part where after you had brought her back, she didn't survive," he uttered. "She died, Mason. On that cliff, outside that cursed church, she died. It wasn't you who brought that child back; it was *him*. *He* brought her back, and she didn't grow. For fuck's sake, Mason, she was in a glass tomb for centuries until *he* breathed into it, and then she gained life again. We don't know what she is, other than his. You cannot love her, son. She's unnatural."

He was wrong; I knew exactly who she was, and what she would become. I knew because we'd brought her back. Everyone other than my men thought she was something else. Erie wasn't just special; she was everything. "She is *his* queen, and if you challenge that, *he* will fight me for control. I will not win that fight, father. She was *his* from the moment she was conceived. She is my mate, our mate. You don't have to fucking like it, but you will respect it. If you cannot, we will take her and leave. Those are your options."

"And if she kills us all?" he asked carefully.

"She's heavily drugged, if you recall," I growled and turned, listening as the machines flatlined yet again. She'd known what she was doing, that was a given. "She will receive more drugs while she is under. If it was her intent to die and rid her system of the drugs preventing her magic, she would not be successful." Erie couldn't reach full power, because if she did, no amount of drugs would protect this compound and we knew it. Worse than that, if she came back as what she truly was, we were all fucked. Right now, she thought she was just a druid mixed with our blood, but she wasn't. Erie was ancient, older than this world itself, and when she remembered that, God protect us because she would unleash hell on anyone and everything that had ever trespassed against her.

"And you will continue with her?" My father asked, his hands balling into tight fists at his sides.

"I will make a child with her, yes."

"I'm asking about after she's given birth, Callaghan. Carolina has agreed to raise your son as her own."

"You think I plan to kick her out after she gives me a child?" I stared at him, watching as he lowered his eyes to the ground.

"Carolina deserves this for the son you sacrificed for the greater good. She lost him too," he muttered as I snorted.

My darling wife had fucked anyone who would allow her into their bed, including the man who thought I was his son. I wanted to remind him what I was, that I had never been born, but created. "And she has had other sons with other men, and that list includes you, Father. I have never stood in her way from moving on. My son will not be hers, and he will have a mother."

"Are you sure she will want him or be safe around the child? She seems more inclined to end her life than live it with you, son."

"We are done," I growled as I spun around, moving

back into the chair that had been placed against the wall.

"Brain activity is back, but her lungs continue to fail," the healer stated as he adjusted the meds that he was pushing.

"And the wounds, why are they not healing?" I asked.

"Because she used poison to prevent the flesh from healing correctly," he swallowed as he explained what it had done, and how long it would take for the wounds to close. "It will be a long process for her body to fully heal, no matter how immortal she is. The poison damaged the tissue, burning it badly. It did the same to her lungs, which means she will begin to feel it. She will die several more times as her lungs continue and fail, trying to take in air. She will continue to suffocate and die," he said softly as the men groaned and shook their heads. It was fucking torture to watch her come back, only to fade away violently.

Death wasn't something new, or something we didn't know intimately. It was part of what we'd become, and every death took us to the one thing we'd lost. We replayed that horror every single time, as a reminder of what we'd sacrificed for who we had become so long ago. It was a visceral thing we replayed, the horror of it, the loss of the one thing we had loved the most. It was why every time Erie killed me; I spent days away from her with the damage she dealt me.

That anger wasn't on her, nor could I direct it at her since she had no idea where I went when I died. I'd known what I was doing, and the monster within had shown me a life that would be bigger than anything I'd ever imagined; a world where there was no death, no

pain for our people. We were their people. The sacred people they had protected before war had come to their lands. Those who had escaped formed the Knight's Order, then the Templar Knights, and last, but not least, the Freemasons. Together, we kept out the monsters that craved to destroy the human race.

"She cannot be placed into a coma so that she won't feel it?" I asked.

"I'm afraid it would alter her mind even more than she already has, and it is fragile and yet healing from the electrocution she suffered."

"So she has to suffer through it," I growled.

"I'm afraid so, but I have added pain medication to the nulling medication. She is still receiving fertility medicine at your father's behest."

I stared at her, watching as her eyes opened and she turned, staring at me until a moan exploded from her lips. Her body bucked against the bed. The noises she made coiled in my stomach as nausea pulsed through me while she screamed silently. The sound of choking on fluid as her lungs gave out was maddening, filling the silent room as we all watched.

"Why would you do this?" I asked, already knowing the answer.

If she were to escape me, she wouldn't be able to do it without her magic. I feared she'd try to kill us all for what I'd done, but that couldn't happen. I couldn't allow her to kill the children who weren't immortal yet, nor the women who carried the next generation within them. I'd made a vow to keep these people safe from harm, and the one thing that could harm them was her.

I reached for her chained hand, slipping her tiny

fingers through mine, lacing her perfection against the scars that adorned mine as I placed a soft kiss onto it. She awoke, only to die again. Lance reached over and turned off the monitors, canceling the alarm that told us when her death was coming.

"You can't keep doing this. You know that, brother," Rhett said softly. "Your father is right, and I hate admitting that out loud. Erie is toxic, toxic to herself and us. She doesn't know any other way to live. Sometimes, that which is broken cannot be fixed. It's time to do this the way she knows how."

"And what would you have me do, set her free?" I snapped.

"That cannot happen," Uther stated. "Arthur either kills himself or fights us until we kill him. Not to be the asshole who says it, but he's made some very dark ties as well. He's hunting her to breed her, and when he does catch her, he will have the witches with him. How else do you explain that weasel dick besting us and remaining out of reach for this long?"

"It may not be the witches," I announced. "The druids wanted her pregnant, and then they wanted her to die. Only a few people know how to end her life, and they are on that very small list. I think it is time to start hunting druids."

"That would mean war," Lance said from where he leaned against the doorway.

"It won't be our first," Uther shrugged.

"And it won't be our last," Rhett said.

"To save her, we would go to war, when she takes her own life from us," I muttered. I watched her open her eyes and search the room, settling on me as a smile flittered over her lips before she started to suffocate again. "Did you see that?" I asked.

"She's definitely got some brain damage if she just smiled at you." Uther snorted and then laughed as he patted me on the back firmly.

"Do you think that I should tell her that she died and was reincarnated by that which lies within me?" I asked the room.

"I think it wouldn't help her to know she died and was brought back, or at least knowing she is who she is, because if I were her, I'd be pissed at what you have done, and that girl is mad enough already," Uther replied skeptically.

"She wasn't dead," Lance injected. "She never rotted to bones. She just *slept*. I mean, considering whom and what she is to me, it makes sense. They aren't like us, so you shouldn't expect her to be like us or even think like us. It doesn't matter that she's unaware of those things; she is still the creature she was originally born as, just weaker now."

"She wasn't fucking breathing. For fuck's sake, she was in a glass tomb," Rhett argued.

"But she never truly died; when you die, you rot," Lance countered.

"Do you think she'd hate us for not telling her that, for that entire time we protected her? That we built a fucking castle around her, waiting for my queen to awaken?" I growled.

"I don't think you should ever tell anyone that story, as she was an infant and you were a grown ass man. Some shit you just don't ever say out loud. I mean, I knew she was your mate, and you knew, but the world wouldn't have understood that the monster that you held told you how to bring her back from the dead. They'd have tied us up and burned us alive, and even if we came back, that's one way I never want to go out." Lance chuckled.

"Go Erie-proof my apartment, smartass," I said. I stood up, pushing her lifeless body over as I lay beside her, curling her against my side as they watched. "I'm done letting her suffer to save us."

"About fucking time," Uther snorted. "And for your information, when she remembers who she is, you take the blame this time."

"Go," I ordered, holding her as she woke once more, only to slowly suffocate again. It was taking longer and longer for her to suffocate, which meant soon she'd be awake through it. She'd feel every ounce of pain as she struggled to remain awake, only to die. She'd known what she was doing, but why she had done it escaped me. Unless she wanted to jumpstart something she'd hidden, even from me. I could read her thoughts, knew her mind before she did. Until lately, as if she had begun to sense I was in it, with her and had discovered a way to prevent it. There was nothing I didn't know about her, right down to which foods she preferred and which things she hated. I knew what she feared, and yet I'd given her privacy because she was here, she was mine. She'd earned it, which was why I hadn't known this was coming and hadn't stopped it from playing out.

Now, trying to listen to her inner thoughts, there was only silence. As if she'd removed me from being able to know what she thought. I'd stayed the fuck out of her thoughts, even if it made me look like an asshole.

I had tried to let her live without me fucking her up, or invading her mind, and now, now she'd gone and made damn sure I couldn't read them. And they said she was just a girl; no, Erie Callaghan was a monster who just hadn't put the pieces of her past together yet.

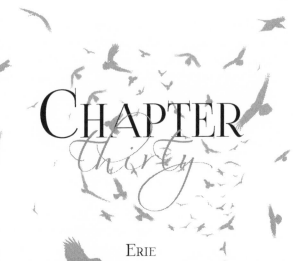

CHAPTER
thirty

ERIE

Beeping brought me out of the deep sleep, forcing my eyes to open as I searched the room for the incessant noise. My arm pinched against the IV, stopping the deadly toxin that was being pushed through it into my system. I could smell Callaghan's nearness, feel the heat from his body while it pressed against mine as he held me. His beast was so close to the surface that his magic was tangible in the room, and it offered comforted me. I could also sense the others like him, standing in the room, waiting for me to awaken from what I'd done to myself. My arm moved, hiding the evidence of what I'd done as I slowly turned to face him. Only it wasn't the Nordic blue eyes that held mine when I did, it was the eerie glowing blue of the beast who watched me from within the human who housed him. His anger was thickening the air around me as he watched me carefully. He studied me as if he expected something to happen.

I opened my mouth to speak and then hissed as pain

rocketed through my chest, burning where my lungs refused to open and expand. Forming words wouldn't happen as I whimpered, hissing through what should have been breathing life into me. My body bucked against the bed, a silent scream that never formed playing in my head as my chest began to burn fiercely, my brain becoming starved for oxygen. Callaghan's arms reached out, pulling me into his body as he watched me struggle for air. My hands grabbed on to him, holding him close as the panic of suffocation lit within my mind, and the tissue began to turn blue where I held him against me. His mouth hovered next to mine, those glowing eyes watching me as his mouth closed the distance between us, kissing me, he blew life into my body, as if he knew how to fix me. I gasped for his kiss, letting his oxygen heal me from within.

"The next time you throw away what I have given you, I will stand by and watch as you suffer the consequences, precious sweet girl," he growled and his body seemed to grow, dwarfing mine as he crawled above me, staring down at me. His fingers lifted, pushing the hair away from my face as he watched me closely. "I do not enjoy watching my mate die, or knowing that she chose death over being with me. You won't do this again, ever. Your life is precious to me, even if you do not think it is. Do you understand me?" he demanded.

"I do," I whispered through the dryness of my mouth. It came out huskily as my eyes dipped to his lips, which curved into a seductive smile. I rolled him until I was straddling his waist, uncaring that my entire ass peeked out of the gown I wore, or that his men watched us.

"You get off on dying, woman," he observed with a

sexy smirk.

I didn't answer him because it wasn't a question. I just stared into his darkening eyes that filled with lust as the ancient beast within watched me and every minuscule move I made. His nostrils flared, and I leaned down, kissing his lips, his tongue jutted out, claiming mine as he allowed it. It wasn't a rough kiss; in fact, it was so fucking gentle that I wanted to sock him in the head and tell him to stop being a pussy. His lips curved up in the corners as he rolled on top of me and stared down.

"Punch me in the head, woman?" he demanded as he watched me. "Fucking try me," he growled as his mouth crushed against mine, stealing the air from my lungs as he kissed me until my insides combusted and my moans were only captured by his mouth. When he pulled away, there was no glow to his eyes, only Callaghan staring down at me in wonder. "Nice try, Erie," he growled as he grabbed my arm, righting the IV.

I had gotten what I needed to know: he was inside my head, listening to every thought I made. I had no privacy or defense against him. "Oh, Callaghan," I smirked.

"How's the pain?" he asked.

"I enjoy it," I hissed.

"I gathered that when you decided to bathe in chemicals with a fucking alarm clock."

"It was electrifying," I uttered as I wiggled my brows.

"Straitjackets are an option, sweet girl. Do not fucking test me after what you just did. You have no idea how far I'm willing to go to protect you, even from yourself."

"Except from you, the one thing I actually need protection from," I snapped as I pushed him off of me, and slid onto my side. "OD incoming," I uttered as I felt the first of the intense sickness rushing through me. My body arched as the first tremors pushed through it, the foam filled my throat, and then I felt weightless as the medication I'd been preventing from reaching me rushed through my system.

"Erie, this isn't fucking funny," he growled as he grabbed my chin, staring into my eyes as they rolled back in my head. "Get the fucking medic, now!" he shouted as he tried to hold me down, his head resting against my stomach as he waited for them to come. When they didn't come quickly enough, he ripped the IV out of my arm, and I barely hid the smile that tried to spread over my lips.

"What happened?" the familiar voice of the medic asked as he entered the room.

"She's awake, or she was until she fucking OD'd," Callaghan snapped as something made a strangled noise. "What the fuck is in that IV?"

"The nulling medication and the fertility meds," he wheezed. "The only new thing was the pain medication we added to give her some comfort so she wouldn't continue to suffer."

I felt my legs healing as the poison seeped from my body, and I pushed against it, forcing it from my system while the blood oozed out. I wasn't an idiot, nor did I fail to plan every detail, down to the exact thing I had known they would resort to doing. While Callaghan had pushed the meds, my body had bled them out just as quickly as he'd introduced them.

"She's fucking bleeding out!" Callaghan growled as he continued to hold my thrashing body down while they pushed the drugs to make my system work harder.

I'd rebooted my brain with the electrocution. Obviously, I'd come back with brain damage if I'd wanted wild beast sex willingly. But mostly, if I had wanted to come back as me, I'd have to send the other bitch away for a while. The slices to my flesh had been to force the poison they pushed through me out, knowing I'd bleed it all out faster than they could push it into me. The poison had been to hold the wounds open, to keep my flesh from healing before I could push their toxins out. Callaghan's hold lessened, and I moved, throwing wild magic against them as I ripped my arms from the cuffs. I slid to a halt outside the room and tossed up easy wards, enough to buy me time to reach Fred.

I'd seen him through the deaths I'd suffered, mere feet away from me. I smiled as Callaghan raised glowing eyes on me at where I stood, just out of his reach. He bared his teeth as I smiled back; game on, fucker. I turned, racing to where Fred's cooler sat, slamming my magic against the bars until they cracked and turned to liquid metal. I stepped into the cell, opening up the cooler and smiled brightly as I looked down.

"Hello, Fred, did you miss me?" I asked as a bubbling laugh escaped my lips. I reached in and grabbed him up by the hair.

"About fucking time," he said drolly. "I was beginning to think you had forgotten me on your way out, and do you mind…that's my fucking hair," he growled.

"It's not like you have many options for me to hold on to," I snapped back as I started down the hallway, throwing magical barriers up as men came rushing forward. "I mean, you don't have a body and all that jazz, or handlebars. I'm working with what I have. I'm open to placing handlebars on your skull, of course, if you're into that sort of thing."

"Just don't roll me like a bowling ball," he uttered.

"Can't promise anything," I said as we rounded a corner and came face-to-face with an angry group of Templar Knights. "Shit," I muttered as I dropped Fred onto the ground and used both hands to send magic pulsing towards them. I picked Fred up as it hit them, knocking them backward as I watched them melt into goo that covered the floor. *Oops, my bad.*

"Damn, girl," he chuckled. "Wherever my body is, it's got a hard-on."

"Ew, Fred," I said as we started down another hallway, turning left and then right until we hit an elevator and slipped inside.

It was the longest elevator ride of my *entire* life, along with the most awkward one as the boring music played until the button dinged and I stepped off, still holding Fred by his hair. An entire class of children turned and looked at me. I swallowed hard as I tilted my head, staring at them with curiosity at how many there were. It was as if every child left in the entire world was right fucking here. I moved deeper into the room as I silently, awkwardly danced around the kids, who all stared at me. One reached out, and I sucked in my stomach as he smiled.

"They're only tiny humans, why are you doing

that?" Fred asked.

"They're trying to touch me," I hissed as I pulled him closer as screaming erupted around us. "Well, that happened," I said as power rushed over us. I watched as the children all turned, setting their eyes on the source of that magic as if he was a saint. I turned, looking at Callaghan, who stared back with a murderous glare in his glowing blue eyes. My eyes dipped down, staring at the kids who all seemed utterly excited that they'd been graced by his presence.

"Step away from the children, now," he warned barely above a whisper of death.

I swallowed as I stepped back, turning on my heel, and I rushed to the other side of the schoolroom, jumping onto the high railing and I peered down at the layered glass below it.

"No way, no fucking way, woman. That is at least three stories down," Fred hissed with a note of genuine panic in his tone.

"Close your eyes if you're going to be a pussy, Fred," I snapped and turned, staring across the heads of the children who watched where Callaghan was slowly making his way through them, his men at his back. "This is not the time to bitch out on me, man."

"Get the fuck down, Erie," Callaghan snapped coldly, butthurt that I'd played him and he'd lost.

"Oh, I assure you, I plan to get down," I said with a saucy smile tilting my lips as he shook his head in silent warning.

"If you jump, you won't be able to run, and I will catch you. There is no way out of this that doesn't end with you being chained to my bed, not after the shit you just pulled on me."

"Mouth, watch it, there are little ears around," I chided. I gave him a *duh* stare as I held perfectly still, buying myself time to grow enough balls to jump.

"They've heard worse," he said and yet he seemed to look around at them all the same. I wondered if he saw the awe in their gazes as they took him in. To them, he was their savior, their God. To me, he was the devil.

I turned, looking at the sheet of glass that was about to break my fall, hopefully. I turned back, watching as his father entered the room, staring at me coldly. His eyes seemed to slide between Callaghan and me as he took in the situation. The alarm began to bellow as the teacher started calling the children to her, and the Knights began to flood into the room.

"Erie, get the fuck down." Callaghan stared at me, silently begging me to listen to his order.

"If she fucking lifts a finger, kill her," Douglas growled.

"I'm not going to hurt you, Douglas," I purred as I stared him down. This man, he'd been on my kill list since I was a mere child; his crude examination of me had left an impression, among other things he'd done. The way he'd stared at me so impartial, coldly. The things he'd made me watch him do, well, that alone had warranted his death. After that, it had been easy to add his ass to that long list.

"You wouldn't get a fucking chance to do it before they fill you with enough lead to make you a statue, girl."

"Tempting," I said as I dropped my eyes and slid them back to Callaghan. "Catch me if you can, monster,"

289

I hissed as I fell over the edge, backward.

Weightlessness was not the coolest feeling in the world. In fact, it wasn't even like flying; it was like straight up falling. The moment before I would have fallen through the glass, I spun and landed on the pads of my bare feet, oblivious to my bare ass sticking out of the hospital gown I wore. Fred screamed, even after I'd landed on the glass. I stood there, staring at him where he was safely tucked against my body as he continually held his eyes closed, screaming.

"Are you done yet?" I asked with a pointed look as I held him up.

"Are we dead?" he asked.

"No, not unless..." I paused as a cracking noise began beneath us, looking down as the glass spider-webbed beneath my feet. "Well, balls," I grumbled as I pulled Fred against my chest, holding my arms close to my body as it gave out and we started free-falling to the next floor. My eyes took in the Knights on the ground floor, and I exhaled as we started for the next, and then the next, finally dropping to the last one, where I threw myself backward, breaking through the wall of glass that should have been harder to get through, but wasn't. I ended up rolling through the shattered glass as I came up on my feet, staring at women who looked back at me and then glanced at the head that was currently smothered against my breasts.

The hand holding Fred pulled away, and he smiled. "Put me back, woman," he demanded.

"You're incorrigible," I grumbled as I started forward, only for the Amazonian woman from the med center to step out with her sword held in a fighting

stance. I smiled, slapping my hands together, which ended in my slapping Fred's face against my hand, but my magic shot at her.

"Ouch! To the devil with you, woman, that hurt!" he snapped as I watched the Knight go down to her knees. A female Templar, now I'd seen everything. I walked past her, only to feel a sharp stab against my side as I did. I looked down at the sword that stuck out of my side. I pulled myself off it, fully intending to slowly turn around to finish her off.

"She isn't immortal, Erie!" Callaghan screamed from the other side of the glass wall that separated this room from the one in which he stood. My eyes dropped to the woman, and I tilted my head, lifting it again to stare at him as I took in the glass that he stood behind. When I was satisfied that he wouldn't get through it, I looked back down at the woman cowering at my feet.

"If you ever fucking touch me again, I will send you to the devil myself," I warned.

"To save my children, I'd walk to him willingly!" she said emphatically, her eyes swimming with tears.

"Have you not heard? All the devils are here, and we're fucking hungry," I hissed. I walked past her, not bothering to cover the wound that dripped blood onto the floor. I walked past the glass that kept the Templars at bay and stopped, kissing my lips to the glass as I stared Callaghan down. "Don't be upset. I did tell you I would never stop fighting you for my freedom."

"You have one hour, one hour and then I begin hunting you down. I suggest you use it wisely, woman."

"Only an hour?" I asked as I rested my head against the glass, letting the steam of my breath fog over it.

"That is exactly how long it will take me to track you down and bring you back."

I turned, sensing the Knights behind me. "They're immortal," I smiled coldly as I turned, then dropped as bullets began to fly. I laughed on the ground as I rolled onto my stomach, lifting my hand, I used Fred as a prop to look over the edge of the table that sat beside us. My hands worked as Callaghan screamed and pounded against the glass. I stood, my power becoming a palpable thing in the room as I stared through the barrier I'd placed at the women who were huddled together, terrified. As if they feared a monster would consume them, but it wasn't a monster they feared. It was me. I swallowed past the lump in my throat as I picked up Fred, slowly walking away as the pounding increased, and the bullets hit the barrier of wards I held in place to protect myself from their bullets. A full circle of magic surrounded me, protecting me as I moved toward the exit.

I started jogging down the hallway; staring at the glass doors, I began to assault them with my magic, and I busted through. I inhaled the fresh air until more bullets shot at me, nailing my shoulder and my hip as I staggered backward into the doors I'd left. I placed a moving ward around my body, swaying on my feet as blood dripped from the wounds.

"Erie, just a little bit further," Fred said. "I'm right outside the gates, go to me. Go to my body, my Queen."

I blinked as screaming erupted from below while I moved out onto the concrete walkway that they'd built, as if this place was a fucking castle. Bullets slammed against the wards, and I wavered as my magic began to fade. I leaned over the edge, staring down at the fast-moving river that rushed below.

"No, my body. *We* need my fucking body!" Fred demanded.

"I won't reach it," I whispered. "It will find us," I cried out in pain as I hefted us onto the wall, swaying as I stared down, trying to judge where to jump to survive the fall.

"You won't make it if you jump, either," he argued.

"I won't be captured, and what's the worst that happens? You get free?" I uttered as I fell forward, tightening my hold on Fred as we toppled into the water. I gasped as the cold water bit into my flesh, renewing my strength to escape the icy death that fought to keep me in the river. When the fuck had it formed rapids? I sucked in air as we went under, and my feet kicked off the bottom while the current tried to pull us down. My hands moved, slapping Fred's face against the water with every stroke as he gasped and gurgled and I fought to live.

Once I reached the other side, I crawled onto the bank and threw up water as I turned, staring back at the Templar Knight who watched me with a wicked smile on his lips. He'd changed into full armor, and instead of giving chase, he watched me beat the shit out of myself, get shot, and wane the magic which was my only defense against him.

He'd known I'd escape, and he knew I wouldn't have enough energy to fight him if he caught me. I turned over, pushing up from the ground as I grabbed Fred and started towards the car I'd hidden outside of his compound for when this day came. He thought he was the only one who had game? I had game. I had a fucking back-up plan for my back-up plan, and another one in case it failed. I'd spent years backing those plans up, and I'd be damned if I ended up being tied to his freaking bed. Although that beast was more than just a beast in the sheets, he made me ache at the mere thought of him. Throaty laughter sounded in my head, and I closed my eyes.

"Is that so, sweet wife?" he uttered hoarsely. *"Run, little one, for this time, I am hunting you, and I enjoy it, and when I catch you, and I will, I will do more than just chain you to a bed."*

"Of course he's in my fucking head again."

"Did you just *swear*?" Fred asked. We both turned as something tripped through the bushes and landed at my feet. "My body!"

"Great," I growled as I helped his body up with my free hand while holding his head with the other. "We need a sewing kit. It's time."

"Time for what?" he asked.

"To become the queen again, of course," I hissed. "I'm tired of the games, and tired of pretending to be weak."

CHAPTER
thirty-one

I<small>NSIDE THE ABANDONED CHURCH</small> THAT SAT ON hallowed ground, I stared down at Fred, who watched me through terrified eyes as my power filled up the room. My fingers touched on the smooth edges of his severed flesh, searching for the arteries and whatnot while I began the process of making him whole again. The light above the sarcophagus he was laid upon swung above us as the sultry song played low from the car stereo outside; *Scars* by Boy Epic, one of the songs that I sang within my soul. His blue eyes watched me, knowing I didn't fear what he was or what he controlled. I could smell his fear, taste it as he studied me, the cold detachment that I exuded. I had a much scarier monster chasing me, one that lived within me. It wasn't the beast who terrified me; it was my reaction, as if I sensed that I belonged to it. But something even scarier within me was waking up, and she wasn't evil, she was war.

"I'm going to tell you a story about a girl." My finger began to loop the nylon thread through the curved needle I held. "It's about a very young girl, one who viewed the world as a beautiful place where she felt cherished. She was very naïve in her views of the world, but she knew no boundaries, or what would become of her as that small child she had been started to reveal what she was, unknowingly. She had been given the world as a playground, with a champion who protected her as best as he could, until he could no longer refuse the commands of the Order he followed; unbeknown to him, they needed him away from her to do very bad things while he was away. I'm sure that I don't need to tell you who that scared little girl was, do I? No? Good. I remember his face as he left me within the walls of that hell, so fierce and proud of the curious being I was becoming. At first, he came back to see me often, until the wars started taking him further and further away from me. That's when it changed, when everything changed. The druids loathed me for how I'd been created. I was barely five when Dane, the Headmaster of the druids, began to beat me; his hands were as large as clubs, and they punished me for things I held no control over. My magic was wild; it was a part of what I was, who I was. I grew stronger than any of them, but there was a part of me that changed every time I wielded it. I started to envision things, a world I didn't know. So I buried it, let them think I was weak.

"The first beating was brutal, but the second one, that's when they placed their woad upon my flesh. I fought the druids, doing everything I could without wielding the magic I held. They beat me into submission until my only option was to lay there as they held me down, using multiple needles to pierce my flesh with the blue ink. Back then, tattoos were not the same. It was a brutal process that only those of iron will and strength could withstand. I remember the sound it made, the searing pain as they pushed it through my flesh. It took them days to paint my face, my arms, and my chest with their blue ink. Afterward, I was hung naked from the wall, a reminder to all that I was not human. I was a monster in a little girl's body," I whispered as I pushed the needle through his flesh, connecting it slowly. "I'm sure they would have done worse to me had they not feared what I was. You see, they left no inch of me unexplored as they searched me for the mark of the devil. Luckily, my untried cunt was, to them, what the gates to heaven are to you: forbidden, untouchable, a sure way to allow the darkness in. For days I hung there, convinced that my Knight would return and save me from the horror of what they had done to me. Yet day after day, as I hung there, starving to death with the ravens pecking against the scabs of the markings and the ink, I lost hope.

"Eventually, knowing he would return, they brought me down and whipped me as everyone watched until they'd torn my body to nothing more than a bloody mess. Tied to a post, I healed, unable to die because something had denied me such an extravagant thing as escaping the torture. For me, there was no way to escape the pain that they delivered. I was free of it after several days, free to become their servant and tend to their chamber pots, to clean their rooms. Never allowed close enough to the other children to ever know what it was like to be loved. Weeks after they'd scarred me, I was sent to the bathing house, for my odor offended a visiting lord. One of the druid's whores, well, she wanted to sell me to that lord, because he enjoyed the flesh of young children. She washed me, touching me as she examined my tits and other…things, or the lack of those things. According to her, I would bring silver or more for what lay between my young thighs. Once I had been washed and violated by her, I was pushed into a dark room with the lord. He was grossly overweight, his breathing was heavy, and even in the dark, I felt the demon that waited within his flesh. The monster who craved to hurt the child I was. So I destroyed him. I freed the demon, knowing that I was strong enough to face it, and so it died there, on that dirty floor at my feet." He hissed as I went too deep with the needle before I tied the end, cutting it before I began to thread the needle again.

"I was beaten again, for defending that which was not theirs to give. That whore was my first taste of human blood. I set her on fire as she took me back to her home, intending to use me to bring her coin. I remember the smell of her flesh as it sizzled when the flames kissed her skin, burning so hotly that she began to melt. I was fascinated by it, how flame burned through tissue before reaching the meat, how her hair created a different colored flame than her flesh. After she'd perished, I played in the ashes that had been left from her corpse. I was, of course, still a child, and I felt free of those people for the first time since my Knight had abandoned me to them. I was on my own then, able to hunt the other druids who had beaten or painted my flesh. One by one, I hunted them down until I was seven, when I watched the last one burn to death in his home, where he, of course, had felt safe from the monster that had begun hunting him and his druids." My finger held

the nylon as I snipped it, tilting my head to listen to the noises outside.

"After I'd slaughtered them, I headed towards Ireland; it called to me, as if it was a part of me that my child's mind couldn't understand. Callaghan, of course, found me in a small fishing village where I'd been trying to work for coin to pay a captain to take me across the sea. Those people in the village never bothered me, never came close as they offered me jobs to gain my fare, but then I think they wanted me to leave their lands. To them, I looked like an orphan, abandoned and dirty, carrying death with me. It was, of course, my disguise; no one touched the dirty ones. He took me to a new compound, a stronger one. One that held no chance of escape," I whispered thickly as I rethreaded the needle, knowing he hadn't realized that every stitch would be a single one, which took a long time to accomplish putting an entire head back onto a body.

"Years passed, and while I had kept the secrets of the last druid compound, no one had guessed which enemy had murdered them all, so I watched them. I studied them, acutely aware of the animosity that they felt at having me within their grasp. You see, to them, I was this unnatural child, born of one of their own. Druids do not breed women, and those who held magic were murdered by them for their wrongness at birth, and yet there I was, a female who outranked them all in skill and power. They kept their distance at first until one boy dared to touch his lips against mine. My fault, of course; for me, any attention was welcomed as I'd been starved of it my entire life. I was the child of evil, born from a magic so horribly terrifying that the Gods themselves had banished it. That boy, the one who kissed me, I had fallen in love with him, or so my young mind believed. I thought that one day, he'd give me the world. He promised it to me, kissing me before I had ever realized his intent. I didn't understand the magnitude of what he'd done until he'd lifted my skirts, forcing himself on me. I pushed him away, and the others, they'd stood watch so that he wouldn't be discovered. We were, of course. As the Headmaster's son, he wasn't punished. You see, Arthur was born of Knight and druid, like me, but he was born male, and I was not. I'd thought that maybe he out of everyone would understand me. That maybe I'd found a kindred spirit, but he only wanted to hurt me too.

"When his father discovered us, I was chained to a post and used to show them proof of what I was. Druids were not immortal, not like the Knights. They died, and so being lured to me was a death sentence. Arthur stood in front of me as I was stripped naked; his eyes were horrible as he took in my naked flesh. I begged him to tell his father the truth, and he only smiled, watching as I was laid bare before him. They'd brought in every male child to watch me be humiliated before them. One hundred lashes were delivered before he invited the boys to defile me, or more to the point, what had remained of me. He encouraged them to piss on my tainted flesh, to spit in my face or openly hurt me in much darker ways. Arthur though, he wanted to push things into me, so he did, through the tears in my flesh since he couldn't penetrate me the way he really wanted to, not with everyone watching him.

"So instead of raping me, he pushed rocks, glass, anything available to punish me as his father watched him through proud eyes. Hours, it took them hours of abusing me to grow bored, and even then, the abuse didn't stop. I prayed Callaghan would come, that he would protect me and stop them, but he didn't come back. He could never come when the abuse started because he never understood why he was ordered away before it began. His father was aware of what I had suffered, often coming to observe it as the abuse unfolded. My Knight was purposely sent away so that I could be tested; to see what I could endure before my body gave out until I was broken. To see if I was evil, I guess, or if I was willing to lose my soul to the darkness to defend myself," I explained as I dabbed the cloth against the flesh I'd finished sewing together, staring at it to be sure the stitch was placed thickly enough. "I knew what they wanted, what they feared, and I'd long since stopped using the magic. I let them believe I was weak enough to be abused and controlled. I'd learned to hide what I had become from everyone, even my Knight.

"When my spine broke, I laughed at them. I looked Callaghan's father right in the eye and laughed at what they had done to me. Callaghan thinks he knows what happened, but I've never told him the truth. I never told him that I had fallen in love with his enemy, Arthur, or that he was the reason for that beating, and that I had earned that beating for my weakness. I deserved it for thinking I was good enough to be loved. Callaghan wouldn't have understood it, the reason I believed I had loved Arthur. The isolation and the abuse I suffered at being their servant, it was debilitating to the child I'd been. Arthur was different, like me. He knew I wasn't evil, not to begin with, and neither was he. His evil was created. I created it within him as I ripped him apart and promised him that he would never know what pleasures my evil body held. It created madness in him, knowing that he would never have what he thought he'd earned. Anyway, after my body had become useless and broken, and month after month had passed of lying in my own waste as my body slowly became a dried-out husk that resembled a corpse, Arthur came. He whispered into my ear that he had sent a message to Callaghan, that he wouldn't let my untrained pussy be wasted as I turned into a husk of dried flesh; *it*, after all, was all he wanted from me.

"He wanted me with a fire that burned within him. He didn't love me; he craved me. Like madness within his mind, he wanted what he couldn't have. Months after Callaghan had saved me, I hunted them all down, every boy who had defiled me that I had considered a friend. I guess I was naïve for believing they wanted me as one. You see, my body was changing, as were theirs, and I was the only female of their age that resided within those walls. So one by one, I hunted them down like animals and put them out of their misery. I knew Callaghan watched me, but I needed him to see me, the real me that was hidden. Arthur, though, he was so much fun to take apart. I started with his cock, showing him it would never be worthy of being used on me. I ripped him into pieces, and then, he vanished, and I sensed he was different than the others I'd slaughtered. The Knights only vanish during their first death cycle, which alerted me to what he truly was. Unlike the others I'd murdered, he didn't stay dead. His mother was of Templar blood, like mine. When they learned of this, he was rewarded for his lineage and sent to the Knights to be trained, while I was locked into a cage that held me until I was old enough to earn my keep. Bound by magic they assumed would hold me to them, I was released. Their mistake, of that, I am sure."

"You've killed anyone who has ever wronged you; who could be killed, anyway."

"Of course I have, Fred." I shrugged nonchalantly. "Anyway, I tried to sleep with Callaghan when he healed me, but he looked at me with such utter disgust on his face that, after that, I hid who I was from the entire world, hid who I was becoming. I buried myself so fucking deep that to anyone looking at me, well, they'd have seen a broken girl, a confused, damaged girl that held no intelligence. I am not stupid, Fred. I am not simpleminded. I am the only female druid, and I have become more powerful than the highest trained male they ever had at five years of age. I had outranked them all by the time I was ten, despite having no one to teach me spells or show me how to strengthen my craft. So I hunted people. I hunted down anyone who preyed on the innocence of those not strong enough to fight back. I let myself die to see how I came back each time. I know which type of death can trigger a body to come back stronger, to strengthen the mind, or to numb it from pain. Make no mistake; I am broken. I have so many fucking cracks that you could look through me and know how jagged my every edge is, and I wouldn't care if you looked through me and found my soul was missing. I have been beaten, I have been broken, and I have died a thousand deaths without ever feeling a single one of them. I am stronger because I've been given no choice but to become stronger. Broken people are terrifying because we know how to continue surviving, no matter what happens to us.

"I know why I was brought back, and what I am to do, and while I see the justification for such an effort, I will not be owned. I have killed tens of thousands of people in every way imaginable to see how they died from those wounds. I know how long a body takes to drain from a simple nick to an artery. I also know where to miss each vital organ to avoid death until I am ready to deliver it. I don't feel emotion when those around me die, because I've never cared for a single person in a very long time, until you. I prefer you without your hands and arms because, without them, you would never hurt me. You need to know that I am giving them back to you, and if you turn against me, not even Lucifer himself will be able to stop me from reaching you. I assure you, I am much more powerful than he is. The magic within me is ageless, more ancient than even Satan himself. I won't hesitate to destroy you and your entire army if you so much as lift a finger against me. You can either be by my side, or in my fucking freezer. That choice is yours to make," I said as I finished sewing his head back on with the skill of the finest surgeon. "I assure you, the only side of me that I have allowed you to view was the side of me that I wanted you to see."

I stepped back, staring at him as he sat up slowly and tested his head. "I should want to hurt you, mistress," he purred as he jumped off the sarcophagus and grabbed

my arms, staring into my eyes as he lowered his mouth to my ear. "I really just want to bend you over and fuck my anger out on you, but you have a bigger problem coming at us. He's close, and so are the witches, my pretty little queen. You should run because I plan to as well." He stared at me as a sinful smile lifted to play across my lips.

I reached over, turning off the recording device that I had set in front of the door. "Oh, Fred, I'm not even here, and ew, no, we're never fucking," I said as I smiled and stepped back, watching as his eyes took in the differences between me and the clone that had put him back together. "Did you really think I would trust you? You've wanted me dead for months now. Trust is earned. Prove to me that I can trust you and I will find you when I am ready. Now, I want you to slip back into your position as the leader of Hell's army. If you choose otherwise, I promise, I will fucking destroy Hell itself to reach you."

"You want me to slip away from Lucifer with half of his army when he is hunting some bitch and her boyfriend, don't you?" he scoffed as he touched my hand, staring at the likeness. "How did you do this?"

"It's a simple cloning spell. It's magic that I used to force the monsters hunting me to look in all the wrong places. I'm going to need you to think bigger, Fred. I want *all* of Hell's army, and I want them scouring this world for those witches. They are here, hiding from us. I want to know where they are. I want to know if they fucking sneeze. Make sure the demons keep their distance and that their presence isn't detected. I don't want them to see me coming until I decide it is time to take them down."

"You expect me to turn all of Hell's army against Lucifer?" He laughed until his eyes met mine. "You know who I am, don't you?"

"You're the High Prince of Hell, *Lust*. Of course, I know who you are. I told you, I'm not stupid. There has been nothing I've done in the last five years that hasn't been premeditated. The demons I killed inside Vlad's bar, they would have challenged you against turning Lucifer's army against him. So they had to die, and a little lie was all it took to finish them off. I also killed your brother, who was stronger than you. Couldn't have Sloth getting in our way, now could we? Plus, I needed his death to make tongues start wagging in Hell, which forced you out and into my world. That was why you surfaced and started slaughtering humans you assumed had knowledge of who had murdered your brother, wasn't it? The only thing I didn't plan was slipping on a beast's cock and liking it. But shit happens, and I did. Now he is inside my head, prowling as he hunts me. The thing is, I knew he would be. As I said, I have trained my body to become a weapon. Callaghan and what is within him can still only access what I allow them to now. I did suffer electrical shock recently, and of course, that makes things trickier for them, not me. I closed that part of it off to him, the part that thinks and plans. Not my preferred way of blocking him, but I made do with what I had."

"You're really the one who was promised by the seers," he said as he covered his mouth with his hand, watching me. "You're the Queen of fucking Darkness."

"I'm so much more than that, more than you and

your minions will ever fully understand. In less than five minutes, that beast is going to come through those doors, drawn by the music and the scent I left on purpose before I abandoned you here to secure the thread needed to put you back together. Into the tomb you go, Asmodeus. I can't have you fucking this up now. Through the tomb is your Hell Gate; take it, and wait for your orders. Tick-tock, Fred."

"If you planned all of this, then why the fuck were we in their goddamn compound at all, woman," he demanded with his mouth opening and closing as he watched me.

"I needed to check their defenses and figure out where Arthur is hiding. He and I have unfinished business to discuss. I also needed to know a few other things, which I learned in my time there. I know a way to kill him, finally."

CHAPTER
thirty-two

I SLIPPED FROM THE COVER OF THE DARKNESS AND shadows smiling. I slowly walked up the stairs to the Guild, feeling the beast as his magic reached for me. I turned calmly, staring at him over my shoulder, I slipped through the wards I'd placed that not even he could pass through. Meeting the Fae hadn't been an accident either, however, them being present as I'd slaughtered demons had been, but shit happened for a reason. Plus, I had never counted on the desperation of the Templar race that had created the pesky necklace. Not every plan could be foreseen, and yet I hadn't minded the pleasure that was delivered because of them.

I turned, sitting down and watched him with the other Knights as they slipped from the darkened alleyways and stood around the edge of the barrier. My heart sped up as I took in the glowing blue eyes that made butterflies explode within me. I felt him deep inside of me, his endless pacing as he realized he was locked out and couldn't reach me.

He paced right in front of me, staring me down as I smiled up at him with victory shining in my eyes. I'd known the Fae had slipped back into Faery, just as I knew there was a portal in the catacombs that led into the harem inside the Horde stronghold, even if they didn't. Once upon a time, before Alazander, the previous Horde King had discovered it; the druids used the portal to save a woman from his clutches. I stood up, dusting off my ass as I stepped close enough to inhale his masculinity, which I craved. I didn't crave him; I wanted this beast to devour me. To give me the silence inside my mind that only he could.

"You want me, woman, I can smell it on you," he growled angrily as he tried to beckon me to him with the shared lust we felt.

"I do, I want to ride you so badly that I ache with it," I whispered huskily. "I want to slide down your cock slowly and let you fill me until I burn from how full you make me. Do you want that too?" I asked huskily. I smirked, watching those ancient eyes narrowing as he smelled the desire my sex put off.

"You do know that when I catch you—and I *will* catch you, wife—I'm going to fucking destroy you. I'll make you so fucking weak with need that you will beg me to come, but you won't come, not unless I allow you to. I'll show you an entirely new meaning of torture," he uttered as his claws lengthened, and those beside him followed his cue as they struggled against the monsters they held.

"I'm counting on it," I said as I remained in place.

"They won't protect you from me," he whispered. "They can't interfere; no one can."

"They're not," I said with a shrug. "Not that they are aware of, anyway. Plausible deniability is something that not even the Gods can charge another with interference if they had no knowledge of committing a crime."

"Smart, but the Gods won't think twice about hurting them should they prevent me from reaching you. That womb belongs to me. It aches to be filled. You know it, and I know it."

"Does it? It may crave your child, but I do not. I do not crave being made into a slave again. I will never be a slave to you or anyone else. I am done being hurt by your people and mine. I am your wife, one you have failed to protect over and over again because no matter what happens, you refuse to look around you. Ask your father why my spine was broken, and who wielded the whip that severed it. Ask him who allowed my face to be painted and my mind to be punished for disobeying him as he craved the woman I would become. Ask your father, Callaghan. Ask that bastard who touched my innocent flesh first and defiled me, or how I knew what fucking was. Yes, I threw myself on you, but only because I watched your father fuck his whores while I was tied to the same bed, forced to watch him as he took them again and again. Practice, he said, so that I would know how to please him when the time came. Only he became impotent, didn't he?" I smiled coldly as Callaghan shook his head. "You never wondered how you were called away every time I was hurt, you never even questioned it. Who sent you away from me? Who sent you on errands that any simple Knight could have done and then off to wars that weren't yours to fight? You and your men are and always have been the strongest of your kind, housing beasts that can kill with

a mere thought of their mind, and yet he sent *you*. He sent you away from me because our bond was unnatural. He craved what you had become, and then he craved the one thing in the entire world that held your attention. I have never been real to him, merely a cure."

"He would never cross me," he hissed as anger pulsed from him. "You want me to murder my father? That's low, Erie, even for you."

"No, not murder him. I want you to open your eyes. You are his sword, his greatest accomplishment. You, who he wished to protect from my poisonous cunt. If he loses you to me, he loses you all. He knows that, he's always known that. He told me as he bent a whore over and took her before me, staring at me the entire time. I was *nine*, Mason. You were on a crusade to protect Knights who had come into a precarious position, but when you reached them, they weren't even there anymore, were they? He has a cross on his chest with the Templar Knights motto beneath it instead of around it as is custom. I'm guessing that he couldn't stand that pain of his clavicle being tattooed, which was why there were only a few dots placed where it should have been. I know, because I stared at that tattoo instead of into his heartless gaze where he wished me to. He also has three scars above his right hip; one was sewn incorrectly and left a gash wider than it should have. On his cock is a nick from a blade, which I know because he came on my face to make sure I knew that when the time came, he'd put it into my untried body."

Callaghan shook his head, but he knew. I could see it burning in his eyes as he stared at me with horror glowing within them. He knew the only way I could speak with the knowledge of those scars was if I'd seen his father naked.

"Erie, fuck!" he shouted as he looked away and then stared back at me with pain in his eyes. "You were mine to protect."

"You failed, not because you didn't try, but because everyone around us made sure that you did. You failed to see the snakes in the grass that never wanted us together. I threw myself at you to stop it, to stop the abuse that I knew would continue the moment you left me again, and it did. Because time after time, your father sent you away so that he could watch me be tortured. He craved it as if punishing me brought him joy. Probably because the one time you disobeyed him was because you were with me. He didn't want you with me, and he knew that if and when he broke me, someone would still be called to use my womb. He promised me that I would carry his seed and that you would never want me. He told me you couldn't stand the sight of my face or what he had told them to do to it. When you denied me, when you looked at me with disdain, I knew what he said was the truth. He reminded me often of what he would do to me. Then he just stopped, because you told him that I was your mate, but that I wasn't just your mate, Mason, I was the mate to the monster within you. See, I could never piece together why he had so suddenly backed off of me until your beast mounted me. I then knew what had scared him so much that now he just wanted me dead. He is currently working with the druids on a plan to kill me after I have given birth to your son. *Our* son," I hissed. "It is his goal to get the cure and end my life before I can taint you or his grandson. Frasier is aware and has been your father's best friend since long before you were born, which is why you have not killed him yet. Don't

worry, right now they're making peace with their Gods. I don't need you to save me. I just need you to stay the fuck off me long enough that I can save myself."

"What the fuck did you do, Erie?" he demanded as an explosion erupted from a few blocks away. Everyone moved, ducking against the attack, except me.

"I set their world on fire," I smiled softly. "Just as I will continue to do until every last druid is dead. Next, I begin hunting witches. Don't worry, your Templars and Masonries are safe from me, well, most of them. My list is growing smaller lately, which is good I guess, since y'know, you and that beast have been removed from it. I do like that cock," I smirked as I turned away from the anger burning in his eyes and sauntered up the stairs of the Guild. "Fuck you later, Callaghan."

"Where the fuck do you think you're going, woman? You just blew up an entire fucking building of innocent people!" he shouted.

I turned and stared at him. "Innocent? Innocent! They beat me; they put things into me so they could track me. They touched me just because they could. I was the dirty little secret that they used and abused when they decided to. I was sent out to murder women and children, Callaghan. To slaughter entire families just so the druids didn't have to pay them what they were due. I have spent years accumulating an underground railroad so fucking deep and protected that no one has or will ever find it. You and your Knights were supposed to protect the innocent, not the guilty. You have protected the rich and privileged at your father's behest since the start of the Order. Me? I've collected those who needed me, those who held their loyalty above all else. Every single person I was ordered to murder at the behest of the druids or *your* father, I saved. They are not innocent; they tried to put that blood on my hands because to them, *I* didn't matter. According to them, I have no soul. *I* have a soul, Mason. I have a fucking soul. I feel it with you. I know who I am. I know I'm yours and that you are my home. I can't be what you want me to be because they broke me. I have so many fucking cracks that I can't hold myself together, and when I try, I just end up with more."

"Erie, come *with* me."

"I can't," I whispered as a single tear slipped free. "I'm not *done* yet."

I turned, walking away from the one thing in this world that I craved. The one man who turned me inside-out and made me *want* more. He was dangerous to the monster inside of me, that craved to play with his, to the woman I wished to be. I wasn't able to become what he wanted or needed. I never would be. Life had thrown me into the flames and watched as I'd burned to ashes. What had come from those ashes was deadly, precise, and yes, a little crazy. My entire world had been created to bring me to where I needed to be. I paused on the stairs, and I turned my eyes to the Druid's Den as more explosions rocked through it, moving the maze of floors beneath it. Several other buildings in downtown Spokane joined it, and I smiled while I looked away, pushing into the Guild as I started making my way to the portal. I prayed that the Gods chose me to punish, and not the Fae. They had extended a branch, and I'd been afraid to reach for it, but now, now I needed them to start the next step of my plan.

CHAPTER
Thirty-Three

CALLAGHAN

I STOOD ON THE ROOFTOP OF THE HIGH-RISE BUILDING, watching as the fires she'd lit continued to burn around the city. The bottle pressed against my lips and I drank deeply of the amber liquid before I passed it to Uther, who snorted as another building exploded. Hours had passed since I'd felt her leaving this world, and still, buildings continued to detonate all around us. She'd set the entire city ablaze right beneath our fucking noses. We'd rushed back here and searched for anything that could explode within the compound, unsure how she had brought this city and the druids to their knees.

"I think she's made her fucking point," Uther hissed as he tipped up the bottle, chugging it.

"It isn't a point. This isn't a statement. This is her revenge for what she's endured, and it's terrifyingly beautiful, just as she once was."

Rhett cleared his throat, and I knew what he was about to say. He said it anyway. "I've seen the scars she told us about."

"We all have," I admitted through anger that burned at what we knew to be the truth. It didn't lessen the blow or the knowledge that we'd been blinded by our trust in Douglas, and the orders we had never failed to obey.

"And, what do we do about that?" he countered.

"I don't know," I admitted. I felt bile pushing against the back of my throat as her words played out on repeat in my head. "Rip his fucking spine out, let her do it? I don't know. If she wanted him dead, he'd already be dead."

"I found this," Lance said as he set a recorder on the ledge of the building and pushed play.

We listened while she recanted her tale, the blow after blow that hit me hurt more as I listened, forced to take in everything she'd hidden. The coldness in her tone, and utter lack of pain with each description of those she'd murdered as a mere child, to the assaults she had survived. She'd skipped telling the demon of my father and his lusting over her, which I knew had been to protect me. This woman who had survived enough pain to last fifty lifetimes had left out things about me, about the Templars that she hadn't had to. Erie's only fucking crime was being born, created from the one thing that could save us. That didn't mean what slept within her was innocent, but the girl who had been born of the cauldron…she was.

"And we thought she was broken, she's a fucking serial killer," Uther snorted as he lifted the bottle before handing it back to me. "One with premeditated methods that she has perfected in the last century," he uttered as he turned, watching another group of buildings as they crumbled to more blasts and eruptions.

"She is very broken," I whispered. "Broken and hurt so deeply that she doesn't feel anything anymore, and worse, she's pissed. Life holds no value or meaning to her anymore, just like before. She cracked today, though, speaking to me. She called me Mason. She used my name and said she had a soul. She wants to be saved, but she doesn't think she can be anymore. We fucking did that to her, our people and hers. We made that girl think she is a monster who doesn't matter. My own father violated her. I don't know if she can be saved, but I have to try before it is too late. Already the witches seek her out, and if they find her before she's returned to her true form, they will destroy her, and we will lose everything."

"And you think she can be saved? She's murdered hundreds of people today alone, and we are still watching them die. She smiled as they lost their lives. She's madness, maybe beautiful madness, but there's just some madness that can never be stopped. How many people are on that fucking list of hers? There may not be anyone to save by the time she finishes completing it." Rhett tipped the bottle, downing the last of it before he reached down and grabbed another. "Of all the fucking things I miss about being mortal, it's getting piss-drunk and forgetting the problems we have."

"You realize the buildings that just went down were the druid's living quarters, with their families in them," Uther growled as the flames reflected in his eyes.

"Their mates were moved last week, they were relocated because of a gas leak," I uttered as my eyes narrowed. "Erie was here with us when that happened."

"You think she spoke truthfully about her underground railroad?" Lance asked as he tipped a bottle of vodka upside down, chugging it. I watched as he polished it off, unable to gain more than a simple buzz no matter how much we drank and knowing that bothered him the most. He'd sacrificed the love of his life, the one woman who he'd cherished above everything.

"I think I wouldn't put shit past her anymore. She's planned everything down the last detail. She slit her flesh to drain the meds that were constantly being injected into her, while using her own poison to keep them open. She knew what type of nulling medication we used, knowing it combined with the mix of toxins she used, would keep her from healing. She used electrocution to keep me from knowing her mind as she formulated her escape, but also knew it would keep me from learning her position; everything she's done has been of her own free will. I think she has orchestrated everything to where she needed it to be and used us all to make it so. I didn't see it coming. I thought I could save her, but this entire time, she wouldn't let me."

"Erie isn't the type of woman who needs to be protected. She's the type of woman you need protection from," Uther chuckled. "She's a wild card, a fucking Celtic woman who set the world ablaze just to show us she could."

"She didn't have the demon with her, what the fuck was that about anyway?" Rhett asked. "I mean, she got herself to that medical ward to free him, as well as herself, right?"

"He couldn't hurt her," I laughed bitterly. "She kept

him as a friend, her version of one she could trust. She took the head of the High Prince of Hell, one who runs Hell's armies, and she kept him in her fucking freezer like a pet. I'm guessing he fits into this plan somewhere. I just have to figure out where. She's got people helping her, that much is a given. She didn't get out of here to plant those bombs. She told them where and trusted them to get the job done. Erie had the wives and children removed from the housing complexes. She planned that knowing with the grid being down, they'd be forced to move out of the city. She knew the druids were meeting tonight, she knew my father would be there. He can't be killed, but she knew he would feel it, would know it was her. Erie is also aware that he doesn't heal like us, and that it takes him time. She took away the chance of me killing him with her being elsewhere. Erie isn't crazy; she's fucking brilliant. She's shown us what she wanted us to see, and this entire time, she's been setting up fucking dominos."

"So what is the plan now? Prepare for the end of days and let it ride?" Rhett asked. "It's not like we don't deserve it, but then, it won't be us dying. It will be everyone else that we are forced to watch perish."

"End of days? No, I'm going to walk right into Faery and take my girl back. She may be brilliant, but she's mine. She knows it and feels it, and as much as she pretends not to care, Erie does. She won't let those children die. She saved the druids' mates; she protected their children. Erie is cold, she's broken, and she doesn't think she can be saved, but she won't let innocent people pay for things that they didn't do. She could have left those women and children in that building and blown it, and then it would have been the end of the entire druid race in the United States. Instead, she protected them because that is who she is. She's more Templar than she is aware. We fight to protect those who cannot protect themselves," I uttered. "The moment I tell the Fae the truth, they'll no longer have deniability of interferences. They may have it now, but once they know, she won't let them protect her. She's faulted in this life, inflicted with humanity. Because deep down, she fucking cares about who lives and dies now. She's one of us and always has been. *Non nobis, Domine, non nobis, sed Nomini tuo da gloriam,*" I said thickly as warmth flooded my chest for the woman she'd become in this lifetime, blossoming within me, giving me hope for the future.

"*Non nobis, Domine, non nobis, sed Nomini tuo da gloriam,*" they chanted, and we all smiled as the past crashed against the future.

Erie was mine, and no one or anything would stop me from getting to her. I couldn't just run in with swords drawn, but not even the Horde King would stand against the beast I held within me. It was older, more calculating and deadly than he wanted to deal with. Besides, I didn't want to fight them; I just wanted her back. The beast within me craved her touch. It wanted her as much as I did, but where I wanted to love her and fix her cracks, it wanted what she gave to him, bare fucking bones. She wanted the mindlessness that took away the pain, if even for a second. I wanted to heal her, to fix what had been broken. I exhaled as I looked around at the men. They had no idea who I had brought back, or why, but if I was right, and the witches had awoken to hunt her, I'd need to bring the real owner of her soul back.

"Get the horses ready and wear your strongest armor. We go for war, but we avoid it at all costs. I can't watch more children die due to this curse. The Horde may want to protect her, but they're held to the laws of their lands, and we can use it. I don't like it, but we're out of fucking time. I have two months left to knock her up, or our child won't be born in time to save us."

"Pony up, bitches, we're going to Faery," Rhett grinned.

"It's not a good thing," Uther snorted as he shook his head.

"How many Templars can say they've ridden to Faery with the intent to confront the King of the Horde to release a maiden?" Rhett laughed and then paused as everyone raised their hand except for him. "Why the fuck do I always get left behind?" he asked.

"You were young, unable to control the beast that chose you. Couldn't have you facing off with Alazander and creating another war, now could we?" I scoffed. "We already had a war on three different fronts, and someone had to get the High King's daughter back. He hid her within that harem knowing the other kings wouldn't touch her. She was, after all, mortal and played a servant to Kiara, and was unsubstantial to his cause. We also went in to get Laura back so the druids would stop whining about it. That one we did right in the middle of a war within their own court. It was easy enough unless you consider the women inside that tomb."

"Whatever, let's just go, *Mister I been to Faery enough times that I could draw a damn map*," he muttered beneath his breath.

"You asked," Uther chuckled.

"You did," I snorted.

"Let's just get this shit over with," Lance groaned.

"To the ends of the earth, and whatever it brings, gentlemen," I said as we started forward. My throat bobbed as I imagined her with the men of Faery, now unleashed sexually. Erie wasn't that girl, but then she wasn't the girl I'd thought she was either. I swallowed down the pain of her betrayal, knowing why she felt we too deserved to die. My own father had prevented me from protecting her, and that created a hatred that burned deeper than anything else. He'd allowed her to be tortured, to be brutalized, which, now that I knew, it made perfect sense. I'd been so focused on saving her that I hadn't stopped to think of how he knew certain things about her.

He knew how to null her powers, which would have taken scientists time to perfect a serum. How I'd been gone every single time something had happened to her, and Arthur, his fucking obsession with her. I hadn't even considered that or where he had come from. She'd known, she had hidden it from me, but why? Why hide it unless even then she had begun planning her revenge? This woman, this beautifully broken, chaotic woman that made my blood pound and my body ache, was brilliant. The one thing she wasn't was fucking heartless, or at least she wasn't *yet*.

"Is now a good time to tell you that Erie kept all of your corpses in the basement of the shopping mall?" Lance asked. "She also set them up to appear to be having a tea party. I had begun to wonder where the corpses were being hidden. She even dressed your naked corpse into a pink dress."

I laughed as I turned to look at him, and my smile
fell. "You're fucking serious?"

"Dead serious, I'm afraid."

"Fucking Erie," I laughed.

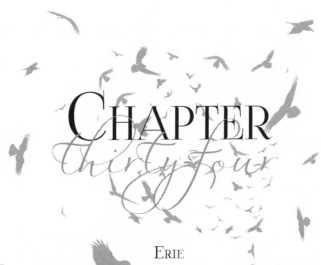

CHAPTER
thirty-four

ERIE

I STOOD UPON THE BATTLEMENTS, STARING DOWN AS
the men below it trained. Zahruk was covered in sweat,
and God love him, the man was all muscle and sexy Fae.
He moved with precision, ageless knowledge that he'd
perfected. Every move he made, I learned, and every
once in a while, he'd peer up at me as I studied him and
the way he moved. Not his body, not the fact that he was
beautiful and lethal combined, but because he was cold,
like me. I was still staring at him as he wiped his face
off with a towel and then disappeared before my eyes. I
leaned over, searching the ground below me until hands
touched me.

Spinning around, I stared him down until my eyes
lowered to the washboard abs that pulsed with brands.
I sniffed him, noting that he smelled nothing like
Callaghan and then I sighed with an ache in my chest
that I couldn't understand. I lifted my stare, watching as
he examined me with a curious gaze.

"You stare any harder and I may start to think you want me."

"You're not ugly," I stated as I took him in once more and then lifted my gaze to his.

He laughed coldly as he stepped closer. "Do you want to fuck me, Erie?"

"Do you want to have sexual relationships with me?" I returned, carefully watching his eyes as his pupils dilated. Something within him peered out at me and, sizing me up, he lifted his hand to touch my cheek, pausing as I flinched, only to drop it, a sad smile playing on his lips.

"I think you'd be wild in bed, but I also think that heart is taken by another. I can smell him on you, which means you've been marked by something ancient. If I thought you were my girl, you'd be bent over screaming as I drilled that sweet pussy of yours until it dripped and sang for me in approval."

"Why don't men ever watch their dirty mouths? I mean, do you think a woman wants to know that you will make her come, and she's supposed to just fall down and spread her legs apart, like come and get it, big boy? Those words slay me? I don't get you creatures."

"Fae, or men, Erie?" he scoffed as he leaned in closer, invading my space with his dominating presence, and yeah, okay, maybe those words had affected me. It could also be the male Fae pheromones oozing from him that was alerting what my brain thought it wanted. One or the other, it was working.

"Are you going to kiss me?" I asked, watching as he smiled and then he did just that. His lips pressed against mine, and I opened for him, moaning as his Fae magic washed over me. His hands settled on my hips, and then he pulled back as his eyes locked with mine.

"What the fuck are you?" he demanded as he backed up. "You're not just something created; you're something brought back."

"Does that make you not want to fuck me?" I asked as I smiled coldly.

"You know that I'm Fae, right? There isn't a pussy that I wouldn't fuck; just because it scared me wouldn't stop me. You, woman, terrify me. You make me crave shit that I don't want to crave. You know that though, don't you? I don't think you want this; you want the one you're fighting against. I get it, I do. But are you really going to let them all die? There are children involved, Erie."

"I was a child once," I said as he stepped back, watching me. "I *wanted* death."

"Gods, Erie, you plan to let them die," he uttered as he stared at me like he didn't know me at all, and well, he didn't. None of them knew who I was, or who I was becoming. Once they did, they would cower before me, and I'd lose them and whatever friendship I was trying to forge. What I was, well, we didn't make friends.

"I don't know what I have planned for them. I murdered thousands of people, innocent people, for merely being part of what sought to destroy me. You want to see the good in me, but there is nothing good to find within me. They did this. They need to pay for their crimes."

"What did you do?" he asked carefully.

"I killed every male druid of breeding age or older," I said with a shrug as I turned away from him, unable to watch the hate fill in his sapphire depths. "They

murdered women and children to teach men of other species a lesson. They sent me to slaughter innocent people like I was something that held no soul and wouldn't feel what I did to them. Zahruk, I've killed so many people that when I close my eyes, it's all I see. I hear them, and I laugh. I don't cry or feel bad. Does that mean I am bad?"

"Did you enjoy killing them?" he asked as he moved to stand beside me and he leaned against the edge, staring out over the land that spread out before us.

"Some, yes. I craved their pain because I can no longer feel it. It's like I'm numb, and I'll never feel again, but then Callaghan touches me, and I feel home. I hate it, and yet I crave it. I am his; I know that. I can't go to him like this. Like this broken fucking thing that needs to be fixed. He believes he can save me, but I don't want to be saved. I've learned to live with who I am, what I am. I am who this world forged me to become in order to survive it."

"How many innocent lives have you taken?" he asked.

"Too many to be redeemed," I admitted as I watched the children beneath us run towards their waiting parents. "When I was first freed of my cage, I did what I was told. I murdered entire families to be released, just to be able to smell fresh air or feel the sun on my flesh. I had to; I had to figure out how to remove the spells that held me beneath their thumb. It took time, so I did what they said so I could survive long enough to make them pay for doing what they did to me."

"That isn't on you," he said as he folded his hands and leaned over, watching the kids. "We do what we're told to do when we have no other choice. I murdered hundreds of thousands of innocent Fae, merely because I was ordered to do it. I didn't blink, not fucking once. I just fucking did it to survive my father. I murdered babes in their cribs, mothers as they fed them," he admitted as his hands turned white against the memories. "I did whatever it took to keep my brothers safe, including taking the head of the second-born son to appease my father that I was willing to fight Ryder for the crown should it fall to him."

"I guess I'm lucky that I had no siblings. I may have killed them too," I admitted as I turned, studying him. "Did your father really cook the Winter Court's children and feed them to their parents?" I watched him swallow before dropping my gaze. "You guys are seriously twisted here. I may have to hang out for a while."

"You won't," he laughed as he stared at me. I turned, gazing back out over the land as I tilted my head. "Oh, wildfire, you're evil, but you're not that fucking evil. You don't plan to let them die, not when you can stop it. People like us will spend the rest of our lives trying to undo the wrongs of the past. Just as you did when you saved the rest of them."

I blinked, and I pulled my power to me, turning to stare at him as the air grew thick around us. "You need to tell me how you know about my people!"

"Calm your pretty tits, woman," he scoffed. "You think I allow anyone close to the King without knowing every fucking minuscule detail about them? I watched you, and when you didn't go back because you were stuck in the Order's compound, who the fuck do you think had food dropped to them? I'm not against you, never will be unless you threaten those I care about. You are not evil, Erie. You're just like me. So fucking twisted that we push those we want away because deep down, buried so fucking deep no one can touch it, is a heart. It's easier to bury it, to hide that it ever existed because it's been broken and abused, and the only way we know how to survive anymore is to forget that it is there."

"You fed my people?" I asked as I let the magic fade away. "I don't even do that," I frowned. "If they're not willing to help themselves, neither am I. If they're weak, this world will destroy them."

"Then how the fuck did you earn their loyalty?" he asked.

"I gave them a choice. Follow me or die. I offered my protection, but it comes with a price."

"Which is?"

"Loyalty," I said softly. "If I don't have their loyalty, I won't hold their respect. If they don't respect me, they die. I cannot have snakes in my field, for one miscalculation and everything I've worked to build will fall. I cannot fail. I will not fail."

"You know he is coming here to get you, don't you?" he asked.

"I'm aware," I uttered as I leaned against his arm and we watched the sun setting behind the mountain range that surrounded their fortress.

"Erie, just because you are broken doesn't mean you're not fucking beautiful. Sometimes we need those cracks to let the light back in. The darkness is there, so we remember, but it also lets us see the beauty within it. Broken things are often the most beautiful. Also, woman, you're touching me."

"You kissed me, so I guess this makes us even."

"So now I can touch you because I kissed you?

Should I fuck you so that I can hug you, too?"

"You like that cock where it is?"

"Noted," he laughed, and I smiled, staring out of the beauty of their world. "Two fucked up assholes. That is what we are, girl."

"I don't mind it so much anymore. I've accepted my demons, but I don't think I can be what Callaghan needs. I can't be a mom. Mine left me on the floor of a church to die; I think she prayed for my death. What if I am like her? What if I hurt my son?"

"So don't," he said so calmly that I lifted my head, staring at him as if he'd grown another head. "Look, Ryder was terrified of being a father. Synthia was horrified at the idea of being a mother. You can't judge who you will be as a parent based on what yours did. If those two have done anything right, it's those kids. You won't be your parents, who, from what you said, weren't even willing when they were pushed into that cauldron."

"You're not as big of an asshole as I thought you were," I admitted as we watched the Horde King moving below us.

"Thanks, Erie. Don't tell anyone that shit. And if you ever need me, I'm right here, girl. I will protect you, even at the cost of my own life."

"I don't need to be protected. I can destroy the world at will; the difference is, I don't want to. I want to fix it. I want it to be a world where no child suffers needlessly. If I have to set it on fire to make them fear what I am, so be it."

"Well, that wasn't ominous at all."

"Don't worry, Zahruk; I'll protect you."

CHAPTER
thirty-five

I STOOD OUTSIDE THE ROOM, LISTENING TO THE FAE speak to one another with respect. A total stranger, and just like that, she was considered their family. My eyes moved to Zahruk, who smirked, watching the intensity on my face as I stared at him. He knew I was leaving, and he didn't try to stop me. I almost wished he would, and yet I knew, I knew I would never let those children who had stared up at my Knight with wonder die. Not even if it cost me my life, which, if everything the seer said was true, may come to pass.

I pushed off the wall, moving to the middle of the room as I waited for them to cease their endless banter, and then whispered my goodbyes, knowing it may be the last time I saw any of them.

"Am I pregnant with puppies?" Icelyn asked, and I paused mid-step, staring at her as my mind raced to figure out if that was an actual option here. I mean, we were in Faery and Danu was fucked up about the rules of her races, and I needed to know the answer before I left here.

"No," Sinjinn said as he shook his head.

My heart slowed as I watched the love in his eyes, which almost wiped out the disappointment of her not carrying puppies. I almost laughed, almost, but the look of sheer terror on Icelyn's delicate features made me pause.

"They'll be normal, Icelyn," he continued, assuring her.

"Fire and ice, and nothing nice," I snickered as they turned to stare at me. "I'm leaving; he comes. Congrats on those babies though, they're going to fuck some shit up when they get older."

"Who comes?" Icelyn asked.

"Callaghan; he is relentless. That Templar needs to find his God again because I tire of being hunted. And if he had his way, we'd be having puppies together, you and I. I'd make a horrible mother, but you…you'll be great. Maybe after I blow him up, we can do some girl time, yeah?"

"Um, okay?" Icelyn replied, staring at me as if I was insane.

"It's a date, in a non-sexual, I'm-not-going-to-lick-your-face sorta way."

"Erie, be careful," Synthia warned, her eyes filling with sadness. "They are running out of time. He won't be able to prevent the others from hunting you any longer. You've reached the ten-month mark for the extinction of two races. They will be working together to capture you."

"They'll try," I agreed. There was sadness in my tone, which I knew settled into my eyes, something I couldn't hide as I turned to leave the few friends I'd actually made who hadn't been in my freezer, which would have been cool, admittedly, but I didn't think they would hurt me. "If I don't come back, thank you for allowing me to be here," I said thickly before I laughed and chewed my bottom lip while I considered what a normal person would say. "It's been fun."

"You could stay here with us."

I stared at her as I shook my head sadly. "And bring yet another fight to your gates? You have enough going on, and this is my fight. This fight is one only I can wage against them. No; if it happens, it happens. Know that I went out smiling, and they just went out with a bang."

"We'd fight for you, Erie. You're one of us now."

"Synthia, that's sweet, but this is war. Don't go ruining my glory with this mushy shit. I've lived by the sword, and I will die by his sword. I've always known my fate and never feared meeting it head-on. I'll go out on my terms." Synthia moved closer, hugging me awkwardly as everyone watched us, including Zahruk, who I glared at as he smirked. "What the fuck are you doing? We don't hug; hugging isn't badass. Eww, that was just awkward."

"Come back, Erie, come back to us alive," Synthia said, undeterred by the way I shrugged it off.

"Not if you plan to hug me again. That's a hard limit for me." I didn't know why these assholes kept hugging me, but I hated it. It was too...normal. Like they'd decided I was family, and they shouldn't. I wasn't family, I was born alone, and I would always be alone. Even among them, I felt utterly alone. Like a part of me was so broken that it would never be set back into place correctly. Waving over my shoulder, I headed down the long, winding hallway towards Eliran's medical unit.

On the lower level, I paused, staring at Olivia, who was being examined as Ristan held her hand, kissing it as they laughed over the sound of static thumping. She was massively pregnant, and any day now, she'd give birth to her child. I frowned as I watched the love they shared, visible to anyone with eyes as it shined from both of them.

I craved what they shared, but I knew I'd never have it. I felt it deep inside of me as if I was cursed to be alone until the day I died, which wouldn't be ever. Eliran lifted his gaze to me and smiled until he noted the look on my face.

"I'll be right back, Ristan," he muttered as he poured disinfectant on his hands and moved to where I stood. He stared at me, his knowing look both bothering and unsettling me.

"So look, I need a few things. I also need to know that you won't tell anyone what they are," I said as I crossed my arms over my chest, staring pointedly at him as I dropped my gaze to the counter, which was lined with specimens and other things.

"You want something kept secret from Ryder and Synthia?" he asked, lifting a dark brow in question.

"I don't want it; I need it. They are not a part of this, and whatever comes from it, that's on me. I don't want them to think they can protect me from what has been foretold if it is true," I admitted as I swallowed hard and then whispered into his ear as he exhaled. "Can you do that for me?" I asked.

"I can, but you're not alone," he uttered as he pushed

his fingers through his messy hair. He shook his head. "I have what you need, how many do you want?" he asked.

"All of them," I replied, barely above a whispered sigh.

Callaghan

The Horde stronghold was spread out over forty city blocks wide, like an actual city of its own. It was exactly as I remembered it from when I'd come here the last time before Ryder was even knee-high to Alazander, and the beast within his father had just begun to catch the madness. My gaze drifted to the army of Fae that stood between us and it, along with the King himself that was walking in the shadows of the fortress with his second in command close to his side.

"So what now, we just walk up and knock on the gate?" Rhett asked as he took in the impressive size and structure of their stronghold. It was impenetrable, but there were ways around that too.

"They're aware that we're here," I muttered as I watched the shadows moving. "Look beyond what your human eyes see, and sense."

"Jesus," he uttered as the armor the Fae wore changed, making them visible.

"Impressive, aren't they?" Uther snorted. "Didn't expect the King to be the one to greet us," he muttered, impressed by the balls of their newly crowned King.

I wasn't; I'd watched him grow into his own as he became a law unto himself through strength and patience. I'd known who he would become, and when his father fell, I'd been one of the assholes cheering on the sheer size of his balls. "Ryder doesn't fear anything. He's like we are, a caged beast that only wears a mask so that people and creatures don't fear him," I replied.

He stopped mere feet from the army of Knights that stood shoulder to shoulder with me. We'd brought force to show them we could, so they knew I wasn't leaving without her. I didn't want to cause problems, not when I respected the shit out of him, and them—not to mention what they were doing—but too much rode on Erie carrying a child. The entire world would die if we fell, and that was something we hadn't made known to them yet.

"I sure hope you thought this through, Callaghan. You don't march an army to the gates of my home unless you damn sure plan to use it." He shook his head, angered that we were here, but if it were his world on fire, he'd have done the same.

"I don't do anything that I don't intend to follow through with, Ryder. I will use whatever force I have to get her back. There are things playing out that you and your kind have no knowledge of. You are interfering where you have no right, not to mention, where the Gods themselves have no right," I argued, watching his men as they closed rank around him.

"She isn't here," Synthia said. "She left to face you."

"She is here; I can feel her. More than that, Goddess, that which crawls inside of me, smells its mate. Just as your beast can track you by scent, mine can track his *wife*."

"Wife?" she asked as she tilted her head, studying me as she sent her power out, sensing our strengths and weaknesses, and no doubt finding nothing but dead air where we stood.

"Erie is mated to the creature I hold. She knows it, just as it knows her. She's mine by right of the cauldron and the Gods; you meddle where it isn't your concern. Just as you did when you thought to freeze me and let her escape me—you can't freeze other Gods, for the record, Synthia." I smirked as her eyes narrowed, but more than that, I felt her distress call reaching from this world into the others. "They won't help you either, because they know what happens when you fuck with fate. You think Destiny is a fickle bitch, try Fate for a change, and you'll know true pain."

"We'll see," she said as she waited.

I nodded, folding my hands slowly, letting the beast take in the situation as my eyes glowed and studied Ryder's. His was the same size as mine, cut from the same ancient cloth. Golden eyes watched me, noting the beast within me as we sized one another up. I saw the moment recognition lit in his gaze. The moment he sensed the likeness, the same cloth we'd been cut from. He should have noticed it sooner, but then Danu masked most of her creations beneath the guise of civility, and she had enjoyed her secrets.

"You fought my father," Ryder growled as his hands fisted at his sides and his head lowered as if he would strike against me.

"A few times, yes."

"Yet you couldn't kill him," he hissed as a smile lit across his face.

"It wasn't that I *couldn't* kill him," I assured him evenly, knowing he was young, younger than me, and that his beast was itching for a fight. "It wasn't his time to die yet. Fate is fickle like that, and had we murdered the King when you were so young; you'd never have become King. You weren't ready. So while I could have killed your father and ended his reign of terror, what would have replaced him would have been worse. You had to be ready to face him because you had to be able to hold that thing inside of you. So we waited, and when you were ready, you didn't need us to fight that battle for you."

"I was ready to be King the moment I crawled from my mother and drew breath into my lungs."

"To be King, yes," I replied. "To hold the beast, no. No, you weren't. It would have chosen another because you were too young. Everything happens for a reason, everything. I was here when you were a child; many of us were. I slaughtered countless creatures of the Horde to save one woman from that madman. You watched me from the walls of this very stronghold as I fought your father and took her back."

"So, what now? We fight for another woman?"

"I don't want to fight you," I admitted carefully, showing no fear to the beast that craved the fight beneath his veneer of calmness. "Erie is too important to walk away from. If my people fall, so too will your world."

"I'm going to assume you can prove that," he challenged as he stood straight, staring right at me.

"Lucian can verify it," I said as I turned my gaze to the creature who had answered Synthia's call, along with his men. Lucian smirked at Synthia before he paused, taking in the tense scene before his midnight gaze held mine, and his smile vanished.

"Well, isn't this a fucking shit show," he grumbled,

studying me before his gaze swung to Synthia and Ryder and then slowly moved back as the tick in his jaw hammered. "Nothing good can come of this."

Synthia studied Lucian and his men before she swung her pretty violet eyes back to me. "It doesn't matter; you're not taking her from us. She is so fucking broken that one more crack and that sliver of hope she holds is gone. She will shatter, Callaghan, and if she does, it's game over for her. Her mind is so broken that it radiates from her. You did that to her, you and your people. You think I'm going to just fucking hand her over and betray her?"

"Synthia," Lucian hissed as the air grew thicker and more Goddesses popped into their line. Lucian rolled his eyes as he crossed his arms over his chest, unhappy that she'd called back-up for her back-up.

"I'm not handing her over to him to be a fucking slave. She deserves better. None of you understand how fucked up it is to have your entire life planned out, right down to the use of your womb. She is broken because of what you allowed to happen to her. You may not have partaken in it, but you sure as shit didn't save her from it either," she said sternly and then smiled as the air thickened again with who she had summoned.

Mórrígan appeared, and I almost rolled my eyes. And then Destiny was there, staring between us before she hit the ground, right beside Mórrígan, or more to the point, the one who pretended to be *the* Mórrígan. I studied their prone position as they bowed at my feet much to Synthia's dismay.

"Get the hell up, what are you doing?" she hissed as she stared at them in horror and then lifted her eyes to hold mine.

"They can't get up unless Callaghan allows them to," Lucian said as he watched me; his smirk was pure evil as he sized me up. It would be a good fight, of that I was certain. He wouldn't kill me though, no more than I would end his life, so a fight was pointless, and we both knew it. We all had parts to play that entire worlds depended on. "Why are you here?" he asked without spilling what I was, only because he knew I'd return the favor.

"I'm collecting my wife," I said.

His eyes swung to Synthia and then landed on Ryder. "You have Erie here? Are you fucking insane?" he snapped as his men stood silently behind him, ready to do whatever he ordered.

"Who the fuck is he," Ryder asked, his beast stirring within him.

"Don't ask questions that you're not ready for, Ryder," Lucian grumbled as his midnight blue eyes locked with mine. "You know she hates you, right?"

"As much as your woman hates you, Lucian," I growled. "Luckily, you solved your issue, which landed us in the middle of an apocalypse, but your mess, it started my mess earlier than planned. Now the clock is ticking, and I have two months to secure a child before the Templars begin to fall to the plague that was promised. You know what happens when they fall."

"I do," he said. His eyes held mine before he lowered them and turned them on Synthia and Ryder. "I'm going to say this once, and I need you to fucking *hear* me. If Erie doesn't go with him, you won't have an earth to go back to, none of us will. It won't be there.

If the Templars fall, so does mankind." He shrugged. "Lena and I will have somewhere else to go, but I'm guessing your unnatural attachment to that world, and your bleeding fucking hearts will want to do what is right."

"Fuck that," Zahruk snapped, stepping from the shadows. "You fucking broke her. You let them rip that girl apart until she thinks she is unable to be fixed. You let them destroy her, and now you want her to save you? Fucking earn it."

"You like my wife," I hissed through a cold smile as I studied his determination to protect her. "I get it; you're like her, broken by a father who enjoyed watching you hurt things," I uttered. "Ryder, to give you an idea of who I am, I was here when you were a child. My beast is the only beast that fought your father and didn't lose to his. Yours is young, way younger than mine is. I have more, an army of beasts that heed my call to arms. I will fight to save my people so that the monsters that wait just outside the veil do not enter that world. I am the protector of men and those who cannot fight against the evil of that world. You have your own world, and I have mine. I won't harm her, but I can't stop this from happening, and neither can any of you."

"She isn't leaving here," Synthia snapped as the air grew thick with power.

I watched them prepare to fight as Lucian's words fell on deaf ears. "So be it," I uttered as we allowed our power to escape the tight confines we held on it. "I will fight to have her, but I don't want this. I won't watch the world die, not again."

Erie

I hefted the bag onto my shoulder as I thanked Eliran, who looked at me as if I was insane. Maybe I was because this was just another part of a bigger plan. I exited the stronghold and stopped in the garden as I waved my hand to drop the wards I'd placed before they could attack me. Power pulsed over my flesh, and I gazed around, peering at the garden to pinpoint the source of the disturbance. The hair on my neck rose as I slipped past the unguarded exit and then frowned.

What the hell were they thinking to leave it unguarded? I straightened as more power pushed through the air, thick enough to slice through it with a knife. I rounded the gates and closed them as I started towards the front of the stronghold, worried that the war had come to Faery at last.

My eyes took in the situation before me, and I flinched as Synthia stood beside her beast with Zahruk at her other side, swords drawn as she stared at Callaghan, who remained calm as if the sight of the Horde preparing to fight didn't even faze him. Lucian was beside them, and women bowed before Callaghan as I slowly got closer. It was the most awkward thing I'd witnessed in a very long time, as if neither side actually wanted to attack the other one, but was going to do it anyway. Then it hit me, who they were fighting over. I watched them preparing to fight each other as I uttered a cry of horror and rushed towards them. I screamed as they lunged to engage. My hands pulled at my hair as I let out a resounding pulse of magic and denial at what was unfolding.

"No!" I screamed as I watched them pausing to look

at me where my hair pulsed, floating with the magic that pushed from me and filled the air as thunder exploded and lightning crashed around me. "No, no, this doesn't happen!" Tears slid down my cheeks as I moved to stand between them.

"Doesn't look like she got very far," Callaghan growled as Zahruk stepped in front of me, protecting me. I placed my hand against his chest and shook my head.

"This is not where you die," I uttered thickly. "I'm not worth this. I'll go," I said as I turned to look at Callaghan. "You don't touch them. You hear me? They don't know who or what I am. You don't touch them."

"I told you, and I warned you that there was no place I wouldn't follow you."

"You have no damn right to be here," I whispered through clenched teeth.

"I have no right? You're willing to let the world burn just so you can get revenge? I understand your pain; I know you deserve to hurt them as they have hurt you. That is where it ends. You are not willing to watch innocent people die; I know this because I know you. You are mine; you will always be mine. If you die a thousand deaths, you will always return to me, Erie. *To me!* You are mine, I brought you back!" he shouted as his wings unfurled. "You may not feel me in human form, but you know me in this one. You feel me, woman. I know you do. You're my world, you've been my world since you stole my fucking heart and made me feel what true love was even if it was hell and chaos, but *you* chose *me*. We are running out of time, and I can't let this continue. I wish I could give you all the time in the world, but I can't."

"Out of time for what? To knock me up?" I screamed as I ripped the backpack off and dumped it out in front of him. I reached down, picking up test after test as I threw them at him. "You asshole!" I cried as I punched him in the jaw and then watched him slowly turn to look down at the pile of positive pregnancy tests that littered the ground. I moved to throw another punch, but he grabbed my arms, pulling me into his body as his wings wrapped around me. His forehead pressed against mine as he exhaled slowly.

"My Erie," he uttered as he held me cradled in his embrace. "You will be okay, I vow it to you. I will protect you. Nothing can change this. I know you feel me, as I feel you. You are my home, my wife."

"It won't be okay. Nothing will ever be okay! They deserve to pay for what they did. I can't do this," I said as I pushed away from him and stepped back. "I'm not ready to do this with you. You want me to play house, be a mother, but I don't know how to! I didn't even have one, how am I supposed to know how to be one? I am evil; I know I am. I crave blood and flesh, and the way it sounds when it is severed from a body. I've murdered thousands of people, innocent people. I don't deserve to give life when all I have ever known was how to take it away! I am not doing this!" I screamed as I hugged my stomach.

"Erie, you've already done this before, and you were beautiful as you carried my child. You just don't remember it. They took you from me, just as they took our son who grew in your womb."

"Are you insane? I have never had a child, never!"

"Erie, you have lived before. You have conquered worlds before you were ever born into this one. You are over a thousand years old. You're the Queen to my King, the granddaughter of the Dagda from which you were reborn. Only those of his line can be brought back with the dark power, just as that is the only thing that can take their life from this world. You are one-third of *the* Mórrígan. You are Éire, the mother of Ireland, the one who gave it life and became their patroness. You are my wife and the granddaughter of the Great Kings of Ireland. Our child will be a Prince of our people. The Templars originated from the people you ruled over, the Tuatha Dé Danann. On your death, we left Ireland to escape the creatures of the sea who we thought had helped murder you. We became nothing more than myths that they whispered about to their children, and their children's children, so that we were forgotten. I kept you safe until you came back to me, but I was under oath to the Gods to protect those who needed to be protected, or they would never allow you to come back to me. You and me, we defended the realm together. We always have since you claimed me. We protected it together after you defeated me in battle and claimed me as your King. You told me that we would fight together, to whatever comes, and whatever end we meet, we do it together."

"You good?" I asked as I stared at him in disbelief. "Did you bump your fucking head on the way in here? I am only one hundred years old." I stared at him as my mouth opened and closed, unable to even process what he said. "If I am what you say I am, then how come everyone thinks I am evil, or better yet, why do I crave destruction?"

"Because you are one-third of the Mórrígan, and you crave war and death, just as Mórrígan here does. Ask her, Erie. Ask her if she feels you as strongly as I do. Rise, Mórrígan, and welcome your sister back from the grave," he growled.

I turned, staring at the Goddess who rose and tilted her head. "You didn't; tell me you didn't do this! The Gods would riot and rain down hell on us if you brought back War!"

"You thought I would allow her to slumber until the others decided she could rise? She's slept for over a thousand years as a newborn babe, gathering her power to her. She was promised, and therefore, cannot be taken. Now welcome your sister back before I take your fucking life," he hissed barely above a whisper.

I watched as the Goddesses moved, one slipping beside Synthia as the other one moved to stand before me. Her eyes watched me, her hand lifted, and I recoiled as I moved closer to Callaghan, who wrapped his arms around me, placing his clawed hands over my womb.

"She will destroy us all," she whispered. "You understand that, right? Can you feel her mind, her emotions? You of all people know that of the three, she craved blood, chaos, death, and fucking war! You shouldn't have brought her back yet!" she hissed before she vanished.

"She sounds lovely," I uttered as I turned, staring up at him. "Am I being punked? Because you lost me at a thousand years. I am turning one hundred this year, and you're not invited to my party."

"I know exactly how old you are because I carried

you with me and built a fucking castle around you to defend you. Erie, you were born before this world was overcrowded with mortals, but you're not what she says you are. You are mine, and everything else doesn't matter. We need to get going; you set a few fires that are close to my compound."

"You mean your dad's compound? No, I don't think so. I won't be anywhere he is."

"Erie, I never planned to keep you locked in the compound. I only stayed there because you needed to see the people, to know they needed to be saved. You think you're the only one who planned ahead?"

"Fine, but don't think I intend to stay there. I will not be your prisoner. Plus, I don't like you, and I have people to kill, shit to blow up, and a world to destroy. I'm a very, very busy girl these days."

He snorted and whispered against my ear softly, "Tell Synthia and Zahruk that you will be okay. They worry about your mind breaking, and we all know that Goddesses do not break so easily." He pushed me forward, and I turned, eyeing him as my jaw ticked.

I stared at the pair who watched me with unease as they'd learned what I was, and what I would become. I chewed my lip nervously as my gaze turned, holding Lucian's with familiarity before I dropped it and swung my eyes back to Zahruk. He'd promised to defend me with his life, and had proven he was willing. Synthia had told me she would fight for me, and so she had tried.

"I'm okay; he won't hurt me. He needs me alive to help him."

"Say the word, and you won't have to go," Zahruk said.

"This is my fight, not yours. I feel him, you know? It's like we're connected on a deeper level, which I can't explain. I promise that he won't hurt me, because if he does, I will get free again and murder his ass, like usual. Maybe you can come visit sometime. I don't think he plans to keep me locked up for the entire time, right?" I asked, turning back to Callaghan.

"That depends on you, wild one. You might enjoy what I have in mind for you."

"I doubt that," I uttered as I looked back at the Fae, knowing that if I didn't go, they would fight and that not all of them would survive. That wasn't something I could live with. No, I hadn't thought that any child could withstand living through me dying, but yet one had. It wasn't in my plans, and it had definitely thrown a wrench into what was coming.

CHAPTER
thirty-six

I WALKED THROUGH THE EMPTY HALLWAYS OF
Callaghan's extensive home. He'd built it deep into the
mountain at the edge of Spokane, hidden deep within
a valley. It was a compound big enough to relocate the
entire Templar people who, even now, were too close to
the chaos that was unfolding in downtown.

I paused as I looked at a portrait of an enchantingly
beautiful woman. Long flame-colored hair blew in the
wind as she looked out over a cliff into the ocean. I felt
Callaghan behind me and slowly turned to face him.

"What happens now?" I asked carefully.

"Now I destroy that pretty cunt of yours and
make you beg me to come. Smelling your arousal and
watching you saunter away beyond my reach isn't
something I will allow to go unpunished. Knowing you
were around men who are sexual creatures as that sweet
pussy wanted and craved to be fucked, it made the beast
a little unhinged. He wants to punish you."

"And you?" I asked, feeling my insides heating at

his words.

"I want to watch you fuck him," he smirked as he stared at my lips. "You smell excited, woman," he uttered as he backed me up next to the picture and his eyes slid up to it. "I have to admit, watching your cunt stretch around us is the hottest thing I've ever seen in my entire life. Watching you demand more, begging to be destroyed by us, you're a wanton little thing, aren't you, Erie? I can smell that pussy weeping with the need to be fucked already," he whispered as he pinched my chin, lifting my mouth to his.

He didn't kiss me; his lips hovered above mine as he watched me. I didn't know what I craved more right now, my Knight or my beast, who took me to new limits I'd never dreamed of reaching. I inched forward, but he pulled away. He smirked, and I narrowed my gaze on his.

"You kissed another man," he growled as he lowered his mouth to my ear. "I'm going to remind you of what and who I am as I stretch that tight cunt as far as I can. You will never allow another man to touch what is mine. I have loved you since the sun first spread over this earth, and while I have taken whores to my bed, and even a wife in this form, I have never loved another woman. Come, we crave you. You get this one pass because I assure you, I crave no other woman, nor have I touched another since you were reborn into this form."

"You scare me with your intensity," I uttered.

"Good, it should. You are my home," he growled as he threaded his fingers through mine and pulled me behind him. "One day, it will come back to you. You've only been awake for a short time."

"You are insane; you know that, right?" I asked as I followed him until he stopped in front of an arched doorway and pulled it open.

Inside the room was the world's largest bed, done in midnight blue and cream blankets. The walls were painted in murals of rolling green hills and water that spread out onto the ceiling. I let my gaze fall to the swing that hung down from four ceiling posts with lengths of chain attached to them. I walked to the swing, pushing it as I turned around, staring him down as he watched me.

"What is this?" I asked as I tried to ignore the burning lust that saturated the depths of his gaze.

"That is where you will be chained as I torture that sweet flesh. It's a swing, one that you'll be bound to as we show you why it's not a good idea to kiss other men knowing that we felt it. You knew, and yet you did it anyway. Your shock treatment didn't take away our ability to feel your pleasure when you're close to us. So when that sweet cunt wept for him, you knew we felt it clenching with the need to be filled."

"I kissed him," I admitted as I turned back, pushing the swing as it moved. "I needed to compare you with someone else. It's not like I've had a lot of experience with other men, so I needed to know what I felt, and what others could feel like."

"And?" he asked against my neck as his lips sent a shiver racing through me.

"And I wanted you still," I whispered as he ripped the spaghetti straps of the shirt I wore, exposing my breasts. "Jealous?" I asked and then felt the power that emanated from him while his hands cupped my breasts as he kissed my neck softly.

"He couldn't soothe that dirty little ache inside of you, ever. You were created to be stretched, to be fucked by me. He wouldn't have even made it to stripping you on that wall before I would have taken his head. I watched you with him. I watched your pupils dilate with his, and then you stepped away, saving his life. We won't share you; three is already a crowd. Wait until he allows us both to fuck you together. You'll like it, my dirty girl. That ass is mine, though, we agreed. You're not ready for him there, yet. You still think you're mortal, bound by the limitations you set for yourself. We're going to wreck them so that you know exactly what you can do with us. Would you like that, sweet Erie? To be so fucking full that you don't know how to exist without us being buried in your tight holes?" he uttered, pushing the jeans I wore down my hips, kissing my spine as he did it.

"I need you," I whispered thickly as his hands drifted along my hips, slowly letting the pads of his fingers skim over my flesh. I felt his nose pushing against my ass as he kissed one cheek before he rose, helping me step out of the jeans.

"I know you do," he chuckled as his fingers explored the wetness of my body that begged to be filled. "Such a messy girl, so wet and ready to be fucked," he growled huskily while he turned me around, lifting me as he sat me onto the swing. I hissed as it started to move, my body adjusting to being off-kilter as he pushed me down onto the long leather back that allowed me to lay on it. His hands trailed over my legs as he pushed them into separate hoops that sat on one side. "Do you have any idea how hard it was to wait for you to be mentally ready to be fucked by us? I had to watch you from afar, hating that you had no idea what or who I was. I thought you were being fucked and it drove me insane, and yet I wanted you to experience life, and to want to be with me on your own," he said. He slowly walked around, staring at my naked body as he grabbed my hands, slipping my wrists through leather cuffs before he attached each one to a separate chain that was connected to the swing. When he finished, he stood back, gazing at me before he pulled on another chain that stretched me out spread eagle, exposing everything to his heated depths. "Helpless looks good on you," he rumbled heatedly.

"I'm never helpless, Mason," I whispered as his knuckles trailed over my flesh and he started moving away from me.

"Ask the questions that are burning in that beautiful mind of yours, my Erie," he uttered.

"I only have three," I replied huskily.

"Ask them, I will answer them honestly."

"What was it like to be loved by me?" I whispered.

"Beautiful, beautiful, and utter chaos. You chose us, both of us. You gave your love freely, but you came with a cost neither of us was prepared to pay. You didn't just love; you went to war to get it. You took everything, and what you gave back was so much more."

"What did it feel like to be with me?"

"Home, it felt like home. Your love knew no bounds, no boundaries. You were something no man or creature could reach for, could grasp. Yet you reached for us, but your love was brutal, deadly."

"What did it feel like when you lost me; when I

died?" I uttered.

"I wanted to destroy the world and join you in death. I wanted to rain down a hell so utterly destructive that no one or any creature could ever rise from it again. It was as if someone had reached into my chest and ripped you from me. The monster inside of me slaughtered everyone who had your blood on their hands. You left a hole that could never be filled when you died. That was the first time; the second time, it was different, it was needed so that you could be brought back to us."

Tears filled my eyes as I stared at the ceiling, more questions forming in response to his answers. "If I meant so much to you, how could you let them do what they did?"

"Druids by nature, are powerful beings. You needed them to teach you how to wield your magic. You needed to know that your taste for blood was natural and that it is part of who you were before this life. I couldn't teach you that and chance you destroying our people, Erie. You once made me promise to protect them, even from you. So I kept that promise, even though it tore you apart. You are war, death, and the darkest and brightest mix of the Mórrígan. Your sister may use and wield the name, but you hold the people. When Danu abandoned the people of Ireland and created the Fae, you took her place. You're their Queen; you always were and always will be. You just have to remember us and find your way back to us."

"And if I can't?" I asked.

"Then we will all readjust and teach you our ways. There is only one Queen who they will honor and follow, and that is you. The Knights, they need this

child to be born, because no Knight of the Order has been conceived; only Tuatha Dé Danann halflings are being born. Our child will be both. You're the Tuatha; I'm the Knight. You're the promised druid of Dagda's blood who will ignite the flame to burn out the curse. You will prevent the halflings from continuing to die from this curse."

"I'm already pregnant, Mason. I don't know how or why it survived my death, but it did. I didn't know," I said as I continued to stare at the ceiling, uncertain why I confided in him now.

"I know, I can smell him on you now." He loomed over me, staring down in his beast form. "It's time for me to destroy that pussy, as I promised to do, wife. If you cherish your friend, you will never allow his lips to touch what is mine ever again. I don't think his head works as Lust's did."

"Do you plan to actually talk me to death, or can we get to the good part?" I asked, letting him see the fire burning inside of my eyes.

His fingers pushed into my sex as my spine arched, and a moan exploded from my lips. "Oh, my naughty little wife, you're not coming anytime soon. It will be fun to watch you squirm for me, though."

CHAPTER
thirty-seven

MY EYES WATCHED HIM, NOTING THE WAY HIS HEATED gaze slid over my naked flesh. Like a beast preparing to feast on it, those sinful glowing orbs perused every inch of me, leaving nothing unscorched by the heat of it. Mason's fingers slowly brushed over my middle, pulling a hiss from my lips as the sensation sent butterflies pulsing through me. I followed him with my eyes while he slowly moved between my legs, his knuckles skimming the vulnerable flesh there.

I moaned when he pushed two fingers into my pussy, curling them at the knuckle before he withdrew them, licking them clean as I was forced to stare at him. His sinful lips kissed the inside of my thighs, working his way to my ankle before he moved to the other one, kissing everything as he pushed his mouth against the back of my knee.

"Such a messy cunt, does it need to be fucked, Erie?" he purred huskily as he once again settled between my legs. His tongue slipped through my folds, lapping at my pussy until I was crying out as his heated gaze locked with mine. The moment I would have come undone, he pulled away and slapped my flesh, pulling a yelp from me. "Dirty girl, I didn't say that sweet pussy could come for me, yet. You don't come unless I say you can, are we clear?"

"I really don't like you right now." I glared at him as a sinful smile spread over his lips. He shook his head slowly and reached down, lifting his shirt to expose the rippling muscles and tattoos that I longed to taste.

Those Nordic blue eyes glowed as he let his hand slowly trail over the path I wished to taste. He sensed it, noting the hunger of my gaze while he slowly undid the jeans he wore, freeing his heavy cock as that knowing grin turned dark.

"I don't care if you like me; you were bad. You let another male taste what belongs to me. You can come when I fucking decide you've earned it. This mess? It craves me," he laughed huskily as his hand wrapped around his massive cock, stroking it while I licked my lips.

Remaining silent, I ignored his taunt. I watched his body, and his tattoos seemed to pulse to life, glowing brighter as he moved closer to where I was bound to the swing. I wanted him to just fuck me, to ease the ache between my legs that pulsed for him. I wiggled my hips, inviting him to play as his magic wafted over my flesh.

"How full do you want to be, my sweet nymph?" he purred, and then moved to my mouth, staring at it as his thumb traced my lips.

"I need you to fuck me."

"I'm aware of what you need, but I want to know

what you crave from me."

"All of you, Mason. I want all of you," I uttered hoarsely as his thick cock neared my face. I allowed him control as he pulled my body to the edge of the swing. My mouth opened as he pushed the thick tip of his throbbing cock against my lips.

His magic pushed into my pussy, and I screamed around his cock as he hit against the back of my throat. He filled me until every entrance was burning from being filled. Those glowing eyes watched me, noting everything with carnal knowledge as he let his magic start to withdraw, only to move deeper with every thrust. I moaned around him as he reached for the swing, using it to control my body, and he hissed as I relaxed, taking him deeper into my greedy throat.

"That's it," he crooned as he held the chains, using them to increase the speed while I trembled from the sensation his magic created, using it to fuck me as if he'd cloned himself into three men. My body shivered as the orgasm started to build, but he withdrew and smiled down at the anger that shone from deep in my gaze. "Oh, you thought you could come? How cute, Erie."

He moved to the other side of the swing, pushing into my body without warning as my pussy clamped down against his intrusion. His hands once again grabbed the swing's heavy chains, using it to control my body and the pace at which he fucked me. I needed him to go faster, but instead, it was slow torture as he leaned over, nipping at one nipple before his teeth grazed over my collarbone.

One minute his cock was the only thing buried

inside of me, and the next, his magic filled my ass, and I screamed at the foreign fullness as my spine arched. He chuckled darkly against my neck as he slowly kissed it, sucking at the thundering pulse that beat for him alone.

"Too much," I whimpered as he added more, taking every inch of my body until it burned from being filled. "Mason," I hissed as it turned from pain to pleasure, his penetrating stare noting every emotion that played over my face.

"You aren't human, woman. You can take me in beast form, all of me. You have plenty of times before, and you will again," he murmured against my ear before he withdrew, once again preventing the orgasm from reaching fulfillment. "Such a greedy girl," he laughed as he knelt between my thighs, kissing the insides of both before he pushed his tongue into my center.

It knew right where to go, where to reach my core that made my eyes close as a scream ripped from my throat while he fucked me with his mouth. I felt him growing, and yet his mouth pulled away, but his thick magic continued to fuck me until sweat trickled from my brow.

I stared at him, watching as he smirked and stepped back, stroking his heavy cock in his hand, staring into my soul as if he could see through the darkness into the last part of me that wasn't broken. When he got closer, I licked my lips, staring at the magnificent cock that he stroked.

"I need you; I need you to fuck me right now."

"Oh, I know you want it, sweet girl. That cunt is dripping for me. It's too bad; I can't make it come yet. I crave it. I want to feel it tighten around my cock as it milks every drop from my aching balls. But you were a bad girl, and I'm not a fucking bitch who just caves because you get my dick hard. You won't come until I allow it," he laughed as he brushed the thick head of his pulsing cock over my opening.

"Maybe you can have someone else come in and fuck me if you're not going to do it," I growled and then screamed as he entered me without warning. He expanded, filling me until my eyes grew wide, and rounded as I wiggled against the fullness of him as he stared into my eyes, watching me as the orgasm threatened to explode.

He withdrew before it could, and I whimpered as I stared down at my flesh that dripped with the need to be fucked. I wasn't above begging him, not when I wanted him to throw me down and fuck me until my mind went silent and the only thing I wanted was to feel him from the inside, feel him as he dominated me and sent me spiraling into oblivion with the pleasure he gave me.

"Mason, please," I whispered as he lowered his mouth, licking through the slick wetness of my arousal as I watched his golden head. His beast stared at me from within as those intense blue eyes lifted to mine, while he fucked me with his tongue. My head dropped back as his hands wrapped around my thighs. That tongue slipped through the wetness, driving into my core like a madness he couldn't contain. I screamed as the orgasm peaked, pulsing through me until he pulled away, stopping it from reaching anything more than a painful need that ached to be filled.

"I think you need some time to think about what you did, don't you?" he asked as he pulled up a chair and sat in front of me.

"I think you need to fuck me," I growled as I felt his magic pushing against my flesh, pinching my nipples as he watched me moaning against the sudden onslaught of magic. It pushed into my wetness and then poked against my ass as I shivered at the foreignness of it. I opened my eyes, staring down at him, and then whimpered as pain rushed through me while the magic filled my body. He groaned as he watched me, his eyes hooded with lust while my body trembled with the fullness of him fucking me in both places without so much as touching me.

The magic against my nipples tightened until it felt as if magical clamps had been placed there. I rocked my hips, knowing that no matter what I did, I wouldn't come or find release until he wanted me to.

"That's a tight ass, Erie. Do you like me fucking it?" he asked.

"Mason," I hissed as the orgasm started to build. "I want you in me, I want you fucking me until you write your name on my soul," I pleaded.

"I asked if you liked me fucking that ass," he growled as the magic decreased until the orgasm receded, unable to reach more than a state of unfulfilled aching that created sweat against my neck.

"Yes!" I cried as I trembled for more.

"You are naughty, aren't you?" he asked, his hand stroking his cock as my gaze dropped to the pearl of cum that slowly trailed down it.

"For you? Yes!" I agreed, my eyes continuing to watch that pearl as he smirked, knowing what I needed and craved. "Every piece of me aches for you, Mason," I admitted and watched as he rose to his feet, lowering his mouth to claim mine, his tongue pushing against mine, fighting me until all I could do was take what he gave me. His tongue captured mine, stroking it as he dueled against it and pushed into my body. That thick cock mirrored his tongue, wrecking me until I was moaning with the impending orgasm, but the moment it started to bloom, he withdrew, chuckling at the frustration that came out as a scream from the denial that slithered through me.

"So close, Erie. That sweet pussy is so close to coming, isn't it? It aches to be fucked." His eyes watched every emotion that played over my face as my frustration turned into anger while he smirked, lowering his mouth to my thighs where he kissed the inside of them, licking through the dripping arousal of my cunt until he slowly brushed the heat of his mouth over my thighs again, kissing his way to the back of my knees as he worked the chain. My legs lifted until I was poised on my ass, hanging in the air as he pushed the swing away from me. Suspended, exposed, and vulnerable to him as he slowly stepped back, staring at my flesh that wept to be filled, clenching with need.

"This is torture," I snapped as I struggled in the chains, noting that no matter how awkward it felt, it didn't hurt. I was literally suspended in the air with my legs in front of me, next to my wrists.

"It's the best kind of torture, my beautiful queen," he laughed and lowered himself to his knees and started to ravish my flesh as if he was starving.

I screamed, and everything inside of me tightened as he pushed that devilish tongue into my pussy, using

it to drive me to the edge, only to withdraw the moment the orgasm threatened to release. Once it had passed, he did it again and again, until tears streamed from my eyes as the ache turned painful. When I thought maybe he would allow it, he lifted and leaned his head against my breasts, sucking one between his lips, letting his teeth drag over the sensitive tip.

"You're so fucking wet, Erie. So fucking hot with the need to come," he uttered as he rubbed his cock against my opening, his hand sliding through my hair and yanking it back as he stared into my eyes. "I'm going to fuck you, and you're not going to come yet. Do you hear me, woman? I'm going to stretch that cunt out, and you're going to stop the orgasm from reaching climax. If you come, I'm going to move to that ass, and when I finish with it, you'll know what real torture is."

He pushed into my body, and I groaned as he filled it, pushing against the one spot that would guarantee I exploded the moment he started moving. The noises he made alone sent me teetering on the verge of no return, and as he slowly began rocking his hips using the chain to control my body, my eyes rolled back in my head.

"So fucking good," I uttered as he moved painfully slow, filling me until it ached. "I need to come for you," I whimpered as my body clenched down on his massive cock. His mouth crushed against mine as he slowly continued to move in my core, and the moment I started to fall over the edge, I shook my head as I fought against it.

"That's it, my sweet girl," he encouraged as he rested his forehead against mine, staring down at where he filled me completely. "Such a good girl," he whispered as he pulled out, letting me see what he'd forced me to take into my body.

I wasn't even sure how he'd managed it, but he seemed to enjoy me knowing that he'd fucked me with his wrecking ball cock that seemed to have endless possibilities. The moment he'd withdrawn, I closed my eyes and hissed from the loss of his heat.

He did it for hours, fucking me, forcing me to fight the one thing I wanted most until he released my legs, and then my arms, holding me up merely by balancing me on his thick cock. My legs burned as I wrapped them around his waist, my arms draped over his shoulders as he moved us to the bed, and then lifted me from his throbbing cock. He slowly pulled my body off of his and pushed me down onto the bed before he spread my legs, sucking against the swollen flesh that ached from orgasm denial.

"Look at how swollen you are," he muttered as he kissed my flesh, uncaring that I lay there, silent as he stroked the needy flesh with his tongue, tongue-fucking it until I was whimpering again, writhing on the bed to be given the one thing I needed most.

"You're going to kill me," I warned as he continued to lick my cunt to a burning need that trembled violently through me. He chuckled against my flesh as I lay there, boneless as tremor after tremor of need circulated through me. My hands fisted his hair, holding him to me, and his eyes watched me, noting every minuscule reaction that I had to his mouth and the pleasure he was delivering.

When he detached my hands and pulled me up without warning until my lips were against his, I moaned

as he smiled against them. "Are you ready to come?" he whispered huskily as the candles around us leapt to life. The lights in the room dimmed as his blue ink glowed against my flesh.

"Yes, please," I murmured as I claimed his mouth hungrily. "Please fuck me," I begged as he pushed my body down on his swelling cock. He'd come so many times that I'd lost count, and yet he never tired. He held me on the brink of orgasm several times, stopping everything the moment I'd gotten close. He'd done it until my body turned against me, following the rules he'd placed as it betrayed me. He growled and pushed me to the base of his thickness and then slowly, so fucking slowly lifted me before he kissed my neck. "Faster," I urged.

"No, woman," he laughed darkly. "You will take what I give you. This flesh is mine, just as you are. I want you to know what it feels like to be cherished, to come so fucking hard that everything inside of you screams in pain and pleasure. I want you to feel me," he hissed as he pushed me back, rocking his hips as his magic washed over me, filling the room until I was whimpering while he consumed me from within.

"Mason," I whispered huskily as he sucked against my nipple, lifting those eyes to mine.

"Erie," he uttered as he lifted above me, staring down at me.

He gripped my hips, and he leaned his head against mine, fucking me slowly until the orgasm started, only to stop as my body refused to let it come. I cried out as he started moving faster, fully aware that my body worked against him as he fucked me until I screamed as blinding pleasure consumed me. My body bucked and took his deeper, spine arching from the bed as I wrapped my legs around him, screaming his name. Everything trembled, aching pain ripped from me with white-hot pleasure that made everything else fade away as he slammed into my body over and over again until he rolled us, grabbing my tits as he lifted his hips.

"Ride me, fuck me, Erie. Come for me," he demanded, and I did, riding him as magic pulsed from both of us and the candles extinguished from the storm of our magic combined. He grew, filling every inch of my body until I lifted my eyes to the ceiling and howled while the orgasm ripped me apart as he watched me. "You're the most beautiful thing this world has ever created," he growled thickly as he rolled us again. "This pussy is a fucking mess, wife. I think when I've finished fucking you, I'll lick you clean," he chuckled as he pushed my legs to my chest, staring at where we were connected before glowing blue eyes held mine. "The next time you flirt with someone else, I will keep you in a state of need for weeks, fucking this messy cunt until once again, it fights you to get what it needs from me. You may not remember me, but your body does. It knows what and who it belongs to. Test us again, and you will know what real orgasm denial is, and how much it can hurt."

"Fuck me," I begged as I shivered and trembled around his massive cock.

"Who do you belong to, Erie Callaghan?"

"I belong to no man," I uttered as I pushed against him.

"No, no other man could handle what you are."

"I am yours, Mason. I'm yours."

"You're damn fucking right you are, Erie," he uttered as he fucked me until neither of us could move. When he finished, and my eyes could barely remain open, his lips pressed against my belly, drawing my hand to it as he kissed it. "You carry our son, wife. You carry our future in this body. To me, you're my world, woman. Remember that, because I've hidden you from the Gods, even from the seer who could only foretell what you would endure being reborn. Your sisters thought you were a mere child of the cauldron, but I knew, I knew it was her outside that church on the day you were reborn. I hid you so fucking deep inside your new soul that not even they felt you until I was ready. Now the entire world is ours," he uttered as he rose to stare down at me, pulling me into his arms and kissing my shoulder.

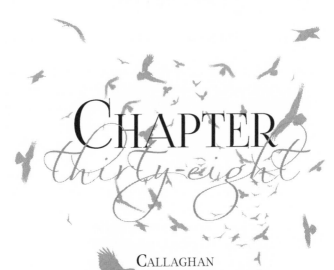

CHAPTER
thirty-eight

CALLAGHAN

FOR DAYS SHE'S BEEN SUBDUED, WILLING TO GO TO war with me in bed and to meet me head-on with her ever-growing need to be with me. It was pure bliss, as we'd been before everything had happened. I was content to stay as we were, with her beneath me, writhing for more, and yet I knew it wouldn't last. It never did with her, not because she didn't want it, but because she was restless, and didn't understand why.

"What news is there?" I asked Lance, who was pacing in the oversized sunroom I'd built for my bride when I'd had this place built with her in mind.

"There are markings all around Spokane. Seven new markings today alone, with the trifecta or pentagrams at points of power, strategic locations made to connect. My guess is, the witches are done waiting for us to fuck up. They're calling her out, and sooner or later, those markings will ignite, and when they do, Erie will be unable to ignore them. It's only a matter of time before they connect, and it sends out a pulse to bring her out of hiding."

"I need more fucking time," I growled as I pushed my fingers through my hair. "She isn't ready, and the only way that has ever worked to bring her back quickly is fucking brutal. If I have to do it, I will lose her, but it would protect her."

"She carries your son in her womb, Mason. He is the hope for the people we have protected until she returned to her rightful place. It's not ideal to bring her back by forcing her mind to recall the events of the past, but we're running out of fucking time. You've brought her back like this before, and while it ended in her death, she came back. If they catch her, they could end her life for good. There's also the curse that they placed that we will have to deal with. And here's the thing, I'd rather have a pissed off pregnant Goddess who hates us, rather than a dead Goddess you can't bring back. It's her third life, Mason. You can't bring her back again, and you know it."

"I can't lose her, not again."

"So you kick-start her mind, what's the worst that happens other than her leaving?" he asked as Uther watched us from the shadows of the room, silently.

"I lose Erie," I admitted. "I hate to say it, but I've fallen in love with the shell that houses the Goddess. Erie has an innocent side to her that drives me wild, and while Mórrígan is lethal and beautiful chaos, Erie is shy glances and beauty incarnate, and when she learns what we have done, what she has done, I lose that side of her. Balor wants his wife back, but she's in that room sleeping in the most perfect form that she has ever embodied. He never had to sit aside and watch Mórrígan fall in love with another as I did. She preferred him to me, and even though I have never wanted anything or anyone more than her, I prefer that broken form that looks at me as if I am the sun that lights her world on fire."

"You can't have both, and sooner or later, she will remember who and what she is. Already fights are breaking out around us. The Fae were going to fight us, and they're unaware that her presence pushed them to act on her behalf. It didn't matter that Synthia was a Goddess herself, she was driven by a need to wage war and fight us because Erie had stayed with them mere days, Mason. She is War, and wherever she is, it will follow her. The Gods will notice that she is back, and I, for one, would rather she face those twisted fucks as their equal. If you don't, you chance them finding her as a broken, unhinged being that doesn't stand a chance against them on her own," Uther pointed out carefully, his tattooed eyes flashing, the design pulsing against the bronzed flesh of his arms. "She's weaker this time, and she's also been tortured, beaten, and abused on our watch. We did this to her, even if it was unknowingly, we failed her. That's on us, not her. If she hates us, we deserve it."

"My fear is not losing her completely, because I know she will always come back to me. It's her being fully formed, seeking the revenge she craves. If Erie is the Mórrígan when she seeks that revenge, the entire world will suffer in her wake. She will set it on fire, and when she rises from the ashes, there may be nothing left of it. She doesn't know that our people are hers, or that she is the one who cursed them, and us, to our fate.

If I'm forced to bring her back with violence, she may damn well respond to us with the same."

"Mason, we've followed you since you joined her army. We would follow you to the end of this world and into death if you asked it of us; you know that. We're brothers in arms, and have been since the sun first rose in Ireland and bathed its beauty with its grace. Whatever you decide, we will stand beside your choice. Our only worry is that she cannot be reborn again. This is your last chance to get it right and to get her back. If we fuck this up, it's not just the end for her; it's the end of this world and everyone attached to it." Uther shrugged. "Whatever happens, we're with you."

"I need one more night," I muttered as I stared at the bedroom door, where the Goddess of War slumbered, oblivious to what she was about to be put through.

"Orders?" he asked, watching me with a sadness I loathed.

"Erase the marks around town, and buy me as much time as you can. Bringing her back like this was violent last time, and it will take time. Ward the compound against the Gods and anything else that may be coming for her. We brought back War, and doing so is going to create a war which this world has never known before. Now we have to save her by breaking her again," I said softly, watching the door as the sun set, casting it into shadows.

Standing up, I moved through the room which had grown heavy in silence; I knew they wouldn't speak again. I knew them as I knew the beast within me; their beasts were similar to what I held. We belonged to the sea, to a world where monsters could belong and not be hunted or trifled with. We were from a different time, and so was she. We were from a time when Gods warred against one another, testing each other and the races that they struggled to create. It was why Danu had built a new world, creating the Fae, abandoning an entire race as war had fallen onto the land, and my Goddess, the Goddess of War and Battle, had come to defend them.

Erie, however, would be lost to me when Mórrígan returned, and I loved her. I had fallen in love with who she was in this lifetime, the innocent smiles and the way she lit up as she took in some new marvelous thing that she'd never seen before. The way she'd responded to way too much sugar as her sweet tongue had licked and discovered cotton candy. The way she watched me with a longing, confusion marring her expressive eyes as she tried to place me from her past.

Erie was chaotic, beautiful, and yeah, fucking broken, but there was so much light inside of her that every fucking crack let a little more of it out. Synthia was wrong, and while she'd been underneath the enchantment of the Goddess of War unknowingly, she didn't see her as I saw her. Erie was born to rule, to wage war against ancient races and bathe in their blood. I'd watched her do it a thousand times before and I knew I would again, even if she never returned to her Goddess form. Either way, I had to make a child with her to undo the curse she unleashed upon us.

Our people depended on it, and I'd made a promise to her, always to protect them. I'd done everything I could to help them live, to flourish in this strange new world and adapt as it changed. Now she was back, and I was going to lose her if I didn't let her go. The problem

was that I loved her enough to let her go, even if it cost me my fucking soul.

Inside the room, I watched her sleeping, oblivious to the horror that she was about to endure. Sitting beside her, I pushed her thick red hair away from her face. Her lips curved into a smile as she dreamt of a home she'd never seen or touched. Ireland, every dream she had was of Ireland and the way the waves crashed against the shore angrily. The thunder that rumbled as lightning sparked across the grey skies. Ireland was beautiful, terrifyingly so, and yet I'd had no problem leaving it when she had no longer been there. She craved it, the eerily beautiful and haunting landscape which was bathed in blood from one end of the island to the other.

"Little one, I need you to remember that I love you. I've always loved you from the first time I laid eyes upon you, until now. I wish there were another way. That I could spare you from this, from everything," I uttered as I curled against the lithe frame of the body she'd been housed within.

The child had been born of magic, but it hadn't been dead. Its soul had melded to hers the moment she took control of it, sharing its mind and soul until hers had been earned. Gods and Goddesses had to earn a soul, unlike mankind. Once they'd done enough good to offset the bad, they became immortal. Mórrígan hadn't earned this soul, Erie had. Together, they melded into one being, and yet somehow I knew, once Mórrígan was free of the tethers we'd placed to conceal her until she was strong enough, Erie would cease to be a part of her.

I'd lose her. And the worst part was, *I* loved Erie more for her innocence, and those shy smiles she gave me. Mórrígan had only looked my way because of what I held, and yet Erie wanted me. She fucking wanted me, and she was perfect, and I was going to destroy it because, in order to save the woman I've loved for the last seventy-five years, I had to let her go.

"Mason," she uttered sleepily as she turned, staring into my eyes as a shy smile lifted the corners of her lips. "I'm starving."

"You want me to make you some food?" I asked, hiding the pain that smile caused me.

"I don't want food; I want you."

"Say it again," I whispered.

"I want you, Mason. I want all of you."

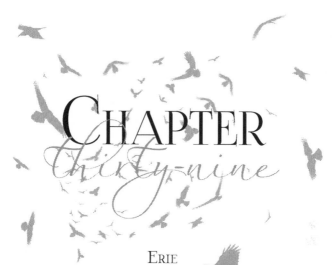

CHAPTER
thirty-nine

ERIE

I STARED OUT THE WINDOW ABSENTLY, WATCHING THE sun as it rose over the rolling mountaintops that stretched out in the distance. The wheat fields below me swayed as the breeze caught them, bending the green shoots as it rolled off of the mountains. A few workers tilled the back fields, probably planting spring crops into the muddy rows of fertilizer. They looked like ants so far from the mansion from where I watched them working. It was a familiar sight, to see the workers out tilling the fields with horse-drawn plows. My gaze swung back to the sunrise, watching as it turned from orange to red.

A song slipped from my lips as I watched it, craving another land so far away from this one with everything inside of me. A land of green rolling hills and magical sunsets that bathed the soul as it crested below the rocky shorelines. I sang the Song of Exiles. It was a song I'd learned and listened to many times before, until it was engraved in my mind, my soul. I didn't sing loudly since

I knew Mason slept in the other room just beside me. I'd slipped from his embrace, moving into this room to think without his touch removing rational thought from my mind.

I could feel his men being drawn to the song, knowing they watched me from afar as it slid from my tongue, filling the room in the sad notes. I craved the lands we'd left so long ago, the land of my birth, and where so many turbulent things had befallen me, and yet so many good things had happened there as well. It terrified me, knowing that Callaghan spoke truthfully, and I felt it within me, the words he spoke. I was sure a lot of what he said was his version, and mine was still buried inside of me. He'd told me how he'd taken care of my body, treasuring it as I healed from being reborn. Somehow, I knew our past was a lot more twisted than what he'd told the Fae.

Turning, I paused, looking at Callaghan, who watched me with something glowing in his stare that terrified me. Love flared in his eyes as I watched him taking me in, his heavy stare landing on where my hand rested on my stomach. This man terrified me more than an army of demons that had stormed into this world. It was mostly because I felt connected to him. I felt him within me, listening to my every uttered thought or plan. He was somehow a part of me, and no matter what I did, I couldn't eradicate him from my soul.

Swallowing hard, I took him in slowly, drinking in the sight of him as my heart began to roar deafeningly in my ears. As if the mere sight of this man, this creature, sent my blood boiling to a roiling need. I marveled at his perfection, the sculpted pecs that were covered in tattoos, and the abs that pulsed with every breath he took, reveling at his strength. Dipping my eyes lower, I took in the V of his hips, knowing just where it led and how massive that cock could grow as he fed me pleasure that was so wild, so wicked, that it beckoned to my blackened soul. He didn't move, didn't inch forward as he watched me eating up the sight of him in nothing more than a pair of faded sweatpants. He looked as if he was created for pleasure, carved of marble to represent masculinity in its purest, rawest form.

"Am I your prisoner now, Callaghan?" I asked as I watched him carefully.

Callaghan's eyes cut to his men as he lifted his chin in their direction. One by one, they left the room until only he, and I remained. Pushing from the wall, his magic wrapped around me, slithering over my flesh with a comforting touch that pulled a whimper from my lungs. His heavy gaze locked with mine as he slowly walked to me. Turning me around in his arms, he pressed a kiss against my ear. His lips skimmed over my neck, kissing my pulse as it kicked into gear, unable to ignore the way he made my body ignite with need.

"What do you see?" he asked, letting his hands moved to cradle my flat stomach. "What did you see outside that made you wish for our home, Erie?"

"The men who tilled the fields, and the rising fire that bathed the land in its heated embrace," I admitted, albeit hesitantly.

"And when you longed for it, was I there with you?" he whispered.

"You were right beside me on the Cliffs of Moher. We watched the sun rise and then set as the men behind us tilled the fields, even though they were barren."

"And did you see the Aran Islands?" he asked huskily as his hands lifted, spreading over my waist as he placed another kiss against the flesh below my ear.

"No, we couldn't see beyond the glowing sun. We just stood there, watching it rise together. As if nothing could touch us there. I think you were angry and yet it didn't matter right then. It was strange but insignificant." I rested my head against him as I closed my eyes, inhaling his scent as I fought to calm the wild beat of my heart. "Are you mad at me?" I asked.

"You left my bed," he growled as he pulled me closer, if at all possible, as we watched the sun rising in the sky. "I don't remember giving you permission to leave it. I missed waking to see you curled against me, little one."

"I didn't ask permission. I needed to think without you touching me."

"Thinking is overrated," he murmured as he pulled me with him to the couch, sitting down as he placed me onto his lap, still within view of the rising sun. "We used to sit like this and watch the sun rising in Ireland."

"I don't remember that," I said as I turned, staring into his glowing eyes which alerted me that it was no longer Callaghan who held me in his arms. As I stared at him, he changed, mutating into the beast, and my breathing hitched, unable to stop it as I watched him turn from man to monster.

"I'm going to help you remember who you are," he uttered as he watched me crawling off him to sit on my hindquarters on the couch, just out of his reach. "Scared of me, Erie? When I first met you, I wanted to rip that pretty fucking head of yours off. You called me a Heathen King, and maybe I was. I had invaded your lands with the sole intent to remove you from power. You were the Goddess of War, and if I could bring you to heel, no one else would have ever tried to move against my people or me. You use to bathe in the blood of your enemies upon the battlefield, this fiery queen that left death and destruction in her wake. I've watched you do it a thousand times before from the shadows, and I've never craved anything as much as I craved you. I craved to dethrone you, to have you kneel at my feet in submission, but without waging war against you, you'd never come out of that perfect fucking palace that caged you beyond my reach. So I flooded your shores with my men, and I sent you my demands. I wanted your throne so that I could force the right to make you kneel at my feet. It enraged you that a Heathen King like me would dare demand someone as powerful as you kneel before me at my feet like some weakling. I'd known that the moment you received my demands, war would be unavoidable. I craved it against you until you answered with your demands. My throne and my entire kingdom destroyed by your hand. You didn't offer anything, only what you knew, which was war.

"You see, war back then had no code of conduct. There were no rules that we played by or followed. That was why, when I stormed the shores of your pretty little island and watched as you waged battle against men twice your size with no fear, no hesitation, I knew I had to fight you. I should have known by the way you held your own against men that it would be a fatal mistake to bring my armies against you, but something in those pretty blue eyes made everything else irrelevant. You feared nothing, no one. This tiny wisp of a battle queen who met my armies on the open field with her pretty tits on display, painted in the woad of the Celtic warriors. The skirt you had worn barely covered your legs, hanging between those pretty, sculptured thighs. I didn't know what I craved more, your throne or just to fucking touch you once.

"I watched my men rush towards you, and you didn't even flinch as you dismounted from your great warhorse and smiled while you withdrew your blades, quickly showing that you were not one to trifle with. Instead, I stared at you, watching your swift, well-placed blows that you landed as you cleared the field of men effortlessly. They fell to your blades, one after the other, until you stood on a pile of corpses beneath your tiny bare feet. It was then that you looked over the dead, and those full, sensual lips curved into a smile as you caught sight of me, watching you slaughter my men. I was oblivious to the war that raged around me, unable to take my eyes from your perfection. You were so fucking beautiful and wild, my perfect vision of what a woman should be. I remember being lost in those blue eyes, drowning in them as I watched you from afar while you slowly moved towards me. You were so otherworldly, a vision of grace. Your blood-red hair caught the wind at the same moment your skirt did, and fuck, I wanted to sink my cock into your sweet, naked flesh more than I wanted to take your head.

"That was how you brought me down, woman. You knew why I'd come, and what I craved from you, and you wielded it like a blade held against my throat. You

promised men the pleasure of watching you fight, only to remove their heads before any could ever tempt you to sin with them. The virgin battle queen who had never been touched by man or beast," he chuckled huskily as his eyes grew heavy with lust and memories. "I was so enthralled by you as you stared me down fearlessly that I didn't even hear the men beside me fall to your army as the battle continued all around me. It wasn't until my legs were kicked from beneath me, forcing me to kneel as you leisurely made your way to where I had been brought down before you, that I understood how so many men had died at your feet. I expected death, to have my head removed the moment you reached me. Instead, you slowly knelt in front of me as I was placed into chains by Lugh. He was your second in command, remember him? He was the only man to live that had ever touched you. Not sexually, no, because you weren't created to fuck, you were created for war.

"You brought me to my knees, Erie. Your brazen beauty and skills for war took down the Second Fomorian King. Only one other monster had ever brought them to heel and ruled them. Only one other man had ever ruled them before, and he had walked away from them to rule at the side of a Goddess. You though, you'd known I would fall to your beauty because all men who had come before me had done the same. You had no code, no honor, and the only thing you understood was war and how to win it. Men trembled before you, but I wouldn't. You told me to beg for my life as you sat there, gazing into my eyes with no fear whatsoever, and I refused you. You kept me alive instead of murdering me, as was the custom back then. Instead of chaining me to the walls of your dungeon, you had me chained in your bedroom. To me, it was a fate worse than death, because you knew how to break me where countless others had failed before you.

"There, you stripped bare and bathed as I watched you. Me, the King of an entire race, forced to watch the untouchable queen bathing. I'd have given anything to touch you, to taste your sweet cunt just once. The longer I hung there, the more I wanted to hurt you for forcing me to watch what I could never have. I wanted to drink your blood while I fucked you. I wanted you to scream my name as I took your life while you rode my cock, and I told you as much a million times. I asked you as you bathed before me in that room how many other men had been chained as I was, in your private chambers, and you replied with only *one*. Never before had a man even entered your room, let alone been blessed enough to watch the Goddess of War bathing, until me. I begged you to fuck me, to give me what no other man had tasted as I waited there, knowing you would give me death eventually. Yet you didn't; you kept me chained there like I was some fucking pet. So there I stood, unable to do anything else as I watched you moving around your room, naked as the day you were created.

"For months I stood there, watching you ponder what my fate would be. You still waged war, battling my people, who fought against you to free me from your cage. Day after day, you returned to me covered in the blood of my people, telling me in every little detail how they had died. On the fifth month of captivity, you slid a chair in front of me, watching me as I fought to free myself of the chains you'd placed me in. I was beyond

hearing you, beyond feeling pain anymore, and you knew it. You knew I was going mad, and still, you made me listen to your pretty mouth when all I wanted to do was fuck it. You told me how lacking my armies were without their Heathen King to lead them in battle. You placed their inability to win against you on me. I wanted to slit that pretty throat to make you stop speaking, but worse, I wanted to feel it wrapped around my cock as you sucked me dry. You were my fantasy every night and day until I knew I was going mad from the need to be buried in your naked heat.

"I'd wanted to hate you, and instead, I craved the sound of your voice and your endless stories. Then that day, when you moved that chair in front of me, and you bared that beautiful cunt to me, I knew nothing else, I wanted nothing else. I hated myself, and I hated you for making me betray my people—or what I had felt was a betrayal. So I hung there, watching the untouched Goddess of War as she spoke of murdering my people. I was lost in the sight of you, baring your untried cunt as you pushed your tiny, unskilled fingers through its slick arousal. You didn't care that a captive Heathen King watched as those tiny fingers dipped into that sweet heaven. The smell of your arousal flooded the room, and you knew I responded to it, to you. It exhilarated you that my cock stood erect and took notice that your pink flesh was wet and ready for me. I don't think I could have hated my weakness more as I listened to the sweet noises you made and came undone as I hung there, helpless to even cover the shame of my ejaculation from where you watched it. You stood up and moved towards me, touching it, lifting one arousal-covered finger through the mess I'd made watching you, and then as I watched you, you fucking tasted me and moaned. As if you'd enjoyed it.

"You see, I knew what you were doing to me and that you wanted me to crave you. I knew you hunted my family with your armies, and even as you slept in the same room with me, others continued to hunt them. It was only a matter of time before you discovered where I had hidden them away from you. Days turned into weeks; weeks turned into months. Every day you would return covered in blood, you placed that chair in front of me, knowing I craved you. I dreamed of tasting you, of running my fingers through the thin patch of crimson curls that would be wet with arousal from my skilled fingers. You became my fantasy in that room. You were the one thing I craved even more than I craved freedom from those enchanted chains that held me. I didn't dream of home anymore. I didn't dream of my beautiful daughters or my wife who longed for the day I no longer mounted her flesh to breed a son that would become my heir. But you, you were the most beautiful creature in existence. You were meant to be savaged," he said as he pushed me back, pulling my legs apart as he stared down at the thin patch of crimson curls. His fingers trailed through it as his eyes watched mine, continuing his tale as he absently played with me.

"One day, months after your endless torture had begun," he growled as his thumb found my clit, absently moving it in a circular pattern. "After what felt like an eternity of hanging there helplessly, forced to watch this sweetness with no chance of taking it, you returned with a wicked smile on those lips. The air around you crackled with your pleasure, and everything inside of me stilled because in your hand was a bloody bag. I was sure you'd found my family. I prayed that you hadn't, but I knew better than to underestimate you. I knew what I had done would result in their deaths at your pretty little hands. Instead, you withdrew my brother's head and held it in front of my face, watching the emotion play over it. You, the Goddess of War, watched the pain flicker in my eyes as if it was foreign to you. You couldn't understand why I felt such a great loss for a man who had fallen to your blade. You demanded I tell you what I felt, and why I felt it. You left his head in the window, forcing me to watch as the birds tore it apart as they pecked him to nothing more than a rotted skull. You went silent for days afterward when I refused to give you what you wanted to know. Eventually, you got rid of it, and when you finally broke the silence, it was to talk to me of battles, strategies you'd used against my people. Then, as if you hadn't just told me how you intended to murder the rest of my family, I watched the most beautiful creature ever created sleep *peacefully*. You looked so fucking innocent as you lay there, sleeping dreamlessly in the giant bed you'd built out of the skulls of your enemies."

"I don't want to hear anymore," I uttered hoarsely as he pushed his fingers into my body, watching as I arched my back, giving him more access to what he wanted.

"I don't care if you do or not. You will remember who you are so that when I fuck you, you look at me as you used to. When I kneel at your pretty feet, you will understand the gravity of it, but more so, you will understand that when I kneel beside you and redo the vows we took together, you will remember that you loved me enough to become my bride. That you loved both of us."

"And what if I don't want to be her? What if I stay me, and we don't do this. We don't go down this path, because apparently, I was a horrible person. So how about I just stay me, and you be you?" I uttered as his fingers pushed deeper into me.

"No, no, you don't get to forget him or me."

"Him?" I asked.

"You loved both of us, Erie."

"How is that even possible?"

"You'll see; we're not even to the best part of how horrid you were before the dynamic of who we were changed. That's not the point of this, wife. The point is to remind you of who you were, and who you have to become. Evil is here, and it is hunting you now. If you're Erie, you're dead. I didn't come this far to lose you again. I don't know if you can ever be brought back again, and you carry my child now. You carry the hope for our future, and I never stopped loving you or feeling your loss. I won't lose you, do you understand that? I'll fight for you, even if I'm against you to save you. I've had to do bad things to you to get you back weak enough to survive."

"That doesn't make sense. None of this makes any sense!"

"It will when you remember us and who you are."

CHAPTER forty

I WATCHED HIM WATCHING ME, HIS WORDS CAUSING my heart to race against my ribcage. He leaned over, kissing my belly before he lifted those glowing eyes and smirked. His fingers moved up my waist, hooking around it as he pulled me up, placing me onto his lap. Straddling him, I studied him closely as his tattoos seemed to glow, studying me back as if there were other things within him, *alive* things. I knew how true that was.

"You weren't a nice person, but no one was back then. It was a different world, and we played by our own rules. If you held power, you could rule over anything you wanted to. If anyone challenged your reign upon a throne, you struck them down fast and hard. You did; you held me in your room for over an entire year torturing me. You knew that I would never cave from pain, so you used the one thing I desired most against me: you. You were the one thing I couldn't have no matter how much power I had or obtained. You had to be given of your own free will. So day after day, night after night, I watched you touching your sweet flesh with those clumsy little unskilled fingers. I knew I was going mad with how much I craved you. I craved you because you made me, driving me insane as you touched that sweetness, and made damn sure I knew that I wasn't good enough to touch it.

"You spread that flesh as I watched you pushing your tiny little fingers through it. You asked me if I wanted it one day, and if I'd give you my soul to taste it. I told you that one day, I'd wreck it as you pleaded for mercy, but that I would grant you none. You laughed and told me that you would beg for mercy from no man," he growled huskily as he pushed me onto the couch, ripping the shirt from my body. "I watched you come from your clumsy fucking touches. The noises you made, fuck, those noises drove me mad. I refused to get hard that day, and it pissed you off that my body wouldn't react to yours. It became so repetitive that I knew the moment you would enter that room, and the moment you would leave it again. Night after night, I feared you would bring a man back to your room, forcing me to watch as he took what I wanted, but it never happened.

"It was then I knew that the rumors of you being a virgin weren't myths, it was true. You fucked that innocent cunt with such unskilled fingers and got off so easily that it pissed me off. No man had ever tasted or fucked you, and you were ancient, timeless. You were a fucking Goddess who had claimed countless lives and had never tasted real pleasure. I craved to be the first, but I knew, I fucking knew that you merely did it to drive me to madness. Then we changed, and every time

you'd get closer to me, you'd get angrier at me.

"You once asked me if I'd murder my own son for a mere taste of your nectar, and I told you that I would never murder *our* son. I remember the fury that shone from your eyes as you informed me that something like you would never breed with a heathen like me. You cut me that night, slicing through my flesh until I died as I hung in your bedroom. Somehow, you brought me back from death changed. I remember awakening different than what I had been, to watch as you lowered yourself down onto my chained body, which laid upon your bed. I watched you exploring my body, touching and tasting it as I was forced to lay there, unable to take what I craved from you," he uttered as his fingers pushed into my body and I arched into the heat of his mouth as his tongue flicked my nipple. "I begged you to ride my mouth, and you laughed, saying that my heathen tongue would never taste this sweetness," he growled as his head lowered, as his tongue slipped through the wetness that craved him. He lifted his head, smirking coldly as he watched me shiver with the need to find release. "You eventually pushed those tiny fingers into that virgin cunt and rubbed this sweetness over my lips, watching in rapture as I licked them clean for you. My cock rose, and those tiny fingers of yours wrapped around it, stroking it until I came for you. I remember your eyes burning with curiosity at how my body reacted to your touch. My sweet virgin queen who murdered men for fun was using me to learn their weaknesses, and I didn't fucking care. After that, you sucked me off with that hot mouth, swallowing everything as you licked those lips clean, knowing how much I wanted to destroy you.

"You used me, every night there was something new you did until one morning I awoke to that cunt rubbing against my hungry mouth. I'd never tasted anything so fucking sweet in my entire life. Not until you showed me what heaven tasted like as you came over my mouth, dripping down my chin with your first orgasm that wasn't self-given.

"You came for me, crying out as I let my tongue fuck that tight, naughty cunt. The next night you rubbed it over my cock, staring into my eyes as I watched your nipples harden while your pleasure blossomed. You killed me after that, ashamed that you'd allowed me to taste and pleasure you, but again, you brought me back because you weren't finished with me yet. The mighty Queen of War was weakening against the man she hated most. You were ashamed that you enjoyed me, using me, letting me do what no other man had ever done before. After that, you stopped for a while," he murmured as his fingers continued to drive into my body and his eyes burned into mine. "You needed to remind yourself of who you were, who I was. I was the opposing King in an endless war. I'd trespassed against you, rising from the sea to destroy you and your mighty people. I felt you pulling away, the confusion that drove you during that time.

"You feared me and what we did together. You told me it had to end because you were the conquering Goddess of War, and you had to finish it. I thought you meant me, idiot, that I was. You left me there that day, in your bed as you dressed for war, painting your face in woad as I had watched you many times before. That day though, something in you had changed, and it wasn't for

the better. You didn't return that night, or the next, or the next one, even.

"A few days later, you came into the room with another head, one that ripped a piece of my soul out because of what it meant you had achieved. You had wanted me to feel it, to feel your strength over me. You wanted to punish me because I made you crave things you didn't understand. You'd found my wife, the queen of my court, and you had murdered her. You placed her head on my stomach and watched as I came undone. Watched me as I shed tears for the woman I'd taken as my wife, and you fucking enjoyed it. You enjoyed my pain, knew I had cared for her at one time, and you had taken that away from me. That night you tried to arouse my passion, and I wouldn't let you," he snapped as he withdrew his fingers, slowly licking them clean as he moved up to sit between my legs on the couch. "I knew you'd killed my children as well, but not even you were that heartless to bring me their heads."

"I don't want to hear this anymore," I whispered as the images played out in my mind.

"No, you wouldn't want to hear what a murderous, heartless bitch you were back then, but I wasn't much better, either. It was a different time; we played by different rules. If you conquered a monarchy, you killed the entire bloodline. You made sure no one rose up to oppose you, and I'd invaded your lands. I knew what you would do, even as I wanted you, I knew their fate would be to die at the end of your blade. You were the Goddess of War, Erie. You thrived on death and war," he muttered as he pushed the tip of his cock against the slick folds of my flesh and I moaned loudly as he watched me with an evil grin curving his lips.

"You left her there, in the bed we slept in together, until the stink of her rotting flesh became too much for you to bear. You threw her away and then when you returned again, you were covered in fresh blood from battle. You'd killed thousands of my warriors and told me of your victories as I tried to block you out. Your name was earned in the blood of my people. I remember watching you strip down to your flesh and straddle my hips as you rocked that needy cunt over my cock, telling me how you'd enjoyed slaughtering the weak ones the most, that those who couldn't survive war had no place being in one, you said. You pushed this flesh against my cock, taunting me as you laughed in my face at my defeat at your hands," he hissed as he pushed into my body only far enough for the head to be clenched by the tightening walls of it. "You fucked up though; just one little slip-up and I took it from you. You were there, just like this, hovering over my cock as you told me that you'd finally murdered my entire court. And then I did this while you were distracted, telling me of your victories," he snapped as he pushed into my body fast and hard, enjoying the scream that tore from my throat as he invaded me. "And that is what it sounded like when I took the untouchable Goddess's maidenhead from her. Your sweet flesh pulsed around me, and I took everything. I hurt you, and you fucking loved it. You could have gotten away from me, but you didn't even fucking try. Instead, you rode me, throwing your pretty fucking head back as you came around my cock with my name on your lips like a fucking benediction that you cried to the other Gods. We were enemies, born to

hate each other and yet we craved each other like star-crossed lovers. We were created to destroy one another, but in your body, I found sanctuary.

"You, the queen who had murdered my family and taken everything from me, became my home. We went to war against one another, and you won, but what I won was so much fucking better than anyone could ever understand. I lay there, buried in heaven as you told me that you gave my wife to your men to rape, and how they had murdered her before you took her head to present to me. My unwed daughters, chained to poles and used as target practice by your archers, and all I could think about was how tight your needy cunt was, and how perfectly I fit into it. I hated myself, I hated you, and I couldn't stop fucking you. It was like whatever magic you had used to bring me back from death had changed everything inside of me. You cursed me, and then you blessed me in the same fucking breath. You could have gotten away from me, for I was chained to your bed." He started to thrust into my body painfully, driving his rage into me as I whimpered and pleaded for mercy, mercy that he wouldn't give as he retold his tale.

"You told me everything you'd done as I fucked you, driving my rage into your tight, untrained cunt. No, Erie, you don't get to ignore me or our history anymore," he said as I covered my ears with my hands, continuing to come around his cock as he fucked me with so much force that I'd be bruised. I fucking loved it, but hearing what I'd done to him, it haunted me as the images played out through my mind. "You boasted of how you'd murdered and ruined everyone and everything I'd ever loved, and I cried as I fought to destroy you in the only way I could. I, the King of Heathens and Beasts, cried as I fucked the most perfect woman in creation. It was then that I heard it, the insecurity in your voice, and the underlying pain as you told me what you had done. You didn't want to hurt me; you wanted me to understand that I had no reason not to be with you. You wanted me to love you. You were alone. All alone in a world you didn't understand or know, and you wanted what those pathetic mortals around you had. *Love.* You wanted someone to love you, but you didn't understand how it worked or happened. So you took everything I loved and made sure nothing stood in your way. You were War, and, war…was what you knew, what you craved. You knew that if I were ever released from those chains, I would go back to them, so you, with your skills for war and battle, used them as you took everything away."

"Stop," I whispered as tears slid down my cheeks. "Just shut up."

"You were the Mórrígan, the Goddess of War, and you were alone in a world that wasn't yours. Men fell at your feet, except for one: me. You craved connection, and yet you wanted it freely, so you took me because I refused to kneel at your pretty little feet. I was the only man who could withstand your magic, the power that you couldn't contain against the mortals that made them bow to your power. They worshipped you, and you wanted something real. You craved me because I was a monster, like you. I craved blood, craved flesh-to-flesh contact that wasn't from someone being unable to withstand this magic we exhume because of what we are. You didn't want to be alone anymore." His mouth

crushed against mine as he expanded, growing too large as he filled me until I was whimpering against him. "You wanted to be loved, and you thought that I had already found it, so you took everything from me."

"No," I whispered as tears filled my eyes. My body trembled, shaking uncontrollably as he pushed me over the edge, watching as I unraveled while he fucked me relentlessly. "You're lying."

"Yes, you did. You had every right to do it, and we both knew it. I was the only one who knew why you did it, the real reason you murdered my family. You took my kingdom, my world, and held me, prisoner. You kept me like that for years, chained to your bed, never forcing what we shared, but indulging in what I needed. You fucked me for days sometimes, and then one day, you wanted to know what it felt like to be touched, to be fucked *by* me. You released me, and I fucking wrecked you for hours. I made you scream until even the Gods knew I'd taken their Goddess of War and shown her what monster she had craved between her pretty, silk thighs. I broke your neck, and when you woke from the endless slumber, you were chained to your bed. The same bed I'd been chained to for over a decade.

"Of course, you had no idea what or who you'd craved, and when I showed you who and what I was, you didn't care. I released this monster, shedding the human I'd shared his body with to face you on that battlefield nearly a decade before it. My wife, she feared the monster inside of me, which was how I learned to use a human to allow the world to see one thing, as I controlled him from within. The problem was, once I had become a part of him, I weakened without a body.

So I found another who was strong enough to house me, one who craved you enough to be willing to watch what we did, and never play with you unless I allowed him to do so.

"You see, I wasn't the only man who wanted what you would never give up. So I made a deal, because he was in love with you, and had been since before I ever stormed your rocky fucking shores. You didn't mind the beast; in fact, you said you preferred him to humans because he wasn't a lie. Not so with my bride, who wept when we mated, unable to even look at me as I planted my children in her womb. She hated me, and what she was forced to mate with, so I hid what I was from her, from the world. I changed to fit the world, which was something you had never done. I showed you me, the monster within, and you fucked me harder. You opened up these sexy thighs and wiggled your tight cunt, inviting the beast to play with it. I fell in love with you then, knowing that I no longer had to hide what I was to be accepted. You *loved* me, Erie. You loved me without care, allowing me, the King you'd conquered, live. In that time, you became my soul, the other half of me, and when I freed you from that bed, you didn't leave or fight against me. You took me until even the beast was sated, and we were happy. You were a murderous bitch, but you had given me mercy. You just didn't know it, and neither did I.

"So if you think you're leaving me, think again. I will chain you to the wall and fuck you when I want to, just as you did to me. I didn't ask for this love; you wanted it. You chose me," he reminded me, and I exploded around him as he lifted me, stopping the orgasm prematurely as

he once again flipped my body over. "You think I don't know what is inside your mind, Mórrígan? You may have been able to play dumb, but you messed up. You killed the druids systematically and used that brilliant fucking brain of yours as you strategized, which tells me that you're coming back already. Erie is a shield, and even though it takes time for you to come back to me after you've died, I can feel you here." He placed his hand against his heart and then tapped his forehead.

I shook my head as I watched his smile turn wicked and he reached down, pinching my clitoris as I exploded again, screaming his name while his mouth crushed against mine. Memories of what he'd said I'd done played out in my head, and yet I wasn't sure if they were memories or images he'd placed there with his words. I felt him growing, and I screamed as it burned with pain. He lifted his mouth from mine, staring down at me, and I detonated as my eyes lost focus, the orgasm ripping through me painfully violent. He didn't stop until I was sobbing, my nails digging into his flesh as his wings extended behind him. I was so busy screaming and hurting him that I didn't even realize what was happening around me. Something pushed against my ass, and I pleaded as his mouth lowered to my pulse, sucking it as he growled loudly. I turned my head, staring back at Callaghan, who kissed my ear as the beast claimed my mouth.

"I want to play with you, too, woman," Callaghan growled.

CHAPTER
forty-one

I WHIMPERED AS THE BEAST ENTERED MY FLESH AGAIN, even as Callaghan pushed against my ass, filling me. It was brutal and beautiful as the painful fullness of them consumed all coherent thought. My arms were around the monster's neck, holding on to him as they both fucked me. I hissed through the pain, uncertain I'd survive both of them at once. I was too full, my body clenching as it burned from where they took me. Someone held my waist, lifting me as they moved me to the steady beat of our hearts. They found the perfect rhythm and continued to silently dominate me as my body hummed with pleasure and delicious pain that sent me over the edge without warning.

"Mmm, that's a good girl, fucking take us deeper. You can do it, Goddess; you were made for us both. Do you feel us in your body, fucking your dirty holes?" the beast asked hoarsely as his glowing eyes watched me. I opened and closed my mouth, only soft whimpers escaping past my lips. "You're not mortal, you never

were, and you never will be, my Queen," he snapped as my mind refused to accept what was happening to my body. They worked together as if they held the same mind, touching, kissing, and fucking me until I shattered so hard that tears streamed down my face. They used my arousal against me, using it so that they could go deeper, harder, faster, and all the while, I whimpered and pleaded for more.

My eyes rolled back in my head until I felt them moving me, and the beast withdrew as Callaghan moved us again, sitting onto the couch as I screamed from deep in my chest while he pushed further into my ass, filling it until I was helpless but to lean against him. He chuckled against my ear as the beast watched him, spreading my legs as he held them apart, inviting the beast to join us again. He didn't at first. Instead, he just watched me being fucked by Callaghan, his cock wrecking my ass as I moaned and came undone while his fingers pleasured my aching flesh. It ached, but it felt fucking unbelievable as he ruined me.

"I think our naughty little Goddess enjoys being fucked like a dirty girl," the beast uttered as he stroked his massive erection, watching as my pussy grew wet with arousal from my ass being penetrated.

"Do you remember this?" Callaghan moaned as he slammed me down on him, using my hips to control the beat to which he destroyed me. "Do you remember us wrecking your sweet holes for hours as we took what no other man had ever tasted? I remember watching you from inside of him, feeling what he felt as he let us fuck you. I remember the first time after we'd connected as one, when I watched him doing what I'd craved to do a million times before. The sweet fucking noises you made as he stretched your cunt wide with that monstrous cock of his. I watched you taking it and pleading for more, fucking begging for more, Erie. You knew no mercy and wanted it from no one, not even him. You go to war with everything you do, including fucking us. Your body weeps to be filled, to be taken until your mind grows silent. Look how wet that naughty cunt is right now, how much it weeps to be fucked too. Come for us, sweet Goddess. Scream our names as that sweet flesh is fucked."

The beast knelt between my legs, licking the mess they'd created as his eyes stared into mine with blue flames dancing in their turquoise depths. "More, Callaghan," he uttered as he pulled back, pushing his fingers into my pussy as he stretched me. "Do you remember this? The feeling of being helpless, destroyed by the men you loved?" he asked as he continued to push his fingers into my body while Callaghan rode me from behind.

I shook my head as a whimpered moan escaped my throat. "No!" I sobbed, my body covered in sweat as they brought me to release and then stilled as the beast rubbed his cock against my opening. I shook my head as he watched me, his eyes searching mine until the tremors of the pending orgasm had passed. "Please, I ache for you," I mumbled as he smirked cruelly.

"Do you remember the first time he let me out so that we could both fuck you? You showed fear for the first time. The Goddess of War feared two men destroying her tight pretty holes. You knew who I was then, that I was your second in command who had been

assumed lost in battle, but I wasn't. I'd been watching you, touching you, falling so fucking deeply in love with you as you smiled at me with love burning in your pretty sky blue eyes. I'd never felt more alive than when I'd agreed to be a part of him, just to know what it felt like to be touched by you."

"It hurts," I murmured as I dropped my head against Callaghan's shoulder and rocked my pussy for the beast to take. I wanted them; I wanted them both to fucking destroy me as they promised to. I wanted them inside of me, owning me until I knew nothing else.

"We're just getting started, Erie," the beast warned, watching my flesh as his thick cock pushed against my swollen pussy. He pushed into my body, and I tensed, arching against him as Callaghan waited for me to adjust to them both inside of me. "You feel that? Feel how your body stretches for us both to fuck you? You're so tight, so welcoming as you house us both in this quivering, messy wetness. Erie, you're fucking perfect. I can feel you clenching and sucking me off already. Such a dirty little thing, aren't you, fucking both of us. Do you want to come for me? Come on, move for us, work these cocks like you used to, sweet girl. You always did have a thing for monsters, my sweet, naughty bitch," he purred as he leaned over, nipping one pink nipple between his teeth before he let his tongue trace the round peak of it. "Do you remember what my wife looked like before you took her head?" he asked as he lifted, showing me the pain that burned in his eyes at the memory. He grew until I was clawing at Callaghan's thighs to get up and away from the thickness that ached and burned until I screamed for him. "She was beautiful, like my daughters." Hurt flashed in his eyes, but also, a love that terrified me. It was two things that didn't belong together, ever. It was a cataclysmic event that forced me over the edge, and instead of ignoring it, he rocked into my body, letting me ride each wave of pleasure as it hit and ignited in my core.

"You think to leave us after we brought you back yet again? I promise you this; it won't happen as you expect it to. I will keep you chained up, tied to the bed to use as I wish, just like you did to me. You craved me; you took away everything I loved and kept me as your pet. Now, now you will finish what you started with me. You will give birth to my son, and you will be mine as you promised to be before. There is no escaping our fate; you made certain of it. You did this, sweet wife. You made me take vows before the Gods, pledged your love before them, and then you told the mortals how to murder you when you feared to birth my monstrous bastard into his world from your perfect body. I should have known you would resort to a way out of it because after all, you only wanted to fuck me. A child wasn't part of our bargain. I won't let you go again, ever. It's my turns to do it to you. Now come, because this pussy can take a lot more than it is, and I need to give you everything."

"I'm not her!" I growled as I clenched my body against him while he grew, watching as he stretched me until I was sure he'd tear me apart as I shook violently around him. I could feel the blood that my nails had drawn from Callaghan, and yet neither stopped fucking me even as we all tried to destroy each other in the only way we knew how.

"You are my wife! I know you are because we created you. I brought you back from death twice now to ensure you wouldn't create chaos with your presence. You're the Goddess of War, but you're not the same one who slaughtered my family. You're different; you're our Erie now. My sweet, claimed mate who cannot escape a fate she forced onto herself by her own selfish choices. I won't let you go, nor will you escape me again. You did this, you wanted this, and now you have us."

Callaghan's hand grabbed my breasts, squeezing them while the beast lowered his hand, rubbing his fingers over my clitoris until I opened my mouth to scream as white-hot pleasure made me buck against them. I went over the edge again and again from what they were doing to me. The beast's other hand grabbed my throat, preventing my scream from escaping. I whimpered as I moaned, the pain, the pleasure, the mindlessness building inside of me until all I could do was ride their cocks as they took me to heaven and showed me the gates.

"That's my good girl," Callaghan purred against my ear.

"She's so pretty when she comes undone," the beast said as he stared down at where we were joined.

"I think we should keep her like this for a while. Make sure she feels us inside her greedy holes. I think you need to take a turn in this ass; it's fucking amazing. So tight and needy," Callaghan crooned as they both slowed, knowing I was on the edge of coming yet again.

"Please," I whimpered as the room started to disappear around me. Stars exploded in my vision, taking me away from the room and into the skies, soaring past pleasure to a precipice I hadn't known was even possible to reach. His hold loosened, and the beast lowered his mouth to claim mine.

"I do like it when you beg me," he laughed huskily against my mouth. "I wonder how durable you are this time."

This time?

"I don't know, third time's a charm, right?" Callaghan laughed.

I felt like I'd entered the *Twilight Zone* and was starring in the longest episode they had ever produced in filming history. My body was lifted, and the slick sound of them leaving it filled the room as I was placed onto my feet. I swayed as the beast caught me, lowering to his knees as he placed my leg over his shoulder, nuzzling into my core. Callaghan lifted the other, pushing it onto the monster's shoulder as he buried his tongue in my pussy, fucking me as he stood up. I gripped his hair as he laughed against my sore flesh. I stared down at Callaghan, seeing him for the first time without his beast in his soul. He was evil, pure and simple. Black veins slid over his flesh, pulsing as he stared up at me with the eyes of a demon prince, and yet I knew he wasn't. He was the First Fomorian King, the King that had abandoned his people for a Goddess. I trembled as I opened my mouth, and the beast increased his attention to my cunt. Callaghan watched me, his blonde head tilting as my mind tried to place him.

"Callaghan?" I whimpered hesitantly as my mind struggled against the pleasure and piecing everything together.

"In my true form, my precious Queen," he chuckled

as his magic washed over him, and he watched me riding the beast's face as he cradled my hips, holding me to him as he cleaned the mess he'd created in my core. "Don't you remember me?" he laughed harshly as he watched me coming undone for the beast. "I shouldn't be surprised, but then you never did notice me until you thought me some warrior you could control. I was there with you when you brought the second king down to his knees. I was an insider who watched you from the first moment you entered the court and became the Queen of the Tuatha Dé Danann. I chased you, but you never even so much as glanced in my direction. I struck a deal with the beast; I got to have you with him, and all I had to do was become his vessel. How does it feel to have fallen in love with two Fomorian Kings after you promised to murder both at one time or another?" he laughed huskily as he watched me coming for the beast who had pushed his tongue deep into my pussy, forcing orgasm after orgasm to rock through me before he finally stopped, letting my body slip down his chest. "It's time to hear my story, Erie. Don't worry; I'll let you rest as I tell it," he hissed as he pushed me towards the couch, watching as I fell down on it, my flesh swollen and bruised; his eyes burned where he wanted to be buried. "For a few moments anyway; I can't stand to be out of you right now. Victory is only making us need to fuck you more."

CHAPTER Forty-two

"I HAD WATCHED YOU SINCE THE FIRST MOMENT YOU entered our court. A court I'd fought to get into and be accepted, right before it began to fall to yet another war. I had many skills, none of which you even noticed. I slaughtered thousands of men at your side, and not once did those pretty eyes ever turn to me and see the man who stood beside you. I was your match in every way, born for war, to wage it, to win it. I was a fucking king that stood beside you and abandoned my crown in order to do so. I watched you ruin lives, bring down the strongest kingdoms to their knees, and you flourished with every new kingdom you destroyed.

"I fell in love with you, and you never even looked my way. So I waited and watched as you fell for him. Night after night, I stood outside your door, listening to the noises you made for him, praying that someday you'd make them for me too. You knew I was there, knew I listened as you fucked yourself in front of him, but you never admitted it. So, I bid my time, waiting

years, and years as you sent me to hunt down his family so that you could slaughter them. It was your right, and I got it, you would look weak if you hadn't sought them out and destroyed them. Even with how long it took with your half-assed effort to find them, your men started to snicker behind your back."

His hand cupped my chin as he took in the bruises that covered my flesh. His eyes smiled darkly as he lifted them, noting the fear in my own. "You heal, you're immortal. That cunt has taken a lot more than that, Erie. Where was I? Oh, yeah. The men started to lose faith in their queen, sure that, when she'd begun riding a monster's cock, she'd lost her focus. So, I struck a deal with the beasts, to join and become one in order to have you, and protect you if your own people turned against you. He'd allow me into him so that I could have you.

"That's neither here nor there. We lost you, and while we were fighting to bring you back, I fell in love with another. I had taken her to heal the pain of your loss, as it had taken over two hundred years to bring you back to us. I had a child with her, even though I'd never stopped craving you or mourning your loss. Then you returned, and you destroyed me without even knowing why you did it. You took everything from us, everything we loved because that is what you do. You crave warriors, and you have this need to take everything away from them so that you are protected from them hurting you. I was happy with my wife, settled into my new world and happy without you, or so I tried to convince myself. But I still wanted you, because you were the love of my life, and I had lost you to a war I hadn't even known we were waging."

I pulled my legs up against my chest, letting my hair shield my body as the beast sat behind me, pulling me to him as Callaghan let his hand skim down my thigh.

"Do you know why you are the cure for the Templars? Because you are the reason they are cursed in the first place, so we thought it's only fitting that you be the way it ends," he said as he knelt between my legs, pushing them open as he stared at me.

"No," I uttered as I stared at him. "That's impossible, I wasn't even born yet."

"Mmm, but you were. You found me when I'd discovered a new God to serve. I was a warrior of the Holy Knights, bound to serve the one God that wasn't filled with trickery or hatred of the mortals. He loved them, and I found a new purpose among them. I found a purpose for our people, Goddess. I have been King of your people since the day of your first death. The day you died, he hid within me and allowed them to think he had abandoned them in his grief, and I ruled over your people. The problem was that we couldn't separate, and we both craved you. So, we started searching for a way to bring you back because you didn't get to leave us after what we'd gone through to have you.

"Call it an obsession if you want, but we were monsters who couldn't let you go because the type of love we had isn't ending, it's a beginning that continues long after worlds have been destroyed or died out. I remember the moment you returned to us, newly born and yet fully formed, your first rebirth into an entirely new world. You found me on the battlefield, searching for your home. You offered yourself to me, sensing that which slumbered in my soul. You felt him within me,

and even though you didn't recognize me, you did him. I fucked you in that place of death, unable to deny the lure of your untouched flesh as you offered it to me.

"Hours, I fucked you for hours until the beast stirred once more, sensing your return. You wanted me, but you knew I was taken. So, you started what you're best at war; driving pieces into place so that you can take what you want without repercussions or the chance of losing them to lesser beings," he said hoarsely as his knuckles dragged over my silken flesh. "You were the sweetest temptation, and like a fly to a web, I was snared. I knew your game because I'd watched you play it many times before. Of course, you had no idea who I was, or that I'd once served you. I knew the moment you found out that I had a family that I cared for, one I cherished above all else, you'd seek to destroy them. I left you that day on the field to return to them, and you couldn't stand it. You raged that you were no man's plaything and that you would not be ignored or abandoned. You craved me, what was inside of me. I had to protect them against you, though I didn't count on how dirty you fought when you were angry.

"You tried to murder my wife, Carolina. You tried so fucking hard until you realized she carried my unborn son. I knew the moment she had him; you'd begin hunting her anew. It was one thing the beast and I had agreed on: protect my wife and our unborn child at any cost, even if that cost was your life. We knew we could bring you back again, of course. No matter how hard we tried to stay away from you, that devilish addiction to you and what you made us feel with you brought us right back every time. It wasn't something you could ignore, the way you fucked, the way you loved; it was an addiction that no man could ignore. You were created to be wanted, to lure men to their deaths, and no matter how hard we tried, not even we were immune to what you offered us so freely.

"I thought that if I spent enough time with you, that you'd understand that I loved you more than I could ever love Carolina, but when she birthed my son, I fell in love with *him*. He was the one thing that made me able to withstand the lure of you. I knew that if I stayed with him too long, you'd want his life as well. So I distanced myself from them, but I'd already caught your attention in my absence. You couldn't stand to think that I may love them too, but then you weren't created as we were. A Goddess of War couldn't understand love could be given to more than just one person. You were cold, unloved, and unaccepted by even your own people. They feared you, feared you and your sisters would destroy them all considering what you brought with you in your nearness to anyone or anything. Chaos and war weren't welcomed around the Gods for fear they would wage war against one another, so you were abandoned. That meant anytime you felt the threat of abandonment, you destroyed everything that could make it happen to avoid it. I thought I could love you enough and that you'd leave my family alone, but I was wrong.

"You wanted everything I could give you, to know what it felt like to be wanted again. I'd spent enough time with you that you tasted the love you craved, and when you felt it strongly enough, you fought to keep it. The moment I fell in love with you, *I* signed the death warrant for *your* people, Erie. You didn't know it though, because you didn't recognize me yet. You didn't sense your people because you weren't looking for them; you were following your path home, to him, the beast within me. You didn't know who I was, or why you were drawn to me." His eyes searched my face, studying it as he swallowed past the lump in his throat. "All you saw was a proud warrior, an immortal among men who you wanted as much as you wanted him. So you did what you do best, you went to war on innocent people, your people, to take everything that stood between us away. *You* cursed us, Erie. You set the demons upon the witches, knowing what they'd do in their desperation to survive. You knew they wouldn't be able to resist the Princes of Hell infiltrating them, and so you captured the generals of Hell's army, forcing them to do as you bid.

"The witches never even fucking did what they were accused of; they just took the blame for a slight they had done to you in the past. That was all it took for you to wage war against an entire coven of this world's strongest, oldest witches. Once the demons had inhabited the witches' bodies and slaughtered entire villages of innocent people, the witches came crawling to us for help, to save them, which you had known they would do. When I refused them help, knowing it would bring all eyes down upon us, they cursed us as we watched them burn, a curse you knew would be placed because you'd given it to them in their darkest hour of need under the guise of one of their own. You sent the demons to them, which sent them to us, they sent the demons to us, and that started everything. You cursed your own people to get the one thing you wanted: me.

"The King, he wouldn't have done what he had unless you'd started the rumors yourself. You and your selfish needs created the chaos that you craved. Once you'd finished with the king, you moved on to the Pope. You knew that both would come after us, knew that it would end in the death of the Templar Knights, which would leave me without a cause in which to fight. I watched you. I watched you as you stood in the crowd while my brothers were burned alive for crimes they didn't commit. You had no idea that I was the new King of your people, or that in cursing the Order, you'd cursed us all to death. You were young, selfish, and couldn't understand why you wanted me. It was never me you craved, in the beginning, but we loved each other, Erie. I didn't even like the woman you had come back as in that life, but the longer I held you, the more I learned that I'd never stopped loving you, even in death. You loved me too, but I fell more in love with you than I ever had with any other woman. I had been obsessed with you before, but that time, I loved you, and you loved me because the beast allowed me to have you in that lifetime, alone. You loved me enough that you cursed our people to get me. It's only fitting that you would be the cure to the mess you created, isn't it?"

"I'm not her," I whimpered, and the beast pinched my nipple, punishing me for my sudden outburst; Callaghan's eyes turned ocean blue, silver hair seemed to grow to brush against his shoulders. Black runes seemingly danced over his flesh as he gazed at me, noting my reaction to his change. He was otherworldly, his body built for war as it darkened until the runes glowed with an eerily blue hue. "I don't remember

any of this," I whispered as tears slid from my eyes. "I'm sorry, I'm sorry for whatever you think I did, but it wasn't me." But it was, I felt it to the depths of my soul, and even worse, I heard the truth of their words, these monstrous tales. I wasn't the victim; I was their monster.

"I don't care if you remember or not. I made a promise to you before I went to war on your behalf. I promised to protect our people the moment I took my crown at your side, wife. I promised you that I would guard them with my life, even from you if it came to that," the beast growled. "Even if they didn't know it, I kept my promise."

"This time, Erie, you will care what is at stake when you go to war against us. Why do you think you carry our son in your womb?" Callaghan asked as he leaned over, sucking my nipple between his teeth, then his eyes lifted, locking with mine. "I lost my son, as the beast lost his, but you will give us another one, and you will love him too. You will be his mother, and God help anyone who tries to touch War's son."

"This isn't happening," I uttered huskily as I felt the beast growing again, his silken flesh pulsing against my back.

"Oh, it is happening, Erie. You started this, and while you may be a genius strategist, we've been planning this since the moment we pushed your corpse into that fucking cauldron and joined two souls to bring you back to us. You just chose two men who were willing to go to war against you to bring you back to us. We've planned this out perfectly, knowing you would never just fall into line if we told you to do. We allowed you the freedom to come back to us, and when your life was placed in danger, we moved up the timeline. There were also other things to consider after your death occurred while we were at war. The world had changed, and beasts could no longer walk among men. Monsters were no longer welcome in this new land, nor were our people, who have pointed ears and tend to glow when you're near them. We hid them in plain sight, and without you close to them, it worked, because their glamour could conceal subtle those things. We'd planned on you remaining with us in your second life, to allow you time to get to know us, but you fucked that up with your petty jealousy. Do you know how you died the second time? I took your life.

"I murdered you outside the Templar Stronghold, where you summoned me, demanding I listen to your madness. You were enraged because my wife was protected, and I'd taken away my son's death from you. We knew you came to take me, to lure me into your fucking web, but that didn't happen. Instead, we set a trap for you. It was the first time *we* fucked you. I ate your pussy...like this," he uttered as he lowered his head, sucking my clit. "And then he fucked you; we made you come until you knew nothing else and wanted nothing else. We took turns ruining you, weakening you without you knowing what was happening. For an entire year, you were ours to share. Helpless, strung up by your own enchanted chains inside the cave that drained you and your Goddess powers until you were nearly mortal. You were so wild with need, unable to do anything but take what we gave you. I fucked my grief out on you, Erie. I wanted to hate you, to strangle you as I fucked this needy cunt, but even being drained, you were too powerful to die. One year, that was how long it took to drain every ounce of power you held, and when you were drained, we fucked you as the life faded from you. You see, you had to die to come back weaker as the cure. You create war with your presence, and to weaken that part of you, you have to be drained and weakened to the point of being a mere mortal. We planned everything together, stealing away the deaths of my family from you, planting you into the cauldron to be the child that was born druid and Templar. You are a battle Goddess who gets off on ruining men. I have watched you ruin men since the moment I first started to infiltrate the Tuatha Dé Danann." Callaghan lifted his head, allowing his demon-like form to shift as he returned to human.

"I am the Fomorian King, and you, you murderous beautiful bitch, you are my Queen and my soulmate. I've planned your downfall since before the land ever stood, long before the stars were ever created in the heavens. You think you can plan a war? You can't even imagine how much we've planned for you together. Instead of fighting each other, we became two entities with a singular purpose who shared one body," Callaghan growled.

"Claiming you, destroying you, and the one thing that has never stopped since the moment you loved us back, loving you. No matter how hard it is or how much you put us through, we *still* love you," the beast snapped. "Some things are just too ingrained in us that no matter how many times we come back, they remain," he growled as he leaned his dark head over, kissing my ribcage. "You still taste like sin and magic, my Queen," he uttered, lifting his head and watching my face.

"Your sister felt you were being reborn when she came to me on that cliff and begged me to protect you, but she didn't recognize me there, either," Callaghan continued, his hand slowly playing with the swollen flesh between my legs. "I felt her; *we* felt her as she appeared in the disguise of a seer. What she didn't sense was that we'd buried you so deep inside an innocent soul, that you were hidden from everyone *but* us. So she came, and then she left there, uncertain if it was really you, or if your sweet soul had finally passed on to another vessel to be reborn mortal. You were hidden in the druid's compound because they alone could shield your presence. The one thing that burned the most was that I cared when you were abused. I shouldn't fucking care, but I did. I saved the bitch that cost my son his life, and now, now you will give him back to me."

"I'm not her; why won't you listen to me!" I screamed as the orgasm ripped through me, contorting my body as the magic assaulted me all at once.

"Ask us if we care? You have her face, her flesh, her black fucking soul inside of you, so everything else is irrelevant. You may not remember who you are today, or tomorrow, but you will come back. You always do. You've never cared who you hurt when you took their lives. You found warriors you craved, and then you took everything from us. You ruined lives, ruined worlds, and never cared who paid the price for it, but this time, this time it is you who will pay the cost. Buckle up, sweet Erie, it's about to get really rough for you."

CHAPTER
forty-three

MÓRRÍGAN

I WAS WATCHING HIM FROM ACROSS THE FIELD AS MEN *died, impaled on spears while my people fought ruthlessly around me. Not a single drop of blood marred the white skirt I wore or the exposed flesh that they craved to touch so much that they fell at my feet. Such a fucking bore, and yet the scent of blood and the scene of utter chaos soothed my soul. Fomorians, heathens from the sea, had thought to attack the race I'd taken over when Danu had created her perfect fucking race in Faery, leaving me to deal with her mess. If they hadn't craved blood and chaos as much as I had, I'd have slaughtered them all and called it a day.*

Exhaling as I pushed the blood-red hair from my face, my eyes settled on the heathen king who fought valiantly. He was darker than the others; his aura alone created a black haze that drew my curiosity to him. The arctic eyes that held mine over the field of death pulled a gasp from my lips. Three men attacked him, and he effortlessly swiped at them. Muscles covered in the tattoos of a warrior's ink bunched beneath the sun's blinding rays as more and more men approached him. Sensing the battle was dying down and that their king was within our grasp, his men tried to prevent the inevitable. It was a valiant attempt, but useless since I'd never lost a battle yet, and I'd waged countless wars.

"Do not let them kill him." It was an order that none would disobey. "I want him chained in my room, and I want the skulls collected from this field and added to my walls."

"He is a monster, one that won't go willingly," my second in command growled, and I turned, smiling into his Nordic blue eyes that watched me with hunger.

"Adonis wasn't either, but I have three of his skulls hanging in my collection. I will distract him; you capture him. Unless, of course, you're unable to, and your skull shall be the next I place onto my wall?"

"As you wish, my Queen," Lugh said, striding away as I frowned after him. Lugh was pleasing to look at, and yet he hungered after me in the same way the others did. He wanted what I could make him and what I could give him. It was unnerving how incompetent some of these beings were, and I almost understood why Danu had left them to create the Fae.

I loathed them all; every single mortal that looked at me as if I'd hung the fucking moon for them. No one refused, no one disobeyed, and I was so sick of watching their dove eyes go gooey for my flesh. As if I'd allow any of them to touch me. I pushed my hair away from my shoulder, exposing the globes of my breasts as I started towards the creature that fought his way through the masses as if he'd face me head-on. As if he thought he would make it to me, but I'd trained these creatures how to battle the correct way since Danu hadn't bothered and then had whined about them being weak. Warriors were made, not born.

His eyes lowered to my breasts as the wind rushed over me, and he paused, lifting glowing blue eyes to mine. He wasn't man; he was other? He was a beast among mortals. My thighs slipped from the skirt as I paused, lowering to the ground to push a soul from a corpse and send it to Hades. The heat of his gaze lingered on my exposed thigh as their club found its mark against his head, taking him down to his knees.

Too easy, I mused as I lifted back up from the ground and slowly walked through the bloody battlefield while he watched me with a look that I actually enjoyed. Strange, that he was a beast in a land of mortals and timid creatures. Chained, he looked almost human except for those glowing eyes that watched me with a hunger I didn't understand. He either wanted my head, or to fuck me, or fuck me as he took my head. It was really a higher chance on the one which ended with my head off while we did the other, with the way he watched me.

"You're mine now," I said as I knelt before him, where he had been kicked to his knees. His heated gaze lowered to the woad on my chest that was embellished and flowering scroll that twirled around my waist and arms, until it reached up to dance upon my cheeks. "You have been dethroned, and are now my prisoner, heathen from the sea."

"You're nothing but a whore who sits on an empty

throne of lies," he hissed.

"Such flattery from a heathen king? Tell me, do you want to fuck me? I can sense your need, the bloodlust slipping from you as something else replaces it. Do you think I'd let something like you touch something like me?" I uttered thickly, hating that my body clenched at the mere idea. For as long as I could remember, my body hadn't responded to man, woman, or beast.

I stood up, staring at him while he watched me. His nostrils flared, as if he could scent my arousal. Men were such dogs, always thinking with their cocks. I, on the other hand, wanted to push the beast down and ride him in the blood of his people. I wanted him to know that I'd conquered him; me, a mere Goddess, even though he was three times my size.

"I will kill you, bitch."

"You will try, as many others have, and fail as they did. I wish you luck though, as this life is tediously boring already, and I'm surrounded by lovesick idiots, so do try soon."

"Release me and fight me, whore."

"Mmm, I can think of many other things to do with you, which you will not enjoy. Why would I face you when you would just lose? I am created for war, born of the kings of this land. You, you are of the sea and nothing more than a heathen who tried to reach for what was not his to take. You challenged me, and you lost," I said softly. I studied his heady stare as it lowered to the exposed thighs that the skirt didn't cover. My gaze lifted to Lugh, who stared into my eyes, unwilling to gape at my nakedness as the other men were doing. Maybe they weren't all worthless. "Take him to my room, and then

collect the skulls of his people. Maybe I'll let him eat out of them so that he knows he has been defeated."

I watched as they dragged him off, the hair on my neck prickling as I turned, staring at Lugh, who watched me with something akin to hunger burning in his eyes. I smiled at him as he nodded and started away from me. He was different from the others as well. I'd considered killing him a few times already, but the bloodlust he offered on the battlefield with his skills kept me sated, and I didn't need his death to feel whole. He alone defied my orders or thought to touch my flesh without permission, and I found him charming because of it. He knew I could end his life, and yet he thought the price worth it to brush against me in battle where everyone else stayed far, far away from me to avoid contact.

I dismissed him as he moved through the line of those who watched as we took their king away. The smile that graced my face was anything but kind. To drag Balor off in chains was a mockery to their race as they watched their brave king being carted from the field of battle. I turned, moving towards the warrior king, who held my gaze. Sleek muscles were covered in blood, bathed in his men's and mine. His shoulders were erect, not bowed as were the other kings I'd defeated. This one was proud, strong. He'd be fun to break into pieces.

"What about the other prisoners, my Queen?" a soldier asked.

My eyes locked with their king's, and I smiled as I walked towards him. "Kill them all so that the next man who thinks to conquer me is warned of what happens when men reach for what isn't theirs to take."

Inside my chambers, with him hanging in chains,

I stripped naked, watching his eyes take in the sight of my flesh. It was a sight men never lived to speak of once they'd gazed upon it, not that many had. Those eyes though, the way his pupils dilated and constricted, made me want to show him more. He didn't seem impressed, nor taken with my beauty as he should have been. He should have at least been screaming or fighting, something other than staring at my naked flesh as I bathed the blood of his men from my skin.

"You don't think I'm beautiful bathed in the blood of your people?" I asked as my hands cupped my heavy breasts while I moved closer, enjoying the taut muscles of his stomach, and my hand lifted to explore them. He recoiled as if my hand offended him. I laughed, and my tongue slid between my teeth as my power slid through the room.

"Your fucking magic doesn't work on me, whore."

"Always with the whore," I mused. "I'll tell you a secret, heathen king. No cock has ever entered me. No God, no man, no one has ever pushed their useless thing between my legs. You are not worthy of it, either."

"Ever consider that maybe you're not worthy of them?" he asked, and my eyes dropped to his cock, which hadn't reacted to my body.

His words pushed through my mind as I lifted my eyes to his. The blue glow of them ignited in his eyes, and I smiled, unwilling to show him that he'd found blood with his words. Men wanted me, but they wanted me for what I was, not who I was, and the fact that at my side, they would be untouchable. No one cared that even those born of Gods craved a connection in some way or another. I wanted one man, a warrior who wanted me

for who I was, not what I was. I had been used, tossed around by men since the dawn of time as nothing more than a way to win their wars. Wars I had never craved, nor wanted. Did they care? No, not even my own father had heard my pleas, and when I'd found a warrior worthy of my soul, he'd slaughtered him before my very eyes, showing me that love was a weakness.

Days passed, and yet he didn't cave, but those eyes, those eyes betrayed him every time I stripped down and showed him a little more of myself. I told him of his people, which I had figured would cheer him up, or should have. They were fighting to save him, dying, but fighting their best against a Goddess of War, which didn't bode well for them in the first place. I watched him for hours some days, letting him assume I slept as I stood in front of him with my ability to pass through the veil and watch the living without them knowing I had. He spent those hours hard, and this man had the nicest cock I'd ever seen. He grew larger than anyone else could dream to achieve, and yet he'd shrink it with ease if my body so much as twitched, which was how I knew what to do to break the proud beast who watched me from within his host body.

The next day, I bathed slowly before moving the chair in front of him, staring at him as he watched me. If my father could see me now, sense the immense power I contained, would he still be disappointed in what I'd become? Would it matter? I'd killed him too because he'd hurt me, told me that I was weak, so I showed him I wasn't. I studied the beast who peered out at me, sensing his need. His thick cock rose to alertness as I spread my thighs and smiled with victory. I reached out, stroking his stomach as he sucked it in, shrinking away from my touch. My lips lifted into a cold smile as I sat back, staring at him, and I imagined his kiss, the way he would taste against my mouth if I took his cock into it.

Fingers explored my cunt, feeling his eyes on it as I closed mine. The bloodlust pushed me to find a release, and this was how I did it. Alone, away from men who wanted to use me. Moans filled the room as I opened my lips, gasping as the pleasure built. His eyes were locked on my hand, watching the movement of my fingers as I gasped, starting to unravel. Blue eyes studied mine as if he sensed what others only dared whisper into the night.

The Virgin Queen, the Warrior Goddess of Battles and Chaos, untried by man; untouchable, feared by all. I screamed out my release as his mouth opened and closed. I stood up, rolling my neck as I moved to the other side of the room, uncaring that my arousal slipped down my leg, or that he was inhaling it. Pouring a drink, I slowly walked back to him, my eyes noting that his own arousal had grown, spewing his seed while he'd watched me do what no man had ever done to me. My gaze lingered on his flesh as I lifted one arousal-covered finger and slid it across the tip of his cock, collecting some of the mess that he made. Our eyes locked in silent battle as he watched me lift my finger to my tongue and slowly tasted his salty release. His groan forced a smile to curve my mouth.

"You are evil."

"Most definitely," I agreed, stepping back while I pulled the chair up closer to him and once again spread my legs, watching the muscles in his jaw as they clenched and feathered. "You will never leave this room

alive or tell another of what I do here, so enjoy it. No other man has watched me come before you. Did you enjoy it? You are hard for me again, yes?" I asked as his eyes burned. "You don't want to be hard because of what I did? Most men want to fuck me, but only to own me. I am the totem they wish to collect to win their wars. You though, you want to murder me. Is it because I murdered your armies, or because all it took was me exposing my cunt to bring you down?"

"You're beautiful, but you know that. I want to murder you and drink your flesh as the life slips from your veins while I destroy that cunt. You thrive on war and destroying worlds. You are a monster, and not even that slick flesh between those thighs would change that. I loathe you and wish to destroy you in the most pleasurable way, among other things."

I smiled, hiding the pain his words brought. This strange beast hated me? Maybe he wasn't right in the head. Or perhaps the club had knocked him senseless, literally. I was the one Goddess men went to war over, their puny minds unable to process that I pushed them into it—albeit unwillingly and not on purpose, never on purpose. I craved chaos, unable to ignore the call of it, but that was just who I was. It wasn't that I didn't enjoy a bloody war; it was that I couldn't stop them. I both hated and loved it. I lifted up, kissing his stomach as my eyes gazed down at his cock that twitched.

"You respond to me though," I uttered.

"I'm male, I respond to anything with a wet cunt between its thighs."

I laughed as my tongue traced my lips. Moving to the bed, I let the bottle of wine float in the air, watching the blood-red liquid as it filled the goblet while I lounged naked. Once it finished, I leaned back, uncaring that he watched me while I relaxed against the mountain of pillows, sipping the liquid.

"Do you have family?" I asked, creasing my brow as I turned to watch his reaction. "You do? That's almost sad, isn't it?"

"You touch them, and I will kill everything you love."

"I'd have to actually love something for that threat to work," I whispered as I swirled the wine in my glass. What asshole brought war against another kingdom with a family? That was just shitty parenting. Now I had to murder them or appear weak and watch as countless other assholes tried me to see if I would fall to their blades.

"Your people, your kingdom, I will slaughter every single one of them."

"Okay," I laughed soundlessly. "Start with me."

I dropped my gaze to the strength of his legs, sending the glass floating as I stared at the muscles of them. His cock was larger than any other man I'd tortured, even limp; I wondered if it would hurt and almost craved to feel it. I was such a slutty virgin Goddess because I craved to feel that thing beneath my fingers. Hell, I wanted to taste it and explore every inch of him, and I wanted to feel his strength and see if he could challenge mine in bed. Maybe I should have taken Lucian up on his offer to sleep with him, no strings attached. He loved war, and I'd done him a few favors, he owed me. Plus, he was fucking seriously twisted and a monster in his own right. He probably fucked like a beast, and if he

didn't, well, I could call in a favor and force him to keep it a secret. The chained beast in my room brought my attention back to him, and I lifted a brow as he spoke.

"You want to die, woman, release me. I will help you end your miserable existence." His tone was truthful, and again, the words stung.

"You can't kill me; no one can. Not unless I tell them how to do it. Sleep, creature. I tire," I muttered as I lay my head against the pillows, staring at him.

What would it be like to have someone that would murder others to keep you safe? To be loved like that seemed unattainable, and yet I'd felt it once. Briefly, I'd been loved by a warrior, but he'd been slaughtered as I'd stood there, still as marble as my father ripped him apart, giving him a permanent death because I'd become weak. Love was a weakness, one I'd been taught to exploit.

"You don't control me, bitch," he growled, and I sat up, staring at him through glowing eyes as my hair rose from the power that exploded in the room. He showed no fear, not a trace of it as I approached him. "Do your worst, whore."

"I've been called so much worse than that. We must work your slanderous tongue to teach it new words. Try untouched murderer of my wife and children, see how that rolls off that smooth tongue of yours. Tell me, has your wife heard that dirty, dirty mouth saying such filth? Do you taste her flesh with such words on it? Or do you cherish her, lavishing her with your false flattery? Or does she shrink away from the monster that is hidden within this meat suit you wear?"

"I will find a way to end you, Goddess," he snapped.

My hand touched over his cock, and he hissed as I lifted my eyes to his. He tried to move away, and yet I held him in place with my magic. As I stroked it, he extended as my eyes grew large with surprise. I moaned against the soft silk that turned to steel in my hand, lifting my eyes to hold his as he watched me with a look I didn't know or understand. In all my years of living, I'd never touched one; never even the lover I'd lost had allowed it. I'd killed that part of me, burying it to prevent it from ever being awoken again, and yet this king brought it clawing back to the surface.

"Release me," he demanded huskily.

"You're not immune," I frowned as I did as he asked.

"No man is immune to a woman's touch. Not when she is beautiful and naked as you are. I'd have to be dead to be immune to you." His honesty surprised me, and my frown deepened.

"And your wife, what about her? If I fucked you, would it be she who you wished this magical cock was buried in?" I asked, hating that I read the answer in his eyes. "You love her."

"She is my Queen, of course, I love her," he hissed as he watched me walking towards the bed. "That isn't your question though; you want to know if I would lower myself to rut with you. You want to be fucked, don't you, creature?"

"Would you fuck me, knowing I'm going to destroy everything you love? Tell me, would you sell your soul and everything you love to taste me?" I asked, knowing that his answer could seal his fate.

"I'd rather twist your fucking head from your shoulders."

"I guess if you're into that kind of thing, it might be hot."

"Sit on my face, let me taste you. You wish to be fucked. I will destroy your cunt, Goddess. I will sate your every desire, and then I will take your life. Now, release me."

I lifted my eyes to his, finding them studying me. He wanted to murder me, not fuck me. It was hot, and yeah, so what if his dirty mouth made my cunt peer up and notice? It wasn't wrong to want him; I'd conquered him. He was mine now. "In time, you will come to understand that here, I am your Queen. You are no longer the King, nor do you have a queen. She is being hunted as we speak. Not even your precious ocean will protect her from me."

ERIE

I opened my eyes, lifting them to the chains that held me. Ancient chains that had been created by the Gods to hold mischievous Gods who had misbehaved. I laughed as I turned to the bed, staring at Callaghan, who watched me, and yet those glowing eyes held control. I shook my head, unwilling to let him see how disturbing the nightmares were.

"You can feed me all the nightmares you want, beast, but you can't make me become her," I hissed as I expelled a breath, staring down at my flat stomach. "The chains are overkill, are they not?" I asked as I watched him lifting from the bed.

"Time to fuck, Erie," he muttered as his wings expanded and his body grew. He was the king of an ancient race, and he wanted to destroy me. He wanted me to remember what I'd done, who I was, and yet that wasn't me. I wasn't a Goddess, of that I was sure.

"How about you fuck yourself," I hissed.

"Mmm, I'd rather fuck that tightness that belongs to me instead. Don't worry; I'll let you come, it's more than you ever allowed me while I hung in your chains. Although, waking up to that sweet cunt riding my face was a welcome surprise, and I may return the favor and bruise your esophagus."

"You do know that I don't remember, and I also don't care."

"You will when we take everything you love away from you."

"I don't love anything," I whispered as I lifted my gaze to hold his. "But you know that already, don't you?" I snorted. "You know everything about me, and more. The only thing you don't know is who I am this time. Tell me, was I different last time?"

"You repeat the cycle," he admitted as his hands drifted down to my sore flesh. "You choose us out of the warriors around you; then you proceed to want us. When we don't give you all of us, you start to remove everything that you think prevents us from loving you."

"And yet I haven't done it, have I?" I whimpered as his fingers slid through my flesh, dancing over it with a tenderness that built a moan in the back of my throat. "I have killed you and run from you. Take the hint already. I've not made an attempt to seduce any warrior, you know that. You broke me, remember?"

"No, because you didn't have time to do it yet," he chuckled as he lowered his body to the floor, where he kneeled before my wetness, lifting my leg over his

shoulder. "The world changed, Erie." His tongue slid through my flesh, and I squealed as he pushed it into my body, moaning as he tasted my arousal. "You always tasted of heaven, as if the Gods created you as a reward to warriors for their bravery of deeds. I remember the day you rode my mouth, coming for me and me alone. It was the first time a man had pleasured you. I remember the wonder that lit in your pretty blue eyes. The taste of you as it slid down my chin as my name left those pretty lips of yours. You didn't realize it, lost in the pleasure I gave you, but you screamed for me. Men spoke of it, and I became a God among my race that you thought you had destroyed. The only male alive to ever make the Goddess of War come undone and scream for him."

My eyes closed as I struggled to focus, to understand what he was saying as something pinched through my side. I looked down, finding his teeth buried in my side as his glowing eyes spun and he watched me. Pain ignited as he pushed something into my flesh; black lines moved over my stomach, and I whimpered as he pulled his sharp fangs from me.

"What the hell was that?" I demanded, but my eyes grew heavy as he watched me, his fingers tracing the raised bumps on my side as he stood up and kissed me hard and fast before stepping back.

"Sleep, creature. I tire," the beast growled.

CHAPTER
forty-four

TODAY I'D BEEN PLACED ONTO THE BED, MY BODY allowed to rest as they joined together as one, needing to grow stronger from their recent time apart. Balor and Callaghan had made a deal, one that forced them to remain as one soul, which meant they needed each other to survive. My body snuggled against the beast, needing his warmth so that I could sleep, even though I knew with sleep would come the never-ending memories.

Last night, I'd dreamt of running through endless fields, watching as Callaghan buried his young son. The same dream changed, turning into arrows protruding from the beast's daughters. I'd given that order, the order to murder those girls. I'd laughed, watching as they'd died. My mind sent me back to that moment, over and over again.

I had defeated them, finally. The invaders, who had come onto my shores, slaughtering my people, now bathed the land in their blood. How dare he enter into my kingdom, intending to dethrone me, to make me kneel at his feet like his pet? His demand had been just that. Kneel on my knees before him and take what he offered between my whore lips as his army watched. Service the heathen king and let him defile me as they watched him do so, as if. Now I was forced to kill innocent people because he'd wanted his dick sucked to show his strength over me.

"You think to deny us?" one of the soldiers asked as I stared him down, knowing that sooner or later, his skull would adorn my wall.

"My Queen, if you deny the men the pleasures of these women, they will see it as a weakness," Lugh growled. His turquoise eyes studied me as his hand continued to grip the King's wife by her hair while she swore and cursed me to the Gods.

I studied her utter perfection. She was beautiful, this queen, her bronzed flesh kissed by the Gods. Black hair shone beneath the sun's merciless rays as green eyes the color of jade watched me with loathing. Lifting my eyes, I took in the daughters who cowered behind her, knowing that any sign of mercy would be seen a weakness to these men. I swallowed the anger at their father, for this *was on him. He'd breached my shores, sent slanderous requests to me knowing that I would be forced to meet him in the field of this battle, and that if he lost, this would play out exactly as it was now. This was war, and I knew the game well. I should, as I had created it.*

"Give her to the men," I uttered as I watched her fighting against Lugh's hand that had twisted into the midnight silk of her hair. The men behind him moved to push her daughters, crying for their mother, towards the

awaiting army, and I shook my head. "No, not them,"
I rebuked, anger slicing through me as the men turned
angry eyes towards me. "They are not to be raped."

"They will rise against you if you allow them to
live," he snapped. "The men will see it as a weakness if
you let them go."

"Who said they would live?" I asked, staring into
his startling eyes. Of all the men I ruled, he alone dared
to argue against my words. Pity that I'd taken a vow of
celibacy after losing the one man I'd loved. Thousands
of years had passed since he'd been murdered before my
very eyes, torn apart by my father to teach me a lesson.
Love was a weakness, and if you loved something, you
destroyed it so that it could never hurt you or be used
against you. "Tie them to the posts, and let the archers
use them for practice."

I swallowed hard as they started to cry against the
words that slipped from my lips. This was war, and
they'd brought it to my shores. Danu had abandoned
her people, fleeing at the first whispers of war, but then
she was the mother. Weak to flee in the face of a battle,
and I'd been only too willing to take her place with the
war being waged. I had never been able to turn down a
chance to indulge my need for battle or to use my ability
to decide the outcome of one.

"Lugh, if you ever challenge me in front of my army
again, I will cut your fucking head off and use your
skull as a chalice to drink my wine. I will not warn you
again."

"You could use me for other things that you'd enjoy
much more, my Queen. I am skilled in everything that
a woman could need," he offered, and I studied the

heat that smoldered in his eyes. "You are everything a warrior craves and desires."

"Pray to your Gods that I never look upon you with lust, Lugh. I don't play fair when I aim to conquer."

"Is that why you hunted his family down?" *he asked, watching me for any sign of weakness. He'd never find it; I'd learned from the moment I was created to hide that side of me.*

"I hunted them down as a lesson to anyone else who thinks to storm these shores. My land is not to be plundered. The first rule of war is to show no mercy. A merciful queen is a weak one. I am not Danu; I do not run from a fight, I welcome it." *My eyes moved to the black wings of the crows as they descended on the dead, plucking flesh from the corpses that covered the battlefield.* "If I allowed them to live, it would be seen as weakness, and more armies would come. This is the price he pays for bringing his monsters onto my shores, and he would have had no mercy if he'd conquered me. I would have been raped, murdered, and placed on his walls as a trophy."

"Is that why he is naked, tied to your bed?" *he asked, and I lifted my eyes to hold his.*

"Who is in my bed is not your concern, Lugh. I enjoy having him there, reminding him that I am destroying everything he loves. They speak of what I do to him; do they not?" *I asked, waiting to hear what they said of my bedmate.*

"They think you enjoy his cock," *he admitted as he stepped closer, uncaring that a few feet away from us, the king's daughters were being filled with arrows while their blood escaped through countless wounds.*

His wife screamed as warrior after warrior took her by force. I wanted to throw up at the scene that played out around me, and yet I wouldn't. I showed no regret, no fear or mercy because to do so would result in others thinking I had some, which I didn't. "They say it grows to monstrous lengths, and that you're riding him every night. That you scream his name as he takes our queen," he laughed coldly. "I don't argue what they say, since night after night, the entire kingdom hears your screams as you come apart for our enemy's cock. You're a woman with needs. I don't think any less of you for using what is at hand. I do, however, think that you should use others among your own court as well to quiet the rumors. As I said, my offer stands, and I would worship every single inch of you, my Queen." He bowed as a sly smile lifted his lips, my cheeks burning with his words.

I turned away from him, dismissing him entirely. I stared at the queen, who was between two men, taking them both as she begged for mercy. It sickened me, forcing anger to radiate through me as the men used her for pleasure. The battle had ended hours ago, and yet I still felt unease pulsing through me. Moving to where they raped her, I pulled out my sword, watching as they scattered away from her body while she fell to the ground, helpless.

"There is no mercy in war," I hissed vehemently. "There is no mercy when you invaded our lands. You and your king brought this upon yourselves."

"He will kill you!" she whimpered through chattering teeth.

"He is chained to my bed," I laughed as I lowered myself to push her hair from her face. "He begs to

fuck me," I whispered against her ear. *"He hasn't even pleaded for your life since I first captured him. Not a single mention of the family he has left behind to die."*

"We are not weak, and he is never weak! He loves me! He cherishes our daughters," she whimpered as a soldier moved between her legs. I turned, staring at him as he rubbed his hand over his engorged cock. *"You can allow your men to rape me, but you will never kill us all."*

"Your daughters are dead, your king is soon to join them, and you...you will die here." I turned her head, forcing her to stare at her daughters, who hung to the posts, lifeless as arrows continued to hit their marks in their flesh.

I watched as her eyes filled with tears, and I wondered what it would feel like to love something as much as she had loved her children. To have a husband who cherished her and loved her for being weak. I would never know that love, never in my lifetime, because to love me, was to die. I rose from the ground, no longer interested in hearing her words as I brought my sword up and then down, severing her head while the men watched me.

"You don't need her mouth to fuck her," I hissed when one uttered his displeasure at the loss of her head. I grabbed it, pushing it into the bag I carried before I moved into the horde of men to find the one I sought. When I reached him, I frowned as he turned, watching me with naked hunger in his eyes.

His hand lifted, cupping my naked breast as I watched him with cold detachment. I said, *"When they've finished with her corpse, you will place her beside her daughters. Let the crows feed on their flesh as a warning to anyone else who seeks to wage war against us."*

"You intend to show them mercy?" he chuckled as he pinched my nipple.

"Lucifer, if you intend to rule hell, you must first learn to not fuck with those who enjoy slaughtering the new God's children. I assure you, I have no mercy. Touch me again, and I will prove it to you," I growled as I grabbed his dick, tightening my hold. "You bow before me, or you die just like the others you begged me to murder for you have died. If you plan to cross me, know that I am *War. I am always ten feet ahead of you, and I never fail to bring down my enemies. Now be a good boy and do as I asked."*

Walking away from the battle left a sour taste in my mouth. I stopped and smiled as I felt my sisters materializing beside me. "You are too late to join the battle," I muttered, staring at each one.

"It's not the battle we enjoy," Fódla said as her eyes took in the lustful warriors that were covered in thick, dried blood. "It is the warriors and their lust I've come for."

"You're willing to lower yourself to take the cock of a lesser being?" I asked curiously as I studied her, waiting for her response.

"It is only you who fears lust, sweet sister. You, of course, lost your lover in a most brutal way, but it was a lesson you took to heart. Some of us don't care what we fuck, as long as we can find pleasure," she shrugged. "I heard rumors that you found a beast and have him chained to your bed; have you finally decided to break

that lousy vow of chastity? You murdered his wife and children?" she said as she took in the two women who were filled with arrows beside the headless corpse.

"If they lived, I would die. I need you to retrieve them, bury them with the other ones in my tomb," I whispered, barely loud enough for the wind to carry my words.

"And why not let the crows feast upon them, they're starving."

"They remind me of us," I admitted. "This wasn't their doing, but war is war."

"And now that you've taken everything he loves away, will you let him taste your flesh? Or do you intend to take his head as well?" she countered as I watched my other sister playing with Lucifer openly without fear of being judged or persecuted for her actions. His broad wings flapped in the wind as he showed her his true form.

"I have not decided," I admitted. "I rather enjoy torturing him. He soothes something in me, and I have grown to enjoy his struggles and his dirty mouth. He speaks freely about wanting to rip my skull off and fuck it; I find it refreshing and a change from the others and their dumb, love-struck ideas. I will deliver his queen's head to him tonight. I don't imagine he will have many good things to speak of when I have done so."

"Will you tell him that you murdered his children as well?" she asked as we watched Banba stripping herself bare while Lucifer did the same. Strange vines slipped from his ribcage to caress her flesh. "She is such a hussy...Is it bad that I want to join her; he is hot."

"I won't have to tell him that his children died. They

were never away from his beloved wife, so presenting him with her head should be enough. That's not right, is it?" My beast hadn't shown me wings yet. Maybe I'll cut him open to see if he has some of those hiding beneath his flesh, as Lucifer does.

"Is she letting those things into her body?" she laughed as we watched our sister bending over, allowing Lucifer to use his vines to fuck her as he stood inches away from her. The entire army watched them, occasionally throwing me and my sister curious glances as if we might join the orgy. "It's disturbing, and yet I am wet just thinking about it. Remember what our father did, Ériu. The other Gods have noticed you are once again here, picking up Danu's mess. They fear what you are, and what your presence does to these beings. Wherever you are, war rages around you, around us."

"Am I to go to the slumber, then? What would they have me do? I only joined this world because the call of war beckoned to me. War was already here; I just stepped in and decided on which side to fight. They're bloodthirsty beings. I hurt no one by being here," I uttered, my mind racing with the overwhelming need to scream at what the other Gods thought of me.

I was created to bring war to the lands, to unleash chaos onto their worlds. They feared me, rejected me, and they took everything and everyone I loved from me. They showed me what I was, who I was, and when I'd discovered that I could want something, it was destroyed. My own father had murdered the one being I'd loved more than myself. He'd ripped him apart slowly while I stood there, watching it unfold. I couldn't save him, nor would I have. I'd been weak, vulnerable. Just as the king tied to my bed was weak, his love of those I'd murdered had been his weakness. I'd done what I knew to make him stronger. I took his weaknesses away so that he would be like me, strong enough to stand with me if I chose it.

"You like this king?" she said as she studied me, uncaring that our sister was screaming like an idiot as some puny angel fucked her. "Why?"

"I like that he soothes the monster within me as he speaks of murdering me," I said with a smirk lifting my lips. "His cock grows to the most alluring monstrous thing I've ever seen. I don't love him, but I do wish to feel him within me. Is that a weakness, Fódla?" I asked.

"No, no, it isn't a weakness to enjoy a man, Ériu," she uttered. "It's been thousands of years since you have even kissed a man or creature. Have you ever even taken one between your thighs?"

"No, I had intended to be with one man alone, but he was lost to me."

"You killed our father, and still, you live with the fear that he will arise and take anything you may love away from you again. He is dead; you made sure that he could never rise."

"I loved him, so I ended him. Wasn't that what his lesson was about? Removing the weaknesses that made you vulnerable?"

"You didn't kill us."

"You're a part of me. Together we form a terrifying monster that not even the Gods dare to cross. Besides, you're my sisters. We shared a womb."

"What do you intend to do now?" she asked hesitantly as her eyes moved to the bloody satchel at

my side.

"Deliver the queen to her king, and watch as he falls apart."

"Remind me never to piss you off." She turned, staring out at the men who watched our sister as the angel pounded into her with increasing speed as vines pushed into her mouth. I blinked then vanished from the battlefield, no longer interested in watching my sister play with a lesser being who had been watching me as he fucked her. It was disturbing, and yet he was pleasing to look at.

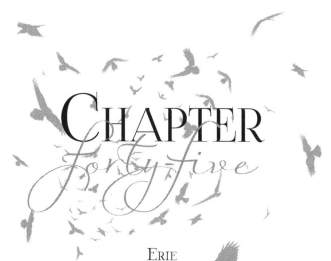

CHAPTER
Forty-Five

ERIE

CHAINED TO THE CEILING ONCE MORE, I STARED AT Callaghan, who watched me, his Nordic blue eyes noting the way I moved against the magic that pushed into my flesh. It was angry magic, magic that filled me entirely as it used me. My body was covered in the sheen of my own sweat as he inspected my reaction, noting the moment I was close to coming, only for him to stop and wait out the impending orgasm. I was exhausted, and yet I craved more. I craved what they did to me, using magic, their flesh, toys, and whatever else they could find to fuck me.

"More," I uttered, lifting my drenched head, staring at him as my arousal slid down my leg. "Fuck me, Mason," I begged.

"Not until you remember who you are," he replied coldly as the magic started again, pushing my flesh apart with vigor as he let it stretch me full while he watched my cunt being fucked at his leisure. "You're such a messy girl today. You're dripping that sweet juice down your legs," he chuckled as he rose from the chair, fisting my hair and staring into my eyes. "Do you remember the first time we fucked? I do because you were untried again, and yet you found me on a battlefield and rode me among the lifeless corpses as you begged me for more. That pussy was so fucking tight, so wet and willing to be used that you let me destroy it, uncaring of being discovered among the dead. You had no idea who I was, what I was, and yet there you were, after countless years had passed between your last lifetimes. You walked right up to me and begged me to fuck that tight pussy. I did, I fucked you so hard, knowing exactly who you were and what you needed from me. You were searching for us, for the beast I held inside of me. It wasn't him that you fucked that day though, and the selfish prick I was, I let you fuck me as he slumbered inside."

His fingers rubbed against the wetness between my thighs before he pulled his fingers up, licking each one clean as I watched him. His hands lifted to the chains that held me, and he released me, pushing my trembling body to the bed, where he re-chained me. Chains that had been specially created to hold even the strongest immortals now held me prisoner to his every desire.

He wasn't playing fair, and I'd begged for hours to come, and yet he refused me. He wanted me lost in my mind and knew that if he drained me to the brink of exhaustion, I went back to that time unwillingly. It was why they took turns, working my body to near exhaustion as he was now, endlessly using magic to weaken my mind to send me back to the murderous bitch that had once played with them.

I'd walked undisturbed through the battlefield, my eyes taking in the carnage of the war that had beckoned me forth to this place of death. A holy war, whatever that meant, had played out here in this strange land. My eyes lowered to the blood that squished between my toes, the familiarity of it felt soothing; it felt right. I was bored, hating that this world was weaker than the last one. I knew I'd been brought back, and yet I couldn't remember anything from the past. My eyes gazed out among the dead and dying and watched as a Knight slid his blade through one of his own men. Mercy? Pathetic.

Stretching my arms, I moved deeper into the field, plucking warriors who had earned their passage into Hades with a single touch as I walked through them towards the man currently dispatching those who had been too weak to get back up. My hand paused on one, lifting my eyes as I felt the power that wafted through the air, slithering over my flesh. I straightened as I watched him moving through the field, deeper into the throng of dead bodies.

Nordic blue eyes lifted from where he'd been searching and held mine. I watched as he slowly moved closer, his eyes narrowing as he took in the white dress I wore, untouched by the blood all around us. I hissed as he closed the distance. He was different, stronger, scarred by battle, and yet masculinity oozed off him and slithered over my flesh. He smelled of home, of what had brought me to this strange land.

"You don't belong here, my lady. It isn't safe for you," he uttered as he held out a chainmail-covered hand, and I stared down at it. *"Come with me."*

I slipped my hand into his, letting his power ignite my own. When he turned to move us away from the fields of death, I pulled him back to me. My dress vanished, and his eyes, those beautiful Nordic blue eyes slid over my naked body with a hunger that I craved. I pulled him closer, letting him feel the wrongness of me, and when he didn't pull away, I started removing his gear.

"My Lady, this is a place of death," he uttered thickly, already caving to the need to fuck me. He was like him, the one I searched for without knowing why. He was my soul, ripped from me before I'd claimed it. "You're so beautiful."

I ripped his chainmail off over his head, pulling his tunic over his head as well as my mouth kissed his chest, craving what I sensed he wanted. His hands yanked at my hair as he pushed his trousers down, lifting me, and then slamming me down on his thick cock. I screamed as he ripped past my maidenhead, tearing it apart as those sinful blue eyes found mine with wonder lighting them.

I pushed him down, needing to ride him as I sensed I had before; needing the mindlessness that came from the pleasure his body could give me. He lay back among the bodies as I lifted up, slamming myself down as scream after scream was ripped from my throat. Every scream echoed off the bodies and through the valley where I rode him with wild abandonment. He rolled us the moment my body started to come undone, and I hissed at being denied my pleasure's release, but his body, the strength of it towered over me as he began to move. Blood coated my back, slipping me further away from him with every hard thrust of his hips.

His kiss stole my breath away, and he thrust into my core, growling as it clenched against his massive cock, burning with an ache that I craved. The pain, the pleasure, the mindlessness that ended the emptiness of being cursed to be alone, he took it all away. Every thrust he forced into my body brought me closer to the edge of release. The dead lay around us, an entire field of corpses, and we fucked to create life. He tensed, coming in me as the world settled around us. His mouth lifted as he smiled down at me, now covered in the blood of those who had died here.

"You were a virgin, and I cannot offer you marriage," he uttered, and the world turned cold around us. I swallowed as I pushed him from me, staring at him.

"I don't believe I asked for marriage, Paladin."

"I'm not a Paladin, I'm a Templar," he said as he stood up, searching for his clothes and armor among the bodies.

"So you are righteous and indignant, and yet you fucked me?" I hissed.

"I am married, happily," he said before his hand moved over his mouth and he stared at my body. "I cannot offer you anything, other than to bring you into the town and provide you shelter in my home for the night."

"With your wife?" I asked, staring at him as I picked up the dress I'd worn, still untouched by blood.

"She is with the King, away from this war."

"I'll come with you." And I would, every fucking way possible. Then I'd take what he loved, because I needed him to look at me as he had, to feel the ache that seemed to never end. He held out his hand, and

I accepted it as I pulled the dress down, even as his heated gaze stared at my bare thighs.

"You're not from around here, are you? Do you have a name?"

"Ireland," I uttered huskily. "I am Ireland."

"Your name is Ireland?"

I stared into his eyes, wondering if it mattered if he knew my name or not. My heart twisted against my chest, aching for what I couldn't remember. I let him pull me against his body as he held me. It felt right, this position against him. His heat filled me, wrapping around me as he lifted me until I was forced to wrap my legs around his waist. Swallowing hard, he shook his head.

"Gods save me, but you're addicting," he growled as he pushed into my body, watching my mouth open as a scream of pleasure escaped. He used me on the field of battle as if I was his to keep, and I let him, feeling him as he filled me completely with his cock. "You are perfect," he uttered as he tensed, coming undone while my gaze slid over the sightless eyes around us.

"I am lost," I whispered. "I cannot find my home."

"I will protect you," he vowed. "I will get you back to Ireland, back to where you belong. Who brought you to this place of horror?" he demanded.

"War," I whimpered as he withdrew from my body, pulling me against his once again.

"You don't belong in a place like this. You belong in a palace, protected from men like me."

"You are a Knight. Am I not protected with you?" I asked as my eyes narrowed and I inhaled, noting that scent I'd been following. I pulled away, searching the

edges of the field for the one thing I craved most, yet couldn't reach. The scent came and went, as if the breeze carried it. I turned back, staring at him while he watched me with heat burning in his pretty eyes.

"You're safe from everyone but *me," he pointed out as he continued to watch me, his eyes following where my gaze had strayed. "What are you searching for, my lady?" he asked.*

"My home; I feel it, but I can't find it," I whispered through tears.

"Home!" I screamed, struggling against the chains that continued touching me. "I want my home!" I shrieked as I fought the chains.

"You have no home," Callaghan uttered.

"What?" I whispered breathlessly as they caressed me, watching me while I groaned and lifted my hips for more.

"You destroyed our home," he uttered. "We tried to teach you that, but you only know war."

CHAPTER Forty-six

MÓRRÍGAN

I LAUGHED AS BALOR CHASED ME THROUGH THE *flowery meadow, catching me and picking me up. His hands cradled my face, as if I was something to be cherished. This creature, he was the moon, my stars that lit up the darkness from which I'd been created. No one had ever looked upon me as he did. His mouth made me feel things, and I had stopped feeling so long ago that I didn't even remember how to until him.*

"When you look at me like that, I see our future."

"And what do you see, my love?" I asked, unable to hide the fear in my voice.

I was war and chaos, and wherever I was, it followed me. It was a part of me that had gone incredibly wrong when I'd been born of magic. I was cursed, and I'd separated myself from everyone, everyone except for my sisters. They were immune to what I was, or what I created, but then occasionally they were a part of me. The three of us became one well-oiled machine that could lay waste to lands, worlds, or whatever we craved to destroy. Me, I craved him. And this man, this man hadn't gone mad with the need to fight in my presence. He was created for me, for me!

"I see us, creating life."

My heart stopped as the power within me thundered at the enticing idea of creating a child, but that was another curse. The Gods feared what I would breed, and had forbidden me from carrying a child. I smiled against his lips, ignoring the panic that erupted inside of my mind as my heart ached.

"You'd want a child with me after I took yours?" I asked, chewing my lips.

"We were the monarchs of two opposing realms. If I hadn't wanted to see you with my own eyes and brought the war to your shores, we'd never have gotten here."

"If I told you something, something important, could I trust you not to leave me?" I asked as the war horn sounded from the palace, and I turned in its direction and frowned. I turned back to find him studying me.

"I would never leave you," he uttered as his lips hovered over mine. "You're my home, and we will create a son together. I want a boy as strong as his mother, who fights at my side when the war horn sounds of intruders." The horn sounded again as he pulled me closer. "You're my world, and I feel you within me. I know you made me immortal. I feel it."

"I did no such thing," I lied as a smile spread over my lips.

"You did it before you even knew you liked me; why?"

"I almost killed you, and I realized I didn't want

to be alone. You may have hated me, but you looked at me as if I was the stars in a sea of darkness, and I wanted that. I wanted someone to see me, to see past the endless war and chaos, and you were immune to it. I know war, so I went to war against you. I know strategy, so I watched you, and every time I disrobed, you would stare at me, and your pupils would grow until this beautiful, inhuman glow lit within them. I saw a man who could stand beside me, not because he had to, but because he might want to. I'm tired of men falling at my feet because they think I will gain them riches or win their wars. I loved before, before I came here. Thousands of years ago, I fell in love with a Demi-God. I wanted the world with him. What I ended up with was standing silently beside him as my father ripped him apart, forcing me to watch it unfold. I couldn't save him, and many others sat and watched as I was taught what a weakness love could be. Three centuries later, I murdered my father because I loved him too. Does that make me evil?"

He stared at me silently as he swallowed past whatever emotion he felt. "How did you get here?" he asked, and I tilted my head.

"Danu, she offered me an escape from the realms of the Gods, as I was a friend of Bilé, her husband and consort. He is the God of the Dead of Ireland, as Danu asked him to become. Then you came, and the war started off as small skirmishes. At first, Bilé came to collect the spirits which wandered aimlessly, but then Danu started vanishing more and more. One day, she didn't come back, and so I went to find her. She was in Faery, a new world she had created. She'd forgone *her own people, left them with no hope of standing against the Fomorians, and so I stood with them. Bilé followed her, of course, because he loved her and they had created a life together. After all, the cost of his collecting the souls and taking them to the underworld through the Tree of Life came at a price. Her bed, for his deeds, once a year until she died."*

"And where is she now?" he countered.

"Knowing Danu, which I do, probably out torturing some pretty little creature with her obsession to control them because she created them," I laughed as his eyes narrowed.

"Is that something all Goddesses do?"

"You're not pretty, Balor," I whispered as I kissed his cheek. "Come, war is on the wind, and I am needed."

"You're pregnant," he said, and I paused, turning to look at him as I dropped his hand. "I should have waited for you to feel it, but I sense him in you. A son, our son, Ériu, say something."

"You sense it?" I asked, my throat constricted as the shadows around us closed in on me.

"I can smell him. You see, when my wife was pregnant with my daughters, they carried a scent, my scent but different. You smell of a child, my child."

"You could be mistaken, we made love nine times yesterday," I stated as I swallowed hard.

"Do you not want a child?" he asked, narrowing his eyes. "Do you not want a child because I am a heathen, and you are not?"

"I want your child," I whispered as my heart raced. "I want to be a mother, but I am War. I am chaos; what type of child would I create?" I demanded.

"Ours," he smiled as he pulled me closer, kissing my forehead. "I go to war, and you, you remain here safe until I return."

"I am the Goddess of War and Chaos, do you plan to think me weaker because you've planted something in my womb? I destroy worlds, husband. I fear no man or war and only become stronger when the world is bathed in chaos."

"I know, but I have not killed anything in days, and you slaughtered an entire continent of men abusing their women two days ago. You agreed that I would become your king, and I have yet to wage war in your name. Let me do this."

I stared at him as his face shifted, and I narrowed my senses on him, wondering what the new person he'd added to him looked like. "Kiss me, and come home to me safe," I uttered and frowned. "Oh, ew, I sound like a whining wife."

"You could never whine, my battle Goddess. I love you, Ériu," he uttered as he pulled me closer, kissing me before he released me and started walking away towards the palace. I watched him until he was out of sight and turned to stare into the shadows that grew around me.

"If you come for me, I will kill you," I hissed to the minions of the demon that watched me, looking for a way out of his debt. "And if you tell the others what you heard, you will never find any rest from me, Lucifer. I will never stop ruining your life."

I stared at Callaghan through strands of wet hair, watching him as his fingers slid over my belly, touching my flesh as he tried to ignite my passion. I didn't allow it. Instead, I let him touch me as he lowered his mouth,

trailing kisses over my flat stomach. He slipped between my thighs, watching me as he began kissing his way up my bound body.

"Please, I don't want to be her, Mason," I uttered hoarsely. "She wasn't a good person. She was evil! Why would you want her to come back?" Tears slid down my cheek as he cupped my face and kissed them away.

"You're not listening to us. You weren't evil. You were lost, broken, and unwanted by the other Gods. They were afraid of you, as were the mortals. Being a Goddess in a world of mortals wasn't something you ever wanted; it's what was available to you. It's why you never stayed in a place very long before you met Balor, because wherever you are, war comes, as it's drawn to you. You're a fucking battle Goddess from a time long forgotten," Callaghan whispered as he gripped and lifted my chin, forcing my swollen eyes to meet and hold his. "You were loved by two men, two men you destroyed because you wanted them to love you. You were lost when I met you. Searching for him, and yet you took me because you wanted me. You made me love you, and then you started to take the people I loved away from me. I allowed my son to die so that I could save our race from you. You brought us down because you went to war against me to obtain me. The druids helped me find a way to prepare for the curse you'd started on our race. I gave up what I loved the most to be fully connected to the beast within me, and to undo the curse that you were about to place upon our people. I sacrificed him for the greater good, but also to bring you back through the cauldron. Because the maiden who came back, she was stronger than we could handle, and war followed behind you as you searched for us, you just couldn't see it because you were reborn without your memories.

"You were this beautiful creature in the chaos of a maddening war. I'd lost my brother that day, and I was searching the field for his corpse when this beautiful maiden appeared. I loved you; I fell in love with you again, even though you couldn't remember me. I had stood beside you through countless wars, longing to taste you, and yet you'd never seen me until that day. It was as if you'd never lived before. There you were, searching for the piece of your soul you'd given the beast to make him immortal like you, and you found me instead. I would have given you the world, and yet I knew that would never be enough for you. You needed chaos, and to be the only thing that I loved. He awoke soon after I had taken you on that battlefield and we made a plan together. I knew what you would do because I'd watched you do it before. What I didn't count on was how far you'd go to achieve it. When you began hunting my family, I made the deal with the druids to make a sacrifice to protect myself and our people from you. I sacrificed my son's life to become strong enough to withstand your allure, and to be able to end you if I had to, but also, it took a life to bring back a life from the cauldron. Had I known then that we'd created life on that battlefield when we lay in the blood and chaos, I'd have chosen you, Erie. Now you carry our child again, and I won't lose you. Do you understand me? I won't lose you again. You have to remember who you are so that what is coming for us doesn't win."

"And to be safe, I have to remember who I am? Why can't you protect me?"

"Not who, what," he muttered as he wiped away a tear that slid down my cheek. "What you are, Erie," he growled as he watched me. "I can't protect you because they've awoken Hecate, and you're the only being that's evil enough to make her kneel at your feet." He let his hand trail down over my stomach, drawing circles over it. "You have to finish this life," he rumbled as he sat up, staring down at me where I was chained with my arms above my head, my legs suspended in the air.

"As what, your fuck toy?" I demanded hoarsely.

"That is what you did to me when you captured me, was it not?" the beast chuckled, and I turned, staring into his black flesh as he watched me.

"I don't remember," I whispered. "You can feed me all the fucked up shit you want to, but the thing is, I don't want to be her. I like me. I like this version, and I'm sorry that you don't, but this is what you get," I hissed before I sniffed the air and wrinkled my nose. "I need a bath," I growled, and he snorted, flicking my hardened nipple.

"Mmm, you smell like sex and magic, and personally, I prefer you like this, creature."

"Don't call me that," I snapped.

"Or what, *creature*?" he asked as he sat up, stroking his cock.

"Put your wrecking ball penis away," I said thickly.

I really had to get out of here, now. I needed to get outside, to escape past their defenses and think about everything that had happened. I turned away from him as he stroked my cheek. His throaty laughter irritated me as Callaghan watched.

"Tell me, Erie. What would you give us for a bath?"

he asked, his eyes slowly sliding over my abused flesh.

"Go away," I whispered thickly, and I closed my eyes, already half asleep even though my mind begged me to remain awake to escape the nightmares they continually showed me.

I stood outside his compound, my heart hammering against my ribs as I processed what he'd done. He'd let them murder his fucking child to protect a people that weren't even his. How could he believe the lies the druids told him? Why wouldn't he listen to me or face me? I spun around as a crowd of men was brought out of the compound, bound and gagged, then the King and his men placed them onto the pyres to burn.

I stood in the crowd, jaded by the man I'd fallen for. I didn't understand what I had done wrong or why he preferred her to me. He'd protected her as he pushed me away, like I was some monster he couldn't distance himself from fast enough. I'd sought him out, and he'd set guards upon on me, watching from his wall as they tried to hurt me. I'd never felt angrier in my entire life. Why would he do that to me? I had no access to my memories or my magic, and so they'd manhandled me, stopping just short of rape because he'd called a halt to it before I was left bleeding in the mud. It had been weeks since I'd seen him, and I'd done everything in my power to stop him from murdering his son, and he'd stopped me from helping him. If I got close to him, I was seized and removed from the area. They'd bound me to a fucking tree, leaving me there to be sought upon by men who had tried to rape me. I'd left their skulls on his wall, and yet still, I couldn't reach him.

He'd told me he loved me, that I was his world, and

the next day, he'd left me. My hand cradled the babe that swelled in my stomach. His child *that he didn't even know grew within me. I stepped back from the guards who marched through the crowd as the Templars were brought out, broken, and abused. My heart clenched as I closed my eyes against their once proud faces, now drawn and haggard from abuse.*

Scanning the crowd, I found my Knight watching me as I smiled softly, my hand pressed against the child we'd created. I started to move towards him, but the anger I felt from him stalled me. I backed up, ignoring the chaos and the screams as the men were set ablaze. Instead of watching it, as my soul cried for, I stepped away, turning and leaving the field where their screams filled the air. I had to protect what we'd created together, even if he didn't want it.

I had to find my home. A home where I could birth his child safely, where no one could harm him. A child I would love that I could raise to be better than I was. He'd know love, know that he wasn't created from pain or rape, and love freely. I felt eyes on me, turning to stare at the Knights who had been hidden beneath cloaks as they approached and surrounded me. I didn't fight them as I looked up to find Callaghan moving through them, grabbing my arm as he pulled me through the crowded road. He pushed me into the field where I tripped, stumbling until I righted myself and turned on him, glaring at him.

"I'm going to tell you this one time, and one time only. Leave, because the next time I see you here, I will murder you for what you took from me, monster. That screaming you hear, those are my brothers burning for

something you started." His grief poured off of him, a loss that I couldn't understand.

He'd let them place a curse on his child, and he'd held him as his young life was snuffed out by that curse. His wife, his precious fucking wife, had learned of what he held inside of him and she'd wanted nothing to do with him. I wanted him; I wanted to hold him and promise him that once she was gone from this world, we'd be free together.

"You think you can tell me what to do?" I asked, and watched as he withdrew his sword and held it in front of him to strike fear into my heart. "Your blades do not work on me," I hissed and then screamed as he lunged, pushing it through my stomach. "No," I uttered as I lifted my eyes to his. "He was mine!" I screamed as the air grew thick around us, my magic igniting and sending bolts of lightning crashing into the ground around us. "You will die! You all will die!" I screamed as I moved forward, pushing his hand away from the blade as I withdrew it from my womb, whimpering as I felt the life of my unborn son slipping from me. Something slammed against my head, and I stumbled, and more blades cut through me until I landed on the ground, lifting my eyes to his. "My baby, my home!" I whispered before consciousness slipped away from me.

I sat up sobbing as I screamed for the son I'd lost and grabbed my stomach protectively, only to be yanked back by the chains. My anger pulsed through me, directed at Callaghan as I turned, staring at him as a sob escaped. Tears streamed down his cheeks while he watched me.

"I told you that you were a mother, Erie. And that

you would have been an amazing one," he uttered thickly, his eyes watching me as tears rolled down my cheeks. "I only wish you'd shared that with me before that night."

"You *murdered* our son?"

"*Our* son?" he asked as his brows drew together.

"You are driving me crazy! I don't know what is real or isn't anymore. I know I fucking hate you both! I am not her, nor do I want your fucking love."

"You wanted my son," he uttered as he leaned over, wiping the tears from my cheeks.

"No, Callaghan, *she* wanted your son. She wanted something to love her, and you took it away. She was looking for him, not you. You just happened to be there, and she fell in love with you. It isn't a crime to love someone, is it?"

"It is when you curse an entire fucking race to achieve it! My son, Erie, my sweet son, who had yet to even begin living, was the cost to undo what you did!"

"I didn't do it! I wasn't the one who cursed your son! I'm not her; maybe your stupid fucking spell didn't work, ever consider *that*? Do I act like a Goddess of War?"

"Yes, and you're wearing her fucking face."

"That you gave me!"

"No, no, Erie. I gave you her face, and the druids painted the woad exactly how the Mórrígan wore hers without knowing who the fuck you were. Blind fucking druids painted your face and your body, and yet they painted it exactly how you wanted it. Ever wonder why that was?"

"And I guess the abuse, that was just me wanting a

refresher course to our twisted as shit lovefest, wasn't it?"

"That was them knowing and sensing what you are. You are a fucking monster, and no matter how long it takes for you to figure it out, when you do, no one will be able to save you from yourself."

"So what's the plan, fuck me stupid? Murder me a thousand times?"

"Love you! The plan is to fucking love you, Erie. To be what you need, and to create the son that neither of us got to hold. Yeah, it's revenge, because it is the one thing that terrifies you the most. Having to accept what you fear, and a family that you craved but could never fully grasp. You loved us both, so we became one. You were the strongest queen our race ever knew, and you will be again. They're dying while you sit here, pretending to be someone else."

"Not me! Her, you want her, and I'm just supposed to fucking die so you can have her back to love her? Jesus Christ, you really do intend to torture me," I muttered as I closed my eyes. "Just kill me already."

"You don't want to die," he uttered as he climbed back onto the bed, dropping a kiss to my stomach. "You never did when another life was on the line. Not one you wanted, anyway."

"Callaghan, if I'm this monster you claim I am, why would you protect me from the druids? Why not just let them abuse me if you hate me so much?"

"You're not hearing me, Erie. I didn't hate you, not even when I drove my sword through you. I was grieving one son, and I'd lost my wife when I told her of you and what I carried inside of me. I lost everything

because of you, and the only thing I wanted was to hold you. I loved my wife, but she couldn't stand the sight of me after she learned what I had done and what I was. You were created for warriors, meant to be taken hard and fast, and she was everything you were not. I wanted you; I loved you. I hated you for that, for being unable to even look at her after I'd taken you. I failed her; I failed her because I'd been in the arms of a Goddess who gave me everything and held nothing back every time I was inside of her. Carolina was vanilla at best, or whatever comes before it. You, you were unhinged and wild and held nothing back, ever. When you gave yourself to me, you gave me everything. You set me on fire, and I wanted to burn. I hated you because you wanted to destroy me; you ruin those you love because it is all you have ever known. Your father taught you to destroy everything because love was a weakness. It's what you do, and the worst part is, you don't even fucking realize it. You sabotage everything to obtain what you desire while pushing them away to protect them from yourself. You're a monster, but not because you want to be, because that's what you were taught to be from the time you were created until now. Your father enjoyed teaching you to kill; he enjoyed teaching you what weakness was. The thing is, Erie, you murdered him too because you loved him."

"I know you think this of me, but I'm not her, and I don't want to be her. Can't I just be me?"

"No, you can't," he said as he sat back and stared down at me. "You can stop pretending the memories you are having are ours. They're not, they're yours, and we can't give them to you, we can only watch as you relive them through your mind."

"Whatever, Paladin," I growled.

"There's that too; only she called me that. You do as well, and you do it for the same reason as she did."

"And? People have confused the two since the Knights were formed; I know because I studied you and the Knights. I also have it on good authority that you told the Fae you were one, so whatever."

"I have to go away for a few days tomorrow, Erie. Which means my men will be here to protect you. You will be dressed, but since you have yet to ask for food or to use the bathroom, you will remain in this room alone."

"And you'll supply the liqueur for this party?"

"You're pregnant," he said irritably.

"Right, sorry, with all the fucked up shit in my head you keep planting, it's hard to decipher fact from your fiction. One thing I don't understand though," I said.

"And what is that?" he asked.

"If she was a Goddess, how did you kill her so easily?"

"The first time, we don't know how or why she died, only that her body was there when we returned, and men stood around it, covered in blood. *Your blood.* The second time, I strangled you as you writhed on my dick, giving you the death you craved when you lost our child."

"I asked to ride your dick while you strangled me, and you think you want *that* back? Maybe you should get your head checked while you're out."

"Actually, I prefer this version, and we planned to keep you as such, but then the witches showed up, and

Hecate went missing from her tomb, where you buried her before cursing her children. There's also the fact that an entire demon army is out there, waiting for their newly crowned queen to rise. If you meet them like this, they will murder you. Now be a good girl, and don't fight me when I unchain you. I hate the idea of leaving a perfectly good, swollen pussy alone when it's naked and wet with arousal."

I watched him as he unchained my legs and then my arms, and then I attacked, pushing him onto the bed. My mouth crushed against his as I slammed him down, using my hands to free his cock before I pushed it into my body. My eyes closed, rolling back in my head as I screamed while he filled me. His throaty laughter was the only indication that he enjoyed what I had done. He rolled us, slamming into me until I was trembling around his cock.

"This is what I love, this bare fucking bones you give me. You expose your soul when you fuck, Erie," he growled as he gripped my chin, crushing his mouth against mine and I rolled us again, screaming while I came undone around him. "Now rest, because soon he is going to play with you again," he uttered as he leaned over, kissing my head.

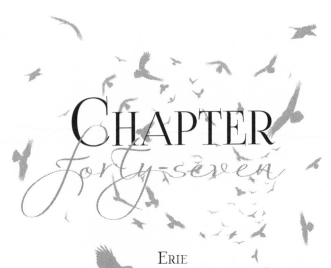

CHAPTER
forty-seven

ERIE

I SAT UP IN BED, STARING DOWN AT CALLAGHAN, where he slept. I looked up at where my arms were once again chained, snapping them free as I whispered a sleeping spell that would render the entire mansion defenseless. I touched his face, staring at him, and then I rose from the bed, moving to my backpack as I grabbed clothing, glamouring myself clean before I pulled them on.

Outside, the air was brisk, and the scent of ashes and sulfur clung to the breeze. I left the compound slowly, unhurried as I moved to the car I'd parked a few blocks from his house, in the woods. I paused as I hotwired the car, then headed towards the Guild the moment it started. I drove until the road became too littered with debris and trash, and then I exited the car and approached the Guild, watching as it lit up, sensing a threat. I smiled, turning to the shadows as I moved towards them instead, sensing eyes upon me.

I listened as the heels of the shoes I wore clicked along on the pavement as I walked towards the hidden Knights. My hair wafted in the wind, sending the scent of rain and fresh grass into it, the smell of Ireland. I paused as I waited for the Knights to emerge and face me.

Arthur was the first one to emerge, and then, one by one, the others followed him out as they circled me. I lifted my eyes to his, and then I rolled them when I found his smile filled with victory. My outfit changed, and my swords slid into my hands.

"That wasn't smart, hiding outside the Guild, Arthur," I uttered. "It was rather easy to find you here."

"You are too predictable, Erie. I like the new digs, easier to take what is owed to me, and I've been waiting a long time to take my pound of flesh and fuck that worthless thing between your legs. I won't be gentle."

"And what is owed to you? The sex you think you earned by abusing me? You befriended a child who had never known love, and you used that against me. The only thing you have earned is death."

"Look around you; you're surrounded, Erie. You have always been less, and will always be less than we are. You think he is going to save you this time? He isn't. You won't get an option to say no to me anymore."

"Oh, no, he's not coming. I put them to sleep until I return to him. You, on the other hand," I said with a dark smile. "You die here, all of you who think to take a woman's choice from her. Your death, though, I'm not going to lie. I plan to enjoy it."

A commotion sounded behind us, and the Knights turned as I studied the man Arthur had become.

Immortality suited him, but like all beings who played with dark magic, it took its toll on him. His skin was pale, colored in lifeless runes that wouldn't protect him, not from me. He'd been with the witches, and I could smell them on him. He thought he was backed by Hecate, but she wasn't shit compared to me, nowhere near my level of evil.

"You seem less...arrogant?" Arthur growled, and his men drew their swords as the Fae and others moved in around us, surrounding his Knights.

"I assure you, I have never been arrogant." I didn't flinch as he moved closer, the scuffling in the alley behind us drawing him to it. "I wouldn't do that," I said as I turned with him, watching as he took in the Fae who stepped from the shadows, staring at me.

"Erie, get the fuck over here, and where the fuck is your shirt?" Zahruk's eyes searched mine, and I smiled coldly as he took me in and then shook his head, watching me.

"Back up, Zahruk," Lucian growled as he stared at me.

He felt it, the power that exhumed from me. Arthur drew my attention back to him as I turned, eyeing him before I disappeared, appearing right in front of him, slamming my fingers through his eyes and ripping him in half, straight down his body. I knelt down, pushing my hands into his blood as I brought it up to my face, painting it before I painted the rest of my body, unable to stop myself as I turned around, standing to stare at them and their horrified, widened stares.

"The fuck, Erie?" Zahruk demanded, and my eyes turned to take him in. "The fuck?"

"Zahruk, you really need to shut the fuck up right now."

"You mind explaining what the hell is going on then, Lucian?" Synthia said as she stared at me.

I was dressed in merely a skirt, my wild hair covering my naked breasts that were painted in woad. I smiled as Zahruk took me in. I could smell the lust oozing from him, his need to feed calling to me as he watched me. He wasn't afraid, but he also didn't want me as my men did; he wanted to fuck me, and that was it. I could read it in his sapphire eyes as they began to glow, revealing his own beast that peered out at me, wanting me.

"That isn't Erie anymore. That is who she truly is. Meet the real Mórrígan, ladies, and gentlemen," Lucian said as a tick in his jaw hammered. I closed the distance between us as my bare feet dragged across the ground until I was close enough to taste his unique scent. Once I reached him, I took in the sheer brilliance of his mask that he'd donned to appear human.

"Pretty shell," I whispered huskily, leaning over, smelling him as I took in the pretty form he preferred when in the realm of mortals. My hand lifted, cupping his cheek before I stood on my toes, and stretched to kiss his cheek. "I like the other one better though."

"I'm still stronger than you, and I'll still kick your fucking ass, Mórrígan."

"Why didn't you come to find me?" I asked, tilting my head with a frown. "Why would you leave me there, knowing I suffered at the hands of weak-minded men?"

"Couldn't, little one," he said, pushing the wild hair away from my face and smiling down at me sadly as he tucked it behind my ear. "You weren't fully awakened yet, and I couldn't feel or see you. You never used your power, which meant it didn't alert anyone to the fact that you were back."

"I needed you, and I needed them. They hurt me, and I didn't even know who I was or what I was. I didn't understand why I deserved to be hurt or why they thought me evil. I was left unprotected in my darkest hour of need, and in my weakest form."

"You are never weak, sweet girl. You are War, and the song of a million battles plays within your veins. You killed them all, and if I'm correct, you also have the druids hiding from what they've awoken. What do you intend to do now?"

"I'm about to take Lucifer's entire army from him and leave him vulnerable. You're welcome. He's hiding in the veil with a small human that you wanted, if *I* am not mistaken. You were looking for him, I found him. I am owed."

"If you take his army and leave him exposed, indeed, Goddess, you will be owed."

"What the fuck is this?" Zahruk asked.

"When a Goddess is awoken from death or brought back, as is Erie's case, they slumber. Callaghan, or Balor as we call his beast, protected her until she began to grow. He left her defenseless with druids, and then somewhere along the way, the Goddess of Battle emerged once more and began planning to set the world on fire. And now, it burns for her as many a man has done before."

"Playing sweet for me, Lucian? You shouldn't, you know I don't like sweet men. And not the entire world or every man burned for me." I smiled at Lucian, who

smirked and nodded his head at the secret we held. "Only those who thought to kick me when I was down will perish. You should never kick the Goddess of War when she is down, because when she gets back up, they go down one by one as they beg me for mercy, and the Goddess of War has no mercy to give. It may be a new world, but it still has the same problems. I have to go, but if you follow me, Zahruk, I will give you back what I have taken from you," I smiled as I vanished.

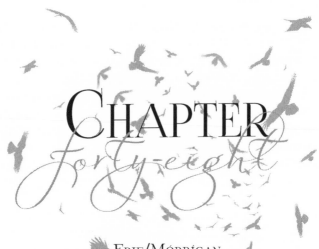

CHAPTER
forty-eight

ERIE/MÓRRÍGAN

I STOOD IN THE SHADOWS OF THE ROOM, WATCHING MY lovers sleep from the heavy magic I'd used to force them into it. Arthur's blood clung to my flesh, dried, crusted, and already flaking off, which was a pity since it felt so good. Callaghan's thick lashes brushed against his high cheekbones as I pushed the memories of our love deep into his subconscious.

I'd loved him; I'd loved him so freaking much that I would have done anything to get him. He was right; I was his monster. I was *their* monster. I didn't love like a normal woman because I wasn't. I'd been through hell before ever gazing into the crystalline, glowing eyes of my fated beast. I'd watched worlds burn to ashes, creatures that should have been invincible being slaughtered, and the rise of mankind. Watched the most brutal and unforgiving race of all time evolve into what it had become today.

He'd killed me, which was true. However, it hadn't

happened as he remembered it. None of what they remembered of me was the full truth. I'd tried to save Callaghan, and the Gods themselves had taken me from my beautiful beast. How they had become one entity was beyond me, but I was glad they had. It had taken a piece of my very soul to make Balor, my beast, immortal like me. It was the most selfless thing a Goddess could bestow upon another being. You had to truly love the being enough that your soul would find a home within them and flourish to keep them alive. Fomorians were only partly immortal, living less than a thousand or so years, and I'd wanted him forever.

Swallowing hard, I pushed more memories into the sleeping pair and watched as they turned over, disturbed in their endless magic-enhanced slumber as I slunk out of the shadows and sat beside them, pushing dark blond hair away from his face. Lying beside him, I placed my hand into his, holding it to create a conduit for my memories of the events to slip into his mind.

PARIS, WEEKS BEFORE THE FALL OF THE TEMPLAR KNIGHTS.

My lips brushed against his, and his eyes watched me warily. I knew he was pulling away, sensing the uneasiness which he felt in my presence. His bright, beautiful eyes watched me as I rose from the bed we'd shared as I grabbed the sheer, rose-scented robe and turned back to let him see all of me. Those eyes that I adored sparkled with lust, even as he lifted from the bed and leaned on his elbow, looking at me.

"You're leaving?" he asked roughly. His eyes were still heavy with sleep as he once more lifted further until

he hung his legs over the edge of the straw bed covered with furs that protected our flesh as we went to war with our bodies. I swayed my hips as he watched, a sleepy grin covering his mouth before something on his mind made his face close down again.

"I have things to do before I can go home."

"You're leaving France?" he asked crisply, eyes slowly narrowing, as if he didn't want me to go and was trying to figure out how to keep me with him. But he did, he wanted me to leave him to his family, and I hated myself for it, but he loved them, and I had no place here with him anymore. I held my memories again, knew what and who he was. He'd loved me once, him and the beast he now housed, even though they hid it from me.

They blamed me for leaving them, as if my sick and twisted version of love had all been a game to me that I'd grown bored of playing. It hadn't, but we'd done the one thing I had been warned against. Together, we had created a child; life had been growing inside of me. So the Gods who feared me had made sure it wouldn't grow anymore. My hand moved to the gentle swell of the new one we'd created before I'd gained my memories and I smiled sadly.

"I need to go away for a while," I admitted. "Will you miss me?" I asked, watching as he hesitated with his answer. "Maybe I will go and find a husband. One who can give me what you cannot offer me here." I watched his eyes narrowing as the beast inside him peered out at me. "I'm sure someone will be able to love me enough for what I am that they offer me more than this. I crave more than to be the whore who waits here for you to need me."

"You're mine. You belong to me, with me. You chose me on the field of battle when we lay in the blood of my enemies and brethren who fell. You don't get to leave me now."

"You have a wife, a son, and a home that would never welcome me into it, Sir Callaghan. You will never leave them, and I almost understand it." I didn't, not when a part of me lived inside of him. He'd taken a wife because they'd expected it of him, even though he'd known I would be reborn sooner or later. I didn't hate him for it, as the years it took for me to come back could be endless, and this world waited for no one.

"You cannot leave," he growled.

"What will you do, chain me to your ceiling and play with me as your need comes? Go home to your wife and child," I hissed as I stripped from the robe and started dressing into the ridiculous layers of the current fashion.

He grabbed me, turning me towards him as his mouth crushed against mine. His hands bit into my flesh as he lifted me, pushing me down onto his massive cock as he walked us back to the bed. There, he slowly lowered me as he used me, uncaring that tears filled my eyes as I watched the love dancing in his eyes as it mixed with his growing anger. He may not want me to leave, but he'd never choose me over his family, and that was part of why I'd fallen in love with this man.

Callaghan wasn't from this era, this new world where men were loyal to one woman. In our days, men took wives, plural. You never married or joined kingdoms for love; you did it to make binding strength and courts stronger. He'd done it this time, never fully loving his *sweet wife, who didn't understand his mind. She was gentle; he was rough. She was a dutiful wife, and he was here, with me. We'd spent months together, and lately, he'd begun to grow distant. So I'd made attempts to rid him of the problem, a wife who he didn't love.*

He lifted my dress, finding my sex wet and ready as I always was for him. He drove into me until he jerked tautly, watching as I unfurled and whimpered while my own orgasm hummed through my body until I uttered his name as he kissed it away from my lips. Those intense blue eyes gazed down at me, his resignation to what was unfolding burning in his endless depths with anger.

"You're not leaving France. You are the one woman I have ever craved or loved this much. You hold nothing back from me, and you give me everything I need. She may be my wife, but you are the one I love. I married her for duty, to bind two houses into one. If I had to choose, it would be you who I wake up to every morning. This isn't what I wanted, but this is what we have together now. It's enough." His hands stroked my breasts, watching me as I struggled to make him hear me, to listen to me.

"Enough for whom? You? I am no one's whore, Mason. I won't play one for you or anyone else. Eventually, she will die, and you will be freed of her. You can find me then."

"I will never be free of her, we made her immortal. Her blood is the same as mine is, Eris."

"My name is not Eris."

"No? Then what is it?" he asked with a guarded look in his eyes.

"It is not what you have called me while you fucked me. I may not know who I am, but I know I am not this

weak *thing that lies about, waiting for you to have time for me. I can feel something inside of me awakening, and I need to figure out what it is. I need to be in Ireland when it happens."*

I felt him growing hard within my body and felt his mood changing from rejection to violence. His thrusts turned angry, harder, driving me over the edge as he barreled there with me. I whispered his name as my lips brushed against his as tears lit my eyes, rolling down my cheeks as I shook my head at his denial. I was toxic, and he knew it. I had done what he couldn't, because I knew he wanted me. If I told him of the child we'd created, he would move mountains to hold me here. I couldn't remember my past, and I wanted this man to be my future, but the stars wouldn't align for us. Nothing made sense anymore, other than running from him and waiting for his wife to leave this world. That, however, would never happen. So I would run alone, and leave him and the home I felt within him behind.

"You're awakening," he mused as he pulled out of my body and rolled onto the bed beside me. "I cannot leave the Knights, nor is divorce allowed within the Order. You will stay with me as we are, and one day soon, you'll understand why."

Two weeks later, after countless dealings with a group of dark witches, I watched from the shadows as the Knights who had once protected them turned them away at their gates. It served them right; their treachery against me couldn't go unpunished. Not when I'd reached out to them for help to conceal the child that grew within me, only to have them send word to the Gods of my precarious situation. So I'd put it into motion to bring the coven to their knees for making my pregnancy known and setting me within their sights.

Mason was inside his precious compound with his loving wife and their son, while my son was unguarded and unprotected from the Gods who would surely murder us once it reached their ears. He knew I was unprotected, only just grasping on to what I was, defenseless as I waited for my powers to grow. He had chosen them, pushing me away as he fought to protect them against me, even though I had yet to try for his wife's life again.

Instead, I had abandoned the house we shared soon after he'd gone back to her. I'd respected his need for her to live, but at the cost of removing myself from the equation. I slipped from the shadows and stared at the demons, who watched me as I approached them.

"It is done, they will burn by dawn," Cade growled. "Release us."

"You will go to the humans' king's court and spread rumors to drive the Templars out of this realm and back into Ireland; nothing damning, just mistrust against them. I need them to return to Ireland, where I can grow stronger, and we can return to what we were once more. It will remove them from here, and allow you and Lucifer to continue your endless torment on these poor humans you enjoy so much. Can you do that?"

"It is already in motion, Mórrígan. You and your Knight will both be removed from this place soon enough."

"Did you need to murder innocent women and children, or did you just get off on it?" I asked icily.

"I got off on it. You wanted them to pay for what

they did, and they are. So will the Knights, and once they figure out what is coming, they will run as they always do when they are threatened," he growled as he watched me. "Is there anything else, your highness?"

"Do not call me that," I hissed.

"You did remove Lucifer from his throne, which makes you the Queen of Hell, your highness," he hissed back, his black eyes glazing over as he watched me.

"Has everything already been set into motion?" I asked, and when he nodded, I struck without warning, removing his head from his shoulders as I watched his meat sack slamming against the ground lifelessly. I held up his head and smiled at his shocked eyes. "I am the Mórrígan, the Goddess of War and Battles, and the current Queen of Hell. When I tell you to cease being obtuse, you will obey, or you will perish as everyone else who has threatened or abused me has before you. Now crawl back to Lucifer and tell him he's next."

"I have no legs!"

"You have a tongue; learn how to wield it correctly. Now go." I tossed him into the woods as I stared at the fires that burned on the high walls of the castle where Callaghan had housed up with his family.

It took days before the Knights began to learn of the rumors sweeping across the land, and in that time, the witches burned outside the Knight's Order strongholds, on display for them to see. It wasn't until I caught wind of what Callaghan had done that I emerged and tried to reach him, yet was turned away with every attempt. Abused by his men, who refused to even listen to me, I started to lose hope.

On my last attempt to reach him, Callaghan himself

watched me from high above the gates of his protected stronghold as I waited, never gaining an audience. The idiot had brokered a deal with the druids, a race full of zealots who wanted the Knight's Order to suffer for removing them from Ireland. I shouted for him and yet he stared down at me with loathing in his eyes, a burning thing that made fear sting against my throat as his Knights pushed and shunned me, forcing me to slip in the mud as he turned away, ignoring my pleas.

Rumors of his loss reached my ears, and I cried for the child he'd allowed them to murder. The druids would pay for their deeds, but the need to comfort him in his darkest hour outweighed the need to avenge. When they came and took the imposter Jacques from the stronghold, I watched from afar as more and more were rounded up and captured, while Callaghan and his men hid in the shadows around them.

The day they burned, I was in the audience with the intention of warning Callaghan of what was coming and why. He had to know why the druids had done it, and that my hand in it hadn't been poisonous as what was unfurling around us. Dominos had been stacked, pushed into motion by everyone who feared my returning to power. Maybe I had deserved it, for after all, wherever I was, war broke out.

In the crowd, I watched him as he glared at me from beneath his hood. The darkness in his heavy stare made my heart race as I slowly backed away from him. He followed me, never increasing his speed as I rounded the bend in the road and turned back around, staring into his murderous gaze while his men closed in around me.

He screamed, his anger palpable as his grief washed through him, crashing into me as I fought to bring my powers to me, to defend myself against the murderous emotions I felt from him. The skies cracked loudly above us as lightning crashed overhead, striking the ground close to where we stood. My hair whipped against my face as his men fully surrounded us. I stepped closer, my hands out palms up as I fought to tell him what had been done and what I carried within me. That he'd made a deal with the druids that had never needed to be forged, but my foot tripped on a wet rock, and I slipped forward. Pain ripped through me as I stared between us, where his blade was embedded into my middle.

"My baby," I whispered. A misstep, caused by the Gods, had taken another life from me. Another child. Another chance at love that would be ripped away from me too soon. Callaghan spoke, but I was beyond hearing him as the loss of the son I'd already started to love turned into hatred.

They would take me to a cave that was placed on six connecting leylines. It was a place where Gods entered to weaken, to begin the eternal slumber, undisturbed. For a year, they'd taken turns weakening me for crimes they thought I had committed. I didn't blame them; after all, I was their monster as much as they were mine. I wasn't what they expected me to come back as, and they'd never intended for me to survive this rebirth, and we all knew it. They wanted to save me, to protect me from coming back with war in my veins. For, as long as War was a part of me, I'd spread it like the rider of the apocalypse. That was something even the Gods themselves feared and wouldn't let survive. So they *drained me and pushed me back into the cauldron, but this time, this time they took parts of me away until I wasn't me anymore. You can't take parts of yourself away to fit into what is accepted, but they had no idea of the monster they would create by doing so.*

CHAPTER
Forty-nine

ERIE/MÓRRÍGAN

I HEARD HIS SHARP INTAKE OF BREATH AND TURNED over in bed, staring at the wide blue eyes that took in my disarray of blood and nakedness. I smiled, rolling onto him as I stared down into his shocked, pretty blue eyes.

"My men?" he demanded as his hands encircled my waist.

"Alive, Arthur's Knights weren't so lucky."

"How long have you fucking known?" he demanded.

"That I am the Mórrígan?" I asked, and at his nod of confirmation, I smirked. "Since the day you picked me up off of the floor in that shitty little compound. The moment you brought me back with your soft touches and pretty whispered songs that we used to know from a land long ago," I uttered thickly. "Memories were a lot harder to understand for a long time though. I still struggle to remember things, but then you tried to erase who *I* am from my mind, you thought to make me weak. I played your game, of course, I needed time to heal,

---

time without you watching me. I was weak, and those memories, they were so fucking fractured that it was hard to tell which were real, and which weren't. You took my pieces from me, and then you threw me to the wolves that we had banned from Ireland, *together*. You knew who I was, and they knew as well after a time, but nobody cared enough to tell me who I was. You eradicated the parts of me that you assumed made me evil, and then replaced them with humanity in this pretty little shell. You thought to make me more human, and you shouldn't have touched what I was."

"I wanted to protect you from the Gods who hunted you," he seethed as his hand lifted, cupping my cheek. "Did you think I didn't see them watching us, hunting you down every time the court moved? I knew what you were, so I brought you back weaker each time until you could stand in a world without reigning fire and hell upon it. I didn't touch who you were, Erie, you evolved."

"Did I?" I laughed as I stared down at him with a mixture of love and hatred at what he had tried to do to me, to us. "You were content to let me live a lie, to allow me to believe I had been created in a cauldron. You thought to make me be this weak being who cowers before you, stuck in a situation that you created, and why? Because *you* fucked up? It sure in the hell wasn't because of me that we ended up right here, Mason, or shall we go back to Lugh now? Which one do you prefer I call you this time, lover?"

"Names are irrelevant; you taught me that," he growled as he rolled us and rested his head against mine. "I won't let them take you from me again. I

won't be without you any longer, Erie. I have loved you from the first moment you entered my world and looked right into my soul as if you knew who and what I would become to you. I waited for you, and then I did everything within my power to keep you safe and hidden from the Gods and Goddesses that hunted your newly reborn soul. It took you longer this time, and every time I tried to bring you to the surface, you dove in deeper. I tried, Erie, I tried to get you to come out, and you wouldn't. The world didn't just stop when you died; we went to fucking war. We hid from what you did, from those who still hunt us because of it."

I closed my eyes against his excuses as he lowered his lips to mine, kissing me with feather-soft kisses meant to pull me out of my mind. "Kiss me, Erie. Come back to me," he urged. "Show me how much you need me, bare bones. No more holding back from us."

I opened my eyes, staring up at him before I rolled us again, cradling his mouth as I kissed him hard. I felt him growing beneath me, already craving me as I rocked my hips against his, and he entered me hard and fast. My arm moved, palm up as I whispered a spell against his lips, and I smiled against him as I stabbed the blades into his chest. His eyes widened as I lifted from his chest, staring down at him.

"You should have left me dead," I uttered as my power ignited, causing my hair to rise as the room pulsed with it. He hissed in pain as the God bolt held him immobile, unable to change into the beast that now peered up at me. I lifted my hand again, catching the other blade I'd taken from Zahruk when he'd kissed me. "Speaking of bare bones, shall we look at yours?" I asked as I leaned over, trailing the blade over his flesh. "You forgot to neuter me, asshole. I'm guessing you thought I would be weak enough with only half of the magic I held, but I never showed you what I actually held within me, did I? Neither one of you knew just how powerful I was when I wanted or needed to be. Some monsters shouldn't be brought back from the grave, ever. You're lucky I enjoy you both and these cocks so much…" I rolled my hips and moaned as my eyes lit up again with what he made me feel. "But I have witches to kill, druids to slaughter, and your father's cock to rip off and fuck him with. Shall we take a raincheck?" His eyes began to glow bright blue and I smiled down at him with a languid gaze. "I see you in there, my King of beasts," I laughed as I leaned over, kissing him. "Mmm, home never tasted as good as it does when it bleeds for me," I whispered as I lifted from him. "I do like you both together; it's like a two-for-one deal, isn't it?"

"Don't you fucking do it, Erie," he hissed.

"Erie isn't here anymore. Remember, you didn't want me to be her. There's only so much time to be wasted riding your cock when so much is happening outside of these walls. And what is it that you fear me doing? Killing your father, or your wife? One tortured me, fucking whores in front of the child I was. You forced me to come back, and then you allowed me to be abused, knowing it would take decades for me to even remember who I was, if I ever did. No, he will die for defiling me. No one has ever defiled my flesh and lived to tell of it, and he will be no different. Your wife, you can keep her. But know that she helped them beat me because your father told her who I was and what he assumed I had done."

"You need to stay here, you're pregnant."

"Am I? Because I'm pretty sure I'm not pregnant, *yet*. I just remember how I smelled carrying our child, Lugh. I remember how it felt to touch him as he grew within me. The memories in my mind didn't just stop every time I electrocuted myself to kick you out of it. You just couldn't see them playing out, or read my mind, for a time. It was time I needed without you eavesdropping into my thoughts. You played me for a fool; you think I wasn't aware of who I was this entire time you've been trying to fuck me? I can be Erie if you want me to be her, as I technically am her now. There is no way to remove her. I can continue to give you her eternal thought process if you so desire it, because she is who I have become in this lifetime. But then, I also knew you read my thoughts because you've always been able to, but then I also fried your connection with the whole clock-in-the-bath thing, didn't I? You wanted me, and here I am. Naughty boys, I don't think you remember who the fuck you just challenged to war, but I do. You made me weak, but even weak, I am still the Goddess of War, and plus, I just took back the throne to Hell, which makes me its Queen for now." I rocked on his cock, staring into his Nordic blue eyes.

"Remember, you wanted me back. I didn't want to come back, not to this time. Don't worry; I'll save our people. I'll even save the Fomorians you hide within them. Such as the ones pacing outside the door because they don't hear my pussy getting off. Fuck it, one more time for the road?" I hissed before I moaned loudly, not even having to fake it as he grew, trying to become stuck in my depths. "Wrong body, remember, I can take you both at your fullest length and width. Give it to me, give it to me, Balor, I've missed that magical cock," I uttered, riding him until I threw my head back and gasped as I exploded. The windows shattered as lightning struck outside, close to the open window. The scent of ozone and burning wood filled the room and smiled down at him, ripping out the god bolt, knowing I only needed a few minutes' head start to get away.

I crawled off of him, staring at his open chest as his heart raced. I loved them both, but if they thought this was how they got me back, they were fucking wrong. I wasn't some weak ass Goddess who needed them to save me or protect me. I was one-third of the Mórrígan, and my sisters awaited me outside the gates of the compound. If the witches thought they had a chance, all the better. I'd missed war. I glamoured on a white war dress with gold armlets, fashioning on my gown as I turned to look back at the men I loved. My hair was done up in war braids as I stared at my men and wiggled my brows.

"You're the war that I cannot win, Erie," he uttered as he watched me with a longing that ached in my chest.

"I know, but you should have known better than to play games with me. Don't ever, ever think you're capable of it, or think you're even on the same level as me again. You're not capable of winning against me. Did you never wonder why the shadows betrayed you, Mason? It's because they belong to me. They serve me at my bidding because I am born of the darkness. I may have worn a mask long enough to forget who and what I am beneath it, but make no mistake: I am

War. Eventually, every mask has to come off, and when it does, the monster beneath it is revealed. And I do understand that I owe you an apology for what happened in the past, so like, go unfuck yourself or something, whatever you want to do. You know, like, I'm not really sorry, because it was war, but I did love you in my own way."

"You're a fucking psychopath, Erie."

"I prefer creative genius. And I told you, Erie isn't here anymore. You wanted me, and here I am. Bare fucking bones. This is me, no mask to shield you from what I am this time. You broke the wrong parts of me, forgot that, even without magic, I have claws. I am not violence or malice; I am the end result of what you and yours have forced me to become. But don't worry, all this blood that I have shed brings out your eyes and makes them look really pretty," I said hoarsely as I watched his pupils dilate from pain. "You should use this time to consider where we go from here. I do want your son, and I will get him one way or another. I am owed for what you took from me.

"You, husband, you stormed my lands and murdered my people. It *was* war, and we were brutal to each other as we waged it. You didn't do that back then unless you were willing to pay the price for losing, and you did. Had it been me, you'd have placed my head on your spike and carried me around as your proof of skill. You wanted me kneeling at your feet sucking your cock to show off your mad war skills. I buried your children and your wife in a tomb fit for the Gods; I know because it's *my* tomb where they rest eternally. I honored them and couldn't tell you, because had I made it known, others would have waged war against us. I didn't have a choice because you took that one away from me. I conquered you, and as the victor, your line paid the price as was owed to the families of my people who you murdered. I didn't ask for you to wage war against me, I just fucking ended it. I do not enjoy slaughtering women or children, but to keep my crown and my people safe, I do not hesitate to end it by any means necessary.

"I didn't come looking for a war; I simply slipped into a position to wage the one that raged around me. You knew the cost if you lost it, and you were willing to pay. It is not my fault that I loved you. I didn't understand what love was, or the price it took to keep it. You lived; did you never wonder how you did? I gave you part of my soul to keep you immortal, Balor. I gave you my protection, at the cost of weakening myself to you and the Gods. I didn't tell the humans how to kill me. They found out what I had done to protect you, and when I weakened with your son growing within my womb, the Gods came for me. I would never fall to mortals. I am a Goddess of War. How you thought they could take me down even if I had allowed it is beyond me. You did the one thing that the Gods feared most, you placed your son into my womb, and they did what they do best. They murdered us to protect this pathetic rock that they love to torture so much. And you, you fucked up by assuming I hadn't evolved.

"You, you made a deal with the druids. The *druids*, Mason," I hissed angrily. "They were expelled from our world, from Ireland, because their reach and greed were endless. They wanted everyone to bow to them and their growing power. You removed them from my lands, *by*

490

force. Why would you ever ask them for anything after that? You barred me from entering your stronghold, protecting your precious wife, which meant I couldn't reach you either. I waited outside, begging you to come to me. You thought I merely craved that cock, when in reality, I was trying to save you from the pain you would endure if you listened to them. Yet you ended up facing it anyway, because you refused to hear me. I was trying to save your son's life to protect you from the pain. You killed me because you thought you'd lost him because of me. Your oh, so great sacrifice. A life for a life from the cauldron is what they told you, isn't it? One life sacrificed to save them all," I growled as I sat on the bed beside him, staring into the glowing blue eyes that made my blood run hot with arousal. "I've never been fully alive, gentlemen. The cauldron isn't soul magic, and that is what they used, wasn't it? Soul magic is death magic, and I'd have had to have a fucking soul for that to work. Goddesses are not born with a soul; we earn them. The half of me I pushed into you, Balor, took me over thousands of years to earn and is the greatest gift a Goddess can part to a lover.

"When I found you, Callaghan, it was because you held that half of me inside of you. I searched for my soul, for my home, because I knew what might happen, and I didn't want to lose you. So I placed a beacon into you so that I could find you if the unthinkable came to pass. But you were so worried about what you assumed I was doing that you failed to see I was only removing the druids. I was, until you turned against me. Both of you turned against me, and I couldn't stop the curses that were placed, because you refused to listen. That is why the druids now die," I laughed as he shook his head. "They messed with my lovers and hurt them both. So they will pay for it in their blood. You don't hurt those I love, or me, and live to tell of it. What kind of a wife would I be if I let that slide? Not to mention, serious street cred that I'd have to fix," I shrugged.

"I'm also the Goddess of Battles, which you seem to forget. I knew my future before you did. I planned for everything except you abandoning me to the druids without my memories being present. You left me exposed, knowing that I was weakened to the point that my mind wouldn't grasp who or what I was. You left me to be abused, and I'm not sure I can forgive you for that one yet. Anywho, I have shit to fuck up, a world to set on fire, and payback that can't wait much longer," I laughed as I leaned over, kissing his lips. "I did love you, both of you. Admittedly, I wasn't a good person, but I was trying to be. I was trying to love you, to be with you, and to have a family. Now, I have to go hurt those who want to ruin that. I will be back, so be good boys while I am away?" I kissed his cheek as I stood up. "If I come back, be ready to sire my son. You know, the one you think is waiting at the gates to slip into this world? You and I, we create war. The riders are created, not waiting inside any walls that can or will crumble. Each God or Goddess can breed a rider; it just depends on their time to be born."

I moved to my backpack, slipping it over my shoulder as I turned, staring at them. "Catch ya later, assholes," I smirked as I flipped them off, skipping towards the door before I blew it off the hinges and slammed my magic into his men, pushing them against the wall. Outside, the storm I'd freed raged as I smiled at Lust, who watched me with a heady stare. His gaze lingered over the bust of the dress I wore before I awarded him a pointed look.

"Fred, don't make me hurt you. Where is my new army?" I asked, and I turned, staring at my sisters, who smiled as they stepped from the shadows.

"About time, we were starting to think you'd never leave that dick," Banba uttered with a snort.

"She always has enjoyed those two. I don't imagine she would mind sharing? I mean, both are kings, and who doesn't want a magical growing cock?" Fódla laughed as she hooked her arm through mine and leaned against my shoulder. "That was the longest you've ever been silent. I fear I will miss it," she pouted. "Did I play my part in Faery well enough, or do you think they noticed I was happy you were back?"

"You played it perfect; not even Lucian noticed your acting skills. The druids?" I asked.

"Dead, or soon to be from the poison they inhaled in the sewers, where the rat bastards ran. I still can't believe they made him kill his own child. And they say we're fucked up."

"Any word of my people in the catacombs?"

"The Fae seem to have begun feeding them. One in particular more than any other. A drop-dead gorgeous warrior. Is he one of yours that you intend to claim too?"

"No, Zahruk is naughty, and as much as I wouldn't mind riding him, he deserves something more. I think two men is enough, don't you?"

"I want a harem," she shrugged.

"That's just greedy," I grumbled. I turned, eyeing Fred as he watched me.

"Ladies," Fred said as he snapped his finger in front of our faces. "Your army, my Queen," he said as the demons started to emerge from the shadows. "What are your orders?"

"I think it's time to ferret out Hecate and bring her up to speed on the witches currently running amok here. If she disagrees on what I have planned, she can die with them. I'm going to set the world on fire, and I'm going to fucking dance in the ashes as it burns."

"Um, you did that already," Fred frowned.

"No, I'm just getting started." I turned, staring at the man who watched me from the balcony of his bedroom. I blew him a raspberry before I turned back to Fred. "Let's do this, we have nine months to find those witches and end this curse. While I don't mind being pregnant as war spreads across the earth, it's much more fun when I can join in."

"You intend to carry his child? Even knowing that you will give birth to the rider of the apocalypse?" Lust growled.

"You think I shouldn't?" I asked, staring at him as his mind grasped onto what it meant. "He would not be born evil, and it would be thousands of years before he's ready to take his throne. This world will either be dead or long ended before my son would rise to bring war here."

"My nephew!" Banba squealed excitedly as I leveled her with a cool stare and a frown.

"We're at your command, no matter what you intend to do." His eyes continued to search mine. "There's a certain Fae warrior hiding in the shadows. Do you want him handled?"

"No," I stated as I watched the Fae moving out of the shadows. "He's here for what I took from him, as I promised," I uttered as I stepped closer to Zahruk. Lucian stepped from the shadows, his men closing in around him.

"And so the Goddess is reborn," Lucian growled, his smirk a mix of love and chaos at seeing me in my dress and gold armlets.

"My blades, Erie," Zahruk snapped, and my eyes turned to him as remorse filled me from the anger I felt rolling off of him.

"I'm sorry, but I needed to borrow them," I said as I lifted my hands, catching both as I flipped them to the sharp ends in my hands, and held them out to him handle-first. "The kiss was unexpected but pleasant. I am sorry for the guise I created to borrow them."

"And the rest of it, was that all an act as well?" Synthia demanded as she sifted in. "We went to bat for you, and you're the fucking Goddess of War!"

"I know, and for that, I will join you in your war. I repay my debts. I needed time to gain my strength, and for allowing you to think I was some lost, wounded female, I'm sorry. I did, however, steal Lucifer's army, set a plague loose on the druids who control the Mages, and healed the hole that is tearing Faery apart. Have you not noticed that it is completely closed?"

"You lied to me, to us," she growled as she tapped the toe of her shoe on the ground.

"No, I just didn't tell you who I was because I wasn't fully healed yet. It wasn't to hurt you; it was to protect me until I'd gained my full powers back. I needed to know everything that was happening. I also wanted to help you, because you are of Danu's blood, and you're created stronger than the race she left behind. There's a cave inside Faery, and it holds the answer to saving your world and mine. War is coming to your land one way or another; I can either sway the battle heavily at your side or stand down. That is your choice."

"What would be the cost?" Lucian asked, his keen stare watching every movement I made. He didn't trust me, but then he was older than even I was. I'd given him good reason not to trust me, but then he'd given me many more. We had a love-hate relationship, and yet we'd go to war to protect each other. It was a complicated history.

"I wouldn't ask a cost, nor expect one. You helped me when I needed it the most. I am still Erie, but I am also the Mórrígan. I won't apologize again. If you want me, I will be there when the need arises."

"Just like that?" she asked, her violet eyes studying me.

"Just like that, Synthia. I owed your mother a debt when she died; taking over the people she left behind wasn't asked of me. I chose to do it because I craved the war that was coming for them. I'm not a nice person, but I do pay my debts. Lucian, I need to speak to Death, he took something from me, and I want it back. See that he knows I am looking for him and that I will set the world on fire to find him. Congratulations on Lucifer and your upcoming victory. He is exposed, his army is now mine, and he is waiting for you in the veil beyond man's touch. Don't keep him waiting. Synthia, the Mages are gathered inside Faery; they're preparing to march to your stronghold. I suggest you not allow them to reach

it. Now, if you'll excuse me, I have a world to bring to its knees for hurting my men." I turned, blowing a kiss to the beast that watched me from his balcony with his men at his side.

I'd discovered a lot about myself as I'd fought to come back this time—things such as the fact that I wasn't the hero in this story. I was the antihero, and I was okay with playing it. I was his villain, the one who had brought him to his knees more than once. I was war, dipped in chaos and sprinkled with glitter to look pretty as I waged it. I was okay with who I was because I'd fought hard to come back from what he'd inadvertently put me through. My mind was unhinged, still piecing together the past, but I had the stepping stones to the story of our twisted as shit love tale, and that was all that mattered to me. So what if it took my own suicide to fully wake that which had slumbered inside of me? I was back, and I was about to bring hell down on those who had thought to kick me when I was down.

I'd loved them both for as long as I could remember, and while I wasn't sure what our future held, I knew that until I eliminated everything that stood between us, I'd hold them at arm's length. I was created for war, not love. Somewhere between losing my love and finding them, I'd felt that sliver of hope blossoming and then lost it twice more. We had a turbulent relationship, of that I was certain, but it was how we'd worked. We weren't from this world, or this time. We were ageless, from a time where blood and strength chose who lived or died. I was going to bring our enemies to their knees, and I would secure our future as I'd tried to do twice before, only to fail. This time, it wasn't an option. The difference was, growing in this body, I'd learned love, I'd learned wrong from right, and while I still blurred the lines, I'd go to hell and back to save them both, because they were mine. Or, if it didn't work out, I'd give them everything I had left to give, and leave this world one last time. But if I was going down, I would take every asshole that had hurt them—or me—out as I left it.

~ The End, For Now ~

About the AUTHOR

Amelia lives in the great Pacific Northwest with her family. When not writing, she can be found on her author page, hanging out with fans, or dreaming up new twisting plots. She's an avid reader of everything paranormal romance.

Stalker links! Want to keep up on what I am doing? Follow me below and watch for author updates.

Facebook: https://www.facebook.com/authorameliahutchins
Website: http://amelia-hutchins.com/
Amazon: http://www.amazon.com/Amelia-Hutchins/e/B00D5OASEG
Goodreads: https://www.goodreads.com/author/show/7092218.Amelia_Hutchins
Twitter: https://twitter.com/ameliaauthor
Pinterest: http://www.pinterest.com/ameliahutchins
Instagram: https://www.instagram.com/author.amelia.hutchins/
Facebook Author Group: https://goo.gl/BqpCVK

Made in United States
Troutdale, OR
06/27/2023

10831367R00309